DEADLY CONCEPTION

DEADLY CONCEPTION

Sola Odemuyiwa

Book Guild Publishing

Sussex, England

First published in Great Britain in 2011 by
The Book Guild Ltd
Pavilion View
19 New Road
Brighton, BN1 1UF

Typeset in Baskerville by Ellipsis Digital Limited, Glasgow

Printed in Great Britain by
CPI Antony Rowe

A catalogue record for this book is available from The British Library.

ISBN 978 1 84624 618 0

Contents

Part 1

Part 2

PART 1

1

ADHD Vaccine

Mr Gordon Ferry waited to make his regular contribution to True Brit radio's afternoon phone-in. He was getting twitchy. The twerps were going to run into the news.

'. . . and another thing, what's he doing posing in front of the screen? Trafalgar Square – don't believe it, how much does that cost? A screen showing how many bloody immigrants they got rid of last month: they all go home for Christmas anyway; shouldn't be here in the first place, it's an absolute disgrace, bloody disaster what's happening; don't get me started: can't work – dodgy back and arthritis, my missus' heart's giving her the gyp – angina or whatever – the GP won't say, prescription charges through the roof; my son's back from uni, can't afford it, in hock to God knows who; can't afford to work, can't afford not to work; what have these minister tossers ever done in their lives, except row boats and ponce about in their fucking tuxedos? It's a fucking joke, an absolute disgrace. You know what the country needs? Real people, that's what, real people, people who've seen life, who've won things. I'd have fucking Alex Ferguson me, right now, I really would; he'd do better than this lot.' Carl rang off, wheezing.

'Thank you for your contribution, Carl,' said Roxanne. 'What do you have to say, on line one, Fred?'

'Hi, Roxanne, you well? Carl's spot on, one hundred per cent, think about it, right: we've got soldiers in Iraq, right, in Afghanistan, right, those boys are coming back, no legs, no nothing, right, can't find nowhere decent to live, right, our boys been turfed out the army because can't fight Tony Blair's war no more, right; I'm not being funny, like, but in Lancashire, there's some sheikh geezer or something – ten children in a mansion, we're paying for, like; how's that, eh? How's that right? Answer that . . .'

'Thank you, Fred, what do you have to say, Alan?'

'Y'alright, Roxanne?'

'I'm fine thank you, what's on your mind?'

'Well, we British, we're too soft. Look, before you get me wrong, I don't agree with the Germans and the war, like, but they had the right idea: look after your own; the French did it, with those Gypsies; why can't we? The country's full up; can these MP geezers, these berks, not see? Problem is they don't listen to ordinary folk like us . . .'

'What's your point, Cedric?'

'Hello, good morning, I'm sixty-five, I've not missed a day's work in my life, the pension's a joke – if it was not so serious! I'm sixty-five, where will I make up the shortfall? My house is worth half what it cost me a few years ago, I can't sell it anyway, no one's buying, the guys, and girls, let's not forget the girls, Roxanne, who got us into this mess, they've the nerve to blame the government – that's you and me, mind – blaming *us* for letting Lehman fail, not bailing them out . . . Why don't they give us the money instead of taking more to give to the banks to build up their balance sheets to lend back to us at usurious rates and pay themselves even more bonuses? Something's not right. Karl Marx had a point. We're the lumpenproletariat being taken for fools. I'd draw the line at a football manager, though, they're just as bad.'

'Thank you, sir, we have a vicar, next, Matthew Ravenswood, have I got it right?'

'Hello, yes, it's Ravenswood, good morning, God bless you, we should be careful, our Christian institutions have lasted generations, we should nurture and cherish our Christian heritage, not

4

be afraid to defend it. To those who want to join us in a Christian spirit I say welcome, but if we pull too hard at the delicate fabric of our unwritten constitution we could tear it apart. We know how easy it is to destroy; much harder to mend than to destroy, that's all I have to say.'

'What exactly *are* you saying, sir?'

'Charity begins at home, couldn't put it better.'

'Jack, what's your point? Jack, are you there?'

'Yes, I'm here, your lot may not want to hear this but I'm fed up to the back teeth, I'm taking the kids out, not staying here, you'll have Johnny Foreigner running it soon: Mohammed Husein as metropolitan police commissioner, head of fucking army . . . Look at South Africa: they've had terrorists in charge since we let them get on with it. Same in Zimbabwe: Mandela, Mugabe – we'll be like fucking Zimbabwe soon, finished. I say, are those youngsters knifing people, selling drugs – animals! And we should treat them like animals, like in the jungle, give it back and more, get the bizzies or soldiers to teach them a lesson, lock them up, throw away the key; national service, community service malarkey – a waste of time: lock them up, that'll work, let them rot away.'

'Thank you for your forthright views, sir. Can we move on to the next line? Who's there? Rashid, Richard?'

'It's Richard, Rashid, whatever, this is my say, you see, you know what I'm saying, it's Common Europe, with Polish, Romanians, that's what's killing us; I say we come out, know what I'm saying, tell the lot of them to eff off, not enough jobs to go round, you see, know what I'm saying, I agree with everything else is saying . . . '

'Thank you, Richard, Rashid. Minister, your comments on what you've heard?'

Andy Parkinson, Home Office minister, cleared his throat to put on his most sympathetic ministerial voice. 'Thank you, Roxanne, and good morning to your listeners. I understand their frustrations and concerns. Let me assure your listeners though that we already have the toughest immigration laws in Europe and we are tightening them further. These laws will be enforced. Secondly, we are working to put the economy right. With respect to jobs, we are very committed to a policy of "Jobs in Britain for real British people". Good day to all of you.'

'I'm afraid that's all we have time for, keep it on True Brit radio, the fastest growing station in the land,' said Roxanne.

Gordon Ferry stared at, then chucked his phone across the room. 'Shit, stuff the lot of you. Paula. Paula, where are my fucking fags?'

A week before, at an impromptu news conference on her return from a G25 summit, Lady Frances Davidson, the chancellor, had presented Britain's continued AAA credit rating as a vindication of her economic policies. Soon, however, she was forced to admit to a back room deal with the credit agencies to delay the announcement conferring a new A*A*A* credit status on Brazil and China (effectively consigning Britain to the second tier and raising borrowing costs) until she could brief her Cabinet colleagues. 'We still have the lowest interest rates in the world,' she said.

'Yes, in theory, but not in practice,' said Mr Russell Amiss, shadow chancellor.

With the government still reeling from the chancellor's humiliation, a young woman was molested at gunpoint at a rock festival. Fibres found at the scene were said to match those on a jacket belonging to Jerome Jackson, one of the six accused. All had previous minor convictions. But Jerome had an alibi. He was on holiday in Mallorca with his family. And truth be known, he would rather puncture his own eardrum with a rusty nail than be seen at a heavy metal concert. The case collapsed, but public opprobrium rose as the nation watched the testosterone-ecstatic men, nicknamed 'the Jackson six' by the press, jog out of court, clenched fists pumping in triumph. 'Rude, aggressive, sexually suggestive, insensitive, offensive, an affront to the girl's feelings and to common decency,' said the papers. A television interview with the victim's face blacked out aroused further sympathy for her and anger against the alleged perpetrators.

'I'm an ordinary girl, my parents, ordinary decent folk, they wouldn't hurt a fly. All I want to do is look after nursery children. Is that too much to ask? Is it too much to have the odd night out?'

Exploiting the *Zeitgeist*, the racist but hitherto marginal Nationalists fanned the flame of xenophobia. At a Yorkshire rally the cynical but charismatic new leader of the Nationalists, Mr Prentice Sugarcane – successor to the rotund, Nazi-esque Mr Bruce Tuck – said, 'Nation building is like baking a cake. They thought we wouldn't notice. They've ignored the recipe – the wrong ingredients in the wrong proportion in the wrong order. Our pan's too small and the oven's too hot. Vote this soft lot out of the kitchen.'

An establishment that broke its promise to hold a referendum on the European constitution could not hold the tide against one proposed by Mr Sugarcane on the question: 'In the interest of national security would you support specific measures to reduce non-EU immigration?'

Immigrants were excluded from the vote. The plebiscite was carried sixty-five per cent to thirty-five per cent. The opportunist, Mr David Cazenove – a political socio-biologist, and executive member of the Nationalist Party – abandoned his PhD thesis and, with Mr Aston Colville, MEP – a former mercenary in Equatorial Guinea and Angola – seized on a study among a small group of men of Caribbean origin carried out by the Newcastle Life Science Park, showing that a cluster of ADHD genes were linked with impulsive behaviour and disruptiveness. On Roxanne's True Brit radio show, David Cazenove said his party would 'vaccinate all newborn males of Afro-Caribbean descent against ADHD. If you want to reduce street crime you've got to go to the source, we've got the data, plain scientific data, and if you give us your mandate we can clean up your streets. Seek and snuff out the terrorists, the extremist Islamic organisations. Remember what your grandmas used to say about the 1950s, when it was safe for them to walk the streets at night before the unmentionables arrived on boats – *Windrush* – we'll get back to that.' From hypothesis to thesis to theory and manifesto promise in only nine months.

National support for the Nationalists rose from five per cent to twenty-five per cent. When they won the Cheltenham by-election with a thirty-six per cent share of the vote, the Conservatives panicked, and split. At the general election, the Old Conservatives, nicknamed the Wintertories because of their support for apartheid, fed up with the Liberal coalition, formed a minority coalition government with the Nationalists.

The new government pledged to bring an immediate halt to non-EU immigration and cut the number of resident non-EUs by ten per cent each year. Basing his estimates on the Treasury models, Philip White ('Philip the philosopher'), a military historian, entrepreneur, secretary of RASI (the Real Adam Smith Institute) and member of GOATS (the Government of all the Talents) – or turds, depending on your point of view! – estimated that the programme would save billions of pounds. 'I promise you,' he said on television, 'we will save billions from social security, billions from law and order, billions from health, to give back in tax rebates and to abolish income tax for the poorest.' Russell Amiss called him the 'sophist of billionaire land.' But the right wing press was more enthusiastic. 'Innovative – this policy will be copied all over Europe, just like privatisation'; 'a new socio-scientific and economic paradigm'; 'breathtaking, innovative and ingenious in its audacity,' they cried. Desperate for good news, the financial markets took the announcements as evidence that the government was coming to grips with the deficit. Stocks rocketed, Cazenove and Colville were ennobled. When the secretary general of the Trades Unions Congress, Mr Stewart Ferguson, was asked what he thought of the government's policy, he said he had not been following the story. He was too busy organising a protest march to defend NHS hospital gardening estate services from privatisation.

* * *

8

Bode and Ruth Dacosta lived in a three-bedroomed terraced house on Kingswood Road in Jesmond, a small quiet residential suburb in the east of Newcastle upon Tyne between Sandyford and Gosforth.

'Oh, got a shock, didn't know you were back,' said Ruth.

'Sorry, I forgot to tell you I was due a half day, some inspection at the plant, so I took the day off. What's for dinner?'

'That's all you think about, that stomach,' said Ruth, checking the time and patting Bode's incipient paunch. 'I'll rummage up some yam and sweet potato; with chicken stew. Keep me company,' Ruth said.

'It's nice to get home early for a change. You're not on call are you? I feel as if I've escaped from prison not Northumbria Water. What's happening to me, why do I feel guilty when I take time off?' Bode said. He tucked into his meal.

When Ruth had finished her salad she filled Bode's glass and gave his shoulder an affectionate rub. 'Don't worry. This ADHD vaccine brouhaha will soon blow over. I can't believe they'll go through with it. We'll be able to start a family once the electioneering fever's died down. We qualify for exemption anyway, even under the present rules. Great-grandad Ekundayo came over to study medicine, my grandmother was born here and so was Daddy,' she said.

'Your side's fine then, what about mine, do I qualify through you, or not? They haven't made it clear and they could change their minds. You can't tell for sure what they're thinking,' said Bode. 'Cazenove would have people like me out, passport or no passport, no question,' he said. He sucked his teeth, rolled his lips, swallowed an errant morsel. 'You should read the Nigerian press; absolute berserk they are, they say vagrancy is a ruse, an excuse. They say the ADHD vaccine will neuter young men at birth. It will blind, cause seizures and all sorts of complications.' He got up to fill his glass at the fridge. In a Nigerian accent, he said, 'Ah, ah, oh, you small children, you are much too young to remember, we were told that other vaccine was for this and that

9

disease, oh, but some children could not talk, could not see, oh.'
He sat down. 'I think they're referring to the very rare cases of,
what do you call it?'

'Encephalitis,' said Ruth.

'Yes, encephalitis, can't get my tongue round it,' said Bode.
'And the Nigerians, West Africans as a whole to be fair, are still
going on about the test nuclear explosions in the Sahara; which
they said caused all sorts of diseases: conjunctivitis, headaches,
meningitis, rashes; you name it, they blame it on the explosions.
They preach it in the churches and mosques. My folk in Lagos
say the market women are the worst rumour mongers. The stories
are spreading here, in Britain.'

'But, Bode, you don't believe these stories, do you? You're here,
you know the facts. We can't wait for ever. I'm twenty-eight, I
don't want to wait until I'm fifty, do I?' Ruth got up to switch
the lights on. She traced the edge of her empty glass with her
fingers, staring through its base as if a lens. 'Promise you won't
be cross,' she said.

'That's my fundamental human right, can't sign it away lightly,'
said Bode.

She looked up. 'It's not like that; Anne asked if I would consider
surrogacy. She offered to be a surrogate mother,' said Ruth.

Bode put his fork down, choked on another morsel, coughed,
sipped from his glass and cupped his fist to his mouth. When the
morsel passed, with teary eyes he said, 'Your friend Anne, Keith's
wife, are you serious? It's a wind up.'

'No, she meant it, she volunteered, said she would carry our
baby. She's had hers. She'd like to help us. I said I'd ask you.
Please promise you'll at least think about it, she's bound to ask
me what you said. We go back a long way, you know, and I'd do
the same for her, I would,' said Ruth. She put her right hand
over his. Bode took his hand away. He got up to switch the kettle
on, waited by it till it boiled and made himself a cup of tea.
Then he poured Ruth a glass of tomato juice.

'I'm not angry, it's awkward, you'll sulk if I say no and she'll think I'm ungracious, but I can't agree.' He rummaged in the cupboard for a biscuit, found none and returned to the table.

'We've run out of your Hobnobs,' said Ruth.

'Never mind. Anyway, you have to make an excuse. I don't think I can bear the burden of gratitude. I don't know her that well, she's really your friend, not mine.'

Ruth downed her tomato juice, and dropped her hands into her lap in indignant despair. 'Why aren't I surprised? We'll just bob along then on your tide of apathy, and let life pass us by, like it always does. It's not the first time,' she said, referring to the holiday in a Mediterranean villa a friend had offered Bode but he had turned down.

'Oh, not that again, it was only a holiday. Look, Ruth, you know me, I don't like to be beholden to anyone,' said Bode. 'I'll catch Kiplingitis, white man's burden. They can't look after themselves, I had to have a baby for them, anyway, what will the Holy See say about "rent a friend's womb"?'

Ruth gasped. 'I was going to seek guidance, perhaps special dispensation, because of the general situation in the country,' she said.

'Bend it like . . . MPs, which is it to be, is it legal? Is it allowed by the Vatican or not? They didn't ask the Pope when he came a few years ago. They should have. And again, don't forget the Nationalists, they hate anything like this, anything that questions or muddies their racial purity ideology. I thought they were going to ban surrogacy anyway,' said Bode.

Ruth put her elbows on the table to cup her face in her hands. 'I'm twenty-eight, nearly twenty-nine, I'm just passing time, and time is passing me by,' she said.

'So it is for me too, all I'm saying is the government says it will clarify the law, we can wait for that, can't we?' said Bode. He cleared the table. Ruth loaded the dishwasher, kneeling so that he could not see her crying. She would thank Anne and decline her offer. Use religion as an excuse. Anne would understand.

* * *

The National Youth Crime Prevention Rehabilitation Bill, implementing the ADHD vaccination programme, was the first to be enacted that parliament. The Blood Contamination Bill, passed in response to the haemophilia-HIV contamination scandal of the 1980s, was repealed and the government exempted from vicarious liability. Professor Bears of York University was appointed Czar of teenage pregnancy and social housing. To 'Sus' law, stop and search and DNA profiling, his task force added 'support for the family'– a programme of sterilisation of any incarcerated young black bachelor. Fertility would be restored when the subject got married or reached the age of thirty, whichever was longer. Supporters hoped the policy would encourage the unwanted to emigrate. In the same month, the government raised the retirement age for non-EUs from sixty-seven to seventy-five years. For the unfortunate minority it was 'work till you drop or before you dribble'. Opposition from Liberty and Human Rights Watch was called unpatriotic. For arranging a petition against the measures, Ms Evershed, spokesperson for Amnesty International, was hounded by the tabloids for weeks. They took photographs of her at home, camped outside her house, raided her bins, and to make Ms Evershed look old, published side by side photographs of her and her rich boyfriend's former wife, Kay, when she was at the height of her career as a fashion model.

Ruth waited. But with every friend who had a baby she became more and more broody. One autumn's day she announced to her friends that she was three months pregnant.

Ruth was in a multidisciplinary team meeting one afternoon when Bode rang: 'Laitan has been expelled,' he said.

'Who's Laitan?' asked Ruth.

'You don't know him, I'm just telling you what's happening. He's some guy I know, through a cousin. Works in IT, not married. They raided his flat early in the morning. Police. Customs. In uniform. Smashed his door in. Bundled him on to a plane and that was that. "National security". His front door has still not been fixed. One of the uniformed guys is supposed to have told the local free rag that repairing damage was a waste of taxpayers' money. I think they did repair some property when a lot of EU neighbours complained that theirs would lose value. Apart from that, no one's doing anything; just looking, watching. Sorry to ring you at work, I had to talk. After this, if we get through this, I'm not having any more, sorry,' said Bode.

'Can't talk now, Bode, can't keep ringing me every day at work, everything will be fine, no one's coming for you. You're British, your dad was born here. You, *we* don't know the full story. Maybe this Laitan guy was dodgy. Involved in a scam or such like, he was in IT, after all, I'll speak to you later,' she said. Her bleep went off. The weekly case review of vulnerable babies was about to start.

Bode was right to ask why there was so little resistance to the expulsions. To avoid the public demonstrations seen in France against the expulsion of the Romany Gypsies, a meticulously planned campaign by the Home Office had exploited tribal and ethnic rivalry and tension by classifying the quarry not just by country but by state of origin and tribe. So when British citizens of Lagos State descent were arrested, tried and deported for minor offences – late payments of mortgage arrears, defaults on alimony payments, traffic accidents, tax avoidance, currency and foreign exchange 'irregularities' – there was little dissent or support from erstwhile compatriots. In the first six months of parliament the campaign had expelled about thirty-two thousand non-EUs like Laitan. Nigeria and other African countries were too poor, poorly governed or backward to exert any influence; protests by African Americans were ignored. Republicans and 'moderate' Democrats would not presume to lecture the United Kingdom on human rights.

Many had seen enough or seen this before, in Africa or Eastern Europe, and fled to start all over again – again; the Asians to try to repeat the miracles they had wrought after expulsion from

13

Uganda by Idi Amin. Others were paralysed by fear. Nigerians, forced to choose between the misery of diaspora and the poverty and hunger of home return, chose misery. Anything that reduced their sons' increasing predilection for gang culture was good. Whatever the insults, privations and tribulations, they were better off anywhere. Anywhere, but Nigeria.

In response to a discreet word from the Old Commonwealth, the coalition announced that the term 'non-EU' did not apply to Canadians, Australians or New Zealanders and other groups designated by the Home Secretary. They would be allowed to come and go as they wished as long as they could lay some claim to Britain through some long forgotten grandmother, mitochondrial DNA or a family history of genetic diseases relatively common in North Europeans: cystic fibrosis, haemochromatosis, for example. The Chinese were also exempt; they could refuse to buy British government debt or block business deals in retaliation. Japan, Korea and Indonesia watched the unique experiment in nation rebuilding with interest. The French were amused. The Germans, embarrassed.

Dr Ruth Dacosta was bursting as she rounded the bend to fork left for Sandyford. The traffic-lights were against her. She grimaced. A young man in a convertible screeched to a halt beside her; his expression changed from admiring glance to self-disgust in a fraction of a second when he saw why Ruth sat so far back. *At least he looked*, she thought and smiled at him. He looked away. Beethoven's 'Pastoral' Symphony faded away on the radio. The news, almost always bad, would soon start, so she changed station and pulled down the sun visor quickly before the lights changed. The lights changed. 'It's six o'clock,' said the announcer. Ruth quickly tuned to Radio 4. 'And here is a summary of the news.' Ruth turned up the car radio. 'The Labour Party regrets to announce the death of a patriot and loyal servant, Ms Donna Crout, MP. Ms Crout, who had a majority of twenty-three thousand, died suddenly at her home this morning,' the voice continued. If that was a news headline there could not be much to follow, so she turned the radio off.

Half an hour after she set off from work, Ruth was crawling along behind a funeral cortège on Osborne Road, on a good day only a few minutes from home. She loosened her seat-belt and reclined the seat for respite from baby and bladder. The sight of her front door increased her urgency and she charged in, trampling and scattering the day's post over the doormat and floor. Becalmed and relieved, she switched on the television. After the usual dross, Sir William Dunston, Nationalist Party chairman, came on to announce that the government had finally decided who was to be exempt from the ADHD vaccine. 'In the interest of fairness to those who deserve a larger share in our way of life' the government would amend the Nationality Act. In simple terms, as he explained later on True Brit radio, 'A non-EU was a non-EU was a non-EU child unless both parents had four generations of unbroken links to the country.'

'You've heard?' Bode said when he got in. He sank back into the settee, stunned, looking into space. 'It's my fault, we should have waited,' he said.

'Don't say that,' said Ruth.

'What's there to say? It's an obvious cynical ploy to catch more non-EU victims, and use that to capture Donna Crout's working-class seat at the by-election,' he said.

'I don't know, you're the political man, let's see what we can do, see what others think, we don't know anyone else who's involved around here, perhaps we could find out. Someone may have an idea, perhaps the courts will help, or a support group,' said Ruth.

'I don't know, it's a bit late now, look what they've done. I bet they start their programme soon, even those who thought they'd escaped could be reeled in; who knows? They haven't said anything about that, have they?' said Bode. He followed Ruth to the kitchen. He sat at the table. 'Perhaps we could have the baby in Nigeria?' he said.

Ruth looked up. 'But they would have thought of that, wouldn't

15

they? Will they let us, the baby, back in? Anyway, I'm British, I'm not going to Nigeria to have my baby and have him deprived of his rights here. That's that.' She waddled to the kettle. 'I'm making a cup of tea, do you want one?' she said.

'No. Where is this going? What will we do if we can't stop this? How will we protect our son?' he said. They knew it was a son.

'I know, I can't bear the thought of this vaccination, or even worse, if what those people say's true, but that must be a wild rumour. It doesn't bear thinking about,' said Ruth. The phone rang.

'That's probably someone who wants to talk about the news,' said Bode.

'I'm not in the mood,' said Ruth.

'Neither am I,' said Bode. And the expectant parents dragged themselves up to bed, only to lie awake all night, one not knowing what to say to the other.

The missed caller was Ade, another of Bode's paternal cousins. 'You called last night. What about, about ADHD?'

'Yeah, man,' said Ade. 'I knew you'd be interested, man, but you know already. Look after your woman, man; anything can happen. You can't imagine what's going on, man.'

'What's happened?' said Bode.

'You, this, man, you don't know anything, do you? This ADHD thing is driving people crazy, man. That young girl, Jo Asamoah, it's in the local London papers, that's why you haven't heard. She's married to Osei Tutu, Ghanaian microbiologist; her father's a professor, called Gerald Brass, head of molecular biology at UCL. Do you know what she's done?'

'What's she done? I'm on my way to work,' said Bode.

'She's only twenty-four; she doused herself in petrol and jumped like a human torch off the multi-storey car park near Tottenham Court Road. They say she was at least six months on, but didn't want ADHD vaccine. Can you imagine such a thing, in this country, not Vietnam or Saudi, man? I'm just saying keep an eye on your woman, it's a delicate time for them.'

'Thanks, I don't think Ruth is thinking of taking her life, she's too Catholic for that,' said Bode.

'It's your cake, man. Just called to fill you in, man, bye,' said Ade.

Seventeen other pregnant young non-EU women were to take their own lives that year. Bode heard and read other reports of how, in some areas of the North, out of fear of physical intimidation, non-EU families pooled together to have groceries delivered at home and went to school and work before it got light, to return after dark. He read of how, in this self-imposed siege, rickets, last seen in the 1970s, had returned to the Asian community. Of how the long winter nights, hated by non-EUs, were now, combined with a hooded anorak, their heaven sent camouflage. Christian non-EUs would not work with their Muslim counterparts. Nor would West Indians and West Africans, the former claiming that their stay-at-home brethren had sold them into slavery. The Somalis, thinking that they would be blamed for Islamist bomb plots, kept to themselves. Asians argued that they were Indo-Aryans, Caucasians, just a shade darker than their British aborigine brethren. One Indian businessman, Barush Patel, said the new laws were not for them; they were for the riff-raff, which the government was entitled to expel, not for business tycoons, lawyers, doctors, accountants or pharmacists. Their naivety was repaid several-fold, with contempt from those to whom they clung; and from those they rejected came worse: physical abuse, murder and desecration of religious monuments. Here and abroad. Religious contributors to BBC Radio 4's 'Thought for the Day', rather than condemn government policy, evaded it, peddled riddles whilst London burned, requesting donations for the victims 'of the wave of discontent sweeping our country', whatever that meant.

After two weeks of futile exploration of their options, Bode and Ruth were reconciled to having their son immunised. One evening, a few weeks before Ruth was due to go on maternity leave, Anne saw her drive past on her way back home. She waited fifteen minutes to allow Ruth some space. While she waited at Ruth's door, she admired Keith's tomatoes in the allotment across the road. The door opened with a creak and suck. 'Hi, come in,' said Ruth, her full cheeks blooming, but her eyes looking weary. 'Tea?' Ruth said, quickly turning her back on her friend.

'Sit down, Ruth, I know you're under a lot of stress. I've been thinking.'

'What about?' said Ruth.

'About you, silly billy, who else? Listen, I think Keith may be able to help. He thinks he could maybe bluff his way out of the hospital, the RVI, before the jab. Surely they don't just whisk the baby off as soon as it's born, do they? It's a long shot, I know, but what's the alternative – emigration?' said Anne.

'You're being daft now,' said Ruth. 'They're not stupid, they have all my records.'

'Yes, but you're an EU; when Keith turns up he's a more obvious EU, and male, sorry to say, but it counts, and they may just hand over your baby and off you go. It's not a cunning plan, but it's easy to execute and might just work. The authorities haven't sorted out all the systems yet I'm sure; it was all rushed. What do we have to lose?'

'I wonder what Bode will think?' said Ruth.

'I'll leave that to you, Keith's ready, it was his suggestion,' said Anne. No wonder the plan was so leaky, but generous, thought Ruth, smiling broadly for a change. Anne tapped her friend on the cheek and hugged her sideways across the neck.

'Bye,' said Ruth.

'Bye, see you soon,' said Anne, hurrying back up the road to talk to Keith before he changed his mind.

Ruth wasted no time in telling Bode about Keith's offer.

'Is that all you've come up with all day? Supposing he's caught, he'll be an accessory to deceit,' said Bode.

'Yes, he's prepared to accept that small risk,' she said.

'What if they come for me, I'm the father; they may leave

Keith, because he's an EU and throw me out, or worse, throw me in jail. Where would that leave us?'

'We've been through this. We can try or just surrender; Keith's been extremely generous, don't you think?' she said.

'Exactly, that's the problem, we're beggars, cap in hand beggars, can't even have our own baby without outside help,' he said.

'Can't hear you,' she said.

'I said, can't we do our own thing, for a change. I don't ask Keith about his family.'

'But they're trying to help, can't you see? Is this reason or ego talking? Because, it's my son! I'm going to be there, you can't do anything about it, and I'm not blaming anyone, it's just the way it is; do you not want to give your son a chance of escaping this . . . ?'

'Go on, accuse me: if I was an EU, your life would be much easier; you're the real citizen, our child will be the product of my inoculation with the virus of exclusion, alien virus . . . I'll tell you how I feel. I'm trying my best, I thought I was part of this State, country, a citizen – call it what you like – but I'm a generation short of safety. Now I'm a target for expulsion, exclusion, and my children: they need treatment to be accepted; begrudged gradual assimilation or coexistence is too good for me or them. I'm a father-to-be, of neutered progeny.'

Ruth sighed in exasperation. 'You know that's not what I meant, let's get real here.' She waited, but no reaction. 'I'm going to say yes to Anne and Keith. I'm sorry, but we have nothing to lose.'

'Look,' said Bode. 'How do you think that makes me feel, to be responsible for that, to inflict that on you and my son, my family? You want to know?' he said.

'Calm down,' said Ruth.

'Calm down, you say, how much can I take: insult at work, insult at home, oblique from your friends Anne and Keith. I can't tell them to get lost, can I? I have no choice.' Tears of frustration lined Bode's eyes.

Ruth sat down next to him. 'I'm sorry, I didn't mean to upset you, but give Keith's plan a chance, please,' she said, giving him a hug. Bode stared into his cold cup of tea.

Later that night, after reading blogs from other trapped parents, he brought Ruth a cup of cocoa. 'I didn't mean to go off on one. I don't think your plan will work, but we'll give it a try.' Ruth smiled at him, his heartbeat missed, he kissed her, but was still afraid.

2

Early Mensah

'Congratulations, you have a baby boy,' said the midwife.

'Thanks,' said Ruth. She knew that already, old news, but where was Keith? Her boy was going to be weighed and examined soon and if he did not turn up it would be too late.

'Do you want anything?' the midwife asked.

'No thanks, I'm worried my husband isn't here. He was going to be here, he could be lost.' She tried to sit up but her back hurt, everything hurt. She'd had only a glimpse of her little baby boy and wanted to see him again, to hide him until Keith came and changed the rules.

'I'm sorry, ma'am, we've got some more checks, he's a boy, as you know we've got to carry out more checks and give the jab,' said the nurse.

'We missed a few scans, with work at the hospital. I'm a paediatrician, can't it wait? I've hardly seen him, can I feed him, hold him a bit longer?' said Ruth.

'We're behind schedule as it is, ma'am, doctor. We're supposed to give the jab as soon as possible, for best effect; it's orders and we have targets,' said the nurse. 'I'll go and get the vaccine, it's harmless and painless, they don't even flinch.'

Ruth thought Jean, the nurse, was in the wrong profession, or maybe she wasn't; perhaps this was the new face of nursing. It was almost as if she was too keen to vaccinate her son.

'Okay, we're ready, I'll take a photograph of the injection site, take a matching DNA sample and record the vaccine batch number,' said Jean.

'I'm exempt, my son shouldn't be vaccinated, Lord, I've just twigged what you were talking about: the ADHD jab, it's not for us, get your matron,' said Ruth.

Jean hesitated for a moment. 'I checked, but I can ask again, or get senior sister to come to see you.'

'You do that,' said Ruth.

Jean returned with a severe looking middle-aged brunette, Mrs Malvern, to find Ruth peering into the baby cot.

'Good morning, Dr Dacosta, challenges are allowed, but to save time we'll have to wheel your baby with us to the treatment room. If you're right we'll bring him back.'

'How do I know you won't jab him anyway, even if you're wrong? My husband will be here any time now, he should have arrived, he must have been held up. Can't you wait?'

'We'll give you a few more minutes, but we really have to get on, it's the law, I'm afraid,' said Mrs Malvern.

Where was Keith?

Five minutes later, Jean, the nurse, came back. 'Is your husband here yet?'

'No,' said Ruth. 'I'll have to take him now, ma'am.'

'No, please,' said Ruth.

'Sorry,' and she wheeled the cot out of the room. Nurse and cot were back ten minutes later. Ruth had her head buried in her pillow crying but trying not to sob. When she heard the squeaky wheels she got up and saw the tick, the mark of the jab on her son's left foot. They had failed. Ruth sank back on to her bed and wept loud, body-heaving, saliva-dripping, nose-running, ululating wails. The nurse left a cup of tea on the tray and a menu and tiptoed out of the room.

Dr Keith Hartley arrived at the main hospital reception about ten minutes after Mensah was born. His car had failed to start in the early morning cold weather and he had had to come by taxi. The taxi driver, new to the North-East, got lost, picked Keith up late and had taken him to the wrong hospital entrance, which was locked overnight for security reasons, and there were no directions to the correct entrance. Keith dashed off in what he thought was the general direction of the obstetrics department, but the hospital wing had been renovated since his last paternal visit and he had an appalling sense of direction, a source of amusement at home, but not so funny that morning, with lives at stake. He hurried down the corridor to room 4, but it was the wrong room 4. The room he wanted was in a different wing. A fresh-faced nurse appeared to be waiting for a lift. 'Excuse me, I'm looking for the labour ward room 4: blue; my wife's having a baby.'

'I'll take you, give me a sec, you must be looking for the leeward rooms,' she said.

A midwife came over and asked Keith whom he had come to see. 'My wife, Ruth,' he said.

'I know her, she's lovely, is this your first?' He nodded. The nurse showed Keith into a well lit light-blue room with a shiny tiled floor. Ruth was crying.

'Congratulations, darling,' he said. He kissed Ruth on the right cheek. He knew. Keith did not know whether to hug Ruth, to get her a drink or to get out for fresh air. He did nothing and they both fell silent. Then Ruth started to cry again. She blew her nose into a clump of bedclothes and tissue paper, got up, swished her maternity frock one way and then another in and around her knees. She clumped the frock in her hands and squeezed and wrung it like a sponge. Keith sat down sweating, wiped his face with a tissue from the wall dispenser. The cheap recycled paper scratched his face. He used his shirt sleeve instead. He stared at the dot matrix display of urine test results and the logo of a local waste disposal company on the side of the bedpan. Shifting his attention to the cot for a few minutes, Keith wondered what lay in store for this unfortunate little bundle.

'I should call Bode . . . should I call Bode, yes?' he asked.

'Yes, no . . . yes, he would want to know and I want to speak to him anyway, just to speak, tell him . . .' Ruth said, splashing her face with warm water. Puddles formed around her from the water dripping off her elbows. She looked as if she would slip or just crumple. Keith followed her, bracing himself to catch her, until she was safely back in bed.

'Can I get you a cup of tea?' said the midwife.

'Yes please,' he said, to get her out of the way. Keith returned to the nurse's station. 'Can I make a phone call?' he asked the midwife. She offered him the ward phone but Keith did not want to be overheard. 'Thank you,' he said, searched his pockets as if looking for an important piece of paper, sucked his teeth in feigned exasperation and returned to Ruth. 'I'm going outside to call Bode, won't be long.' Ruth nodded.

Keith went out into the corridor to make the call. 'Hello,' said Bode.

'Bode, when I arrived, they'd given it, given the vaccine,' said Keith. 'Sorry, I'm really sorry. Ruth and the baby are OK, but she's very, very upset. We'll talk later . . .'

'When's she coming home?' asked Bode.

'I think later on today,' said Keith.

'Thank you, you did your best, we'll always be grateful. You've been incredible, both of you, regards to Anne and the kids,' said Bode.

Dr Hartley then rang to tell his office he would be late. For appearances' sake he waited until Ruth was discharged and took her home, in a taxi.

When he got home after work Keith Hartley was too exhausted and drained emotionally to eat a proper meal. 'Toast and a glass of milk, please, I can't eat. What a day! The whole thing from start to finish, I wouldn't like to repeat it even if I lived for a thousand years. What were we, was *I* thinking?' he said. 'That plan was never going to work. But I keep thinking we could have done more.'

'You did your best,' said Anne.

'Yes, but take this morning, was I thinking at all? I must have panicked or something, why did I not drive your car instead of ringing a taxi? Little things like that could have made the difference. And on top of it all, the taxi driver got lost.'

'Fate?' asked Anne.

'Please,' said Keith, rolling his eyes.

'Well, don't beat yourself up, you've gone as far as anyone would. I'm really sorry for Ruth and Bode, but we mustn't push too hard. You've heard about the Misrepresentation of Nationality Act; you could be arrested.'

'Like Matthew, you're right,' said Keith, feeling marginally better. Matthew Sands, a work colleague at the geology department of Newcastle University, had been sentenced to three months' community service for not correctly registering his child's nationality. Although the Hartleys were exempt from the provisions of the Nationality Act and had two children of their own, Anne's grandfather was Colombian by birth, and a redefinition of nationality by the government could, in theory, render them stateless.

'I see your point,' said Keith. 'Can I have an omelette as well?'

Seven days later, in accordance with some vaguely remembered Yoruba practice, Bode and Ruth Dacosta named their little boy Mensah; it was not a Yoruba name, Ruth just liked the sound of it. To some narrow-minded invitees, the teetotal Ruth, with her untidy hair, appeared too jolly or even drunk at the party.

At the end of his week off work, Bode was exhausted. Ruth had hardly moved all week. He made the bed when she got up. When the health visitor, Ms Dreyfus, came to see her, Ruth did not bother to see her out. She fed, cleaned and changed Mensah, and went back to bed. She had a croissant and a cup of tea for breakfast, a tin of rice pudding for lunch and baked beans for supper. When her parents came and Bode's mother called, she came downstairs, spent a few minutes, left them with Mensah and went back upstairs. 'I'm not sure why I'm so tired,' she said.

'We understand,' they said. Then Bode started to lose patience with Ruth's tears and her aloofness, the vacant stares.

'If I'd known you were going to be this miserable . . .'

'What?' said Ruth. 'Go on, have a go, everyone else is, your mum, my mum, I can't help how I feel. I didn't know how I would feel. You haven't been that much help, trotting off to your mates at work. Can't you see: I'm worn out?' said Ruth. 'Go on, go out, I'll cheer up for you, cook, and feed Mensah, make it all right for you,' said Ruth.

Bode took off his coat. 'I was only going round to get some milk, I won't bother. You know I had bad vibes about all this right from the start, you could have had an abortion,' said Bode.

'Thank you very much, just what I want to hear, that you could even dare to suggest such a thing, abortion, how would I feel, to break my vows for what, an inconvenience, take a life, for the government? Bode, you don't know what you've just said. If you're trying to make me feel better, you're not.'

'I'm just telling you how I feel,' said Bode. 'I am allowed to aren't I? I'm just saying: no child, not happy; you have child, still not happy – what do you want me to do? We would have been better off without, knowing we couldn't stop them giving him this jab,' said Bode.

'That's awful,' said Ruth. 'Really unfair, you know we tried, I know it was a dodgy plan, but we tried, but an abortion, never, never! Never use that word in my presence ever again.' And she went back to bed.

One early morning Bode got up to clean Mensah ready for Ruth, and once she'd finished feeding him she got him back to sleep. Bode thought he would try a different tack. 'Okay, look at it this way,' he said. 'Just look at your little pet, isn't he beautiful? This vaccine they've used, suppose we look at it as a sort of prophylaxis, like the other jabs we get as babies and later on. You know, like measles, tetanus, diphtheria, cervical cancer and yellow fever. Maybe we overreacted.'

Ruth flushed, beads of sweat shone on her forehead, she raised both hands to her ears, a half garland between neck and head, and dropped them as if in salaam.

'It's a bit early in the morning for this sort of talk. Don't insult me, I'm wide awake. Don't insult my intelligence.' She sat up higher in bed. Her dribbling left breast hung out of her nightie. 'This is different, and you know it, it's discrimination. Has the jab been tested properly, on whom, on any other groups? Did they vaccinate the shysters who sold collateralised debt obligations to people who could not afford them, or the swindlers who allegedly sold worthless investments and then bet against them, peddled useless pension policies and dodgy endowment policies? The credit agencies that gave their friends triple A ratings and have the front to downgrade sovereign debt? Glad the Chinese are going to call their bluff! Why don't they do research into that and jab *their* children against chicanery, finagling, double dealing, dissembling, white collar crime; why don't they do research into that? Why don't they do research into the kids on the streets: why they're there? And you tell me it's like smallpox vaccination; it's not, you know it and you think I'm stupid. I'm not stupid, I know where you are all coming from – I know. You didn't want me to have a child and now you want to kill him. I won't let you or your Nazi, Stasi government harm him.' She fished frantically for her rosary under the pillow, muttered a prayer, kissed the rosary and made the sign of a cross over Mensah.

Ruth carried on with her Hail Marys, for absolution for her sins, for relief from her torment, or just out of habit. No one knew. Anne and her other friends despaired. Oblivious or indifferent neighbours slept. Out of uxorious loyalty, perhaps, or out of impotent frustration, Bode, a Muslim of sorts, dusted down his long-discarded prayer mat to recite the short, easier suras he had learned from his father. Not having a target, himself, he prayed for whatever Ruth needed. When his desire to pray for Ruth waned, he prayed to want to pray, for endurance, so that Ruth would be consoled by seeing him pray. For weeks Bode

27

prayed longer, harder and louder. Whenever he was woken up in the middle of the night he would say an extra prayer, hoping for Ruth's wishes to recede or be fulfilled; he did not know which.

Ruth prayed too. Does anyone know how hard you have to pray, how long – how much belief, sacrifice, conviction and zeal of exhortation are needed for prayers to be answered?

When his father called from Nigeria, Bode told him everything was fine: Mensah was beautiful. He even asked whether his father would visit. Then his 'aunt' Iyabo rang. She was a Lagos market trader. 'I hear your story in London,' she said.

'Which story, Aunty?' said Bode.

'They tell me you let the Oyinbo people give your son bad medicine. And you did nothing. They say you were at home, didn't go to hospital. How can you allow such a thing? Your father would never allow it, you are not a real man, *haba*.'

Bode was speechless. She went on. 'Your first son, *first son*, they give him something that make him not to have a child and you just sit there like a dummy. You are waiting for them to save you; how can they? They say they don't want you there and you sat there waiting for what? Manna from heaven? You are a nincompoop. You are weak, and your wife, you allow her to wear the trouser in that house. That is not the way back home, I can tell you that even as a woman. No wonder she does not do what you say. She thinks she's better than everybody. We saw it when we visited – some rotten, wet, cold, miserable insult of a biscuit and a cold cup of tea, not even a lump of sugar. You remember when Oluniyi came to visit, she couldn't wait to get rid of him. He'd only been there five minutes, she was asking when he would leave. His course was for nine months; only three months she let him spend there, only three and he said she can't even cook what he likes. All that bland food they eat, he had to manage. Does she think we are starving? As if we have not met any other doctors. So what – her father was a consultant? Well it's your bed, you made it, you must lie on it. None of this would have happened if you had taken our advice and left her. You thought you were an Englishman. Now they've taught you a lesson. We warned you.' She put the phone down. Bode returned to making his supper of toast and butter.

Anne Hartley, Anthea Record and Ruth's other friends worried about her isolation and her prayers. Anne even thought of adopting Mensah. 'We've done enough, remember?' said Keith. Bode's trips out of town got longer and longer until Ruth either did not notice or care. Ruth would not let her parents help, and Bode's Mum had given up, stopped visiting, too easily in some people's eyes.

Bode was on his way back from Harrogate, when his phone rang. 'Hello, are you Mr Bode Dacosta?' said a man unaccustomed to unusual names.

'Yes,' said Bode.

'Where are you, sir?'

'In England,' said Bode.

'I think we know that, sir, how far are you away from home?'

'Who are you?' asked Bode.

'The police. Look, we're only trying to help. It seems there's been some sort of mix-up at home. Your son's been left on his own.'

'What do you mean, his mum's there is she not? Is he all right, is his mum OK?'

'He seems to have been locked in, by accident, sir, we're just making enquiries, sir, you see.'

'What's happened? I need to park the car. Officer, are you still there?' he said after a few minutes. 'I'm about twenty minutes away, is my son all right? Where's my wife? She's a doctor, I hope she's not ill?'

'Your son's fine, as I believe your wife is too, they're safe, we'll wait for you, sir.'

Bode hammered up the bypass into Newcastle. When he got home, Anne and Keith were standing with Ruth. The police liaison officer had Mensah in her arms. 'That's my son, what's he doing with you?' said Bode.

'Please can we go in, sir, we'll get this sorted,' said the officer.

'We'll be off, let us know if there's anything we can do,' said Keith and Anne.

Bode waved at them. 'Thanks,' he said. Indoors, he let rip. He shook Ruth. 'Where were you, where, what happened?'

'You're hurting me,' Ruth cried. He turned to the police. The most senior, a tall, pale, large man with a soft Geordie accent, said a neighbour had heard a child crying in the dark and had broken in to find Mensah locked up alone, a lamp flex wrapped round his ankle; perhaps he had pulled it off by accident and blown a fuse?

'It's not true,' said Ruth. 'I was at work, doing my visiting, I'm a community family paediatrician.'

'How can you visit? You're still on maternity leave; I can't believe that you could be so irresponsible. My baby all alone in a cold, dark room,' said Bode. Then remembering that they still had company, he said, 'Thank you, officer, I'm home now.'

'Thank you, sir, procedure, sir, we'll need a statement from both of you and we have to take your son away for the night for a medical report from a duty child specialist and they'll take it from there. They're very good, but you can see, it has to be done, it is very serious, your son could have died.'

After the assessments and a medical report Ruth admitted that she needed help. Mensah was taken into care. Bode thought it would only be temporary, until Ruth 'sorted herself out', but the Friday after, Bode came home to find Ruth inconsolable. He prayed again, wept with Ruth, but by Monday had made up his mind that Allah was telling him to start a new life. His paternal 'aunt' Iyabo agreed with him with glee.

So Mensah joined the not so exclusive club of abandoned BoNDs (Britons of Nigerian Descent). Membership of this club was granted via unemployment, bankruptcy, ill health, divorce, religious differences, a royal-like yearning for a child of the right sex, interrupted careers or studies and, yes, fecklessness and self-indulgence. Some genuinely believed the State would be more competent custodians of their offspring. They, the parents, could take time off and turn up eighteen years later to reclaim their once-little package. But baggage left unattended, even for a day, gets lost or damaged, and when found, its contents are often no longer viable, needed or useful.

3

Ruth Loses

With both Mensah and Bode gone, Ruth returned to work. She got ready in the morning, drove to the hospital, sat in the car park, and watched the trees sway in the wind. Trees became sea waves, the howl of wind and the rustle of leaves morphed into wave crashing against seafront, alternately close up and gigantic and then distant and minute. Ruth would then go home or to the local newsagent or library to thumb through magazines. Then to the pub. Support from therapists and psychologists was in short supply – savage cuts so no money.

'Dad, they're trying to get rid of me,' she said after her line manager invited her to a job re-evaluation, appraisal and pre-revalidation exercise. But Dr Charles Omughana thought his daughter's problems would blow over with support and time.

'What do you mean they're trying to get rid of you?' he said.

'I'm sure they are, but they're dressing it up as rationalisation, reconfigurations and so on. The hospital's in debt and paediatrics is vulnerable, we cost so much. I've had a hard time, my GP will support that, but they're not having it. I don't have the strength for a tribunal.'

'You must try, Ruth, we're behind you, Mum is too,' said her dad.

So with her parents' support, Ruth tried to sue the hospital for discrimination on grounds of mental health, but the case took so long that she could no longer follow the arguments, started drinking again and lost interest. She lost her job, then her home. So she went to live with her parents. One night when Ruth stole downstairs, as was her wont, to find that her parents had moved the alcohol to safety, she lost her temper. She flew up the stairs, crashed into their bedroom and shook the shocked pair out of bed. 'I know your trick, both of you, you're trying to kill me, aren't you! It won't work. Where have you hidden the booze? If you don't let me have it I'll wake everyone up and tell them what you're really like. Murderers and child molesters. You took my son away. You killed Mensah.'

'Please, Ruth,' said Charles. 'We just forgot to tell you where we put the key, that's all. Look, I'll show you, it won't happen again, but could you help us too?' For your mum's sake, and mine. I've got to go to work. Could you try not to make so much noise at night? We'll show you where the key to the cabinet is. Are you looking for a job?'

'Yes, I'm close,' said Ruth. 'As long as you're fair, I'll be fair, straight, I'll be straight but don't mess me about,' said Ruth. So they agreed she would not rummage around at night. But when Ruth was not out at night partying she was in her room singing and dancing to the latest expletive-laden dance records. When they complained she said, 'You are not happy because I won't let those filthy friends of yours have their way with me, I know because I see the way they look at me, did you invite them, tell me? I have heard about this but did not think you would do it, to your own daughter; I'll tell the police if you don't stop them coming. I will, don't try me. I'll report both of you.'

'She's had a double bereavement, she'll get over it, in time,' is what Charles would say to his wife at these times. Esther was not convinced but did not know what to do either. One day Charles came home to find Ruth standing over a whimpering Esther with a broomstick. Charles quietly called the hospital, and soon, with considerable skill and patience, and by pretending to be on her side, the paramedic cajoled Ruth into his ambulance.

In hospital, Ruth refused to see her parents, so they left money and supplies with the ward staff. 'Have we been too strict?' said Charles.

'No, you spoilt her,' said Esther. 'Modernity they called it, you were for the modern way, maybe that's the problem.'

'I don't think it's got anything to do with us,' said Charles. 'Adolescence, viral infections, mutations – could be anything, even before she was born. We can blame the school, the chemicals in the water, the month she was conceived; you name it, there's a candidate. Watch daytime TV, you'll see. We'll just have to get on with life, we can't go under as well. We have to think of Mensah. I'm not going to surrender him to the State if I can help it.' Charles was referring to their legal fight with social services over Mensah's custody.

A few months later Charles Omughana said to his wife, 'Ruth's coming home today.' Esther beamed. 'They say she's much better, I hope we can get her sorted, back on track. Where's my jacket, I'd better take one for her as well. It's been ages.'

When he got to the hospital, Sister Friends was waiting. 'How are you, doctor?'

'Fine, thank you,' he said.

'Can I have a word, please?' asked the sister.

'Of course. What's happened, is something wrong, is she ill?'

'No, nothing like that, she, she's refusing – how can I say this? – she's not coming.'

'Can I speak to my daughter, please?' said Charles.

'By all means, sir.'

Dr Omughana went to Ruth's room. Ruth was packed but was sitting on one of her suitcases; another, smaller, box was open in front of her, which she appeared to be unpacking. 'Ruth, let's go,' said Charles.

'No, I'm not coming with you, you cannot be my father, to

send me to this place; I will not, repeat not, return to that house. You think I don't know you; poor mother just copes, I'll come to take her away from you, you're no good. What have you done with my son?'

Charles sat down next to her. She moved away. 'Don't you dare come near me,' she said.

'But we've been waiting for you, we've been fighting for Mensah; the house is all ready, your mum's expecting you.'

Ruth folded her arms and turned away, tapping her foot. 'You'd better leave, because I'm not coming, the council will find me somewhere safe. You are not my true father, God knows my real father and He will show him to me; my mother is trapped with you; I'll release her from your bondage in Egypt to a new Jerusalem.'

Charles returned to Sister Friends. 'I'm sorry, what are you going to do?' she asked.

'I'll see if her mother can persuade her,' said Charles. What else could he do? His daughter seemed lost to him.

When Charles got home without Ruth, Esther burst into tears. 'What did you say to upset her?'

'Nothing,' he said.

'I should have come with you or gone myself. Three months she's been away, I haven't seen her, you're sure she's all right?' Esther put her coat on. 'I'll find out myself, give me her jacket,' she said.

But when Esther arrived at the hospital, Ruth refused to budge. 'I'm not going home if that man's there. I'm not going there, you come with me, we'll be safe together,' Ruth said. So, Esther returned empty-handed. The council eventually agreed to put Ruth on the community and 'distant monitoring' programme.

4

Mensah, Marty and Nancy

Under the amended provisions of the ADHD Bill, Mensah's grand-parents and his parents – Ruth, by virtue of infirmity, and Bode, by deserting – had in effect lost all legal rights to Mensah. Charles and Esther were told that anyway they were too old to look after Mensah and they would be barred from seeing their grandson if they continued to cause trouble by taking legal action. But Charles would not give up.

While his grandparents fought for custody, Mensah was moved from one foster home to another. The Snells' first memories of Mensah were of a thin, unhappy little boy with thick, unruly, dark brown hair in a rubber pool with other children in the garden of a large Victorian house on a sunny Northumberland day. Marty was a bookish and athletic man, an engineer with British Wind Fuels; Nancy, a former primary school teacher. Marty and Nancy were resigned to childlessness after several failed attempts at *in vitro* fertilization, and took to Mensah at once.

With his grandparents defeated by the cost, stress and effort of litigation, when Mensah was four, the courts decided that his psychological development was more likely to be secure with the Snells. Then, in an uncommon exhibition of common sense, the council agreed to Mensah's formal 'trans-cultural' adoption.

Every weekend they went shopping together as a family. 'Mensah smiled, he smiled at me,' said Nancy on one such outing, taking off her gloves.

'I took a photo. Do you think I should show it to him?' said Marty. 'Should I go and give it to him now or should we wait? We may frighten him.'

'I can't wait to tell Mum, she said it wouldn't work out,' said Nancy.

'She had a point, when he wouldn't talk or smile even I was getting worried,' said Marty.

'Mrs Bedford, the health visitor, the nice one, not Mrs Harrison, old grumpy, will be thrilled. We're getting through,' said Nancy.

'We shouldn't get carried away, can't be sure whether he was smiling at you or at his reflection in his "Emperor the Mighty" outfit,' said Marty.

'He even squeezed my hand. Well, if that's what it takes, I'm taking him to John Lewis every weekend until he goes to school this autumn,' said Nancy. 'Mensah, hi, did you enjoy the shopping?' Mensah nodded. Then he smiled, with all his face, from ear to ear, and his eyes lit up, still dressed in his outfit. He tried a pirouette. 'Yah,' he said, and he fell over, quickly getting up again. For a second or two, silence. Then he laughed. Nancy and Marty laughed too. Nancy held out her arms and Mensah ran into them.

And so the years went by. Mensah went to a fee-paying Roman Catholic school in Gosforth, Newcastle. His first report card read: 'likeable but prone to the odd violent tantrum if he's kept waiting.' After school, Mensah would finish his homework, but never asked for help. He would come down for his meals, watch the cartoons alone, in silence, and rarely started a conversation. Once, when Nancy went to pick him up from school, Mrs Matting, the class teacher, called her to one side. 'Is everything all right at home?' she said.

'Of course, why do you ask?'

'Well, I am not one of those teachers who works to live, I care about my charges,' she said sincerely. She knew that some of the other teachers, aware of his difficult start in life, made concessions for Mensah's foibles out of guilt, kindness, embarrassment, indifference or was it just laziness? She wondered.

'What's wrong?' asked Nancy, slightly impatient to cut to the chase.

'His computer monitor,' said the teacher, 'it went blank during the maths test and he didn't tell me, he just sat there. I don't know why. Maybe it's just timidity, maybe he was frightened somehow. I know he's good at sums; it's not as if he doesn't know the answers, he just seems very inhibited. And, there's another thing: Mrs Samuels told me that Mensah wet himself in the English story class. He didn't ask whether he could go to the toilet! And of course the children teased him; called him names. Anyway, he hit out and had his shirt pocket torn off in a scuffle.'

'I thought he tore it from playing corridor rugby,' said Nancy. 'If there's anything I can do . . .' said the teacher.

'Thank you, Mrs Matting, we're working on it with support and he's getting better; be patient with him, please. I'll talk to him, but everything's fine at home, I assure you.'

One evening, when he did not come down to do his homework, Nancy went upstairs to find Mensah bawling. 'What's wrong, Mensah, pet?' she said. He lifted his head off the pillow, startled. He wiped his tears. 'It's all right, darling, what's wrong?'

'It's Vince, he's leaving. His daddy's going somewhere else. He's not coming back.' And he started to cry again. Nancy cuddled him, rocking him from side to side. After an hour, during which he appeared to fall asleep, they went downstairs together and he finished his homework. 'Happy now?' she said after they had packed his satchel and she read him a chapter from *Big Pig*.

He nodded. 'Do you think the bear in the jungle would like a piece of chocolate, Nancy?' he asked.

'Does that mean you want some?' she teased. He was silent.

'You see, Mensah, if you want something, or if something's

troubling you, you just have to say, we're here to look after you, we love you, we understand. What are you like?' she tweaked his cheeks.

He nodded. 'I'll go now,' he said.

'Don't you want the chocolate?' He nodded. She brought him a piece of chocolate cake and sat next to him as he ate it. 'Now, let's go and wash your hands.' They went through to the kitchen and she washed his hands in hers and left him to wash off the suds in the warm water. He put his hands out to be patted dry. 'There, there, don't cry,' she said, seeing new tears form in his eyes. But these were different tears, behind these ones his eyes sparkled. He smiled and hugged her. 'Better now?' He nodded. 'I love you more than the rainbow, more than the sea, more than the itsy-bitsy in with me . . .' she said. He smiled and snuggled up. He did not go back upstairs and sat watching the soaps with Nancy until Marty came home.

On the evening of his eighth birthday, Mensah said his birthday cake reminded him of the woman who used to bring him cake when he was in care. 'I don't remember the other ladies' names, I just knew them by smell, some nice, some not so nice, and when they wouldn't put me down, I pulled their hair just a little and stiffened up and wriggled until they did. A beautiful lady who used to cry – she must have come with a nurse or police-woman or somebody like that. She used to bring me cake, ruffle my hair and cry all the time – she came maybe twice or three times and we sat downstairs in a room. I wanted her to give me more cake but all she did was cry and hug me. She looked me over for scratches or rashes. Once she took me to the fair – could have been the Hoppings – and sat me on a ride with a young man. The lady with her said she should not go on the ride. I was a bit frightened but I didn't want to let her down and could see her smiling and worried face down below each time we came past where she was standing. We went back to the home and she kissed me – the other children were watching from the top window. One day they said she was coming and I was ready, but she didn't come, I didn't want anyone to know that I was waiting for her but when it got dark I knew she wasn't coming and I haven't seen her since. I don't know why she stopped coming. No one said. Sometimes the visitors came to inspect us – and we had to be neat. When you came I liked you, and hoped you would stay. You looked kind, with long, light brown hair down your back,' he said. 'I liked your blue eyes – like the ones in the books of fairy stories. But I thought you would take me back. I tried to be a good boy so you would keep me. Have I been good?' he said.

'Of course you have. We'll never ever let you down. We'll never leave you. Never, never!' She squeezed his hand and he leant against her, head first. Nancy, moist eyed herself, was not sure whether Mensah had really experienced or just imagined these visits from his mother.

During another 'little chat' with Nancy one winter evening when he was about thirteen, Mensah told her about some of his early school days. 'The first boy to talk to me on my first day at school was called Vince; then John, then Julian. I cried but so did everyone else. I didn't want you to know that I cried but now I know that everybody else did. Josephine was always behind in her reading but she giggled a lot and the teachers let her get away with it. She was Dutch I think. Bingo, Sister Francesca's dog, scratched Julian and I never saw Julian again. John moved when his grandfather died, but Vince was my favourite. So I didn't have any friends and I didn't want to make new ones. They couldn't be as good as Vince and John.' He told Nancy that when he was captain during the weekly English and mental arithmetic quiz, his team lost because Mrs Schlumber, the teacher, had allowed Terry, her favourite (and her niece!), more time to answer her question, costing his side the game. 'She was always allowing Terry more time!' he said. He did not tell Nancy that he slashed Mrs Schlumber's car tyres in revenge.

'We are very, very proud of you,' gushed Nancy when she heard that Mensah had won a part scholarship to the Royal Grammar School. Mensah was pleased that Nancy was pleased with him. 'The others were not trying, or must have had an off day, RGS is not as good as it should be then if I can get in. Maybe they just took pity on me,' he said.

'No they didn't, you were the only boy from your school to win a place at the RGS this year,' she said. 'You're a clever little clogs, you are,' she said.

'I thought I was clever, but I didn't get a scholarship,' said Marty.

'You did, in . . .'

'Oh shh, Nancy, we're being serious, here,' said Marty.

Later, Mensah won the four hundred metres race for the North East Independent Schools team at the mini-Olympics in London. By age sixteen he was 1.84 metres tall and weighed seventy-nine kilos and was gaining in confidence; but from a low base. Mensah worked hard, largely to please Mr Pates, his chemistry master, who encouraged him to take both the national board examinations and the new Baccalaureate exam administered by the United Nations.

5

Grandfather's Legacy

On his eighteenth birthday, Marty and Nancy knocked on Mensah's bedroom door. 'Happy birthday, Mensah,' they chimed. 'Isn't it a lovely summer's day. Come on down, we've got something for you, downstairs, hurry up, you're a man now.'

Mensah stretched and yawned himself downstairs. He loved birthdays, presents and being fussed over. First he opened his cards and then his presents. In the first box was a portable multimedia GAA (GoogleApple Alliance) player/music mixer, which also allowed the operator to transform songs into different genres. He tried his favourite – Mucous Membrane's 'You Keep Me Hanging Out' – as it might have sounded if it had been composed by J.S. Bach. After that he opened the more practical presents – a new overcoat, Marks & Spencer's vouchers and luminescent bicycle clips. 'Thank you so much, these are great, just what I needed,' he gushed as he hugged Marty and Nancy one-armed and cheek-kissed Nancy. Nancy nodded a signal to Marty and said, 'We also have a present from your grandfather, your mother's father.'

Mensah looked up at them both from the sofa, wondering what this all meant. 'You've never mentioned my grandfather before – I didn't even know that I still had a grandfather. What grandfather, is he here?' Mensah asked.

Nancy decided that she would do most of the talking. 'No,'

she replied, 'he's not here and we don't know where he is either.' 'We love you very much, but your grandfather or his family or the council – we are not sure who – sent us this box soon after you came to live with us. It's just bits and pieces from your grandpa, we don't know what it really contains. It's the right time to have it, before you go away to university. We think you're old enough now . . . don't we, Marty? But we'll do what you want. Lock it up and put it away again if you're not ready. You could leave it like this. One day you may want to pass it on to your own family. You're lovely, come here.' Nancy hugged Mensah again.

'I'll always be yours, won't I? You're not trying to get rid of me?' said Mensah.

'Of course we're not,' they replied. Mensah nodded, an aching lump in his throat. To stifle the tears, he wheeled the cases in a wide arc, turned and lugged them up to his room. He knew they meant what they said and he thought he knew what they meant. In life, particularly in adversity, everyone needs a parachute or parachutes: in family, religion, professions, money, connections, self-knowledge, temperament, experience, education, vocations, or even crime.

After taking a shower, Mensah went downstairs for breakfast and, with Nancy occupied in the garden, rang his friends, George and Santosh, who agreed to meet him at the Metrocentre, to take in a film and a meal to mark his birthday. Mensah returned to his room. He opened the smaller box. A musty aroma of camphor and stale books caused his nose to run and misted his eyes. Inside there was a jumble of books and photographs. In the lid pocket of the smaller case were several data memory sticks. 'Oh, Nancy,' he cried, 'these are old-fashioned, out of date, these memory sticks; they're over twenty years old.'

'If you don't mind me going through your stuff, I'll get Marty to ask Ralph – his computer analyst friend – to put them all in the correct format for you,' said Nancy when Mensah showed her the data sticks. The larger box was also filled with books, diaries and photograph albums and very old mobile phones, but Mensah could not find anything from his parents.

True to his word, Ralph reformatted the data sticks for use on Mensah's new GAA player. On the first data stick was a collage of memories and facts compiled by Dr Charles Omughana, Mensah's grandfather. There was a brief introduction by Charles himself, wishing Mensah a long life and good health and hoping that the contents would serve as a bridge to his past and in time provide pleasure, entertainment and information. The rest of the contents included a photograph and footage of his grandparents' wedding at Newcastle Civic Centre, plus his grandfather's medical graduation ceremony and even the funeral of Bob Notscratch, the manager under whom Newcastle United had won the Premiership and got to the semi-finals of the Champions' League. Notscratch – as any diehard Newcastle fan knew – had died suddenly, pitch side, when Newcastle had conceded a goal against Sunderland for the first time in ten Derby matches. There were also references to major historical episodes: the Brixton riots of 1981, the miners' strike three years later and President Obama's inauguration of 2009. There was extensive footage and photographs of the dawn of New Labour and its landslide in 1997, followed by its shabby demise when, after losing the election, it had tried to hang on, printing money like Mugabe and nearly bankrupting the country. There were autographs of the West Indian cricket team from back in the day – golden names like Viv Richards, Joel Garner and all. There were academic certificates, payslips and contracts of employment; memories of the credit crunch, elections (national and local); footage of Grandpa standing on the touchline while his daughter played hockey; farewell and birthday cards; 2012 Olympics mementos; favourite musical recordings. All this in disorderly juxtaposition on the data stick: as were musings and jokes from patients that were probably not meant to be seen but may have escaped his grandfather's self-censor. What else? Old football match programmes;

half a dozen books by Dawkins, Dennett and le Carré; and scores of Fela Kuti CDs had been downloaded. But the timeline seemed to end when Mensah was aged about two years. His grandfather looked about fifty or sixty years old when the latter entries were made, making Mensah think that his grandfather may have died shortly after Mensah was born; either that or he had gone away, become ill or had simply had nothing new to add?

He could not help looking at some of the more intimate entries. Grandfather, referring to some old flame, had written:

> . . . *she married that layabout Robert, I knew it would not last. Obvious. Now a heifer, knocking on my door after two years; sorry ma'am, this one's not a fool any more. Take your baggage off to some other porter.*

Other entries were more sombre:

> *Attended this interview – overqualified. Last time no experience, other time too good to be true or too old or too unpronounceable – not going to change my name for anyone. What's in a name? Well ask those African Americans – Jones and Ellery and all the rest. It was not by choice. Jews had to do it for camouflage. What disguise do I adopt? Ah, light brown hair, distended abdomen, adult kwashiorkor, so they can patronise me, with aid?*

There was one entry about Ruth, his mother. His grandfather wrote, *Ruth has lost it,* but that was all, and if there was more Mensah did not find it or want to read it.

In his final year, before heading off to university, Mensah wrote an essay for the school magazine in which he described organised religion as an elaborate Ponzi scheme: in the West relying on recruitment from 'backward' countries as the 'flock' in the more advanced societies dwindled; and in other countries predicated on ignorance and fear. Why would a god have allowed his mother and father to leave him to his fate alone in the world?

And he was not the only one. There were still millions of children in the world whose parents were dead, missing or had abandoned them. Or they had bombs raining down on them, dropped by so-called 'religious' countries, and suffered hunger and disease. *Where was God during such genocide?* he asked. China's progress (brought about without belief in a 'conjuring trick with bones') would convince the developing world, particularly in Africa, that their salvation from poverty – if that was their desire – lay in corporeal and not spiritual application. Mr Barraclough, a closet atheist, thought the essay 'emotional' and directed Mensah to Humanist websites.

Once, challenged by Michael Thomas, a classmate, that religion inspired and spawned great music and art, Mensah replied 'so did Nazism and Marxism, have you seen bacteria under a microscope? As beautiful as anything you could draw; worship them then.'

When Martin, a rugby playing zealot, threatened to thump little Brian Holding because he would not recite the Lord's Prayer Mensah leapt between Holding and his assailant. 'If you so much as look at my friend, you'll never play rugby again,' he said to Martin, to his own and Martin's astonishment. Mensah was not sure why he had reacted so. He was powerfully built, but he was no fighter.

Partly because it had a peerless reputation in medical research and partly because he was afraid to move too far away from Nancy and Marty, Mensah applied to only one university, Newcastle. He was not sure why he wanted to be a doctor; perhaps he wanted to be happy by seeing or making others happy? Perhaps it was to emulate his grandfather? But he could not admit to that. Left wing governments and then the Nationalists' selection panels had instructed medical universities to discriminate against candidates with a medical background. Ironic, when Mensah had not even met this offending grandfather. The Nationalists had also introduced a so-called 'Burka' system, using voice scramblers and a panel between interviewers and candidates to ensure that candidates from a working-class background got a fair shout. When Mensah won his place to study medicine at Newcastle it was too late for the authorities to withdraw their offer. In *Youde v. Vice Chancellor*, the European Court of Human Rights ruled against a university that tried to rescind a non-EU's offer to read law.

Mensah's admission to medical school was the first major competitive target he had set and reached on his own account. He took more pride and got more pleasure from Nancy and Marty's pride in him than he took in himself. But he was happy. Free-wheeling on the moors that afternoon Mensah laughed and sang, the wind blew tears of relief and joy past his ears, as he anticipated a more secure future than his past. He was vindicated, as if a weight had been lifted from his shoulders and the fear of rejection that had caused his defensive self-deprecation had finally dissipated. He had got in to a top university just as Mr Pates had said he would. Afterwards, he sat on the park bench to watch the sun set and, as his success sank in, he allowed himself to think that in six years' time he would have fulfilled his ambition to qualify as a doctor.

6

Vince Again

After the matriculation ceremony, Mensah was standing near the Great Hall trying to get his bearings when he heard a loud 'And where are you going?' It was Vince. Mensah could not believe his eyes. Vince, the boy with the ready smile, the first boy to speak to Mensah at school all those years ago, and here he was again on the welcome party for the freshers.

'Vince, it is Vince, isn't it?' said Mensah.

'Yeah, it is, look at you, you're a medic? Mensah, you'll enjoy it here. Look at those muscles! Positively immense; how? You were a little runt. It was your profile, couldn't mix it up with anyone else, even after all these years.' They hugged: Mensah with relief that he had found someone he knew; Vince with delight.

Vince was in the second year of a course in psychology, information technology and international relations. His parents ran a successful recycling and scrap firm in Middlesbrough and when Jeremy, his younger brother, decided to read business administration it took the pressure off Vince to join the family firm. 'Come on, let's go out, to the "Viking Lair" and then see what happens – take it from there. Oh, it's good to see you.'

'Are you sure? Your friends are waiting for you,' said Mensah.

'Nonsense, they won't mind. Hi, guys, meet Mensah: my long-lost prep school friend. He's a medic and he's coming with us.

I've got some stuff to drop off. Won't be a minute,' said Vince, dragging Mensah into the Students' Union building. Then the party of six headed for the Viking Lair, a cavernous pub on three floors of garish Nordic artefacts and loud metronomic music and even more outlandish punters. Throughout the evening Mensah became intoxicated by booze, by Vince, his friends and the pub's wild ambience. At about half past three, Vince sensed Mensah's vulnerability and sacrificed his night with his latest girlfriend, Sophie, to make sure Mensah got home safely.

In that first year, Mensah was the caddy to Vince's pro. The girls loved Vince, and Mensah's percentage of the spoils was much higher than he would have got as a sole trader, at a fraction of the cost or effort. By his second year, though, the student was as good as the master. A quick pint of beer to chill him, his deep voice and his mordant wit supported his solo forages into Newcastle club land. The Casting Couch was his favourite haunt and was usually packed with medical students and hospital staff. If he had not pulled by the end of an evening he would go home with the sore head President Kennedy had if he went twenty-four hours without it, allegedly.

'My system failed,' Mensah said one evening.

'What system?' asked Vince.

'I have a system: when I meet a girl I tell her my birthday is the twenty-second of the month in which we met. That way if I meet another girl the next month and she wants to visit or go out on my birthday there's no clash. But I met Jennifer and Cassie in the same month. On the twenty-second I was with Cassie, happened to look out over the balcony and saw Jennifer and a friend of hers walking up to the main entrance lifts to give me my birthday present. So I told Cassie there was a gas leak; she looked lost but she had to go, smuggled down the fire-escape ladder. She knew there was something dodgy going down. As it happens I had to wait for Laurence to find out when Jennifer had left before we could go back. I liked Jennifer.'

49

'What system will you use now?' said Vince.

'I'm not sure, sometimes it's better to sit it out. I did a few weeks ago: Samantha and Carla met in my room and neither would give way; I left them for an hour, pretending to answer a hospital call, but when they still didn't budge I went out for a run, and asked Laurence, logistic Laurence, to let me know when they'd gone. I haven't seen either of them since. But why worry? It's another month, another account. Carnal time-share can be foreclosed without warning; I'm sure I'm not a majority shareholder,' he said.

At clubs, though only in his third year, Mensah passed himself off as a fully qualified doctor. This one girl, Christina, asked him whether it was true that Swedish scientists had identified a complexion-enhancing sperm protein. Mensah said he was one of the subjects of the experiment and he would be happy to provide her a free trial. 'Or your money back,' he said. 'How many samples would I need?' she asked. 'They didn't say, at least a dozen,' he said. 'Over how long?' she asked. 'Why do you ask? You've got a lovely complexion,' he said. 'I'll pass then,' she said.

At the end of Mensah's third year Vince finished his studies and joined the Home Office, but they kept in touch. In his fourth year, Mensah was elected president of the students' athletics team and met Fifi when they made a foursome to the new out-of-centre multimedia cinema with Tony and Jasmine. Fifi, a javelin thrower, was studying politics. For a few weeks Mensah liked the idea of the presidency and his steady girlfriend. He was in a live experiment to see whether he would fall in love. He wanted to because it sounded so wonderful. Everyone said she was 'just right for him', but how did they know? And he soon became bored and restless – socially and sexually – and vowed to return to his old ways. Sexual proclivities aside, he lacked the maturity and generosity to give up his flexible single life and was not yet ready to let anyone in to his private world of parental abandonment, Marty and Nancy, and his grandfather's legacy. He wanted his old life back, his selective solitude alternating with expeditions to club land, pop concerts, rides on his bike, visits to Nancy and Marty, science. He was busy enough with running the athletics team.

Fifi sensed Mensah's withdrawal. One day, to his relief, she called him 'to talk'. This much he knew: when a girl wanted to talk it was serious and almost always cathartic. Mensah sat next to Fifi on the park bench outside the Students' Union building whilst, unknown to him, his mates watched from the top floor of the humanities department. 'Mensah, you are the most selfish and immature person I've ever met,' she said. Mensah nodded. Silence. 'Don't you have anything to say for yourself?' she asked. Silence again, then a soft 'not really' from Mensah. To argue would lead to negotiation; better to concede her points, for freedom. He did not care if she told her friends that she had dumped him. What did it matter if he was free? 'You know, I know that in there is a much better person, you just can't be bothered, I pity you, if you ever find anyone, I pity her,' she said.

'I'm not that bad, am I?' said Mensah.

'No, I'm sure if you promised to try harder, just be a little bit more considerate, bend a bit, we . . .'

Mensah got up before she could finish. 'It's fine, you've made your point, I'm no good, not good enough for you, I'll take it. Which way are you going? I'll walk you to the station, if you don't mind,' he said.

'I'm fine, I'll wait for Amerie,' she said.

Shortly after his break-up with Fifi, Mensah was walking to the city centre with Jo, a psychology student whom he often accompanied to the station. They were quite good friends. When Jo stopped at the cash dispenser at Haymarket, to check her balance, he waited ahead of her, and as she caught up with him and they waited to cross the road, he looked around to make sure they would not be overheard. 'Jo, is it possible to be incapable of love, just as some people are incapable of empathy?' he asked.

51

'There are several types of love: we think that the swooning, blushing, wistful love of romantic paperbacks is probably unsustainable, but not so if it is transformed into a more adhesive, bonding relationship. If you're asking about the romantic side, I don't know. We have the capacity, but unevenly developed, enhanced or diminished by our experiences; that's the best I can do in five minutes. Why do you ask?'

'Oh, we were having an argument, that's all, with friends. You read some of this stuff in the papers: man killing wife and children because she rejected him, that sort of thing; you wonder what it's all about, who loves whom . . .'

'Those are extremes, not a good example, we don't know the history, jealousy is very powerful,' she said.

'So my friends are wrong,' he said.

'About what?' she asked.

'They say some people aren't capable of love; well, to be honest, just because I'm not one for romantic gestures, one said I'm like . . . what did she say again? Oh, yes . . . I do to love what a rusty corrugated tin roof does to light: absorb it; waste it. She called me the black hole of love. I thought it was some sort of compliment, but she may be right.'

'Oh, don't worry, I know you, you're just a big baby, you'll grow up, you're a late developer. Are you coming with me or going into town?' she asked.

'Into town to get a few things,' he said.

'See you next week,' she said and hurried to catch her train.

Mensah caught the bus. He did not want to carry on his conversation on the Metro. Jo might be right in theory, but Mensah thought the feelings he had for Nancy or Marty did not appear to be those his friends had for their parents or guardians or that he had read about. But he thought he could learn it: use the same cerebral plasticity that enabled him to play the piano, ride a bike or drive a car. To practise he would learn from his friends, their girlfriends. He could simulate, mimic its rituals, copy what others did, when they kissed, exchanged gifts, bought flowers, remembered anniversaries, until he was as good as they were. From love's rusty tin roof to its high fidelity polished mirror; if not radiating, reflecting love.

7

Contamination

That summer was hotter and drier than 1976, 2003 or 2024. It was marked by lawns the colour of urine and peeling beetroot-shaded flesh, even in Newcastle. So hot was it that non-EU economic migrant Anopheles mosquitoes from Europe twice had to elude border patrols: first to get in and then to flee back out, before they fried. The *Daily Mail* multiplied by ten the number of malaria cases in the south of England, but there were no foreigners to blame.

Nancy pottered about the house wondering how to mark Mensah's graduation. A lavish party or gift was out because that would further tie Mensah to them emotionally and he would want to reciprocate. She made a note on a used envelope to 'ask Marty'. Nancy opened the first of the official looking letters. Self-help groups, charities, even genealogical societies and governmental organisations all sent the odd circular, or letter. One of the envelopes looked different. It came from the Home Office, not from a quango or charity. The letter was addressed to Mr and Mrs Snell; so she opened it. The first paragraph referred to 'a state of emergency'. Nancy's unease grew as she read on. The letter read:

In response to widespread public disquiet at the disproportionate number of non-EU-born children involved in knife and street-level crime foreign-

born parents were encouraged to submit their children at birth for treatment that would modify their restlessness, impulsive and disruptive behaviour. Whilst we believe that this policy has achieved its primary objective, namely, to help the subjects integrate into wider civilised society, we are sorry to report that during the course of the programme, batches of the vaccine were contaminated with a dyskaryotin-c gene carrier protein. The effect of this contamination is yet to be determined but it is estimated that it will result in a reduction in life expectancy to about 40 years. Mr Mensah Snell is one of a group believed to have received such treatment. The victims of this unfortunate error, or their beneficiaries, will be informed when the level of compensation due is calculated by an independent team of consultants.

Reference was made to how they were improving the service all the time, how they were on the side of the ordinary citizen; they should remain calm, seek advice from the Citizens' Advice service, their GPs and from financial advisers as the report could affect eligibility for medical, travel and life insurance cover. A number of help lines and websites were enclosed and the letter was signed by A.J. Steward, the Permanent Under-Secretary of State for immigration and foreign nationals.

Nancy opened the back door, leaned against the right jamb for support, turned round, returned to the kitchen and rearranged the fruit in the bowl on the table. Then she sat down and wept.

That evening Nancy waited for an opening to show the letter to Marty, but when he went on about how he had got the better of Steve at tennis, she propped the letter in front of his postprandial glass of wine. Marty lip-read the letter twice, got up, sat down again, legs spread-eagled. He turned away from the table, hunched over the letter as if in prayer or to remould or will away the letter's contents. Nancy stood at the sink, waiting for his reaction. After five silent minutes he raised clenched fists and placed them on each temple, then crashed them down on his knees, banging his left elbow against the table corner.

'We fought world wars to defeat these scum, and now we vote

for them here? Have they forgotten? Did we fight the Nazis only because they thought of the idea first? Did we secretly agree with that form of government?' He was getting carried away but could not help it. 'I've never really understood what this thing, the Nationality Act, meant. I voted for the Nationalists thinking the country needed to be cleaned up. How and what do I tell Mensah?' he said. 'How could this happen? In this country? The original ADHD policy was wrong – it was awful, bloody awful what they did. Now we have this crap, they pretend they're concerned.' Marty was on a roll. 'These people, these politicians, the bureaucrats, the lot of them – who do they think they are, wrecking people's lives?! This wickedness to young babies and their families?' He was exasperated.

'And what were the parents thinking having a child during that uncertain period?' she said.

'You can't judge them like that,' he said.

'I'm sorry, wasn't thinking, it just came out, can't imagine what it must have been like,' she said. Marty sat brooding, bristling. Nancy had never seen him that angry.

'We'll have to find a way to tell him, before he finds out, perhaps we can join one of those patient groups, others in this mess,' he said. He got up. 'I'll call Ronnie. See what she thinks.' Ronnie was Jane Ronsberg, their solicitor. 'And we mustn't tell a soul about this,' he added. Then, in reaction to a faint expression of surprise on his wife's face, he said: 'No, not even the boy!' as if naming Mensah made it more real.

Mensah was looking forward to starting his training at the Royal Victoria Infirmary. It was six months since he'd last had time to contemplate anything other than his final examinations and, before he knew it, spring, his favourite season – the season of promise – had passed him by. With his exams over, time suddenly appeared to slow down. Trees, flowers, the parks – everything looked clearer, brighter, and more beautiful: the girls too. The ones he remembered from last season were now young women, nearly ripe for plucking without breaking the law. He planned to spend a few days with Nancy and Marty while he decided what to do with the rest of his holiday. He would spend the afternoons regaining fitness on his bicycle after three months of hard revision, and in the evenings he would lounge around with Nancy sharing anecdotes and watching remastered versions of her favourite classic weepies. Bliss beckoned.

Mensah set off for a walk he loved, in the shadows of the old city walls and around St James's Park, Leazes Terrace and Strawberry Place, but avoiding the pubs because they were too noisy. Then off to the quayside, another favourite, to admire for the hundredth time the engineering feat that was the Tyne Bridge. All bridges looked wonderful to him. He could not resist the old world charm of the mouth of the river Ouse further up the quayside. After his tour, Mensah sat on a bench halfway up St Thomas Road to eat the Cornish pasty he'd bought at the Haymarket branch of Greggs. He spent a few idle moments basking in his pride to have won a place on the rotation at the magnificently rebuilt Royal Victoria Infirmary whose entrance he could see a hundred metres to his right. He then set off for Nancy's.

For Newcastle, twenty degrees centigrade was especially warm for the early evening of a long summer's day. Perhaps it was *Casablanca* the night before that got Nancy going, but she was crying by the end of the day's movie, about a group of good bacteria that had been killed off by antibiotics promoted by irresponsible and environmentally insensitive multinationals. 'Don't be so mawkish,' Mensah said, but he thought her sensitivity made her sweet and kind.

'Are you enjoying your stay?' she asked him.

'Great,' he replied.

'So am I, have a Bettys' scone,' she said. He adored the scones from Harrogate's premier tearooms, Bettys, and he waited for Nancy to ask whether he wanted a drink. After all these years he still did not want to sound too forward. Nancy brought him a glass of orange juice. She knew she spoiled him, indulged and reinforced his reticence, but if what she had heard of university life had failed she was not going to change him now. He knew what she was thinking because they had talked about his shyness many times. 'You'll miss many opportunities to make friends and enjoy yourself. No one will do it for you. Just try a little harder, for my sake, then. Promise?' But she did not want to spoil his good mood today by nagging. So instead she simply asked, 'Do you want anything else?'

'No,' he replied. Mensah took his snack outside to enjoy the evening sunshine. He knew Nancy liked to think he was the same shy boy he'd been before he went to university. Mensah was not, but he liked to play along because he enjoyed her fussing over him.

Last summer's acer tree was in bloom with red rusty leaves; the Russian vine was winding its way round the trellis he'd erected before he'd started his clinical studies four summers ago. Humming some self-composed nonsense Europop tune, Mensah was as happy as Don Juan's condom. Nancy watched him from the kitchen window and then sidled towards the door. Mensah looked up to acknowledge her presence without encouraging her intrusion until he had finished the scone. Nancy brushed an errant hair back. 'Can I talk to you?' Mensah raised his head and pointed to his full mouth and chomping jaw – he sensed Nancy's nervousness but did not want to talk. 'I need to talk to you about . . .'

'My bedroom, I said I'd clear it,' he said.

'No, no! Not that!' she said. He pulled a face, swallowing the last of his scone. The sticky piece of scone trapped behind his left lower molars would have to wait. 'Do you know why so many people left the country about twenty years ago? You must know that many people fled,' she said.

'Of course I know; the newcomers swamped the country, and the schools, hospitals and housing stock couldn't meet the demand. The country had to decide: keep the immigrants or repay its debts after the second deep recession and the collapse of the coalitions.'

58

'Yes – you're right. Do you know why they had to leave, had to go?'

'No,' he said.

She drew a deep breath and sat down next to him. 'They were frightened, they felt threatened.' She told him about the ADHD vaccine and how many non-EUs were so frightened that they left for anywhere or anyone who would have them.

'Was that why my parents left me?' said Mensah.

'I don't know,' said Nancy. 'It could be connected. That's all in the past, I want to talk about the future.' Then Nancy showed Mensah the letter. He read it, pushed the last scones away, got up and, without saying anything, went upstairs and collapsed on to his bed overlooking the back garden. As he leant further over the window-sill he could see Nancy standing on the patio. Mensah crawled back, sank on to his chest. He felt as if he was wading in treacle. He wandered into his bathroom to splash water on to his burning face, unzipped and zipped his trousers without knowing why. He sat on the toilet fully dressed, his head in his hands. Five minutes later, he had wet himself. Trousers and underwear peeled off, he sat half naked on his bed. He crunched a paracetamol tablet but his mouth was too dry to swallow the pieces and he spat out the wet crumbs. Mensah had heard about the ADHD vaccine but did not think it had applied to him; it was for the non-EU newcomers he had heard of at school. Now they say he was part of an experiment that had gone wrong. He was going to die. Poor Nancy and Marty had wasted their time and money on him. Head on left forearm, Mensah sat on his bed, shadows in his mind. The garden lengthened as – indifferent – the sun set, its valedictory iridescence lost on Mensah who had fallen asleep, dried tear tracks across his nose and under his left ear. Waking up an hour later he saw the spilt tea on the carpet, but did not feel like cleaning it up. He put his shoes over the stain to remind him to wash it off before Nancy found it. Lying there in bed, Mensah knew it was too early to retire for the night, so he shook off sloth and, leaving his bicycle downstairs, he waved at Nancy and shambled along to the Great North Road to sit on the bench overlooking the moors to watch the traffic.

He saw solitary male drivers, probably on their way home, loose tie around neck and other examples of mannered sartorial disarray. Young men and women on a night out screeched past, and a small Ford hatchback with a man and a woman staring ahead, lost or cocooned in their own worlds, stopped not far away at the traffic-lights. Mensah asked himself where they were all going. Were they like him, losers, with hopes unfulfilled or dashed? How many were happy – how many had the jobs and partners they really wanted, with parents and children they were really proud of? Which of them was going home to find a husband or a wife who had fallen off a stool or a loft ladder and broken a leg or worse, a neck? Who was going home to a wife with someone else's DNA up her? Or to a termagant, or a bully incubating a raging temper? Some, he knew, were going home to an empty nothing. Yet, most people he met *were* happy or at least seemed it. Mrs T, who brought the students home-made honey, had been happily married for sixty-five years. Yet for him, yesterday's happiness (if that's what he'd called it) had dissolved in a solvent of misery. The hard-won control he'd wrested from destiny was slipping from him, his assailed defences undermined and twisted, but would they crumble, and he with them?

'The fascists! What are you going to do?' said Vince when Mensah told him his news. 'Is there nothing you can take – drugs, therapy, or do they just want you to wait and see?'

'That's what it sounds like,' said Mensah.

'Are you sure what they say is true, what do the doctors say?' asked Vince.

'They're not too sure what to do either. They say they're waiting for more data,' said Mensah.

'I'm off to Paris for a few months, then to the States,' said Vince. 'Work, I'm afraid. I'll be thinking of you. I wish there was something I could do, I'll call you, come out for a visit.'

'I'm not sure I'll get travel insurance now, unless I . . .'

'No, I see, bugger,' said Vince. 'What can I do? I wish I could help. I just don't understand, this is freaky shit, surely they'll not get away with this.'

'I can't even be bothered, who cares?' said Mensah. 'They say they'll hold some sort of inquiry. Anyway, you have a good time, don't worry about me, I'll still be here when you get back. If the doctors are right,' he added.

For four weeks, Mensah attended the twice weekly counselling sessions for the victims of the contamination, arranged through the local Care Trust. Nancy drove, negotiating the mid-morning traffic on Grandstand Road. Mensah insisted on sitting in the back of her electric car so he could hum and moan in time with the engine. The programme director, Ms Stephens, introduced Mensah to his counsellor, Dr Harry Wagner.

'Good morning, Dr Wagner,' said Mensah.

'Pleased to meet you,' said the doctor, 'I'll show you through.' He ushered Mensah into a long narrow office with a small chest of drawers, a couch and two low seats.

'Are you a psychologist?' asked Mensah.

'No,' I used to be a wind farmer, then I did a course in behavioural sciences, lectured a bit and here I am. I hope I can get to the bottom of the problem. We need to reconcile your predicament with its causes and consequences. Tell me about yourself.'

Mensah gave him a potted history including his adoption and how he had found out about the contamination. 'Well, you are an interesting case, but in my view your problems are twofold: a lack of appreciation of why this treatment was necessary and a need to come to terms with and to accept your yearning for release from your enforced trans-cultural incarceration.'

Mensah did not understand what the man was going on about – this was all bullshit, but it must pay the man's bills. Each session made Mensah feel worse, because Dr Wagner said the eugenicists were not to blame for his predicament. 'You realise that none of this would have happened if your people had not been involved

61

in arson, violent crime and drug taking. You can count yourself unlucky, but we all have to make sacrifices; yours was the price you paid for the good of wider society. Think – didn't this vaccine help you to complete college education? How many of your peers had gone to proper university?' asked Wagner.

'All of those who wanted to,' said Mensah.

'Must I attend these sessions?' Mensah asked Nancy on the way home after the eighth session.

'No, I don't think so,' she replied. 'But we should make sure it does not affect any claims you could make against the perpetrators or the government. Why do you want to stop?' Mensah raised his eyebrows, eyes wide open, a quizzical tilt of his head as was his wont. Did she really need an answer?

So Nancy cancelled the sessions. When asked why, Nancy told the receptionist that thanks to their efforts, Mensah was much better, thank you – he seemed to have made a miraculous recovery. Dr Harry Wagner could tick his boxes, earn his bonus and leave them alone.

8

Pre-registration Year

Mensah started his first pre-registration job at the Royal Victoria Infirmary with trepidation. Each day was contemplated with dread. Sleep did not refresh him. He retired early every night, only to wake up at about two a.m. unable to get back to sleep, pre-bedtime hopes of rejuvenation dashed. Mensah would switch on to a classical music station. Barber, Monteverdi, Purcell? Was it not normal to cry to such beautiful elegiac music? But to still be crying hours later when you should be getting ready to go to work? Mensah ascribed this persistent post-music languidness to lack of sophistication. But everything from Haydn to Sibelius and Mozart, even the 'Jupiter', evoked the same lachrymose response. Barber and Sibelius were understandable, but how, except for joy, could you cry to the 'Jupiter'? Yet, every day Mensah somehow dragged his leaden body out of bed in stages and shuffled the one hundred and fifty metres through the subway to work. So doleful was his mien that his patients thought he was tired. 'You're working too hard, doctor,' they said. Mensah feigned insouciance with a shrug of the shoulders; but to the perceptive, his eyes evinced a deeper malady. Even his old university mates mistook his doleful demeanour for world weariness, but hospital ward cover was shared between so many teams that no one saw him often enough to notice or care.

Nurses put Mensah's apparent aloofness first down to an

affectation – that he had gone all arrogant on them since he'd qualified; then to ignorance. So they asked his advice only as a last resort. That suited Mensah. 'Hey, Mensah,' said Dr Knight, his opposite number on the surgical ward. 'I'd like to see my parents, they're coming over from Hong Kong for the weekend, could you swap duties?'

'Err, I'll see, it may be difficult, I've already agreed to swap with the guy, I forget his name, he's just started, and he's got to go back to collect some of his luggage,' said Mensah. He was just about getting away with psyching himself up to do his rota and was not going to provide cover or swap duties. The nurses exchanged snide glances. When left one on one with patients in clinics or on the wards he was gripped with almost unbearable terror; his palms sweated and shirts clung to his torso with perspiration like poorly applied wallpaper. Once it took him so many attempts to insert an intravenous cannula that Mrs Venables, the ward sister, had to take over.

'Doctor, I see you're tired, we all struggle sometimes,' she said and succeeded first time, but the bemused, pin-cushioned Mrs Parry was left with a painful patchwork of plasters on her arm. To comply with the hospital's infection-control policy, Mensah had to go back to sign and date each dressing.

Mensah avoided any serious untoward incidents but had several near misses, once administering Teicoplanin to a patient with an allergy to the drug. Fortunately the patient's supposed allergy was only a harmless hot facial flush, but he received a reprimand because the alert had been flagged up and written in the notes.

He averted his gaze when addressed. His head dropped first down and to the left and, in the facial equivalent of continental drift, his mouth slipped further with each passing week. A friendly half-volley on the leg stump of a question such as Dr Road's 'What do you think precipitated Mrs Clasper's admission?' – a simple question to which he could have given a dozen acceptable and plausible responses – revealed Mensah's wretchedness. 'A variety of factors,' Mensah stuttered, his tongue a dead furry animal, his heartbeat echoing irregularly in his chest, neck, stomach and his disconnected head.

'Just give me one possible reason,' Dr Road persisted. Then, he sensed his colleague's discomfiture. Dr Road was not a bully. He lowered his voice to a whisper and said, 'Familiarise yourself with your patients' histories – it helps patient care and the rest of us because we can get more done; some of us are very busy, we don't have the time to pull teeth on wards.' Mensah swallowed hard, but his mouth was dry. Later, he ducked the medical students waiting for him to allocate patients to clerk and told Mrs Lumble, the ward administrator, he had to leave early to attend an urgent rescheduled teaching session. At the end of his first month, Mensah, by grinning non-stop, had just managed to reach the government target of smiling in fifty per cent of the photographs taken of him in patient contact.

To avoid contamination, cross-infections and needle-stick injuries, unused opiates and premedication agents, including morphine, diamorphine and propofol, were disposed of in a plastic tub. Accompanying patients to theatre during his surgical posting gave Mensah the opportunity to raid this 'sharps' bin. During his break, and when the theatres were quiet, he crept into the busiest cardiac theatre anaesthetic rooms, took the heaviest sharps bin and, adopting the demeanour of someone looking for a replacement, retired to a toilet or cubicle to shake the contents of the bins on to a paper towel. Using a syringe, he aspirated the contents of the least contaminated of the vials, refilled and replaced the bin. In his room he injected the concoction into his femoral vein to hide the puncture sites from view. He soon became hooked on the thrill, the subterfuge and the direct effect of the opiates combined with the cannabis he bought on the street. Even the aroma of the antiseptic he used to clean the vial excited him. But afterwards, he would sink into even greater self-hating, hand-wringing remorse. After a few difficult days on the ward he learned to avoid shooting up the day before he was on call.

'Dr Snell, is that your new piggy bank, or are you emptying

the vials for profit?' said Sister Gear, infection-control team leader, one evening when she saw Mensah with the sharps bin in the main theatre corridor. Her apparent perspicacity so unnerved Mensah that he abandoned his hospital-based drug-raiding expeditions and sought his highs elsewhere.

When Mensah thought he was getting too fat, he started a diet, which was easy since he did not take any pleasure in eating. He soon weighed less than seventy kilos. When Nancy called he just told her that he had been busy but was fine. She sensed that he was not telling her the truth, but did not want to intrude. Marty told her to relax, Mensah was a young man, finding his way through life.

Mensah spent his free weekends walking around the city centre, eyes down, hands in pockets, ignoring a lifetime of training. Head bowed, shoulders hunched, pigeon-toed, he shuffled along, save for a stone to kick: the comic book stereotype of a sad, bored boy. So miserable did he look, with untidy hair and ill-fitting baggy trousers falling off his thinning waist, that people crossed the road to avoid him!

On reaching Eldon Square, he sat on one of the benches opposite John Lewis hoping to start with a shopper or pensioner, one of those symbiotic but rhetorical one-sided conversations that led nowhere but passed the time. As long as he interjected with the odd 'really', or 'cannot believe it', Mensah could keep them talking for as long as he wanted. Some, seeing the sadness in his eyes, asked whether he was missing his warm homeland and got up to sit somewhere else. Their lives were lonely enough without their own personal live human depressant in a shopping centre! Their grandchildren had warned them of these strange loners who went berserk or got off on old prey. Round the corner in the retail centre Mensah would download a few music tracks. He never enjoyed his selection but, because he was not concentrating, he often went back to choose the same songs he had just rejected.

On the odd occasion Mensah tried to shake himself up by

venturing to the Bigg Market pubs and clubs. He'd get in early, stand in the dark and have a few beers to free him, but it seemed to make him worse. When he ventured on to the dance floor his head and legs appeared to be disconnected; he knew he was supposed to be enjoying himself but he was not. Yet he recognised the songs as his favourites, the ones to which he had danced six months earlier in the bathroom.

One time, Bianca, a blonde, asked him to dance. 'What's your name?' she asked. 'Mine's Bianca.'

'Mensah, I'm not a very good dancer,' he said.

'What are you good at?' she asked above the din. He smiled: it was a reflex smile, a smile from memory of better times, but it was enough for Bianca. To her it was a smile of promise, safety; he was good-looking and not cocky. After a few more dances and drinks she kissed him. He applied himself but did not feel any buzz; he had to get away.

'Should we go?' she asked. He nodded, downing the last dregs of his drink as if in readiness. 'Let's go for our coats,' he said. He did not have a coat. Whilst Bianca queued for her coat Mensah sneaked off home. He had forgotten the episode when he ran into her at Catty's a few weeks later. Bianca tapped him on the shoulder and, head nearly touching his, said, 'You's a miserable loser, waste of space. Why don't you just lie down and die, lock yourself up and let the rest of us be happy. You won't be missed, miserable shitty git, it cost me twenty quid to get home, I looked everywhere for you, I thought you were lost or something, why did I bother? I should've known; waster, fucking waster,' she said. Bianca made her point and showed him to her friends by barging into him whenever their paths crossed. But Bianca's hostility did not stop Michelle, her friend, sidling up to tell him that Bianca was a slag, who left two toddlers with her mother whilst she went out clubbing. She, Michelle, was a nice girl.

'I really am a loser,' replied Mensah to put her off.

'But, but, she says you's a doctor, like,' her voice rising in alcohol-fuelled indignation.

'I lied,' he said, and hurried back to his hospital room on foot, too scared to wait at the taxi rank in case the girls found him.

To Mensah, mischance begat, became or was a calamity. When his briefcase burst open at Boots the Chemists in Eldon Square, the other shoppers helped to pick up his pen, comb, wallet and other sundries. They would not give his accident a second thought. To Mensah, the shoppers must think him pathetic, a man who could not look after himself. Without looking up at them, so that they could not see his tears, he thanked them and hurried away, not sure whether he had settled his bill. For days he avoided the city centre because it reminded him of his humiliation. At the out of town cinema multiplex he stared at the screen taking nothing in, other than the popcorn he bought and chewed like an automaton, but did not taste.

On blowy, overcast days, fatigue, cannabis and depression combined to hallucinatory effect. That winter the crunching on snow of a few pairs of boots sounded like an army on the march. Yet he had lucid days when he recognised that he was not right. To whom could he turn for help? Why should he tell some stranger that he was a BoND – abandoned, adopted – that he did not know where his parents were, that he had been vaccinated against behavioural problems and contaminated with a life-shortening agent and was now struggling with his work? What a CV! A rocket-fuelled boost to a career, or more likely the splash back to earth and oblivion. The only parachutes he had were his grandfather's diaries, Nancy, Marty and himself, but he did not want to involve Nancy and Marty, because he did not think he was worth their bother. He resolved to go it alone, through literature searches and self-analysis. No way was he going to see another counsellor. So he called Jo, his psychologist friend.

'Jo, how are you? It's me, Mensah.'

'Great to hear from you, I've been worried about you. I heard about this contamination thing, I thought of you. Can I help?'

I saw your name in the programme of lectures, wanted to have a chat, about stuff,' said Mensah.

'I'll meet you outside Greggs, Haymarket branch near M&S, say around five?' she said.

The town centre was still buzzing. Mensah and Jo sat on a bench overlooking the city hall, each with a pie. Jo paused, was going to say something and stopped again. 'What?' asked Mensah.

'I know you called but I was going to call you, to ask you a favour, it's a bit awkward and I'll understand if you say no. I'm doing a project on free will, thought experiments and all that. For some time I've been interested in ADHD, its causes and treatment. I'd been thrashing around. Then my supervisor told me about the coalition government's use of an ADHD vaccine, but I didn't think any more of it, until it hit the news again recently. Naturally, they didn't make a song and dance of it, but when the government admitted to the contamination, I'm sorry but I thought about you.'

'It's all right, Jo, I'm trying to come to terms with it all myself. How can I help?' he asked.

'Thanks Mensah, it's like this. We wonder whether we are automatons, but it must be different if you have an extra dimension such as this vaccine that's supposed to change you; no one knows how, but it's there. The government took credit for a drop in street crime, so do they take the blame? Am I making sense?'

Mensah shifted from cheek to cheek. 'You *are* making sense, but you're not going to try to counsel me, are you?'

'No, not at all,' she said. I just wonder whether this vaccine programmes you, or whether the choices you make are freely yours – free choice; is it you talking or are you talking through the mist of this vaccine? Can it be calculated, how much choice do you have, how much were you born with, how much have you got left, does it wear off?'

'I've thought of it myself,' said Mensah. 'I see where you're going; I didn't know anyone else was interested. When I do anything or think, I'm not sure whether what I feel or think is really how I would have felt or thought without the vaccination.

69

It may not matter. Should I just get on with it? But it doesn't stop me thinking it, and when I do I ask myself if I would think this way if I had not had the jab.'

'I don't know,' said Jo, 'you're the doctor; sorry, being facetious; we'll plan experiments, and if I need help would you volunteer?'

'Yes,' said Mensah. 'I've asked my mates whether they go round in circles like I do, but they have not been jabbed, so their answers still do not tell me what *I* would have been like without that wretched jab. Perhaps Dr Wagner, the counsellor, was right. Without the ADHD treatment to make me more placid and attentive, curb me, curb my impulsiveness, I may not have done well enough at school to get this far. But did the treatment tone me down, make me less optimistic, make me expect to fail? It drives me bananas, but it shouldn't; perhaps I'll grow out of it. Maybe because of the ADHD injection I'm some kind of agent of the State? If the politicians claimed that ADHD vaccine reduced street crime, would they be prepared to take the rap if I did something awful? Could I defend myself on grounds of diminished capacity or responsibility?' He put on his falsetto voice, "Oh, your honour, had I not had my daring and impulsiveness bred out of me, I would have pulled the drowning baby's pram out of the pond." Could I join the army, and if I failed in the field could I argue that because of this vaccine I lacked that final, crucial impulse needed to take out the enemy positions?'

'Those are exactly the sort of questions I want to answer,' said Jo.

'Good luck, I'll help if I can, but I can't wait for your results,' said Mensah.

That weekend he spent in cold turkey in his room, which, partly to his regret because he missed them, got rid of the hallucinations.

By spring Mensah's memory and concentration were up to leading the students in discussion groups for half an hour on general topics such as how to approach the patient with cardiac symptoms, but he was not ready to stand up in a lecture room to give a didactic presentation. When the senior trainee, Dr John Nightingale, asked whether Mensah would present at the grand round, just before he could reply, and to his relief, Dr Michaela Dawes (alias Milky Drawers) – a loud, pushy trainee on his unit – said, 'I will, please, I will, I have just the case for that meeting.'

Just before Easter, on a Thursday in the last week of March, Mensah was sitting alone in the top tier of the lecture theatre pretending to scan the pages of an old edition of a journal while he waited for the hospital dining-room to open again after its midday disinfection. Suddenly a buzz came from below him as the room filled for the weekly grand round. He was trapped, as he could still not face walking back along the hall through the hundred or so members of the medical department heading for the meeting. He decided that he was not that hungry and would wait an extra hour for his snack. Professor Dean Prosper was leading the presentation. After going through the history, the professor stopped to ask what the audience thought was the likely diagnosis. After ten seconds or so of silence and murmurings, there was no definite response. If Milky knew the answer she would have shouted it out by now – and she was there in the front row as usual trying to draw attention. A bygone familiar tension and excitement stirred in Mensah when he realised that he knew the answer, but he waited another few seconds hoping that someone else would put their hand up. Mensah signalled his intentions with a just-audible grunt, which, thanks to the acoustics, the professor heard just as he was about to unveil the answer himself. From the podium the professor saw Mensah with his head tilted towards a right hand lifted barely past his ear. 'Yes from the back,' said the professor.

Mensah looked around. The professor was talking to him! He nearly put his hand down; but it was now or never. 'Type five cytoplasmic protein kinase deficiency, sir,' he said, his trembling voice sounding disembodied to him. A rustling went through the auditorium as several heads turned his way. 'Who's that?' he could

71

hear someone whisper. 'Dunno,' said another. He could not believe what he had done – opening his mouth and words coming out in an auditorium full of people, many strangers.

'Excellent from the doctor in the back, p kinase deficiency provides the best explanation for this patient's clinical features. I'll come back to this point later in the summary of the literature.' He nodded approvingly to acknowledge Mensah several times during the discussion, each time he referred to the diagnosis. So pleased was Mensah with his triumph that he forgot his snack and returned to his rooms without his jacket and room keys.

Members of the department acknowledged him with a quick nod of the head and a blink as they passed him on his way back to retrieve his keys from the ward. He ruminated over aspects of p kinase deficiency that evening and thought of a series of questions he could have asked the professor – he would like to have followed up with the professor on which drugs should be avoided; what sort of advice should be given on genetic counselling and individualised medicine based on whether transmission was autosomal recessive or dominant; and whether the new translocation therapy would replace bone marrow transplantation. Mensah made a note to look up the condition again before he went to bed. He could not remember the second half of the afternoon's presentation. That was a blur.

On Friday, the next day, Mensah woke up not at his usual time of three o'clock but at five o'clock. The ward round was flawless. The large block of ice inside the top of his skull appeared to be melting and he knew the answers before the questions were asked. Milky Drawers was impressed, or shocked; but he knew one good day did not a new him make.

As spring progressed, and the days lengthened, walking along Claremont Road to the town Moor was not the torture it was six months earlier. He had his unruly combination of oily afro and Rasta locks cut and bought himself a new suit. Culinary pleasure returned and his waistline grew back to normal. To amuse himself he practised wriggling his bottom like a traditional African dancer in front of the mirror. Then he had his first early morning erection in six months. His old friend that greeted him each morning when he shaved was back. *I never thought I'd see one of those again!* he thought. *Where've you been?* His libido had returned. But he was not yet ready for experiments in love mimicry. He would first learn as much as he could about his contamination.

Mensah met Professor Douglas Burns-Savage in a small laboratory-cum-office. A photograph of Charles Darwin hung on the wall behind him. 'Dr Snell,' he started slowly, 'you already know much of what I'm about to tell you. At both ends of a linear chromosome is a specific sequence of DNA to protect it from chemical damage and to prevent the end-shortening of the chromosome during DNA replication. This sequence, called the telomere, is maintained by telomerase. Mutation or mutations that affect telomerase impair telomere maintenance during development. Impaired telomere maintenance results in prematurely unstable chromosomes. Symptoms have been linked with several mutations in protein sub-units of telomerase, but no one knows which of these mutations contaminated the vaccine used in the programme orchestrated by the Nationalist coalition; and so no one knew then or knows even now how it might affect the patients. We do not know whether the changes were vector driven or directly invoked using chemicals; nor are we sure of the exact extent of the problem. It was a long time ago and, naturally, many of those involved with the programme have moved on. The closest model we have for what has happened is dyskeratosis congenita. This is a condition that results in premature dental decay, greying and increased skin pigmentation, anaemia and a predisposition to cancer. The most serious forms of the natural disease significantly shorten life. We have no reports yet of anyone dying from the disease as a result of this contamination, but we will have to wait for more data from the office of populations censuses and surveys. I assure you that we will investigate this in detail, working closely with all the relevant specialist teams in this country and the international epidemiologists, statisticians and geneticists. Do you want to ask anything?'

'Difficult question, sir, but what do you suggest I should do? What I'm trying to ask is what should I look for, what should I avoid?' said Mensah.

'Don't smoke, and until we know more, probably a six-monthly hair, skin, gum check and an annual bone marrow biopsy. Look to live as full a life as you can, as you would with chronic conditions like diabetes, HIV, depression, hypertension, cancer, coronary artery disease. One consolation: the condition is neither contagious nor heritable. Be positive. Good luck, young man,' said the professor.

Mensah felt neither young nor lucky. 'Thank you, professor, I'll keep up with the literature on the dyskeratotic gene, and I may join a patient-support group.' He would also talk to Nancy and Marty.

Nancy and Marty were enjoying a quiet teatime when Mensah arrived. 'How's our young doctor? We haven't seen you for ages,' said Nancy.

'You look well,' said Marty. 'We were worried about you. Are you looking after yourself?'

'I'm fine, last winter was tough, new job, just a rough patch, but I'm over it now. I'm good now, very good in fact. It was busy, winter months are always busy. Sorry, that's why you didn't hear from me.'

Nancy gave Marty a nervous glance. 'What did the professor say?' she asked.

'He was very positive, very helpful; he says I should have regular checks. There's no treatment, but then there's nothing to treat, no problem, yet. I must admit I've been all over the place thinking about it.'

After a cup of tea and biscuits Marty turned the TV on to catch the football scores. Newcastle had lost. He harrumphed and switched it off. 'Dodgy defence again, gets on my nerves the way they concede goals, I've stopped going. Can't waste my life watching away supporters cheering,' said Mensah.

'How's work?' asked Nancy.

'Work's fine, it's when I'm alone that I worry,' he said. 'What should I do, is it worth the effort – all the hassle?'

'How do you mean?' said Marty.

'To be frank, it may sound morbid, but if I'm going to die young, why study, practise medicine? Would it not be under-standable, rational even – some might call it an obligation – to enjoy myself, pay little tax, add to the tax burden by having as many children as I can, by as many partners as will have me and then leave them all to the State to bear? To leave nothing of worth for the State when I go? I would have done exactly what the vaccination was supposed to prevent.' He put on a high-pitched Home Counties voice: "Too many fatherless children; something must be done, try this vaccine." Wouldn't it be ironic if I went on a spending spree and left them to hold the tab? What would they do then? Throw me in prison? I'm already in prison. Makes you wonder whether communities with low life expectancy, poor educational and professional qualifications come to the same conclusion.' Mensah went through to the kitchen to wash his cup. Seeing the garden in which he had spent many happy days brought pangs of nostalgia. He returned to the living-room. 'You think I'm going over the top, don't you?'

'Mensah, be true to yourself. We haven't brought you up to be like that: you're not the sort of person to bring a child into this world uncared for. We know you too well, we've always been here to share your ups and downs, haven't we? Nothing will change that,' said Nancy.

'Thanks, it means a lot. By the way, did you get the Bettys scones and shortbread biscuits? Nearly forgot, I'd be really sorry if I left them behind.'

They laughed. Nancy set off for the kitchen.

'Marty, at work, do you ever ask yourself whether others have an advantage of sorts, so they expect to be rewarded in proportion to what they put in, their effort and ability? They get recognition, the benefit of doubt, the marginal decisions, just like a big football club?'

'I don't think about it much, some people have a start on others, I agree, but I don't let it bother me,' said Marty.

'I do,' said Mensah.

'Why? It's inevitable,' said Marty.

Nancy sat next to Mensah and put her hand on his shoulder. He put his hand on hers. Marty moved over to sit next to Mensah. 'Keep a diary. In a few years you'll look back and all these worries will be small beer to you. You've got to be strong, it's all been done or seen before, some worse, some better than you, I know what you're trying to say, but does it help you? If it doesn't, cut it out. I could show you footage of young black boys playing football, some even being booed by their own side – bananas, jungle noises. These boys were in their late teens and early twenties, I was a little boy then but it stuck with me. When you came along, it made me think how to prepare you for the wider world. It made me think of what young men, boys even, many others had to go through to succeed.' Marty popped another piece of biscuit into his mouth. 'Your professor may be right. The disease may be mild, or a cure could be found and you could live a long life. You can't control that, people die every day. I could go now, sitting here, tomorrow an accident could end it all or a malignancy mark my days. There's not much we can do about that. But are you not better off than most of the rest of the world? To them, you're the one with the silver spoon.'

'Marty, but . . .'

'Let me finish, it's important. Look what's happened to you, we are all very lucky, this wretched system would have spent fifteen thousand pounds a week on you, it does on every child trapped in the care system, can you believe it? Do you know how many escape illiteracy, criminality and teenage pregnancy? Guess, go on, guess.'

'About fifty per cent?' said Mensah.

'No, ten per cent, what a terrible waste! By a so-called impecunious government.'

'I understand what you're saying, Marty, I didn't mean that I would go on a spending spree, I just wanted to say . . .'

'I understand, it may not be much of a consolation, but in many parts of Africa average life expectancy is still less than fifty years, their fate determined by kleptocrats. I know the stories and so should you. Martin Luther King, Nelson Mandela, Frederick Douglas, Rosa Parks, Adam Clayton Powell – they triumphed over apartheid and Jim Crow segregation. Millions, less lauded, quietly win their battles in their own ways: over medical school admission policies skewed against Jews and Asians; over Third World dictatorships against their own peoples. Try not to feel sorry for yourself. Don't betray their memory,' said Marty.

'That's what Grandpa said, he said something like youth should be filled with work and aspiration, because work winds a spring that builds a fund, of memory, to unwind and release at leisure, like a pension. Thanks, I hope you are right,' said Mensah.

'I am, don't waste energy fretting about failure. Don't dwell on not being born with life's gifts wrapped in a bow. Untie the knot to open life's bounty for yourself. And for others. You make your own luck. The jab didn't turn everyone into zombies,' said Marty. Nancy put the package on the settee next to Mensah.

'Cheers, Nancy,' he said. Marty smiled. 'You know what you need, a wife, she'll make you happy, whole. I'm serious, that's all most men need. Mind you, I don't know what women want or need,' said Marty, winking at Nancy.

'Women are philosophical puzzles, we are unknowable,' said Nancy.

'That's what frightens me,' said Mensah. 'If that beautiful woman in grandfather's archives, my mum, could abandon her child, what stops me abandoning mine? Might as well not bother if that's my pedigree. Who will look after my children when I'm gone? What happens to them if we get an even more virulent politician?' said Mensah.

'We'll be here to support you,' said Nancy leaning against the car.

'When will we see you again? Come and see us soon,' said Marty.

'I will, it was nice to see you, bye,' Mensah said. He waved and drove off.

One evening, Mensah was having a drink with Drew after a game of tennis. Drew had just got on to the respiratory training rotation. 'What will you do after your pre-registration year?' asked Drew.

'I haven't really thought about it, I quite fancy cardiology,' said Mensah.

'But everyone says it's fiendishly difficult to get in. You hear all these rumours. Campbell was told not to bother, too old. Neil wasted time in the wrong pre-registration jobs and all the other stuff. Dr Sanista, you know him, always on TV, the epidemiology guru, he was a brilliant student, wanted to be a cardiologist. That guy, Thomas, who was a locum last year, another who got stuck halfway through his training,' said Drew.

'He said it was because the professor didn't like him,' said Mensah, 'but again all rumours. You don't know what's true or not because it's difficult to tell sour grapes from rotten apples, bruised oranges or egos.' And even as he uttered the words he decided that cardiology was the speciality for him; just what he needed. A challenge. And he did not stop to ask what was needed to succeed or whether he was likely to be any good at it. But to spend the rest of his days contemplating his own death would disable and paralyse, kill him metaphorically, long before the contamination would. He would renew his defences, prove himself again by pursuing a career in one of the most competitive and demanding specialities: cardiology. 'Drew, I'm going to be a cardiologist,' he said.

'Don't waste your time. Who or what put you up to this, what's brought this on? It's gone back to smoke and mirrors again with the latest reorganisation; the attrition rate's gone up, what's wrong with you?' said Drew.

'Maybe I'll find out,' said Mensah. 'I'll buy you a large drink if I make it.'

'If you make it I'll buy you a brewery. I'll borrow my grand-mother's false teeth after she's had breakfast,' said Drew.

To stand a chance of being selected for any training post in cardiology, Mensah needed to stay on a rotation based in the Newcastle teaching hospitals. The revamped Burka system of interviews, in which neither the interviewer nor interviewees could be identified, could once again work in his favour. Mensah failed to get on either the Yorkshire or Scottish rotation but was delighted and surprised to get on to the more competitive Newcastle training programme.

PART 2

9

Timms

Thirty years post-coalition . . .

Jingoism feeds psyches, puffs chests, but does not fill bellies. Just like idol Baal disappointed his prophets in the showdown with Elijah, the economic miracle promised by the racist coalition of the Nationalists and the Wintertories – Old Conservatives – was exposed for what it was: bullshit. And did the electorate wreak its revenge at the ballot box? Only a bill compelling dog owners to use a scoop that converted dog mess into steam, oxygen and a powder that could be tipped down the drains survived the cull of the coalition's legislation.

Patients, unless they knew better, or could afford to say no, went where they were told. Taking advantage of this, and the fudged distinction between commissioner and provider (forced upon government by powerful vested interests and not, as they claimed, a concession to coalition partners), Robert Trishart and his wife Hilary Dunne, acting as courier and punter, 'reconfigured' health services in favour of their own holding companies, becoming, in the process, the first medical billionaires. As one commentator on health policy wrote: 'A radical government would have abolished the department of health itself, and given the people their billions back so that they, the patients, not the entrepreneurs, could decide where and by whom they should be treated.' Fat chance; politicians love power. Reorganisation passed the time and transferred the responsibility to the doctors. A cunning plan and devious trap, because when the reforms failed, the politicians could ride in on publicly funded white chargers scattering blame and legislation like socialists spending other people's money. With trousers full to the brim with billions of your money – 'fuck you' money – Trishart and his friends would not mind taking the blame because they could lend you back your own money, and they and their families could forever live off the interest.

Primary care disintegrated as doctors from poor non-EU countries seeking postgraduate training or greener pastures (on which the service had once relied) shunned the United Kingdom, for fear of the Nationalists' return to power or influence. Doctors opted for the relative independence of 'fee for service' clinic- and hospital-based practice, where everyone was a specialist. Nurses – now university-educated and heavily indebted, but not as arrogant as doctors – were used by the government as Band-Aid for the shortfall in services. Dr John Worth, a former general practitioner and wannabe knight of the realm, relaunched his primary-care strategy to raise money, placate the unemployed nurses seeking a new role and distract the public from his government's failures. So, for receiving care at a nurse-led clinic you got a rebate from your household energy bill to be redeemed a year after the end of that clinical episode, but you paid twenty pounds for each consultation with a general practitioner. Knowing that nurse-led clinics were in short supply, he calculated that you invariably had to pay. To the Treasury, a few locals without access to primary care were 'a price worth paying' for financial stability. 'These innovations will encourage an increase in individual responsibility. If you want a second opinion there's always the Internet,' the Secretary of State, Mrs Jane Duncan, said on *Weekly Scrutiny* to murmurs of approval from her think-tank-sponsored co-panellists. Colleagues critical of the policy were told to resign if they did not like it. Few ever did.

The international cardiac unit at the Freeman Hospital in Newcastle had been taken over by FYAB, a Shanghai-based holding company, on behalf of NWAMD, an Iraq-based energy company. Resistance to the acquisition was fierce and determined, but when forced to choose between a hospital run by foreigners and no hospital at all, the opposition melted as quickly as football fans scurrying away from the scene of a Derby humiliation. As a good-will gesture FYAB also bought Newcastle United, to the chagrin of those Geordies who remembered the relegation season tenure of Sports Direct billionaire, Mike Ashley, as club owner. Newcastle United had narrowly missed retaining the league championship they had won the year before but had won the FA Cup, their fortunes having improved with the appointment of Mirandinha, an English-born great-grandnephew of a Brazilian forward who had played for the club in the 1980s.

David Timms, nine months into his post as pre-consultant in cardiology, expected to be appointed full consultant at Freeman that autumn. Martin Landing had got the job in Leeds and Vanessa Stewart-Endecott was unlikely to want to move from Edinburgh, so there was no serious threat to him here. Even if a strong over-seas candidate applied, David had the advantage of incumbency. Local candidates who failed did so because they had rubbed someone up the wrong way or had not been good enough. David had always been top of his class and had an intimidating CV. His research track record was excellent and he had met several of the opinion formers at conferences and meetings. Some of them knew his parents socially. It should not matter. But it did. That was life, not his fault.

'Tidy up for me, will you, Gani.'

'Sorted,' replied Gani, 'where can I find you when the next patient's ready?'

'You mean the next patient's not here yet?' Timms replied, out of earshot of the other team members who, because they were short staffed, liked to slow down the changeover between cases, to catch their breath and have a beverage. 'I'll be having my sandwich next door and please remind them that I will be using the size 7 French special lubricated, ribbed sheath this time – the patient has a particularly atrophied and shrivelled valve! I'll be back in five minutes, so let's get going, I've got someone to meet at lunchtime: couch, touch, cut, ouch, out – remember the sequence,' said David.

'What's come over him today, won the lottery?' staff nurse Abbado asked the others as she tidied up.

'No, that blue-titted wife of his must have let him have a feel,' said Gani.

Timms went round to the library; something had caught his eye that weekend and had suddenly come back to him during the last case. He flipped through the article. *How many times are they going to publish the same data?* he thought to himself, recognising the authors' names, now in a different order, but still flogging an outmoded strategy for the prevention of reverse remodelling. Walking back to theatre he came across young James Gerard. 'Can I have a minute, Dr Timms?'

'Yes, of course, what is it?'

'Dr Timms, am I asking the right question . . . how do you get to do what you do?' he asked.

Timms smiled. His seniors had inspired him when he was a student. 'Work hard, put the hours in, develop your talents. Use the simulators for example. Forget the outside world. Are you one of these people with hobbies?'

'Yes, rowing and tennis.'

'Dump them, your work should be your hobby,' said Timms. 'I could have done anything I wanted, joined the City, the Foreign Office, or, like my mother, worked with the Treasury. Why did I choose medicine? Because I wanted to make a direct differ-ence to people's lives; not by proxy. Get to the top on merit, not sentiment, not quotas or deprivation indices – all the reforms that let the wrong people in. Otherwise this profession will be ruined.'

'Thank you, Dr Timms,' said a surprised young James and he shuffled off to join a gaggle of his mates by the lifts.

Surrendering to a rumble in his abdomen, Timms turned round to use the toilet, at the end of the corridor. He flushed the cistern once before, and twice after he had finished, cleaning up with the alcoholic gel he carried around with him. Last year he'd experimented with a post-defecating anal deodorant but gave it up because it made him itch. Alcohol gel would have to do. The next case was likely to be more challenging.

Mrs Meissler was ninety years old but a 'good' ninety. 'Good' – a euphemism for biologically preserved, well spoken and middle class. She was from Munich and had had a valve reconstruction and repair at seventy and then at eighty-six. She'd insisted on a referral to David because she had fallen out with Breitner, the famous German cardiologist, and to spite him had decided to throw in her lot with the young man she'd seen explaining his work on the famous online health channel 'Alive'. David glided across the ward towards her. 'Good morning, Mrs Meissler, welcome to England and our hospital; we are very honoured that you have chosen us as your team to look after you; we hope that not only will we gain from our professional collaboration but that we will be able to share a glass of Glühwein one day in Munich.'

Mrs Meissler threw back her head and laughed. She knew he did not mean it. *He probably has little time for his own family*, she thought, but it did not matter. She liked him anyway. He already made her laugh.

David had studied the case records in detail and decided to list her after he had warmed up with a 'routine case' or two just to get him going – much better than a cup of tea or coffee or some other addictive beverage. After he finished Mrs Meissler's valve procedure, which took two hours, he went back to the ward to see that all was well before returning to his room to complete some more paperwork. Here, after reading an American article about the effect of the surgeon's religious faith on operative success, he threw it in the bin with a grimace, dismissing it as another piece of pseudo-scientific fiction. Most of the rest of the day was spent supervising his registrar in theatre. In between cases, he called the head of the research team, Professor John Ferner, based in the medical school.

Before David had moved up north they had collaborated in research using reactivated memory proteins from stem cells to reconstruct mitral valves in which established techniques had failed. 'Hi, John, David here, glad our paper got accepted by the *New England Journal*. We can extend the work to younger patients, I'm sure. Thanks for your input,' he said.

'Yes, thank heavens we didn't have to rewrite the methods section again,' said Professor Ferner. 'Let's wait for the reaction, er, the reception at the AHA was very favourable but the Japanese, er, and Chinese were not so keen. The Chinese man, Hong, came a cropper, he dive-bombed. I wanted to hide. Didn't he have a supervisor? His presentation was terrible. I expect we'll need, er, to repeat the experiments using new nanovectors. We need to be sure that these are safe before we design a larger trial because funding will be tight.' He went on: 'I've got Jane, you know Jane, clever Jane, er, I've got her working on this one. Between you and me I do not, er, entrust major research projects to the same, er, lead. Too risky.' Then, the professor asked, 'When are the interviews again?'

Competition for the next round of substantive consultant posts to be appointed that autumn was stiff. Applications had come from all over the world, attracted by the large sums of money on offer, the most productive doctors' earnings comfortably into mid six figures. 'September or October, but it depends on the board. They need all the main constituents on the selection panel because these may be the last of such appointments for some time – some say five years. If you believe them we are in the middle of a bubble in health care and the hospital is just being more cautious, that's what we are told,' said David.

'They've been saying that for five years. I'll make some calls, but not yet, must keep the powder, er, dry,' the professor commented.

David was delighted. As long as he kept his nose clean, his

backers on side, and maintained his clinical and research productivity, he was home and dry. Humming to himself, he tidied his desk, washed his hands and almost ran to the car park to drive home for the weekend.

David Timms' father, John, a consultant psychiatrist, had postponed his retirement because the government had raided his private pension and retrospectively cut his NHS pensions to plug the budget deficit and reduce inequality 'for a fairer Britain'. His mother, Rachel, an economist, specialised in cultural influences on corporate and national economic performance. Her books *Harnessing Irrational Exuberance* and its follow-up *Redefining Economic Growth* had influenced governments all over the world. She sat on the boards of five fledgling environmental and engineering companies. Her favourite pastime was fell-walking in the Lake District. Their jobs, and John's parents, had kept them in Surrey, but they had stayed after John's parents had died because they were close to Heathrow and Gatwick airports. Rachel was a straight, sensible, strict and unfussy mother who abhorred swearing, lateness and rudeness. She had made sure David was hardworking, neat and polite but largely left him to his own devices. She'd never helped him with his homework, leaving that to John. John had done most of the ferrying to and from school, plays, sports days and rugby at weekends. When David had left home for university, Rachel had devoted even longer hours to work; whether to distract her from her empty nest or because she now had time to do what she really wanted, it was difficult for John to say. He missed his boy; his job, golf and painting were but poor substitutes.

With previous girlfriends, David had been watchful, detached and deliberate. Almost anything – a tiny blemish, a cough, wetness around the corner of the mouth, a runny nose, or the odd hang of a dress – soon put him off. Samples of girlfriends' hair, saliva, blood when he could get it, were sent off for genome testing for traits. If the results were not perfect he dumped her. As soon as he was sure that a girl was not for him he ended the relation-ship; nearly always rudely, sometimes cruelly. They got the message when he demurred at even a doorstep kiss, or simply refused to let them in to his flat when they buzzed. He once asked the secu-rity staff to remove one girl, Becky, from the premises. 'DNA technology is more reliable than the inefficient and chancy tradi-tional rituals our forefathers used for pairing off,' he told Alan, a critical old school friend. David took the male pill but was still wary because he had heard of paternity suits brought by women who must somehow have obtained enough DNA to construct arti-ficial sperm.

Amanda was just right. She had passed his test; maybe she would not have done so a few years earlier, but by the time she came along he had changed, or was ready for marriage. They'd met in London while he was a year one specialist registrar and she was a trainee accountant. She was bright, genetically suitable and compatible, and after four years together he felt it was time to propose. Her parents hailed from Romsey and lived in Newcastle. David reassured Alan, his best man, that he had not married Amanda with an eye to a career in the North-East.

Amanda was the eldest of three daughters of Mr Stephen Lockley, a civil engineer who exploited the government's predilec-tion for wind farms. He knew that an easy way to make a lot of money was to be appointed as a consultant on a government project. Amanda was convinced her fulfilment and destiny was in her own hands. She had clicked with David. But she was not going to be silly until she was sure, and he had only become acceptable to her when a douche sample had shown that he did not carry any of the common inheritable diseases. David had probably tested her himself. It was what a lot of young people did. Pheromones could be faked and bought over the Internet. Now she had returned to the North, she told her dad, 'I hope Mum approves and likes David, but it's tough if she doesn't, it's my row of ducks and I'll line them up my way.'

So David and Amanda got married in October on the Isle of

Skye in autumn when the cold weather would discourage a high turnout. 'We're not going to be one of those stupid, irresponsible couples who leave their children's genetic destiny or inheritance to a lottery,' they said to friends. So, after a week's deliberation, debate and discussion, as they called it, they agreed that they would have first a son and then a daughter. 'We go to great lengths to pass on our material possessions. Why just hit and hope that any product of your loins, your gonads, will thrive in the larger lottery of life!' said David. His children would be as near perfect as possible.

In preparation for *in vitro* fertilization, each stopped taking the pill, selected and presented the range of attributes they wanted for their embryonic son to the specialists at the clinic, provided the respective samples and resumed their contraceptives. Embryos carrying genes for several conditions including haemophilia, cystic fibrosis, Marfan's syndrome, hyperlipidaemia, schizophrenia, breast cancer and various forms of diabetes were destroyed. The idea was that because near perfect children would need very little rearing, their parents could pursue fulfilling careers.

When they sold their central London apartment, David and Amanda moved from rented accommodation to a large semi-detached house off Moor Crescent in Gosforth, a posh suburb of Newcastle favoured by businessmen and senior hospital staff. Amanda was just returning from a walk with Jonathan when David turned into the drive. 'Hi, darling,' said David and pecked Amanda on the cheek.

'We've had a great day, haven't we, little boy?' she said, beaming in to the pram and ruffling Jonathan's wispy hair.

'I'd better get cleaned up,' said David, opening the front door. He bounded upstairs two steps at a time, changed into a pair of jeans and one of the T-shirts Amanda had bought him last winter.

'Aren't we lucky,' he said later while they were in the kitchen. She was cooking.

'You could say so, but I don't feel it,' said Amanda.

'Yeah, but in the round, we've got everything: each other, great jobs and a beautiful little boy,' said David.

'You're so smug,' she said.

'But I'm not complacent, am I?' he said.

'You're certainly not that, just smug,' she said, sipping at the gravy to taste. 'Hmm, should I add . . . ? Was that the door bell?' Amanda went to answer the door, Jonathan stirred and David lifted him out of the cot.

10

Rachel's Visit

Rachel rang her son's door bell at about a quarter past seven. 'It's lovely to see you, Rachel,' said Amanda. David, with Jonathan in his arms, looked over his wife's shoulder. Jonathan burped, curdled milk dribbled down the left corner of his mouth.

'What a nice way to greet Grandma,' said Rachel. 'Come here; he's gorgeous.' Rachel looked down at her grandson. 'Wait until John sees him. You know what he's like with children. He'll probably retire now, pension or no pension.'

Amanda and David went in to the kitchen. 'I'll stay here with Jonathan, I'm not hungry, you go on, have supper,' said Rachel.

After a while David walked in with a tray. 'Bettys scones and tea, to keep you going, you should have eaten with us,' he said.

'Nonsense, I'm fine, it gave me time to get to know Jonathan,' she said.

'Come to Mummy, let Grandma have some tea,' said Amanda, extending her arms to take Jonathan off Rachel.

'I must order some scones and the shortbread biscuits when I get home,' Rachel said.

'Oh, yes,' said Amanda, handing Rachel a towel. The clock showed that Rachel had less than forty minutes to catch her plane at nine-fifteen. 'Can't stay long, I made it a long day after the seminar at the Baltic Centre. I flew in last night with a few of the other delegates and stayed at the Hilton. I promised John I wouldn't sneak in before him, but couldn't resist. He won't mind. It wasn't fair anyway. Could you call me a cab please, David, for the airport?'

'Don't be silly, Mother, I'll run you there myself. Do you want to come with us, Amanda?'

'No, you go, your car's too small for all of us and mine's filthy. Anyway, Jonathan needs a feed.'

Rachel rummaged through her bag for her purse, and stuffed a few bills into Amanda's hand. 'I'm sorry I haven't got much,' she said. 'Here, I thought I'd lost them, a little suit and a pair of mittens, for my favourite grandson.'

Amanda thought she caught sight of a blonde wig, but Rachel closed the bag before she could be sure.

'Your *only* grandson,' said David.

'I like favourite, it's more accurate, because, of all the grandsons in the world Jonathan is the one I love the most,' said Rachel. 'Your definition is less accurate.'

'Let's not argue, you must be right, Mother, we should go if you are not to miss your flight. I'm sure we'll find something to debate before we get you there.'

David had had a tough day and the next day promised to be even busier. It would have been easier if his mother had gone by taxi. David and Rachel rarely had much to say to each other, but as they were both tired this trip was particularly quiet. Out on a long stretch of road to the airport, David said, 'You look well, Mum.'

'Thanks,' replied Rachel. 'When's that job you keep telling your dad about going to be advertised? You need some stability, now you've got Jonathan, don't want to have to move again, I'm sure Amanda won't like it,' she said.

'Any moment now,' he said, 'they're waiting for the go-ahead from the board members based in the Far East to approve the dates,' said David. 'I've started well and all the heavyweights are behind me. They more or less told me so. There's a rumour that one of the other candidates has been asked or advised to withdraw. Even if he doesn't withdraw he doesn't have a hope. I just need to keep my nose clean. How's your work going, Mum?' 'Oh, busy, I'm developing my ideas on comparing organic economic differentiation with traditional measures of economic growth. I'm collaborating with some biologists on a model which can be used by the Treasury. The project will keep economists busy until your little one grows up,' said Rachel. 'I'm also on the committee examining the dyskeratotic gene scandal; the poor victims deserve at least an apology and compensation, but the public's not ready yet.' She sighed. 'But I'll not wear another whitewash,' she said.

David geared down, came out of the roundabout and turned to his mother. 'You're sure you're not raising expectations: creating malcontents, encouraging compensation-culture victims?'

'Most of them probably don't know or understand the issues, or what's happening. They wouldn't have made a fuss if . . .' Rachel looked away and said, 'Call me a busy body, but they need someone to put forward their case. By the way, I hope you don't mind me asking . . . when's Amanda going back to work?'

'No, Mother, I don't mind, Dad should have told you, we plan to have another one straightaway,' said David. 'We want a boy and a girl, so why wait? Afterwards, Amanda can start work again, get into the financial nitty-gritty again properly, without any more breaks. We more or less promised her boss; it's pushing it but that's the plan.' David turned left at an electric charging station. His fuel gauge showed enough charge to last him to the weekend. Turning back to his mother, he said, 'We'll be using Lloyds Bank laboratories this time. I love Jonathan to bits but we wanted him to have blue eyes, and somehow the other clinic couldn't combine that with the other traits we chose. It makes you wonder what else they've got wrong.'

Rachel looked straight ahead. 'I didn't know you and Amanda were having problems – your Dad would have told me; anyway, you got married only last autumn.' She went quiet as David came to a halt at a set of traffic-lights. 'Ah,' she said as they set off again. 'Don't tell me you're using this pre-assignation technique

95

to choose eye colour as well. Your brown eyes haven't done you any harm. Neither have mine. Newton, Einstein, Copernicus, Beethoven, even Barabbas – who remembers what colour eyes they had? Tell me, because I don't,' said Rachel.

'Mother, the clinic asked if we had a preference, that's all, it was as simple as that. We were asked to choose. I just couldn't understand why they didn't deliver, that's all. Everyone else on our side of the family has brown eyes and I thought it would be a change to have a child with blue eyes, like Amanda's. You're not cross are you?' said David. 'You should know – progress, choice, the markets; you write about these issues all the time. These techniques are here to stay; the progress they're making, incredible; we can't turn the clock back.'

'It's the way you said it, so matter of fact,' she said. Rachel leaned over to wedge the bag on the back seat the right way up. As she turned forwards and sat back in her seat, she said, 'What do you do if you don't get what you want?'

'What people have always done, accept their children for what they are,' said David.

'Do you sue the laboratory? It's a commercial transaction after all,' said Rachel.

'You probably could, but I haven't even considered it and I don't intend to, unless Amanda feels very strongly, which I doubt. The legal position might be different if the clinic had failed to live up to the claims in its literature, but we're talking about an option, an afterthought; it's irksome not to get what we wanted, but not a catastrophe,' said David. He slowed down to allow time to assuage tempers before they got to the airport. 'Mum, you're tired, I'm tired, let's talk about this some other time,' he said. He should have let her get a taxi.

Rachel dabbed her nose and cheeks. 'Ignore me,' she said, 'I've had a long day too; it's your life after all. Oh, look, David, there's a gap, just pull in here. I'll call you,' she said as she got out, pulled her bag off the back seat, waved at the car, not David, and set off for the departure hall.

At Gatwick's arrivals terminal, Rachel saw John before he saw her, so she had time to compose herself. 'Hi, darling, good trip?' said John, kissing her on the cheek.

'So-so, I went to see David, Amanda and Jonathan.'

'You didn't,' he said, stopping for a second. 'I knew you would – you dark horse; "I'm not one of those grandmothers clucking around like mother hens,"' he said, mimicking Rachel. 'Ha, now look at you, sneaking off without me,' he continued, laughing.

'Did you know they were using PRD?' said Rachel.

'No, I didn't. Did you?' said John.

'No – it was such a shock, such a shock. David said he really wanted Jonathan to have blue eyes but had to make do with brown. Now they're going to have another one, a daughter, probably also choosing all sorts of traits to design.' She checked the signs for directions while John stopped to wrap his wrist around her bag handle. 'Am I overreacting? I'm surprised I feel so churned up about this, about them. I don't want to lose them, my grandson, but this business of choosing physical traits for children, like choosing underwear from a rack, causes me disquiet. Have I, with my big boots, made it more difficult for them to confide in us, or to decide about another baby, designer or not?'

'Relax, Rachel,' John said. 'What's the real problem: the technique? That they used it? How they went about it? The blue eyes bit, or that they didn't ask you? What if they'd chosen long-lasting knees or crack-proof heels? David and Amanda are happy, are they not? Do you want to hurt them, or spoil it for them? How they decide to have their own children isn't any of our business. Why should they be different? You're going all self-righteous again. Ask yourself whether you're not being as arrogant as the coalition was in riding roughshod over contrary views?' he said.

'I oppose these designer baby Frankenstein-creating techniques, instinctively, except in the most exceptional cases,' she said.

'Who decides what's exceptional?' said John, as he turned into their road, Oaklands. 'I know how you feel, there are many who feel the same way, but let's not lose our son, break up the family, at this exciting time for us, for Amanda and David.'

11

Mensah's Day

A fresh breeze blew across Mensah as he pedalled elaborate, playful curves around dog owners and pensioners making the best of the early Monday morning tranquillity in Jesmond Dene, Baron Armstrong's gift to the city. Mensah was three months into his job as pre-consultant in percutaneous cardiac progenitor cell therapy at Freeman Hospital. His study of bio-magnetic brainwave-operated robotics in treating post-operative complications had been very well received at the last world congress of cardiology. Patients seemed to like him, and reports and feedback from his academic supervisors and the sub-dean for sub-speciality training supported his objective to be appointed to the coveted post of consultant in percutaneous restorative cardiology. Like David Timms and others in that year of pre-consultants, Mensah had a stunning CV.

From his first year as a trainee, Mensah had always wanted to be involved at the cutting edge of cardiology – the repair of mitral valves by gene therapy or replacing parts of valves with new valve tissue grown in the laboratory (percutaneous restorative cardiology). Degenerative general cardiology – nicknamed post-modern or prehistoric cardiology – however, was steady: its practitioners, who were not and did not expect to be trained in the new techniques, treated the patients turned down by the restorative team. The bulk of the work of this department was still coronary angioplasty, but most of the skill had been taken out of the procedure by advances and applications of computer technology. There were even special simulative programs, and if the operator made a mistake, a monitor bleeped and suggested the correct sequence.

That day, Mensah arrived at work at about seven o'clock, an hour before the scheduled start of the lists, to review the patients again even after he had seen them the previous night. By then he had familiarised himself so well with the patients' histories that he could recall the most salient points from memory. He recited the names of the patients he had seen each day while he drove or rode home to Jesmond, a practice he'd learned after those dark early days as a pre-registration doctor. He liked the reassurance of knowing more about his patients than anyone else because it helped his patients and was a defence against ward round humiliation. It was also useful when answering queries or complaints to recall unique non-medical aspects of the case. A patient's recent bereavement, or their child's childlessness or divorce, a grandchild's name, hobby or drug addiction added a personal touch to the response.

'I wish these cleaners would just leave my desk alone, I can't find my list,' Mensah muttered as he repositioned his keyboard and chair and settled down to work. 'Drat, it was here all along,' he said, when he found the list sticking out of a journal where he had placed it as a bookmark. After writing up, editing and reviewing the outstanding patients' case histories he sent them off electronically to the main departmental computer network for editing, attachment of multimedia results and images. Invoices would be prepared for patients and general practitioners, foreign embassies, companies, primary care trusts and families where appropriate. Completing his paperwork, he got ready to go to theatre.

Even after the widespread acceptance of seven-day working, Monday was still different. Monday morning always seemed to start slowly. One trust had paid A.S. Hewd Wink Consultants over half a million pounds for a model of cognitive diurnal biorhythms to reduce the lethargy of the first day of the week, but had found out from a neighbouring hospital that a theatre coordinator who planned the list with the surgeons was a much cheaper and more effective solution.

'Oh no,' muttered David under his breath as Mensah walked in to get changed for the day's procedures. Nine months earlier, just after David had joined the staff, he had asked Mensah to fetch some scrubs. Mensah had sucked in a deep breath, counted to two and said, 'Go and fetch them yourself, you've got hands; if you ever ask me to fetch anything for you again I'll break your face, do you understand?'

'Sorry, I didn't mean to offend, I thought . . .' David had offered.

'I know what you thought, just don't do it again.' Mensah had left David standing half dressed in the changing room. Later that day, Mensah reproached himself for being so sensitive. Perhaps David had made a common and understandable mistake. However, when a few weeks later Mensah saw how, at a UN summit, even the most powerful leaders in the world refused to be condescended to, not only on their own behalf, but on account of the people they represented, he concluded that he'd been right not to take orders from the prat. Of course he would not break his face if it happened again, but he was sure David would not repeat his error. He wondered what he would have done if he had not been vaccinated. Then he might have broken David's face. When David had found out later that Mensah was on the training rotation he'd tried to apologise when he ran into him in theatre the next day. But in reply Mensah had just glared past him and grunted, in acknowledgement or disdain, he wasn't sure which. David was most put out when, six months later, Mensah had joined the team as a pre-consultant.

As part of their regular appraisals, cardiac trainees were required to watch themselves on recordings carrying out various procedures on patients and on simulators. To progress to the next level of technical difficulty a minimum score had to be reached in each of the competencies. Eye and hand coordination, manual dexterity, tendon and autonomic reflexes, concentration as well as blood pressure, heart rate and so on were entered into a private appraisal folder. Each doctor's scores were confidential and kept with all the other assessments by the human resources department. David thought he was the best but could not be sure because, try as he might, he could not hit the highest level on dexterity and autonomic reflex sections. That failure made him uneasy because he did not know the other scores.

'Good morning, sister, did you have a good weekend?'

'I did, Dr Snell, and how are you?' Sister Maria Cheddles was in charge of theatre 2, the most advanced integrated mutant cardiac laboratory in Europe. In minutes, the theatre could be transformed from an operating facility for complex heart surgery to a cardiac catheterisation lab or an MRI and CT scanning room. Medical students peered through their phone lenses to record the action, others sat quietly taking notes, or doodling. Mensah turned to the observation port in the ceiling and, leaning into the microphone, said, 'Our first patient needs to have her conduction system cleaned up. By undergoing this procedure she could avoid having a permanent pacemaker, which would mean that she would keep the heart's normal activation sequence and reduce dizzy spells, palpitations, arrhythmias and breathlessness. I'd like you all to mug up on the mechanisms responsible for degeneration of conduction tissue.'

Mensah turned to Nurse Daviniesta – her features a beautiful female version of a father's face. Mensah did not care much for cleavage. Most were boosted artificially. Legs were real. Puncturing the rubber top of the vial or locating the opening always gave him a thrill when Daviniesta was assisting. She stood ramrod straight, chest thrust out. How did she make holding a vial for local anaesthetic look so inviting? He liked the way she moved the vial around almost imperceptibly, and braced her wrist and the bottle top for penetration. None of the other nurses had this effect on him.

The whole procedure, from infiltrating local anaesthetic to taking the tubes out at the end, took less than ten minutes with Mensah commenting and instructing throughout. Afterwards he asked for questions. 'Ask me something, anything, it does not have to be about medicine. What, no questions?'

'Zilliant,' said John Gerard, the whippersnapper. Mark Tennant, a mature student who was not interested in anything that was not relevant to examination success, watched in silence, probably wondering how soon he could pass his exams and earn some money to pay off his debts.

'Thank you, sister, who's next?' said Mensah as he de-scrubbed and washed his hands.

'I'll just check with Susan,' she said, hurrying into the control room.

'Good talk,' said Professor Rodell after the weekly afternoon clinical meeting.

'Thank you, sir, it was something I knocked together at short notice. It's not our turn to present until next week. It was Phil's turn but he's on paternity leave.'

'Thanks for standing in, anyway, it was very good,' said Dr Crane, a radiologist who had also been waiting to have a word.

Before Mensah could reply, Dr David Timms barged in: 'I just saw Mrs Jones, you know, the one with the pneumothorax; I sorted her out for you — she's fine now. She's happy with my explanation that it was nothing you'd done wrong.'

The consultants nodded their goodbyes and melted away. Mensah could not remember any recent complications — but that did not mean that he had not had one. Every doctor has a hand-held personal device, or PD, supplied by the hospital on which they are notified of complications. The room was virtually empty, but about twenty staff members had heard David. Mensah rebooted his Notebook, entered his password and checked his complications sub-folder. No Jones. David must have made a mistake. Mensah looked up, hurried down the corridor to find him, but he had gone. 'The bastard,' Mensah muttered and returned to the lecture room to retrieve his mini-book presentation.

The rest of the day passed without event. Dr Wissler, the registrar, was keen to do the last day case, so with one eye on the clock, Mensah sat on the sidelines. After that came the round on the day case unit, a review of the patients on the main ward, some more paperwork, and a telephone call to a patient who relied on the hospital for her prescriptions until she could find a new doctor after her general practitioner had resigned. Mensah was reluctant, almost guilty, to leave the hospital, thinking he had left work undone or left others working while he was not, so he twice cycled round the hospital perimeter and then, reassured when there were no more calls, turned for home.

Mensah lived in a small first-floor flat on Forsyth Road in Jesmond, only five minutes from Jesmond Metro station, from which the city centre was only about ten minutes away. He opened his post: a few bills again, and a reminder to pay his subscription to a medical journal that he had not read seriously for a year but to which he had forgotten to cancel the subscription. As the next day was relatively easy – he had only ward work and the medical students to teach – he could relax tonight. So he called to ask whether Vince would like to go out for a beer.

12

Maginot's Advice

The next morning, a Tuesday, as Mensah walked through the hospital's main foyer, he found himself behind Sally, a buxom radiographer. Rather than hurry on, as was his wont, he slowed his pace to walk behind her as she pushed the portable CT scanner, her trapezoid back and posterior sloping backwards showing the outline of her underwear and her sculptured, symmetrical legs, well defined but not overly obtrusive calf muscles just discernible as each stride ended with a little swish of her short shoe heel. In thrall, Mensah walked past his turning, then out of a clear sky he received a message to call Mrs Darby.

'Are you in the hospital?' she asked. He confirmed that he was and called the ward sister, Mrs Mary Toogood, to tell her he would be late. The battleaxe grunted. 'When do we expect you then?' she said. 'Soon,' said Mensah as he caught the lifts up to the academic department on the fifth floor.

Professor Maginot's secretary sat behind a huge desk in a room with six armchairs arranged on each wall for visitors who came to see her boss from all over the world. After a few minutes' wait, Mensah was ushered in to the professor's office. The room was strewn with papers, files and journals. On the wall were four clocks, each telling the time in a different city. Mensah made out Beijing and New York. 'Sit down, Dr Snell,' said the professor, hand combing his ten wispy white hairs back over his enormous pate. He had a way of looking over your head as if at someone behind you, a habit he deliberately cultivated to unsettle the juniors. Mensah took some journals off the least burdened chair and sat on its edge. 'How's your work going?'

'Very well, professor. I'm enjoying Dr Marsh's firm, and Mr Beveridge and Mr Siddell's cardiac surgical teams are also very supportive,' said Mensah.

'How do you get on with the theatre nurses?' said the professor. Before Mensah could reply the professor went on: 'Not easy to win over, are they?'

'I haven't had any problems,' said Mensah.

'Really, even with Samantha?' said the professor.

'No, Professor, even with Sister Beardsley,' said Mensah.

'Everyone has problems with Samantha, you must be the exception,' said the professor.

'I'm generally very good with people,' said Mensah.

A smile disturbed the professor's thin lips, his cheeks unmoved. 'That's not why I wanted to see you,' he said. 'You know the department's looking to expand. Where do you see yourself in the next two years?'

Mensah paused for a few seconds. Not sure where the interview was going, he wondered whether it would be presumptuous to admit his ambitions to the professor. A friend at court would be welcome, but he doubted whether the professor would promise him a job just like that, and an informal endorsement counted for very little on its own. Everyone knew of at least one hot favourite who had been invited to apply for a job, but had failed to bag the prize. 'I see myself as a consultant in percutaneous restorative cardiology,' said Mensah.

'Ah, that's the most competitive sub-speciality,' said the professor. 'That's the team our Chinese board members and financial backers are most interested in. I understand you've told your supervisor, Dr Blake, about your interest?'

'Yes, Professor,' Mensah said, his throat tightening. This was not the start to the day he'd expected.

'Well, said the professor, 'I advise you to consider, give some thought to degenerative cardiology. They're short of consultants and fellows and . . . someone of your abilities would be a great boost to that team, the service and the hospital. I can almost certainly assure you, guarantee that you could make a great name for yourself in that field. The field would be clear for you, absolutely clear. If you go for RC you know what you'll be up against; the decision's yours. A few years ago we couldn't get anyone to apply for RC. We now have a glut and this year is especially strong. We'll be fair, we are obliged to be fair, we back our candidates, but we'd prefer not to have votes split.'

Mensah gulped, his chest hurt and the muscles in his back tightened. His armpits prickled with sweat. 'Thank you, professor, I appreciate your advice. Thanks again.' Mensah smiled, bowed and offered his hand to the professor as he got out of his chair.

'I'll prepare papers for the next round of applications.'

Mensah was turned to retreat, then remembered all the resolutions he'd made to himself and to Nancy and Marty, what he had been through; it all came back to him in that microsecond. He turned round to face the professor. 'Professor, do you give this advice as a professor, as a senior colleague, head of the department, as educational supervisor or representative of the medical colleges or the deanery? The professor blanched. 'I should be having this conversation with my supervisor and he's not due to assess me for months. We don't work on the same firm. I'm as well qualified as anyone else around. I can't see why I shouldn't apply; I have no intention of giving up on restorative cardiology without a formal assessment. But please tell me if I've misunderstood your comments.'

Professor Maginot, who had got up to see Mensah out, sat down again and sighed. His hands shook with irritation at the temerity of this Snell man. 'Sit down, my good man, you may have got hold of the wrong end of the stick here; each sub-speciality needs a unique mix of skills. Look, I've trained several now eminent cardiologists. I'm very, very experienced in directing trainees to the most suitable careers. Let's say my advice is a distillation of this experience; a prophylaxis to professional disappointment. Do you not think so? Surely my opinion counts for something?'

'I do, Professor, but it's my career, my life; I think my fate should be decided in open competition.' Mensah opened the door. He did not stop to exchange gossip and mock flirt with Mrs Darby. Could she have betrayed him to the professor? Had she told Maginot that he'd said he had a head like a coconut? Maybe she did for him in some other ways. He hurried away to the ward round.

Mensah was relieved to see Dr Bell conducting the ward round. Dr Bell was usually brief, his uncompromising approach earning him the sobriquet 'kill or cure'. Dr Bell had to use the toilet a lot because he suffered from an enlarged prostate gland, so when Dr Michelle Gold, the pre-registration doctor, embellished the history with some tittle-tattle about the patient's celebrity daughter, he said, 'Just tell me what you think is wrong and if you don't know, tell me so we can move on and cure the patient.' He went on. 'She obviously has endocarditis; it's going to be touch and go; it must have come from that catheter. Take the catheter out, cultures including for that fastidious one they grew the other day, and let us plasma exchange; we may dampen the immune response. Make sure you replace volume – no pussyfooting!'

'Good morning, sorry I'm late, had to attend an impromptu meeting with Professor Maginot,' said Mensah.

Dr Bell raised his eyebrows. 'It's that bad?'

'No,' replied Mensah. He did not know what Dr Bell meant, but his conversation with the professor was no one's business. 'I had to sort out some ethics committee paperwork. You know . . . red tape,' said Mensah. More prickly, stinging heat spread from forehead to ears.

Mensah finished the round, had lunch and started the afternoon outpatient personal session at half past one. Some clinics were conducted in real time over the Internet, mostly for patients who were stable. Mrs Bretuime wanted to be seen in person because her chest pain was giving her gyp. 'When did it start again?' he asked.

'It never really went away,' she said.

'Looking through your records, it says here that you were fine when they saw you six months ago.'

'Yes, I was good that day, but the day after the pain started again and I have no regular doctor and I've been in agony, just agony, you can't imagine,' she said. 'I live alone and sometimes I think this is the end.'

'Where does it hurt, ma'am?'

'From here to here,' she said, rubbing her left breast area and then down to her left hip.

'How long does it last?'

'It never really goes away, doctor.'

'Is it very bad?'

'It's agony.'

He was not getting anywhere. 'What does it feel like?'

'It's gnawing away all the time.'

'Does anything make it better?'

'When I rest.'

'Does anything make it worse?'

'Lying on one side, maybe my left side, but could be my right, and walking and when I'm stressed. It varies, every day it varies, it's sharp, it's tight, it's up and round the back,' she said.

Mensah was struggling but felt Mrs Bretuime's pain was not due to her heart. The trouble was how could he convince her so as to reassure her? 'You have had all the tests, ma'am, it doesn't feel or sound like it's your heart. Although I'm an expert in the body you know your body better than anyone else. What do you think is wrong?'

'You are the doctor, doctor! One of those new treatments I read on the Internet for bad circulation, do you do them here? The pain is down my left side, which is where my heart is, so I just want to know whether everything is all right.'

Mensah did not want to argue that the site of her pain had nothing to do with where her heart was in her chest. But as the customer was always right he waved her into the adjoining room, and scanned her heart on a portable electromagnetic three-dimensional CT/echo machine. 'Excellent result,' he said. 'I think you have arthritis.'

Mrs Bretuime was dubious. But having already spent over twelve hundred pounds that morning, she decided to cut her losses to return another day.

'This one was useless. I must see the consultant next time,' she told Tara, the receptionist.

Mensah was running late. The next patient, Mr Grant (do you know who I am!) Cardison came in pointing at his watch. 'I'm sorry to keep you,' said Mensah.

'You're not,' said Mr Cardison.

'I am, sir. How can I help, sir? I don't want to waste any more of your time.'

'I don't mean to be funny, but Mr Marsh promised to see me personally,' said Mr Cardison.

'Dr Marsh is away, Mr Cardison.'

'Then I don't think you can help me,' he said and stormed out to tell the receptionist that he did not want to see that arrogant doctor again.

The next patient, Mrs Napoli, was one of Mensah's favourites. Her great-grandmother-in-law had married an Italian soldier stationed in England during World War II. She did not have that much wrong with her but when he discharged her she put on a doleful face and he agreed to another follow-up appointment. She paid up so what was the problem!

The next patient was Mrs Offer. Seventy-eight and widowed, she walked in with her new partner, Arthur. After introductions and a few embarrassed looks between the pair, it transpired that they each had a pacemaker. 'I'd like to ask you a favour, I don't think my insurance will cover it, doctor,' she said.

'Why not?' asked Mensah.

'I've got a pacemaker,' she said.

'Yes,' said Mensah, not sure what she was getting at. The pacemaker was working well last time it was checked two months ago.

'Well, Arthur here's also got a pacemaker, his is on the right, mine on the left, we've just met, you see,' she said. She looked over at Arthur. Arthur winked at Mensah. Mrs Offer blushed. Mensah got it at last. He had never come across this before. Mrs Offer's was on the left side of her chest and Arthur's on the right, so the devices clashed when the new couple coupled.

'Have you decided whose should be moved? We can move it to the other side or bury it lower or deeper. You decide, think it through and let us know. Seeing as both systems are working well I'm not keen to revise either by moving them to the other side; I'd rather not disturb them at all, but we'll see how we can help.'

Such patients cheered him up and gave him hope: that in fifty years' time if he lived that long, even with a pacemaker, he could still be a carnal athlete.

Next was Mrs Wallace, aged sixty-five. Towards the end of the consultation she said, 'I looked after a Mensah; he would be about your age now.'

'It may have been me,' said Mensah. 'Did you know my parents?'

'I'm afraid not. Several of us looked after the children. I remember your name, that's all. You were in care, they said your father had left the country. We still talk about the children we looked after, you know, reminisce,' said Mrs Wallace. 'I've been thinking about you. You know the campaign they have been running in the papers about split families, and lost children, it made me want to ask you. My friends kept saying they had met a doctor called Mensah, and when I asked them to describe you I thought it could be the same boy I used to look after. It just made me think about the past, things we should deal with, secrets, our history, they are important, especially family. It made me wonder just as I was leaving last time; I didn't say anything but it was bugging me. You know how you want things to make sense, out of curiosity. I'll be amazed, delighted, if it is you, if it was you. I'll tell the others. I'm sorry, I've been extremely rude, but if you don't mind me asking, have you seen your parents?'

'No, ma'am,' he said.

He discharged Mrs Wallace from the clinic. She irritated him and he felt she should keep her snout out of his life. Marty and Nancy were enough for him. Why would he want to see his parents if they did not want him? If she came back he would avoid her.

After Mrs Wallace left, the clinic coordinator popped her head around the door. 'Dr Snell, do you mind seeing these three patients from the other list? Dr Flood's been called away on an emergency,' she said.

'I do mind, thank you, I've got to be on the second floor myself,' he said. To avoid walking past the waiting patients in the hall, Mensah vaulted out of the window and walked across the courtyard to enter the opposite block through a service entrance. Later, on his way home, he suddenly remembered that he had not seen the patients on the next day's list, but he was too fed up to turn round and ride back up Castle Farms Road. So he pedalled on his way to his flat, legs feeling heavy and weary with the effort.

Mensah went up to his kitchen, made himself a mug of tea, cupped it in his hands and sat at his kitchen table overlooking his postage stamp lawn and his window basket of shrivelled pansies. Wispy threads of smoke-like clouds drifted across the dark sky and his vacant gaze until a growling motorbike exhaust crashed through his reverie. He called Vince and arranged to meet him at the Green Salle.

Vince and Mensah were regulars at the Green Salle, a first-floor pub on the junction of Ivy Road and Gosforth High Street. With its cubicles and dim lights, cheap drink and simple but ready and hot fare, it was ideal for bachelors who did not like pool or darts. 'Still saving lives?' asked Vince over their first drink.

'Lives and souls, like a priest,' said Mensah.

'Will you ever learn to give a straight answer?'

'Sorry, Vince, work stuff. You know how hard I've worked to get this far; well some bloke, this professor's asked me not to apply for the job I've set my heart on. Here we go again, I'm thinking: what do I do now? If it's not one thing . . . the whole system's crap. It just shouldn't happen, it shouldn't be allowed.'

'Tell me what happened,' said Vince.

So Mensah told Vince what Professor Maginot had said.

'Do you think this is because he has the job earmarked for someone else or because he doesn't like you?' said Vince.

'Not sure,' said Mensah, taking a sip of beer. 'What difference does it make?'

'It could, in emphasis, and how you fight back. We studied this at uni – sometimes there's nothing you can do about traceless discrimination. It's when the field is so good that you can't prove anything, but over a period of say ten years, you just find the same people at the top; it happens everywhere, even in sport, but the professionals are past masters at it. That's why you have to convince those who decide your fate that you deserve a place on the starting block. If they don't want you, you're stuffed. They'll shunt you away from your choice. You know that, I know that, you must see it in your practice: different treatment for some patients; at least, that's what the papers say,' said Vince.

'You're right, but what was it about me that attracted these naysayers? If the professor was acting on his own behalf I still have a chance, but not if the advice has come from some shadowy cabal. I can't be sure whether the professor was expressing his own views or whether he based his recommendations on some other data, hidden stuff. Makes you wonder whether the official assessments are a smokescreen – maybe they've got a secret site where they can be more brutal or honest, put the boot in.'

The food arrived, jacket potatoes, lots of butter and baked beans, genetically modified to bind cholesterol in the gut. The two men devoured the meal in silence. When the waiter came to clear the table, Mensah wavered then signalled for more beer.

'At least I have one consolation – I have warning. Poor John

Dent, he was so conscientious as a trainee, but for all his gifts, they didn't appoint him because he had 'issues' or was too 'po-faced and earnest', depending on whom you spoke to. Others said John did not laugh at the professor's bigoted jokes during ward rounds. John was ambushed. Ended up in a backwater polyclinic, a highly qualified medical clerk, requesting scans and signing prescriptions. Adam Desire, not a patch on John, got the job instead. If that happened to them, I wonder why I'm doing this, am I overreaching myself? It makes you question yourself; you're doing well, at least you think you're doing well, and there's not much to tell you otherwise, then this happens. Someone taps you on the shoulder and says, "Son, you've not got what it takes." I've seen it in others: at school and uni – you remember – students applying to read subjects for which they had no significant talent, and no one with the heart to tell them. Football players who want to manage: we've had a few of those in the North-East. But that's not what he's saying. I just want a fair crack. I'm not saying I'm special and that if I fail it will be a great loss to cardiology.'

'Mensah, you're going off again, on a tangent. From where I'm sitting, they're stitching you up; the bottom line is are you going to apply or not, and fight your corner? Or give up?' said Vince.

Mensah poked a straw through his wet serviette. 'I won't, not without a fight. Stuff the lot of them, stuff Maginot, I'm going to apply,' he said.

They walked downstairs into the cold night's air. The rumble of a passing pantechnicon drowned out conversation until they got to their parked cars. 'How do they decide, what's the process, what are your chances in a fairish fight?' asked Vince.

'Good, I think; my assessments have been excellent, I'm reasonably optimistic, for me, that is, but I accept that competition is tough, but I knew that anyway. There's this guy, David Timms, he's a bit of a prat, but a clever prat, devious – just what usually works in this situation,' said Mensah. 'I'm told his CV's excellent, but he doesn't have a good word to say about anyone, except himself. Elbonics, they call it, elbowing everyone else out of the way. It works. I'm not very good at it, I'm afraid. They think it's a virtue until someone does it back. Then, oh, it's not cricket, but then look at cricket. I digress.'

They walked round the cars on to the safety of the pavement. 'Then there's Lisa Matters, the blonde, thunder-thighed, luscious-lipped, tennis-playing billionaire's daughter. Her CV is probably even better. Well, she's married to Professor Grant of the genetics department. I think he's much older than her, but he must have a sexy intellect,' said Mensah. 'They've co-authored a number of articles: polypills for heart failure and postnatal depression patients: that area in general. For all I know, her husband could have done most of the work, but you can't blame selection committees.'

'Blame them for what?' said Vince.

'I meant, you can understand why they use the CV as a measure of ability, endeavour and initiative,' said Mensah.

'It all depends on what they want: my job needs none of the above; animal cunning, perhaps, charm, looks,' said Vince.

'Be serious, no one knows what you do,' said Mensah.

'Are you saying looks, appearance, deportment play no part? I read somewhere that the receptionist's first impressions are just as good as any number of CVs, psychometric tests and interviews,' said Vince.

'No, but talking of looks, the Burka system could play a part,' said Mensah.

'We had it in the Home Office but it has been quietly abandoned – they rely more on the results of the aptitude, personality tests and the examination papers,' said Vince. 'Who knows, I guess you get what you deserve in the end.'

'I think people deserve what they get more often than they get what they deserve; it's the market place,' said Mensah.

'Isn't that too negative?' said Vince.

'No, reality,' said Mensah.

'Keep your chin up, in a few years you'll wonder what all the gloom was about,' said Vince, getting into his car.

'That's what Marty said, I hope you're all right,' said Mensah. 'Let me know how it goes, see you soon,' Vince said.

In the car, Mensah reflected on his day. Had he been allowed his piddling successes, been placed on the ledge or mantelpiece of aspirations from which they would now gently remove him to hide him in a cupboard, or, if he clung on, from which they would wrench and drop him? Like Boxer in *Animal Farm*. There was no obligation on the rest of the world to enable him to fulfil his dreams, but without these dreams he was, he had, nothing. Was he being selfish? Would yielding to someone more talented not in the end be to patients' advantage? But not everyone thought like that. Everyone was convinced they were the best. His grandfather had managed to be appointed a consultant when it was virtually impossible for non-EUs or women to get a job that anyone else wanted. He'd written that luck, and the backing of a number of kind-hearted members of the establishment had helped him to succeed. Mensah was also inspired by an entry about a bright female who had succeeded in neurology after she had been advised to give up. Times had changed. He was better off than his grandfather. At least he would be a consultant, much younger, in a much sought after speciality, in one of the best hospitals in the country. He stopped at a Tesco corner shop to buy a few toiletries – almost all the independent shops had closed during the Nationalist coalition – and when he got home, mug of cocoa in one hand and tuna sandwich in the other, he watched a brief report on economic migration from Hong Kong to mainland China and another on a fight in the family enclosure at the junior Wimbledon quarter-final between Isme Huran of Iran and Leon Sumerman of Israel. In response, as well as erecting a barrier between supporters' camps, the All England Club would now ask the spectators in the family enclosure to sign a propriety pact. The next story featured an economist explaining why the prevailing economic uncertainty justified further reductions in public sector pay and pensions.

Mensah was furious, so before he went to bed he logged on to his blog site to let off steam.

The next day (Wednesday) Mensah overslept by a quarter of an hour. He cursed and calculated that if he woke up fifteen minutes later each day for the rest of his short life he would be cheating himself of nearly ten days per annum. To make up the lost time he forwent his toilet void and his shave. He left feeling bloated and itchy faced and arrived at work in a bad mood.

Graham Castle was the new gastroenterologist on the block. Shortly after Graham was appointed Mensah had helped him with a patient who had gone into acute pulmonary oedema and ventricular tachycardia during a routine colonoscopic polyp genomic biopsy and washout, and he seemed a nice fellow. Mensah, drawn to Graham's easygoing efficiency when they had worked on the same floor two years earlier, thought his new colleague might understand his plight.

Graham had just arrived at work himself when Mensah found him. 'Hi, Graham, can I have a word? There's this job coming up and I'm not sure whether I have a chance.'

'Mensah, why do you ask? You'll have no problems. You know you are at least as good as anyone else. You've got the qualifications, you've got the experience, and if you have the requisite publications you just need a bit of luck. But if everything else fails there's always the quota system, if that's still around. Heard that it's been used by some to get in; I'm not sure whether it works for your speciality, what was your speciality again?'

'Cardiology,' said Mensah with a knot in his belly. *Quota system!* A system introduced by the Nationalists under the guise of fairness for all in which the government insisted on a proportion of working-class students to be admitted to read law, medicine and engineering, but put a ceiling on the number of non-EU admissions. Mensah's heart and head wrestled for control of his face and mouth; his head won, then his heart. His lips stopped but heart and stomach clenched in revenge, and finally he could not help himself. 'Are you serious,' he blurted, 'could you be more crass! Please, I asked you a simple question as a colleague and you come out with this crap. There's not a snowflake in hell's chance of me qualifying for anything by the quota system except for deportation or some new non-EU vaccination programme. What made you think that Freeman Hospital operates a quota system?'

'I meant to say that you'd be fine, whatever happened,' said Graham.

'Forgive me, Graham, if I did not see it that way. I'm shocked, and I hope I never have anything to do with you personally or professionally again. Just clear off; I shan't take any more of your time.'

Mensah hurried off to theatre, Graham Castle to his endoscopy list, shaking his head. 'Some people are always angry,' he told Sister Bottlebottom at the clinic.

'What are you talking about?' she said.

13

Mrs Patrick

'Good morning,' said Timms.

'Good morning, David, we'll be starting on our own. The boss is showing someone round,' Mensah said. He would rather be working with one of the registrars because he did not trust David Timms. Just because David had been a consultant elect longer than he did not excuse his condescension or his presumption that he was a nailed on certainty for the consultant job. 'A spoilt and privileged man who smiles with his teeth and not his eyes,' he'd told Nancy last weekend.

'Marsh will probably join us after we have put all the lines in – I can't see him allowing us the limelight with his visitor around,' said Timms.

Mensah paused for a couple of seconds to think of an appropriate answer. 'We'll see,' he said.

The list was now not particularly demanding. The first patient, Mrs Gloombury's bidirectional revolving biosensor mitral valve re-replacement, had been cancelled because she had a cold. Yet even with the reassuring presence of Dr David Marsh, the senior consultant cardiologist in the wings, Maginot's advice and Timms' presence increased Mensah's unease. He changed into his theatre suit, nearly falling over when he put both feet through the same trouser leg and burst into the pre-operative annex through the disinfecting tunnel to find the patrician

Dr Marsh already going through the consent form with Mrs Patrick.

'Good afternoon,' Dr Marsh grunted. *This is not good*, thought Mensah. Not the way to impress the deciders of his fate. Even more galling: David Timms had taken his place as first operator.

Mrs Patrick had been moved up the list because of a cancellation. Her mitral valve had literally fallen apart after two previous valve repair procedures – the first thirty years earlier and the latter twenty years later. This time the relatively new technique of growing valve parts in the laboratory and implanting these to repair damaged valves was being used instead of a percutaneous whole prosthetic valve replacement. Mrs Patrick was not suitable for the latter because of the severe scarring from previous infections and operations. She was ninety years old and understood that the operation was to improve her quality of life and for research. Until she'd retired, aged seventy-nine, she had been a buyer for a department store. On retirement, she'd worked as a responsible adult on call to assist the police with juvenile crime suspects. She lived alone, still drove her electric Mini and had sought the attention of the team at the Freeman when she was repeatedly woken up by chest tightness. The operation would cost just under fifty thousand pounds, with half of this waived because of her age and because she had agreed to take part in a research sub-study sponsored by Delsaco, an Indian-based multinational with strong connections with the North-East through its relationship with Stephen Peritt, a former health minister who had recently retired from his Newcastle Central seat.

The doctors reintroduced themselves to Mrs Patrick and started work, self-conscious as Professor Radic from the United Serbian University watched from an adjoining room. Whilst David applied the antiseptic, Mensah tipped the contents of the bowl containing the main instruments, and reclaimed his position as first operator. David gave way. He appeared distracted and twice handed Mensah the wrong end of the guide wires and introducers. 'This is not the usual Cordis stuff. That lady – I think she's from the agency – keeps handing me the manifold the wrong way round,' said David. *Take all the gain and give all the blame, just how to succeed in life*, thought Mensah, quoting from his grandfather's diary. 'Have you given the anticoagulant yet? I had it in this syringe,' said David.

'Yes,' Mensah replied, 'I told everyone when I gave it five minutes ago. Steve did not hear me the first time, so I announced it again and told Sister Mellanby. I'm sure they heard me.'

'Sorry, just testing,' said David.

Sister Sue Mellanby tried to break the tension: 'They don't label these packages properly any more – easy to make a mistake when you take them out . . . I find that sometimes, I really do; rubbish, this modern recycled stuff they give us,' she said.

Other theatre staff tried to look busy filling their charge forms or following Mrs Patrick's vital signs. Under just enough local anaesthetic, and with a small dose of sedative to reduce anxiety but not respiration, the operators turned their attention to Mrs Patrick's vascular access sites and inserted the peripheral and central intravenous and arterial lines. David hoped Dr Marsh would hurry up with his preparations and join them. For a change, he was even relieved that Mensah had taken the initiative. *If we slow down, Dr Marsh will be here soon to take over and I can relax*, David thought. He would try to get through the day and find some way of getting someone else to cover his list of diagnostic imaging that afternoon. He just needed to get through this case and he would make some excuse and get back home to Amanda.

Once all the catheters and wires were in place, both doctors settled down to the painstaking task of repairing Mrs Patrick's mitral valve.

Soft classical music played in the background – a compromise between the silence David preferred and the rest of the team's need for ambient music. Mensah and David were now relaxed. The procedure was going well. Mensah turned his attention to their visitor. 'Professor, we've come to the issue you raised at the last congress of cardiology . . . we were taught to place a few extra stitches in the *in vitro* grown chordae. Allows for wastage – if we lose a few from infarction we will still maintain valve function – we hope! Suddenly the voice of Steve Rayner, senior chief cardiac physiologist, came over the microphone: 'Pressure's down, crashed, people, pressure is thirty systolic, now vt/vf, no vt still thirty.' Mrs Patrick's blood pressure had plummeted. By training and instinct, both operators looked up at once to the heads-up display of elec-trocardiographic and haemodynamic data. All the readings – the pressure, resistance, output, the electrocardiogram – were heading south.

'Oh, shit,' said Mensah.

Mrs Patrick went rigid, then had to be restrained as she tried to get off the table. She screamed.

'Anaesthetist, inotrope, assist pump device five point four, please. Peripheral balloon support, now, fluids please, folks,' said Mensah. Sister repeated the request to one of the other nurses. They had rehearsed this scenario several times in the simulator, but this was real. Mensah inserted the pump into Mrs Patrick's heart while the senior cardiac physiologist scanned the heart. One of the supporting pillars of the mitral valve, the valve they were working on, was torn. It was leaking and the lungs flooded with blood coming back the wrong way. There was nothing they could do – even an open heart procedure would not repair the damage fast enough to save the patient. Seconds later, with a chilling, dreadful croaky rattle and crackle, foamy blood-stained fluid gushed from Mrs Patrick's nose and mouth, coating her teeth and gums in the red emulsion. Just an hour after she had been laughing and joking with the staff, she was dead. A flake of dried lipstick clung to her cheek, and her limp, damp hair hung over the sides of her face and lifeless, pale, ninety-year-old head, revealing her roots and a bald patch.

After Mrs Patrick's body was made presentable, and Mr Andrew Patrick, her son – himself now sixty-five years old – had been informed of his mother's death, Mensah and David retired to the coffee room to compose themselves for the rest of the day.

They still had two more procedures on that morning shift and one major combined open and percutaneous procedure after lunch, if time allowed.

Sister Mellanby notified the bereavement and governance officer and distributed the relevant forms to each team member to state from immediate recall what they had seen. A more formal report would be compiled by the operators and their consultants. Finally there would be an interview and a report compiled to be presented to the relatives, the hospital board and the life and health insurance companies.

'Terrible, terrible, disaster' was all Mensah could say. Nurse Daviniesta thought Mensah was always wistful, even when things were going well, but now he looked particularly miserable.

'Do you want a coffee or something?' she asked. Mensah, leaning back in an armless chair, his head turned up to the ceiling as if in homage, had not seen her coming. He did not normally drink caffeine-based beverages because they made him weepy and tremulous, but out of politeness and implicit appreciation of her concern, he replied, 'Yes, please, I'll have a cup of tea, but no sugar.' He tried not to blink to keep the tears of grief-laden impotence trapped behind his smarting eyelids. 'Thank you,' he said when the tea arrived.

Daviniesta sat down beside him. 'Are you okay? These things happen you know – you did everything you could.' *But I failed,* he thought. *I should have been a lumberjack, a shelf-stacker or a hobo.* Daviniesta sat by Mensah in silence, wondering what to say. 'You're an excellent doctor, everyone says so,' she said eventually.

'*I* don't,' he replied.

Daviniesta got up. Do you want another cup of tea or a bun? I'm going round to the canteen.'

'No thank you, you're very kind,' Mensah replied.

David stood by the sink waiting to wash his mug out. He had scalded himself gulping down a hot cup of coffee. As David turned to leave, he said, 'These things happen – it's in the nature of the work.'

'In a way she got her wish, she said she didn't want to live and wanted to die in bed,' said Rick, the anaesthetic assistant. Gallows humour formed part of the mutual healing process.

14

Post-op Sadness

Few were untouched by the sudden operative loss of a patient. It was one thing coping with the operation in the heat of battle, but quite another returning from the fray to tell a family of their fate: life without a wife, husband, father, mother, son or daughter, friend or neighbour. *Why?* Killed by friendly fire. 'We are sorry.' 'Sorry!' This little word was what you uttered when you interrupted or bumped into someone in the street or waved when you cut someone up in traffic. For some, rehabilitation came through prayer or alcohol or opiates or cigarettes or work; for others, a re-evaluation of their duties, hours and lives. Sometimes, a colleague's sympathetic and professional support, annealed by the intensity of shared emotions, morphed and merged into carnal support, then even wedlock, severing previous covenants. Some would, if they could (or felt they should), offer a scholarship to the orphaned children of the dead, or a pension to the widowed instead. The few who, by chance, had all the reinforcements they needed, or who had seen it before, carried on, unfazed, but the best tribute to the dead is to learn from each defeat, so as never to repeat it.

During quiet periods, just before he went to sleep or early in the morning as he cleaned his teeth, did his laundry or listened to music, Mensah tried to shake out of his head those foreboding terms such as vicarious liability, negligence, corporate manslaughter

125

or inadvertent homicide. The mandatory confidential debriefing and counselling session arranged by the hospital did not help him, and he refused to use his personal and well-tried remedy of cannabis and St John's Wort. She was his patient and he wanted to take his punishment neat.

But for weeks, memories of the disaster were evoked by other anniversaries: the next time he had to use the same theatre or had an observer or visitor in situ; an elderly female patient; or a threat to his punctuality or routine. For a while he would suddenly see someone he imagined to be Mrs Patrick being driven past him in a car as he walked up Gosforth High Street, and on one occasion he almost called out to her in relief that she was alive, only for reality to return a few seconds later when he remembered that she was not. He cancelled visits to the cinema or to St James's Park because he felt that he should not be enjoying himself if Mrs Patrick's relatives were still grieving.

15

Post-op Reports

David Timms telephoned his parents every Wednesday night. 'Hi, Dad, it's me. How's Mum?'

'She's fine, a little tired from her trip, but you know Mum, she's working on the introduction to the minority report she's writing on the dyskeratotic gene scandal. She seems to feel strongly about it. She thinks the government's trying to duck its responsibility to the thousands of innocents affected by the contamination. She has to get it finished quickly before the main committee publicises its recommendations. She's afraid that they'll rule against setting up a judicial enquiry. She doesn't want me to disturb her.'

Conversations with his mother were brief, anyway, a few pleasantries and she would hand the phone to John, but she always came to the phone. 'Is she still angry with me about Jonathan's eye colour? Tell Mother I'm sorry not to have involved her more. Just tell her I'm sorry and we'll talk soon,' said David.

'Don't worry,' said John. 'I'm sure she's forgotten about it – she's under a lot of stress with work and everything. She just won't let up. It's hard going, but she won't listen. Great result yesterday, wasn't it?' Surrey had won the county championship on the last day of the season by beating Yorkshire – imports and all – by one wicket. 'Barry and Pocock's legs have gone, they've had so many stem cell injections they are more plant than animal,' said John.

'Not your best attempt at humour, but full marks for endeavour, Dad. You're still going to Abu Dhabi?' asked David.

'I'm not sure. For one, your mother can't come; work, she says, and then there's you. She wants to be around more now that you have Jonathan. I can see her point. And she'd rather go walking,' said John.

'When do you have to let them know?' said David.

'I think the end of this month,' said his father.

'Let me know what you decide,' said David.

'Your mum and I will come to see you soon, maybe this weekend.'

'It'll be great to see you both, I'll tell Amanda. We're looking forward to it. Bye.'

David smiled, blew Amanda a kiss and called the main cardiac post-operative ward. He gave his code number and the case record of the patient, Mrs Fairy. The robot asked him whether he wanted to speak to a nurse, wanted the latest readout of results or just a summary. He asked for 'summary'. 'She's fine,' the robot replied. 'Tell her I'll see her tomorrow. Good-night.' 'And good evening to you,' replied the robot.

A formal report of the incident had to be compiled within a fortnight. Mensah rang the clinical advisor, Mrs Everton. 'The board will convene the case-mortality meeting soon for the quarter. If medical malfeasance is suspected, Mrs Patrick's death may be one of those discussed in more detail,' she said.

'Should I include Professor Radic's compliments on the team's speed and efficiency in dealing with Mrs Patrick's collapse?' he asked.

'No, we don't want to implicate our visitor. What the professor thought did not help to explain the event itself anyway,' she said.

A few days later Mensah collated all the relevant records from the files and, for perspective, included Mrs Patrick's difficulties with severe breathlessness at rest and the failure of all other available techniques to relieve her symptoms. He dealt with the issues as they were relevant to his own involvement and resisted the temptation to be defensive. He was aware of a number of minor errors in the record such as the inflating pressures and the odd misspelt unit, but he did not think these altered the conclusions of his report and he did not draw attention to them. After a few drafts he left the five pages of text over the weekend and on the Monday read and edited the report once more before he sent it off to the head of clinical governance.

By the end of the week, Mensah had perked up and had a plan. After the clinic he finished his paperwork and looked through his complication list. Nothing serious: a suspected stitch abscess had turned out to be a scab. He put a letter of gratitude from a patient in his appraisal folder and went back to Mrs Patrick's notes and re-examined the data and all the paperwork. He made an appointment to see the counsellor about his career, spoke to the Medical Defence Union about a clinical governance issue and was getting back into a routine.

David's report stressed that he was no more than a bystander, that the recording would show Mensah taking his place as first operator and that it was Mensah who was manipulating the catheters when Mrs Patrick collapsed. In the report he thanked the nurses and members of the resuscitation team but could not comment on whether Dr Snell had placed the devices correctly; it was all in the heat of the moment. David hoped that by drawing the committee's attention to this aspect of Mrs Patrick's resuscitation it would further concentrate flak on Mensah. Mensah could not be discounted as a serious contender for the consultant post. He was not going to let the Geordie beat him.

16

Saturday in Jesmond

That weekend, Mensah returned the bag of laundry belonging to Mrs Snelling that he had picked up in error from the dry-cleaner and was relieved when the receptionist accepted his explanation. On his way to watch the Magpies play Spurs in the opening match of the season, Mensah decided to visit Mr Yardbarrow, the local insurance broker, again.

'Good morning, doctor, how can I help you?' said Mr Yardbarrow.

'I've come about the same issue: insurance; I'm fed up that I can't go abroad because I can't get travel insurance,' he said.

'I'm sorry, doctor, but we do have some new life insurance products.'

'I don't want useless life insurance, I have no dependants, you know that all I need is travel, critical illness and permanent health insurance. Why would I need life insurance, in my position?'

Neither Yardbarrow nor Frankland, the financial adviser, could help. 'Your case is unique and the actuaries can't give us a quote for you because the risk's difficult to assess. The situation has not changed since we last spoke. We may be able to help when there's a government-backed security in place.' He was referring to the action promised by the select committee.

Mensah's tremulous voice betrayed his anger. 'But it's gone quiet again, and everyone knows it'll take years to resolve, if ever.'

He marched out of the office. As he left, a smart new shop on the other side of the street caught his eye. Wondering why the council had changed its policy on preserving the character of the High Street, Mensah crossed the road and walked in. He chose a shower gel and a new brand of aftershave he had seen advertised on the Internet, and made his way to the self-service checkout. Perhaps because of his argument with Yardbarrow, for a few blank seconds he could not remember his pin number, but it came back to him and he keyed in the selected items. Transaction complete, he stuffed the tubes into the ample pockets of his jacket, wrestling with the wrapping of a chocolate bar as he made for the door. Just as he was going to take a second bite he felt a hand on his right shoulder as if in friendly re-acquaintance.

'Good afternoon, sir, you have receipt for that item?'

'Of course I have,' said Mensah, I've just paid for it with my card. Your machine wasn't working properly. I had to key each item in twice. Anyway, I'll show you and that should sort it out – oh, it's here somewhere. So many pockets in this jacket, but it's here somewhere.' For two minutes Mensah rummaged around in his jacket and trouser pockets, looked on the floor around him but could not find the wretched receipt. Then he realised what may have happened. 'I'm sorry, my receipt is probably still in the till or in the waste-paper basket,' he said.

'I'm afraid, sir, I under strict orders to report shoplifters,' said the store detective. 'I'd like you come with me somewhere quiet so I take your statement. In private, not here, I'm sure you don't want embarrassment.'

Mensah looked round him, burning all over with frustration, afraid that they could be overheard. He was sure he had paid for the items. 'Why don't we ask the cashier at the adjacent till – she oversees the self-service tills as well. She saw me having problems with the keyboard. She may remember me. She should. It was only a few minutes ago,' he said.

The detective agreed to accompany Mensah to the till. 'Where's Annie?' he said to Chelsea, a young assistant.

'Annie's gone, she's had a coffee and then I saw her pack her bags, she's got the afternoon off,' she said.

'Perhaps you could check your surveillance camera,' said Mensah.

'The CCTV new, not working,' said the detective.

There was nothing to it other than a visit to the store's security office to explain himself to the senior detective. Mr Aragones, the detective who had apprehended him, spat out his chewing gum into a waste-paper basket, took a few notes, filled out a form. 'Every time, people say we make mistake, always mistake, but no receipt, so how mistake?' he said. 'Fill form and write statement,' he said.

Mensah filled out the forms. While the detective made a folder, Mensah thought of a way that he could convince the man that he was a doctor. From his pocket he brought a list of blood and radiological results and his potted summary of the medical histories of six of his patients. He showed them to the chief detective. 'I have a list here on letter-headed paper just for you to see. I work at the Freeman, I really did make a mistake, I lost the receipt, just a silly mistake, but I paid. I don't have any identity cards on me but this may help.'

'Thank you, sir, you know, they may say anyone can have this list. Can I keep it? I'll send the report to headquarters. Head office says report everything. Mr Rodder says we must improve all our arrests and numbers, our security, you see. You see, it's more than my job's worth . . .'

Mensah left the shop with his chest hosting the Grand National. He was furious with himself for not keeping the receipt safe and humiliated by what he thought was the sceptical and patronising tone of the detectives. But after a few minutes turning all his pockets out again Mensah gave up and set off for the match, promising himself that if the Magpies won he would go to the cinema and if they lost he would go home. They won, but he went home anyway.

Mr David Aragones, the store detective, was not sure Mensah

was who he said he was. To him Mensah looked just like those people who sold T-shirts at the roadside in Madrid, and other main Spanish cities, or played football, very well, he admitted. Their children wanted to be singers, models or actresses and he did not know any who were working as doctors. He did not like Mensah, a bit too cocky. The next Monday morning, Aragones called the hospital switchboard. 'I would like to report shoplifting. He say he member of your staff.'

'Have you informed the police?' the voice asked.

'No, my boss say to talk to you first, to keep quiet, like,' he said.

'I'll put you through to the human facilities, resources and occupational therapy section,' she said.

'Hello,' said Aragones, 'a man say he work here as doctor has been caught shoplifting, can we talk?'

'I'll ask my secretary to call you to make an appointment for you, can I take a few details?' said Ms Sherry.

133

17

Suspension

At about four o'clock on a Tuesday afternoon, six weeks after Mrs Patrick's death, Mensah was sitting at his terminal skimming through the latest edition of *Circulation* when the departmental porter, Mr Gerry Banks, handed him an envelope marked 'private and confidential'. Scanning the letter quickly for key words, his heart dropped. The letter was from the chairperson of the clinical effectiveness committee, Dr Marsh, suspending Mensah from duty with immediate effect and threatening him with further disciplinary action if he did not produce within ten working days a satisfactory response to specific allegations of professional misconduct. Mensah read the letter again, checking to see that they had the right doctor. He could not remember doing anything that could be construed as unprofessional. Perhaps he was guilty by default: of omission rather than of commission.

Stapled to the main envelope was another letter from the head of the nursing division of clinical governance, Mrs Patterson, asking him to comment on a report that Mrs Patrick had asked that the procedure be stopped just before he inserted the intraventricular assist device during her resuscitation. That in continuing with the procedure, Mensah had disregarded the patient's wishes and her human rights. *'Allegations of disrespect or contempt for the autonomy of the patient are taken very seriously.'* Mensah was also accused of shoplifting and betraying patient confidentiality by leaving material and private clinical records in a public place. Enclosed were copies of the scraps of paper with patients' names on that he had given the store detective to prove that he was attached to the hospital. The letter concluded by reassuring Mensah that he would be granted relevant but restricted access to the hospital network, from home, to enable him to prepare his reply from the case records. After that, a disciplinary committee would convene to decide his fate.

He had heard how consultants had been disciplined and sacked. A typical Trust-engineered sacking or suspension would involve a consultant who was usually older than average, who may not be open to 'new ways of working' and who would not call bull-shit aromatic daisy chains. Either that or someone who had fallen out with management or was not making as much money for the hospital as expected. A patient or carer making a general obser-vation or simply filling in a questionnaire about the service they had received – such as a late appointment, a missing result or papers; late communication or post-operative discomfort; or other complications – would be encouraged, during a conversation, to resolve the issues raised by making a specific and formal complaint. The target consultant would then be required to respond to the complaint within a specified deadline, say fourteen days. An intem-perate e-mail or response expressing indignation, even if justi-fied, or an inadequate reply, would be used to skewer the target or entangle them in such a web of red tape that this of itself – without prejudice to the merits of the original complaint, not to mention the potential adverse effect of the stress and time involved in dealing with these queries on the clinician's practice – could result in the consultant's suspension, then dismissal.

Mensah did not think he had done anything to deserve suspen-sion or dismissal. He had handed the scraps of paper to a detec-tive and not left them lying around for anyone to read. But with his track record of bad luck, anything could happen. Mensah called Ms Sherry in human facilities. 'You'll need to find a replace-ment for me,' said Mensah.

'That's all in hand,' said Ms Sherry.

'When will the consultant job be advertised?' asked Mensah.

Ms Sherry was rumoured to be very close to the chief executive, who had appointed her to the Trust when a local law firm, Flapping and Floundering, or whatever they were called, was taken over only to close a year later. 'I'm sure the appointment will be made before the end of the year because Mr Li Tang, the chairman of the Trust, chairs all important appointment panels. He always comes to enjoy the English autumn. I can't tell you when the interviews will be held though,' she said.

'Thank you,' said Mensah.

'You're welcome, but remember, you can't apply if you're under investigation for professional misconduct and I see that you have two disciplinary points,' she said. No doctor with two or more disciplinary points could apply for a consultant job and points stayed on the record for six months. Disciplinary points ranged from two to a maximum of ten, depending on the severity of the offence. A total of ten points in a calendar year meant automatic dismissal. 'You have two disciplinary points, and two suspended,' she said again to rub it in. Mensah had forgotten. What he thought was a minor disagreement over Tom, the ward cardiac physiologist's repeated late arrival at work had turned into an allegation of bullying, and Mensah, rather than contest the silly accusations, had let the points, which were due to come off his record in two weeks, stand. He now wished he had not been so blasé. His suspended points came from a patient complaint. Mensah had said, 'I'm just going to amplify this incision' as a way of indicating that he had to make a deeper cut, precisely so as not to cause offence, but Mrs Aldcock, a large woman, had insisted that he'd called her ample and demanded an apology. So he'd apologised.

'I should have contested those points,' he said. 'Oh, and do I still have to see the careers counsellor next week?'

'Yes, as long as it is not in a clinical area,' she said. 'For confidentiality, you could meet her at her offices,' she offered.

Mensah put the letter in his pocket and called the Medical Defence Union. There was a delay while they checked his subscription and membership details, then a friendly voice advised him to write an account of his role in the procedure leading up to Mrs Patrick's death. The adviser did not think the Defence Union was likely to deal with Mensah's case before the consultant jobs were advertised but she would contact him if there was any progress. Mensah then called the British Medical Association to speak to its conflicts adviser. The Association had split into 'Consultants' and 'GP' sections, and the pre-consultants and other trainees, caught in the middle, were given low priority. As there were so many pre-consultants in his shoes, he might as well have been reporting the loss of a pair of socks to the police.

Mensah cleared his desk, stood staring at the paperweight, a present from his patient, Mrs Adgey. Refocusing, he put the gift down and rustled through his desk drawers. Through tear-filled eyes he read the postcard he kept to remind him of a pleasant summer holiday, and smoothed the photograph of Mr Ask, a decorated veteran of the Second World War (a gift to his grandfather he kept to remind him of the sacrifices others had made for freedom and to remind him that those frail old patients on the wards had once been dashing and virile). He threw in the bin the scraps of paper on which he had scribbled medical terms he had not had time to look up. They no longer seemed that important. Mensah tripped over his left foot and nearly fell as he half ran towards the centre's main foyer, oblivious to the charity shop receptionist trying to catch his eye, or the shouted 'Hi, Mensah, you lost your bet,' from Alison, one of his favourite cardiac physiologists. Then his skin prickled with anxiety as he heard the hubbub from just round the corner reminding him of the video conference on cardiac injuries caused by explosives in the Gaza strip. David, Lisa, Farrier and a group of other trainees were walking towards him. Lisa saw Mensah just before he could turn into the safety of a corridor leading to the secretary's offices.

Mensah shouted 'fine' down the empty corridor to feign the end of a conversation and walked towards his colleagues.

'Hi, how are you both? I thought I saw a rep in one of the offices. I'm off to prepare next week's meeting. When are you presenting?' he said.

'I gave mine only a fortnight ago,' Lisa replied. 'You remember, you were sitting right in front of me in the front row.'

'Sorry,' said Mensah, 'I'm a little distracted, our recent calamity.'

'Oh, sorry to hear about that. Have you finished all the reports? Not one for the CV, you know what the board will do if there's a formal complaint. They'll take the easy way out and stop you doing restorative cardiology,' she said.

Mensah, detecting a hint of *schadenfreude*, fumed but could not think of a retort. David stepped back half a metre, to enjoy the whiff of animosity. Mensah turned to David. 'Whilst we are on the subject, have you heard anything else about Mrs Patrick?'

'No,' David replied, 'have you?'

'I don't think so, it's dragging on a bit,' Mensah replied, trying not to lie again. He headed for the library, walked along the whole length of the sixth floor and down the staircase, emerging from the back entrance of the main hospital block.

18

Career Counsellor

'Good morning, Dr Snell, I've looked through your file and I
hope I can help.'

Mensah nodded. 'Good morning, you may well be able to,' he
replied, pulling up a chair. 'Though I have to admit that I don't
know how.' Mensah was sitting in one of the offices Ms Lovell
shared with one other official who was out for the day visiting clients.

Ms Lovell opened her folder. 'I'm accredited in counselling
and professional advice. The hospital employs me to resolve the
staff's professional and personal problems; the latter in so far as
they affect the member's ability to perform their duties to the
high standards demanded by the hospital.'

Mensah swallowed. At first blush, he knew he was not going
to enjoy this session. He had never found counselling useful. He
half expected her to read him his rights. Another box-ticking
clinical governance busybody, but he had to cooperate. Ms Lovell
produced another sheaf of certificates. 'Sign here please to confirm
that you have seen these documents.' Mensah initialled the docu-
ment and looked up. 'On a scale of one to ten, how close am I
if I say that you are at a professional crossroad?'

Mensah was not prepared for this line of questioning. 'I would
say zero, but how do I know? Crossroads, halt, detour: I don't
know which, honestly. Perhaps I am approaching one, but I don't
think I'm there yet,' he said.

Ms Lovell opened another file. She appeared to be reading from a pro forma. 'Do you consider your barriers to progress professional, personal or both?'

'I have no personal issues,' said Mensah. 'I'm looking to apply for a consultant job, my patient died. I cannot remember the patient asking me to stop the valve repair or even resuscitation. We were in the middle of an emergency, for heaven's sake. I don't remember her asking me to stop. What was I supposed to do – leave her to die? Years before, a patient, Mrs K, I can't remember her name, insisted that if anything went wrong she was not to be subjected to salvage procedures. The consultant asked her to restate her request to the theatre team before the operation. As it happens, the complex angioplasty went without a hitch. But even these orders are subject to interpretation, they are ambiguous; what happens if the collapse is iatrogenic, or due to faulty equipment, or to a reflex drop in blood pressure or heart rate? These scenarios have not been tested. We need to consider these issues carefully,' he said.

Ms Lovell crossed her legs. 'Go on,' she said.

'Then I've been accused of shoplifting. It was a misunderstanding and I'm sure I will clear it up with my bank or some proof of payment. I could argue that this was caused by professional considerations – worry about career progression and . . .'

'Let's concentrate on the professional then,' said Ms Lovell. 'Is it fair to say that you are obsessive about your career, this consultant job you are applying for; that this has become all consuming, that it may even have contributed to your patient's death? Have you asked yourself whether your work-life balance is adequate? I'll give you an audit diary to fill from memory. See if you can remember how many of your free weekends you can recall. Just off the top of your head, there's no right or wrong answer.'

Mensah knew he had spent most of his time in his flat recently. What would that prove: that he was lazy, unbalanced or conscientious? He filled in the form, circling the options most closely matching his activities. 'This form does not address my concerns,' he said, handing it back.

'Ah, so you are having a personal crisis then – should I put that down in your file?'

'No, no, I don't know,' said Mensah.

'You must have been very upset by Professor Maginot's advice,' said Ms Lovell. Mensah missed a beat. She knew this as well. How much more did she know about him? Ms Lovell went on. 'Who is to say whether he is right or wrong? Why do you pick this line of work; to help yourself or others?' Mensah was going to reply 'to help myself' but Ms Lovell said, 'I understand that cardiologists do not starve. Be honest. Your sub-speciality is quite well rewarded, have you not considered the possibility that your motives are financial? Would you not enjoy doing something else, would that make you a failure? Failure at one career may spur you on to better success in another.'

'You miss the point,' said Mensah. 'I've not failed. Had I failed I would be asking different questions. I'm here because it is likely that I may not be allowed to reach the point at which I will have a chance to fail, or succeed. I was hoping that someone like you might help me make sense of that, what I'm going through. I expect with your qualifications you have come across this before?'

Ms Lovell listened, making notes on her laptop. For a moment Mensah thought she was sending an e-mail to Maginot, but he slapped down his paranoia, only for it to resurface when she asked, 'You're not working at the moment?'

'Yes, I am,' he said. 'That's an internal misunderstanding which will soon be resolved.'

'I understand,' said Ms Lovell.

What did she know about it? Mensah's chest and throat throbbed and ached with the force of his thumping heart. For a split second he felt light-headed and his chest empty as a particularly hard beat thudded round and reverberated into his neck. Then half a dozen alarmingly rapid beats followed. He steadied himself then got up. 'Thank you very much, Ms Lovell, one day I hope to be as good at my job as you are at yours.'

Mensah was not impressed. Fancy her asking him about money. Of course we all want to help people – like politicians, even army dictators seize power protesting that they seek to govern in the national interest. No doctor wanted to be a billionaire or buy a yacht, or fancy holiday homes, cars, mistresses. They all wanted to help people. Why should he tell this stranger that self-affirmation trumped material success, that he placed the need to impress himself above all else? That to prove himself he had sought a difficult summit? Failure would tag him – to himself and the world around him – as a loser, as worthless, just as it would for anyone else in his predicament.

19

Mensah Looks to the Past

Immigrant life must be like watching television in another man's house. Mensah, whingeing and raving to counsellors or colleagues about his predicament, would evoke, at best, empathy and indifference; and at worse, pity, contempt and aggression. To complain to Nancy and Marty again he thought risked alienation by identifying them with his persecutors. *What if they had voted for the ADHD policy?* Mensah thought; then, *Not Marty and Nancy*, he said to himself. Yet, perhaps it was because Mensah missed the indefinable affinity of a shared bond, outlook, history or blood that he thought of looking for his birth parents. Or, did he want to show Marty and Nancy he was hurt? Or perhaps he was just curious or spurred by the comment Mrs Wallace had made about family. Or was it because he no longer wanted the fake version he was now an expert in peddling, but real unconditional love, as writ on his mother's face in his dreams? Or because he wanted, through re-acquaintance with his heritage, to imagine what sort of person he would have been if he had not been vaccinated; wanted to rearrange and take control of a life assembled and moulded by government agencies and now manipulated by his superiors? Or perhaps it was just a phase, a yearning, which, like other passions, ebbs with time. If he found his family, would they think him inferior, a dirty secret because he had been in care? Or would they resent or despise his modest achievements? What if they were dead? Perhaps he was just confused, afraid and needed new anchors or bearings to support him if he failed? Or, if he failed, he could say to (or about) them, 'There you are, I knew I had no chance.' If they were successes he could meet his guilty parents to gloat, to read the charges before he passed sentence, for he had already prosecuted and convicted them. Damned they were by those photographs showing his miserable face, small sad eyes, bowed head and his untidy hair. Charged and convicted they were for his sojourn from home to home, for leaving him to the lottery of the game of pass the little one. What would they say in mitigation? Could he commute their sentence or forgive and acquit? Would his case collapse when he met them? If they said that his life had made him stronger, a better person, a better doctor even, could he retort that he would rather have been a happier child? Stuff the profession, any number of people could do his job, but no one could live this life for him. Unintended benefit was no defence, his parents were guilty, absolutely.

Cardiology was so much easier than this, with its manuals and three-dimensional scans, its devices and well-defined outcomes and processes. No manuals, levers or drugs could tell Mensah what to do or what to expect in life. Mensah spent the next few days reading about adoptees' reunions with their birth parents. Many were welcomed like prodigals, but several had had the door slammed in their faces. His research over, and after a week's rumination, Mensah gathered courage enough to ask Nancy's advice. 'Perhaps I'll cope better if I know how others like me have coped with the same problems. Grandfather's boxes are great but I need more, to be closer to these roots. Something more tangible, a body, a feel, a touch, a smell, not an image I've created of them but what they are. I know it's a risk, but I know I can cope. I may be rejected, but that's why I need your support.'

'You know we want the best for you, whatever you want. We want you to be happy and fulfilled,' said Nancy. 'We'll be there for you, as long as we are around.'

A pang of fear went through Mensah. He had never considered

Marty and Nancy's mortality. 'Marty and I know who our parents are, so should you,' said Nancy. 'We just want you to be happy and content. Look through your grandfather's papers and I'll dig out papers of the court proceedings. It's a start. Then we've got the hospital and birth certificate; the council will also have some information. Be prepared, though, for the worst. Call me after your rummage.'

Mensah found his scanned birth certificate on one of his grandfather's data storage devices, but the names were illegible. He did not want to risk turning up on the wrong doorstep.

'All I can remember is that your mother's name was Ruth. We can use that to get another birth certificate through records at the Royal Victoria Infirmary and the Birth Registry. They centralised it during the coalition but it has since been over-hauled,' said Nancy.

The Registrar traced the birth and reissued a birth certificate to Ronnie – Jane Ronsberg – their solicitor. Now Mensah had a start; his father's name was Keith Hartley and his mother Ruth Hartley. But when Nancy rang the Hartleys they refused to meet Mensah.

Three days later, Vince called Mensah. 'Mr Hartley says he will meet us, but not at home,' said Vince. 'I said we could meet at the Meadows in Ponteland.'

Vince had offered to help as an intermediary in the search for Mensah's parents and had come up trumps. Vince drove. Mensah, sweating with anxiety, sat in the front seat. Halfway to the hotel, he said, 'I wish I hadn't started this.'

'Don't be silly, if you don't go through with this I'll never talk to you again, it's just cold feet, it's natural,' said Vince.

When they got to the hotel, a three-storey Georgian building with a fountain in its foreground, Hartley was already waiting. From his seat he saw the two men walk in to the hotel foyer, Vince and Mensah, the one he had lent his name to save. A lump came up in his throat. If Anne, his wife, could see this; Anne, who had warned her husband that Vince could be the front man for a '419', a West African hoax. She would kill him if she found out that he had given in to Vince's ever so gentle but persistent and persuasive arm twisting. He did not imagine that people like Vince existed and were paid from public funds. They knew everything. More than they should. Keith thought of his own children, their sheltered lives with their parents, wanting for nothing. In the aftermath of the recession life was harder for them, they were all unemployed, but they could look back on healthy, happy and secure childhoods. Mensah had lost out and he had a persuasive advocate in his friend Vince.

'Is this one of your tricks?' Mensah asked Vince when the receptionist pointed Keith out. 'No way is that my dad.'

'Trust me,' said Vince, out of Hartley's earshot. 'Good afternoon, Mr Hartley, this is Mensah, thank you for coming.'

'I guessed so, pleased to meet you, glad to be able to help, I've got about half an hour,' said Keith Hartley.

'I'll leave you to it,' said Vince. Mensah and Keith sat down at the veranda table.

'Mensah, you're the double of your mother, I knew as soon as I saw you . . .' Hartley choked for a minute. 'Ruth, your mother, and Anne, my wife, were very close, like sisters. It's a long time ago. Shouldn't rake over old coals. I have to admit, I put it all behind me, too painful what happened. Ruth Dacosta was her name. I can't remember her maiden name, neither can Anne, it's a long time ago. Ruth tried to protect you, I don't think she thought you would come to harm, it was the principle of it. Anne and I still talk about that morning I went to the hospital to try to smuggle you out before they gave the jab. But we failed. The rest you know.'

'How do you mean smuggle me out?' said Mensah.

Keith told Mensah about the planned deception, his masquerading as Mensah's father, the hospital, the taxi, the jab, how upset Ruth was. 'I'm sorry we couldn't do more, if we had perhaps things would have turned out differently,' he said.

'Thanks for trying, my parents were very lucky,' said Mensah. 'Lucky?' said Keith.

'Yes, lucky to have friends like you, it must have been a very difficult time.'

'It was, but we had little to lose,' said Keith.

'You say that, but not many would've done what you did,' said Mensah.

'To be honest, after so many years I had laid those events to bed, but the scandal, the contamination fiasco brought it all back to me. When your friend called me I thought I must do something to help.' He paused and put his hand on Mensah's. 'Poor you, it must have been terrible for you, how are you coping?'

'It was, but I'm fine, but that's not why I'm here.' Mensah took his hand back. 'I'm trying to find my mother, I need to,' he said.

'I'll do what I can to help, of course I will,' said Keith.

'You've been very helpful, I'm very grateful to you for coming. I have her name, can I call on you if I need any more help?' asked Mensah.

Keith shifted in his seat. 'Of course,' he said.

'I understand, I won't impose, perhaps I'll get Vince to ask, he knows what to do, he's very good at that sort of thing; Vince the discreet, we call him,' said Mensah. They both got up, Keith to use the bathroom before he left, Mensah straight for the exit.

'What did you think?' asked Vince when Mensah got back to the car.

'It makes sense, it's plausible. It's strange, to speak to someone who was present at my birth but who is not my parent,' said Mensah. 'How did you get him to come?'

Vince shrugged. 'I asked him, explained that he owed you at least a few minutes, appealed to his conscience, his guilt, his own good fortune,' he said.

'I don't blame him for not wanting to get involved. I've got to find her, my mother, she's Ruth Dacosta, if she's still Dacosta; I just hope she's still alive. Is this what other people have to go through? It's crazy, what do I have to do, what will I find?' said Mensah.

'We're in it now and we're in it to win, you can count on Nancy, Marty and me, we'll help.'

Vince called again a few days later. 'Good news,' he said, 'I've found your grandfather, Dr Charles Omughana, but he's old and frail as you'd expect. He's in Wylam, in a residential home. My contacts tell me that he moved from his own flat in Jesmond to a warden-controlled flat in Wylam but moved again when a routine medical revealed mild cerebral vascular disease. He was started on the new dementia drug, Reconsiderate. His wife, Esther, died ten years ago and he faded for two years, but he rallied again, according to his carers, for the sake of his errant grandson and daughter. He's lived there for five years – they couldn't find a next of kin, I don't think they tried very hard,' said Vince. 'That's where the trail ends, or begins,' he said. 'I could take you to see him; we'll explain who you are, take identification with you and some of the memorabilia and we'll see what happens.'

'Thanks, I've got so many questions for him, but if he's so frail will he remember what happened to his daughter, my mum, and what made them fight for me when my mum didn't? She didn't seem to want me. Will he be able to explain the diary entries about my mum and her early life? Why did the entries end when I was just a baby? So many questions, but will I find the answers?'

20

Grandfather Omughana

The residential home called the 'Departure Lounge' had set an appointment for teatime. After a few wrong turnings, Vince and Mensah got their bearings on the one-way system of the recon-structed 'green' A167. Mensah, reinforced by three layers of clothes, trembled with anticipation, apprehension and the cold north-east wind. When Mensah pulled in to the residential home's gravelled drive it was raining. Mensah parked the car, his right heel trembling against the car floor. Vince waited in the car. Mensah walked up the gravel drive and through the main door. The foyer was quiet, with no one in sight. Mensah thought of leaving, but the receptionist had seen him arrive. 'You must be Dr Snell,' she said from behind Mensah's right shoulder. 'I'm Anne Reedy, main receptionist, pleased to meet you. Did you find us all right tucked away here? I'll show you in, I just need to make sure Doctor is ready. All the residents have a sleep after lunch. I'll check with sister. Please sit down.'

Mensah did not want to sit. Cues prepared you at job inter-views, dental appointments or meetings. For this reunion with a grandfather there were no cues, or hints at what to expect: no smiling relatives returning from their meetings; no one walking briskly away as if never to return or glad to be going; no one looking back up through misty eyes at their relative's window as if for the last time; no one walking hand in hand with their

149

mother sharing a joke; no thunder-faced man who may have been written out of a will. No cues. So Mensah stood. Then he sat down, found the chair too soft and low and was standing again when Ms Reedy returned to lead him to his grandfather.

Grandfather Omughana was sitting in the corner of a large room with a bay window overlooking the front of the building, a room he chose so he could eavesdrop on the car park conversations. He cranked up to about one and a half metres tall in his slippers when Mensah walked in through the open door. As the old man shuffled towards his grandson, Mensah thought there was a hint of the stoop of Parkinson's disease, but there was vitality in his grandfather's eyes, and the wispy tufts of white hair on the side of his head gave him a quizzical look. Mensah shook his grandfather's hand, hard from alcohol antiseptic gel and years of 'scrubbing'. In place of nails, both little fingers had hard, concave, corrugated pulp. 'Good afternoon, Grandpa.'

Dr Omughana looked up at his grandson. 'Good day to you, young man. Have you come to see me? I still ask that stupid question – it's like when we say, "You're back",' he said. 'What's your name? Have you come with some news about my grandson? He's not ill is he? He was always catching something. Coughs and sneezes and . . .' His voice tailed off and he looked as if he was going to cry. The old man sat down and looked away.

'Do you want a cup of tea?' asked Ms Reedy.

'Yes, please,' Mensah said, to break the ice. Mensah pulled up a chair and sat close to his grandfather. 'I'm your grandson. I'm Mensah.' Silence. Dr Omughana picked up a stress ball and squeezed it in his hands, his face in puzzled tension. He took in the timbre and pitch of Mensah's voice, his prosody, demeanour, his face, from brow to the set of his mouth, and distilled them through instincts honed from years of clinical experience. His face dropped a notch, in recognition, regret or whimsy, and then he smiled, with lips, cheeks and eyes, his face lifted, eyes shining, furrowed brow unfurled, tension released. He knew.

'I don't know what to say, I don't know what to say, we didn't know what to do,' he said. 'I'm sorry, I, we never forgot you.'

'I brought photographs of you and me taken when I was a baby,' said Mensah.

'Can I see the photographs, please?'

'Yes, Grandpa,' said Mensah.

Mensah's grandfather put his stress ball down to look through the half a dozen photographs Mensah had chosen. 'Oh, oh,' he repeated. After his first pass, he went through them again, pausing to stare ahead as if trying to recall, retrieve and savour again the atmosphere on the day the photograph was taken, before he went to the next image. 'I never thought I would ever see these again,' he said. 'Mine got lost when we moved. You'll not believe it but I spent years looking for these, like a sort of Silas Marner. Esther, your grandmother, thought I'd gone bonkers. I knew how much they meant to me, only I knew; if that's bonkers so be it, they'll never understand. I hope they never have to ache for loss like we did.'

He looked at Mensah again – at his face, his nose, then his eyes and back to his nose. 'You have Ruth's, your mother's features. Do you have more photographs of her? I have if you need any; it was your photographs that I lost. What do you do now?' Mensah told him. 'Ah, another middle-class unquantifiable professional – symbiotic,' he said. 'I'm getting quite dizzy, my heart's pounding; it must be those tablets, or excitement.'

Mensah pressed the call bell. A beautiful nurse came up to the room. His grandfather's eyes lit up for a second and then faded in nostalgic, impotent lust. She took his blood pressure and pulse, checked his temperature, asked him whether he had taken any medication, and reassured him that he was all right. After the nurse left, Dr Omughana got up to use the toilet. He was gone for about fifteen minutes. When he returned he grimaced with arthritis as he sat down. 'Can I keep the photographs?' he said.

'Of course, Grandpa,' said Mensah. His grandfather stared at one of the photographs, the one with Mensah, Ruth and himself in Ruth's back garden, a few weeks before Mensah was taken away. Ruth looked severe, but vulnerable, leaning towards her father's right shoulder, which was braced for his daughter. He looked troubled.

'That silly, irresponsible Bode, he just left her, left her with his child, in the lurch. My Ruth, my child, devastated. She could not look after you as well as she wanted. How do people do that to their own children? They're not ill, they're healthy, they are in a developed country, they have children and just leave them like goats to the elements. Like wild animals. No, wild animals are better, they look after their own. Then they go and have some more, get bored and leave those as well. Anyway, enough analysis, he left. Naturally, she couldn't cope, she had a demanding job, she was a doctor, you know.' He'd been told that the council, during one of its spates of hand-wringing officiousness, had taken Mensah in to care on a neighbour's tip-off. 'We tried hard, we went to court, to appeal, and we lost – they said we should have got in earlier. We knew there was something wrong between Bode and Ruth but we thought it was the stress of having a new baby, the coalition's vaccine, coping with work. We tried to help but did not want to intrude. We were all angry, afraid, but what could we do?

'When they said we couldn't look after you it nearly finished us. Ruth lost her job, we lost contact, that's why I left the diaries and bits and pieces. I would have kept a proper diary, I had always planned one for my grandchildren with jokes and anima-tions, things to enjoy, family history – I put some of the angry passages in for balance. I'm in life's departure lounge passing on tips to you as you wave goodbye. Did you like my poems? I hoped, but never thought I would see you again; as for your mother, I still hope.'

Mensah's eyes filmed over. He looked down, to hide his face. The nurse came back to ask whether they wanted anything. Mensah asked for a cup of tea, his grandfather for a glass of fruit juice. They drank in silence. Sitting there sipping tea, Mensah was not sure how much his grandfather knew, remembered, or chose to tell him about Ruth's fate.

His grandfather shuffled to the door after Mensah. Mensah gave him a gentle squeeze about the shoulders. 'I'll be back soon with some more photographs,' he said.

'Don't leave it too long, don't forget I'm in the departure lounge, not long before I fly away.'

Heavy-hearted, Mensah watched his grandfather turn round and, with a stoop and a limp from mild left-foot drop, walk back to his chair. Mensah stopped on the landing to blow his nose and wipe his face. Composure regained, he walked downstairs to find a relaxed young couple waiting at the reception desk. Mensah puffed his chest, sucked in his abdomen, nodded a greeting to the couple and, not trusting his voice, waved at Ms Reedy and walked to his car.

With Hartley's information, Mensah traced his mother to an apartment over a small community centre library-cum-bookshop in Walker. A rusty, peeling signpost to a former Church of England primary school marked the entrance to the centre. Mensah drove through the gates past an overgrown front courtyard to the converted classroom block. He stopped by a woman dressed in a pink dress, with flat shoes and a scarf pulled down over one ear. She seemed in a hurry. 'Excuse me, ma'am, I'm looking for a woman, she works in the bookshop, Ruth Dacosta.' The woman leaned her left elbow on the car window frame and scratched her left eyebrow through the scarf.

'Dacosta, Dacosta,' she said.

'Do you know her?' asked Mensah.

'Very well, I do, I think she said she was going away for the week.'

'Where can I leave a note, a message?' he said. She pointed in the general direction of the signpost to the library.

'There,' she said, and hurried away.

Mensah got out and climbed the stairs to the library. It was locked. He walked all the way along the corridor, then back again and came downstairs. A greying middle-aged woman came out to meet him. 'How can I help you, sir, are you lost?' she said.

'I'm looking for the woman who works in the library or book-shop; she lives upstairs – Ruth?' he said.

'Did you say Ruth?' she said.

'Yes, ma'am, do you know her?'

'You've just missed her, she knocked on my door a few minutes ago. She may be gone a while, she didn't tell me where she was going.'

'What was she wearing?' asked Mensah.

'Pink dress, headscarf,' she said.

Mensah's shoulders and face dropped. 'Can I help you, did you see her?' she said.

'Yes, I think that was my mum,' he said. Her eyes lit up then lowered in recognition and sympathy. She brushed her skirt, flicked her shoulders.

'Can I make you a cup of tea?' she said.

'Yes, please,' he said, holding on to the low front wall because his legs felt hollow. 'I hope you don't mind if I stand here, ma'am, I feel a bit light-headed,' he said.

'You're all right,' she said. 'I'll bring you a cuppa. So you're Ruth's son?' she said.

'I am,' said Mensah.

'Come here,' she said, and gave him a hug. 'Are you okay?' she said. 'Known Ruth for ages, she's been in hospital. They'll keep her this time, I bet they do; they have a system: bloods and satellite like – they'll find her. They can tell if we're off. Even before we do. I know where she goes when she's like this,' she said. 'They'll take her to the North Shields Brain Mind Hospital on Newcastle Road. Her nerves, they say, stress, or whatnot, it all gets on top of her, we look out for her. We've all been through it, I have with my nerves, but I haven't been in for years. I take my medication. Don't see much of the other lady who runs the shop with her, Mrs Dexter, but she may be away, said she was going to see her daughter on the coast. They don't do much business. All that fuss when the shop was opened; no one wanted to have a community rehab here at first; now it's all right.

'My boys have grown up, left, the council helped. Mine still come to see me, you know. Always going on about her son, saying he was taken away. We didn't believe her, just thought it was part of the stress. She says why don't they help her look for her son? But she does not say anything to the nurses because she's afraid she will be chucked out or locked up. She knows things, you know, doctor stuff; she must have learned in hospital, she can say the drug names, no one else can, even the doctors canna do it.'

Mensah perched on the wall with his now cold cup of tea. She smiled. 'You've got her face, big ears and funny head. If you're not hers, you're a good copy, like,' she said, and laughed. 'Sorry,' she said. 'I was lucky, their nan helped. Can you give me your number, I'll give it to Molly, Mrs Stellar, when she gets back. She'll know how, what to do for the best, like.'

Mensah tried to say something appropriate, but all he could say was 'Thank you. You've been very kind, ma'am.'

'Call me Laura,' she said.

Mrs Stellar called Mensah later that evening. 'I'm not sure what I'm doing, but Laura said you're kosher, like. Ruth lost her job; no job, no family. She just does what she's told. She takes her treatment. No fuss now, she hands herself in or they come for her, or they find her, always the same place: Jesmond High Street. Never any problems, not like in the old days; they've got the monitoring nearly right: it's still not great but better than it was. She's as right as rain when she comes back. A little embarrassed, she does go on a bit when she's ill; always about her son. She said she lost his photograph, thinks she can find the photo shop on the High Street to make her a copy. That's where she goes. To photo shops, just walks and walks until they find her. Glad you're here, she's had enough suffering; no one should have their kids taken away like that, not now, not any more. Even murderers: they get probation, time off, don't they.' Mensah nodded

155

over the phone. 'I'm down as a sort of next of kin, I could contact the hospital to ask if they'd allow you to visit. I think it's good if you saw her in hospital whilst she's under observation. That way she'll be in the best place if there are any problems or set-backs. I've been through this myself; seen it in others. I looked after disturbed children and children who'd lost their mums early. But don't expect too much. Leave it with me, I'll get back to you.'

'Thanks, bye, bye Mrs Stellar,' said Mensah.

21

Ruth

Mrs Stellar called that weekend. 'Mensah, I'm sorry, pet, I didn't know that you didn't know about Ruth, her sickness. We spoke out of turn, really sorry, like, we didn't use our brains one iota, not sure what we were thinking. Must have been a shock to see her, miss her and have us talking about her like that. Sorry.'

'To be honest, ma'am, I was just relieved that she's alive, that I can find her, ma'am. I didn't know what to expect, really.'

'Pet, can you go to the hospital to meet the ward sister and matron? Preliminary, like, got to be sure, like; you can see, they don't want some guy turning up causing ruckus for the patients. We've had pranksters, voyeurs, con artists. Last year Mr Denbies and another patient, Mr Frenshew, were done over. Life savings filched before the real family sussed; it was all gone: they took advantage of Mr Frenshew's delusions. Nearly a million he lost.'

'I'll do what the sister wants,' said Mensah.

'If they're happy they'll let you see Ruth; if they're not they'll call the bizzies.'

Later, Vince and Mensah were talking together about his preliminary hospital visit.

'How did it go?' asked Vince.

'I went, I saw the two nurses on duty, left them a copy of my birth certificate. They didn't think a recording of my grandfather's voice was needed yet.'

'Where to?' said Vince.

'Home, straight home,' said Mensah. 'Somehow, this is different,' he said. 'With my grandfather, I could still be clinical, rational, but to think that I saw my mum and we didn't recognise each other; I was that close yet so far from making contact. Didn't even touch her; it's so different, Vince, difficult to describe.'

'It must be,' said Vince. 'It's biology, you're made up of half of her, you're looking at yourself, feeling for her and yourself at the same time, that's why it aches so much.'

'It's more than that: it's the loss; the reality was so mundane, you want bells and fanfare when you meet your mum, not what I saw last week, it's . . . dashed expectation. Grandpa was old, not ill. Mum's ill, still ill. Nerves, they call it, it's more than that; what sort of nerves affect you for decades? My hand shakes playing pool, giving a speech, going out to bat, even at work: that's nerves. They're ill; I wish society would grow up. Maybe if she'd had early treatment she wouldn't be in this mess. It's not "nerves". I don't know how I'm going to cope, Vince,' he said, tears welling up in his eyes. Vince stopped the car. 'Counsellors, they were useless. How will I cope, can I face it, Vince? What if I make her worse, by turning up?'

Dr Lamb, one of Ruth's consultants, met Mensah the next day. 'Nice to meet you, thank you for all you're doing for my mother,' said Mensah.

'I'm one of a team,' replied Lamb. 'She's done well. Unfortunately, we cannot get her out of these cycles, these relapses. The longest we have gone without a relapse is a year. Compliance is not an issue because we use micro-pellets and these can be activated by us from the hospital when the drug levels fall or appear to be inadequate. We can also explant old pellets, replace them with the same drug or change to use new combinations of pellets or single poly-pellets. For Ruth, and one or two other patients, we also use the tracking devices. Most of the other patients in the programme have fewer relapses; but they probably did not have the same history.'

'Do you need any information from me?' said Mensah. 'I don't have much, but if I can fill in any gaps . . .'

'It's OK,' said Dr Lamb. 'As far as we know, Ruth is the only patient who has lost husband, son and contact with her parents more or less simultaneously. She also lost her profession. Friends rallied but there was only so much they could do. The Friends of the Hospital visit the patients and help with administrative bottlenecks. Otherwise Ruth has been alone. Generally we do not oppose contact with friends and relatives, but this is unique. This is the longest interval between loss and contact we have had so we'll have to consult the literature and discuss it at the multidisciplinary meetings. They'll be as concerned for your own welfare and the welfare of your family as for that of your mother. Sorry to be technical. Ruth has none of the usual chromosomal microdeletions. We've moved away from looking for specific genes for mental illness. Imbalances between glutamate and gammaaminobutyric acid are implicated, but we're still scratching around when we see really chronic cases. Do you have any questions?' Mensah shook his head. 'Don't hesitate to ask. Let me know if you need any more information.'

Mensah got up and shook the doctor's hand. 'I'll take you through to see the archivist, she's good, she'll fill you in. She's too much sometimes; shut her up if she overloads you.' Mensah followed the doctor in silence, head bowed, concentrating on getting to the next stage in his bizarre day.

Mrs Wetherall, the archivist – the griot – lived up to her reputation. The receptionist rang a bell. 'She's in there somewhere, in the archive room. I'll call her on the loudhailer; no modern stuff here, she says,' said the receptionist. Suddenly, with a rustle of heavy plastic curtain, there she was, a small, wizened woman with a large unfettered bosom rubbing her hands with wet, heavy-duty industrial paper.

'Hello,' you must be Mensah.' She looked pleased to be needed or to be of service or interrupted. 'Come in,' she said. Her office was a tiny prefabricated cubicle in the corner of the room. She sat behind her desk on a bench with her back against the wall. Mensah sat opposite. 'I bet they've told you what I'm like: I'm the joiner, I join lives together for relatives like you who've lost contact, don't relish their lot, but I enjoy helping, just like you do. Stop me, ask questions, I'm here at your service.'

'Thank you, it's a great relief, you've all made it much easier for me, you've been tremendous, thanks,' he said.

'I've compiled a summary, but most of it's up here.' She pointed to her temple. 'Your mum, Ruth, spent many years in a branch of the Maudsley. When she improved, but not enough to go back to work as a doctor, and when it was clear that she was not going to get much better, she was re-housed. Then they found her some work in a library, away from those who would have known her in her youth. Monitoring is through a combination of blood tests. They also use a subcutaneous chip that feeds blood level results to a central station where her sleep patterns, movements, dyskinesia can be followed. Before she suffers a relapse we nip in and she's back in hospital before she gets too bad. We use other chips. When the depot injection levels fall the chips activate the pellets, deliver a boost then increase the maintenance drug dose. We have several hundred similar patients, it's very successful, but not very well publicised. I'm not sure whether that's a good thing, it's not my business. Don't ask me, I couldn't tell you; it's a sickness like any other so why hide, pretend it doesn't happen? It's hard for relatives. Many important people have been through us; most once, some more frequently. Others have sisters, wives, husbands, sons; you name it, they're in here. They're not on gap years or working in Australia; they're on our programmes. And we're proud of what we do.'

Mensah could not take any more. His mother, a paediatrician, had ended up in a community bookstore arranging old paperbacks no one would read. It was now his duty, his responsibility to see it through; no longer a way of escaping *his* fate by trying to explain his mother's. 'Thank you, Mrs Wetherall, you've been very helpful, your work should be better recognised and I'm sure it will. Can you show me how to get back to sister? Thanks.'

'You're very welcome,' she said, holding out her hand. 'Through that arch, yes there, you'll find sister's office signposted.'

Mensah came out expecting the same fresh, bright day, but was greeted by dark, dense clouds and the cold, as if a gigantic igloo had been suspended over the North-East. Sucking in a deep breath, Mensah whispered a 'come on', thrust out his chest and set off for the sister's office. She had left Mensah a timetable setting out a course of counselling he needed to complete before he could be allowed to see his mother. The programme consisted of a series of multidisciplinary meetings, to help communication with the team, and a provisional date for him to take the plunge.

Then, two weeks later, Mensah was ready. He waited in the matron's room for his appointment. Matron – Mrs Thomas – arrived breathless. 'Sorry to keep you, I had an impromptu meeting with a patient's relative. I hadn't forgotten, I know you're very busy. Do you want me to come with you?' she asked.

'Yes, you may be able to help me to get through to her,' Mensah said.

'I've found that it's better for family to meet the patient by themselves,' said the matron, smiling. 'Trust me,' she said, 'we've seen this many times.'

Mensah walked behind the matron as she glided along the corridor across a clearing, down a few stairs and through a privet hedge into a courtyard. A dozen or so women were sitting in a near circle. Scanning the group, the matron said, 'That's your mother,' pointing Ruth out to Mensah. Ruth was sharing a magazine held by another patient who had just turned the page over. 'Wait for me,' said the matron. She hurried over, whispered to Ruth, who looked up at Mensah, smiled and got up to walk towards him. 'Ruth, I'd like you to meet Mensah. Would you like to come with me?'

Ruth looked at Mensah. He smiled. He was more nervous than he had been with his grandfather but tried not to show it. Ruth turned towards Mrs Thomas who led them into her office, taking Ruth in first, and signalled to Mensah to wait for her. Five minutes later, Mrs Thomas returned to get Mensah. Ruth was sitting in the room with a bible in her hand; small, slim, beautiful triangular face, hair tied in a bun at the back from which it threatened to escape. Her hair was dark brown, highlighted by frizzy, crinkly lines of grey. She greeted Mensah with a polite, tired smile. She held out her hand. Mensah caressed and shook it in both hands. He started to sob, first reluctantly, chest heaving, head bowed, hissing, face turned away from his mother, then loudly in shameless surrender. For nine minutes he could not look at his mother. Whenever he thought he was ready, he would break down again. Ruth withdrew her hand and patted Mensah on the back. 'Why are you crying?' she asked.

'Excuse me,' he said. 'I'm sorry, I'll be back soon.' The matron escorted him out of the room. Mensah walked around the courtyard. Fortunately, it was deserted. The corridors were always cleared for these meetings. After ten minutes, Mensah felt ready to go back in again.

When Mensah returned, Ruth was reading her bible. She looked up at him. 'How can I help you, sir, the Lord is the answer to your prayers,' she said.

Mensah wanted to say he didn't think so. 'You may be able to help me. I just want to talk to you,' he said. Nobody else could do this for him. He had thought of this moment. How would she respond? He was here now. He spat out the words. 'I'm your son. I'm Mensah. Mensah Snell, because I was brought up by Marty and Nancy. I don't know whether you met them. My real name is Dacosta.'

'Everyone is my child, my son,' his mother replied. 'We are all God's children.'

'I'm your son,' he said.

She looked up. 'My son, you say; you were dead and have come to mock me, to dupe me, to torment me. What have I done to anyone to deserve this?' She licked her lips, smacked them, muttered, then, eyes lowered, smiled. 'My son, what will they try next? They now want to kill me. They're trying to force me to admit strange young men into my family. I have no son. They've done it before. When I protest they say I am mad. Do I look mad to you? I am intelligent. I can see what they're doing before they do. One of the doctors is a bad, bad, man. Stay away from him, will you, or he will harm you too.'

Mensah sat beside her. Who did he ask? There was no help desk, no software, no consultant to bail you out. Compared to this, suspension was small beer. Mensah sat there listening.

'They're all mad,' she said. 'Why do they sit around during their meetings talking about men and children, whispering to each other, falling out, arguing? The things they say about each other, when they think I'm not listening, and then they smile in public. Who is really mad? Only Mrs French who cleans this place is any good because she does not like dirt. She is clean like me. She is a proper Christian, like me. The others are going to hell. So will you if you continue to have anything to do with these people. Men are animals. They lock us all up here, for what, to abuse us. It shouldn't be allowed. But who is Prime Minister, a man! The chief consultant is a man. They won't listen to a woman like me.'

Mensah waited until Ruth had finished and waited some more to see if she would start again. Ruth picked up her bible. He had to ask. 'Do you know where I can find my dad?' he said. Ruth looked up, waved her index finger at him, fury writ in her wide eyes.

'Are you my son or are you his nephew or those Nigerian family people of his, the crooked, evil man? How, if you are my son, *if* you are my son, can you be the fruit of the two of us, our union? He must have raped me, that animal man, evil pervert; you know he molests girls: that's why he left. I wouldn't allow him to use me like a cheap towel. I have my standards, don't ask me about that man, I can't even mention his name, not a Christian, a godless man; if you mention his name again I will not speak to you ever, ever again, evil, evil man. You are not like him, maybe you are or you wouldn't be asking me about him. Your father; he's not your father, when I see your father I'll show you; you'll know a wholesome, handsome man, not that monster you asked me about.' She hollowed her cheeks, smacked her lips, perhaps dry from the medication or dehydration or talking so much or not being used to talking.

'Don't have anything to do with that matron either, two- faced cow,' she said.

Mensah left the room. He was right not to have brought Vince or anyone else with him. He had seen her now – it was not what he had expected. All he had was emptiness. What had he expected: High Art, violins, or tears and embraces?

Matron was waiting for him when he emerged, red-eyed. 'How did it go?' she said. Mensah shrugged. He stifled his tears. 'A cup of tea?' Mensah nodded. He blew his nose.

'What can I do?' he asked.

'Be patient,' she said. 'If you stay in her life I can assure you that you stand a good chance of helping her to get much better. The consultants will modify her regime, to take your presence into account. They are very clever with the new-generation eidomic scans. They'll find out whether your visit has changed the balance of neurotransmitters and neurotransmission. Try to come regularly; I know it's distressing, but you have made contact now. We're here to help.'

On the other side of the fence, between patient and professional, Mensah could not concretise the clinicians' dispassionate description of his mother's symptoms. It was as if they were talking about someone else. No lump, tissue, scan to feel or examine or monitor. Everything was so surreal. Surreal because this was not a brief, self-limiting flare-up of an appendix or an arthritic knee, but an illness in which treatment was not directed at part of the patient but at restoring a semblance, reconstructing, as close as possible, the patient's essence. Not like mending a fractured leg, but like surgery on a plastic mind, any improvement in function an acceptable compromise, like a graft. Except in his dreams, Mensah did not know her. She did not know herself, so she could not tell the doctors about herself as she would about a refashioned neck, cheek bone or set of teeth and say, 'Yes, that's exactly how I wanted it.' No matter how they tried to reimagine her, she could not be that self again, ever, but she could be called well.

Mensah witnessed, suffered and learned of his mother's involuntary, automatic, spontaneous insensitivity, her torrents of abuse, bursts of apparently aimless orgiastic activity, then torpor, her trust and paranoia, laughter and tears, in dress and undress. And in his dreams he saw his mother not as the hand-washing saint, but as a grotesque. He dreamt once that Ruth was cured and that they were sitting on a park bench in Gosforth. He was telling Ruth about his early life but not about the ADHD vaccinations, the dyskeratotic gene contamination, or his suspension. He told her of a fiancée, Hermione, and how he was going to get married and be a consultant cardiologist at a top teaching hospital. She nodded, smiled and, as if to punish him for his deceit, turned into a grotesque again. Mensah was torn. If Ruth got better, he could not risk a relapse by telling her the whole truth about his life; but he did not want to lie to her either.

Mensah wanted to relive his childhood, this time with *this* mother, but when she was well. To relive the dream in which his mother's serene and loving face smiles at him whilst she washes his hands was now impossible. That was fact, but had he come into her life at the peak, nadir or middle of this condition and could he make a difference? How did he fix it, or would she get worse, and, if she did, would he be dragged down with her? Why, how had *his* mother ended up like this? Confronting Ruth's illness had shattered his dreams. Instead, he would have to spend the rest of his short life looking after her, supplanting her as the meat in the sandwich of care between generations. And where would he fit Marty and Nancy? To what, to whom could he turn for answers?

For the first week after he met Ruth, Mensah was consumed by his mother's illness. He sat at home lost in thought about her and forgot to call the hospital to ask about his suspension. When Vince came round one evening he found Mensah in his pyjamas, ready to go to bed at nine o'clock. 'Uh, oh,' said Vince. 'You're not going all soft on me, not if I can help it. We need a plan, always a plan,' he said.

'I'm tired of plans,' said Mensah. 'I'm not getting anywhere, it's like I'm trying to hit a small target at the bottom of a bucket of water with a piece of spaghetti. Impossible.'

'Never mind all that, let's try, at least in stages; that's how we've always worked, haven't we?' Mensah nodded. 'During the day, work on your defence, see what you can find out about the process – any weaknesses; ask your defence people; anything you can do during office hours you must do. In the evening, if you want, we can go out or you can go to see your mother; you must go, if only for a few minutes.'

'It's easy for you to say,' said Mensah.

'That's why I'm saying it. But it's true, and you know it too,' said Vince. 'Do you want any help with the dry-cleaning? I can collect that and get in some groceries. That's all you need: clothes and calories.'

'I'll be fine, I'll get my laundry, it'll give me something else to do,' said Mensah.

Mensah dressed smart-casual for the visits to his mother. He did not go every day because he thought the staff would ask how, if he was a hospital doctor, he had so much free and predictable time off. If he needed to speak to the consultants he went during office hours. They told him Ruth was making progress: extra dormant sodium potassium channels were being activated, which should attenuate the more hallucinatory and delusional symptoms. She was by no means ready for discharge yet. They still were not sure whether she would accept Mensah as her real son or another mirage, but they could hope that her memory of her early adult years would return. In the past she always seemed to score well in her recall and retrieve sessions when she went into remission, so they hoped that she might do better this time.

When Mensah met young families, in the park, street or supermarket aisles, envy – for what he thought he had lost – then guilt – for thinking it because he'd had Marty and Nancy – merged with vicarious pleasure. Could he, would he, ever, himself, hold or be held in a paternal embrace?

From Freeman, no news, only rumours. Interviews for substantive posts might be postponed because the chairman was delayed in Saudi Arabia.

He called Nancy to tell her his progress. 'I was just going to call you,' said Nancy. 'How's it going, can we do anything?'

'Well, Grandpa's doing well, I'm seeing him again soon; Mum, I don't know how to talk about "Mum". Seeing her sort of explains what happened, but not the whole picture. It's like a three-legged stool with a leg missing. I'm afraid I'll let her down.'

'Don't be silly, Mensah you're putting too much pressure on yourself.'

'I know, but I can't help thinking that if I let her down, don't support her enough, I will have failed as a son and as a person. Fail as a person, fail as a doctor.' Nothing meant more to him but to succeed as a doctor.

'It doesn't follow: there are some strange, but extremely gifted doctors who are hopeless as people; I'm not saying you are a psychopath, just making a point. Don't drag your mum into everything,' she said.

'I may be afraid for myself, as well. If my mum could break down like this, what chance do I have with my triple whammy jeopardy card marked with family history, ADHD vaccine and contamination?' Deep down he feared that his awful pre-registration winter adumbrated worse to come, and could he cope if, as had happened to Grandpa Omughana, his own child fell ill?

'Your mum's case was unique. She needed more support. You are not going to be ill, you are not, because you have us,' said Nancy. The doorbell rang. Mensah ignored it.

'Nancy?'

'Yes?'

'I've got to find my father. Grandpa may remember something. Is Marty there?'

'No, he's popped out, forgot to get the picture hooks I asked him to get me, so many times, so he's gone. He shouldn't be long.'

'Give him my love, I'll let you know how I get on,' said Mensah.

Ruth was not guilty; she was ill. His grandfather was not guilty; he was old, and at least he'd had a go, but what about his dad, what had he done? Anticlimax threatened. But perhaps he would have better luck with his father than with the first two, if he could find him.

On an overcast Sunday afternoon, Mensah went back to see his grandfather. When he knocked on the door, there was no reply, just the hum of a radio. Mensah edged the door open. His grandfather's feet were hanging over the left corner of the bed. Hippos thundering through his chest, Mensah swung the door open hard and ran to the bedside. The old man's head was flopped over the other side of the bed. He stirred, rolled over, and a streak of saliva drooled from the left corner of his mouth. He had fallen asleep, reading a newspaper. 'Oh, you're here, Mensah, what time is it?' Mensah gave him a piece of tissue paper. 'Give me a second, I'll tidy up, sit down, you look ill.'

'I'm fine Grandad, for a moment there . . .'

'I read on my belly, when my back hurts, old habit, I'll be back in a minute.' Through the open bathroom door Mensah could hear his grandfather's weak urine stream, then his electric toothbrush and the click of a pull-switch. 'Ha, all I need is a cup of tea and I'll be OK,' said his grandfather.

168

'I found Mother,' said Mensah.

'Really, where?' said his grandfather.

'She's doing some work, I saw her, it's going to take time. She's not bad.'

'Can I see her?' said his grandfather.

'Yes, I spoke to the doctors, the ones who looked after her before – they advised us to wait; I haven't discussed it further with them yet. I haven't told Mother either. She's only just getting used to me, but I'll bring her to see you as soon as I can, as soon as they let me,' said Mensah.

'How do you mean, is something wrong, can they deny a father contact with his daughter? At this time of my life I've seen everything. I know how things were when we lost her: she barred us. Your grandmother died sad. We lived with her, just tell me what's what.' So Mensah told his grandfather all Mrs Wetherall had told him. 'Poor girl, poor Esther, poor girl,' was all his grandfather could say, on his chair, his back bent, head lowered, grey-haired wrists on knees.

'Are you all right, Grandad?' No reply. 'Grandad.' He looked up, with moist eyes.

'Yes, my son, sorry, I thought I could take it; I will, at least she's alive, we can help her. I won't let her down.'

'Grandpa, can you help me?'

'I'll do anything to help you, Mensah, what do you want?'

'Do you know where Bode went after . . .'

'After he abandoned his family,' said Mensah's grandpa. 'He ran off to Nigeria. Leaving unpaid traffic fines and parking tickets. Guess who had to pay the bills? Ruth! Sorry.' He paused, he looked to see whether he had hurt Mensah's feelings. 'I don't think he's been back, but I can't be sure; you ask *me*, a man who didn't even know where his own daughter was. Try the customs and excise people; they keep offenders' names on files; if you're owing, they track you down, and if you come back they'll find and fine you or lock you up. You know how strict they are now.'

'Thanks, Grandad, I'll see what I can do to find him. Are you all right? I must go now.' Mensah rang the bell for the nurse. She appeared a few minutes later with his grandfather's order: thin lamb cutlets and some vegetables. Mensah waited until his grandfather started his meal, hugged him and hurried downstairs. His grandpa did not look up.

Through the Nigerian subsidiary of Longlife Insurance Company, Mensah employed a local detective: Mr Chudi Uma, used by British-based lawyers representing Nigeria-based clients. He found three Bode Dacostas who were of the right age to be Mensah's father.

22

Bode

The next week, Mr Uma learned that Bode Dacosta was at one of Lagos Island's famous all-night parties. Mr Uma instructed the band leader to keep Bode there until he arrived. Baba Ibeji, the master drummer, obliged by encircling Bode's party, regaling him with ever more improbable tales of Bode's wealth and sexual exploits. Mr Uma, his white shirt drenched in sweat, arrived an hour later, paid off the drummers and had to shout to make himself heard over the music, conversation and the passing traffic.

'Mr Dacosta, are you Mr Dacosta?'

'What?' asked Bode, the rim of his light-green cap dark with sweat. He leaned forward, trying not to crease the white lace *agbada* resting on the back of his chair. 'And you are?'

'Mr Uma, sir,' said the detective, bending over, hands behind his back. Bode liked that, respect.

'What can I do for you? I have no money,' he said.

'No, I'm not after money, sir,' said Mr Uma.

'Everybody is after money. Olu, listen to this man who says he's not after money. Is he serious? My man, make your point, what do you want?' Olu squinted at Uma, as if he was some museum specimen, and guffawed.

Mr Uma ignored the lackey, the hanger-on who scraped by on crumbs from his superiors' table, hoping one day to hit the jackpot, a contract, or get close enough to deceive or dupe his

171

master. 'Excuse me, sir, I do not have much time to waste here, it is people from overseas who sent me to you about an important matter. About your son.'

Olu, antennae buzzing, stopped fondling the girl sitting on his lap. 'Olu, watch out for the driver, I want to talk business with this man,' said Bode. He led Mr Uma into a small living-room. An old woman was sitting in the corner. A young woman, probably a house girl, was feeding the woman some sort of gruel. Bode greeted the woman, identified himself as the host's business partner, and sat down. 'Tell me again, it is quiet here so don't shout,' he said.

'Sir, your son, Mensah, he wants to see you, he asked me to track you down. I didn't want to talk this business in front of everybody. I have respect for delicate matters, that is why the overseas lawyers use my services.'

Bode sized up the detective. 'Show me your identity card,' he said. Mr Uma gave Bode a card. 'Uh, everybody has a card nowadays, I don't mean to disrespect you and your card. 419 people everywhere.'

One of Bode's friends, Lati, had been done by a con artist using forged DNA samples. 'You can check my bona fides with London. Check my information. I am not here for money; it is about your son and your family. If you don't want your private life to become a topic of Lagos gossip, check with my offices. I will contact London to let them know that I have seen you.' Bode wiped his face with his symbolic chief's white handkerchief.

'I'll check, if you give me wrong information, you are finished in Lagos, you hear me? So make sure your facts are correct,' he said.

'My facts are facts, sir, I will go now, sir, you have all my numbers,' said Mr Uma, and he leaned over to shake Bode's hand.

Bode staggered back to the party but left for home soon after, leaving his *agbada*, which had been trampled underfoot, draped over his chair.

Mr Uma rang again the next morning to ask whether Bode had followed up his leads. Through his hangover, Bode recognised that Uma's story had the ring of truth and his story checked out with the High Commission and his British contacts. But no way would he go to Britain. If Mensah would come to Nigeria he would be delighted to meet him. His doctor son. Who would have thought it? Mr Uma set up an evening for Bode to speak to Mensah over the phone and plan the itinerary. Bode made sure he was alone, he did not want his new wife to know that she had a stepson. It might upset all her calculations for his estate when he died and she could start to make life difficult for him.

At about eight o'clock Bode took the call in the garden out of earshot of his neighbours and house help. 'Hello, is that Mensah? Good, Allah is great, I'm delighted, praise indeed to Allah, how have you been? I hear your voice just like you are next door. When are you coming? It doesn't matter because I'm always available; fix a time and I will come to collect you. It is good you will know your roots.'

'Nice work,' said Vince when Mensah told him his news. 'When do you go?'

'As soon as I get a visa,' said Mensah. 'Can you keep an eye on my mother? Don't tell them I'm abroad – anything can happen. I'm not insured, but the premium if I got one would be incredible to go to Nigeria; so I just won't bother. Haven't got much choice, because I have to go. I don't think she'll be discharged before I get back.'

After the usual mayhem at the Nigerian High Commission, Mensah was granted a visa for three weeks' visit, though without access to the northern part of the country. More conflict there, he presumed, but no reason was given.

Bode Dacosta lived in Eko Atlantic City, a planned district constructed on land reclaimed from the Atlantic Ocean and served by an overland light-rail network. He moved there from the rebuilt quarter of Lagos, to which his ancestors had returned from Brazil after the abolition of the slave trade in South America. These returnees, the Aguda, played a prominent role in introducing new trading and agricultural techniques to West Africa in the early nineteenth century and were still the most prominent traditional families on Lagos Island. Related to the Oba of Lagos, the family interceded in land disputes between the traditional and secular realms of government and wore its own royal colours during traditional ceremonies.

Bode planned to meet Mensah at the airport but lost his nerve at the last minute and sent his driver instead with instructions to drop Mensah off at the hotel and return to pick him up later. Lagos, a metropolis of twenty-five million, had a new airport, 'Unknown Nigerians' Airport, in honour of those who had suffered under dictatorship and died in the civil war. Some also said it was to honour those who had died at the hands of unknown soldiers during army rule to remind people not to let their guard down again. The old airport, named after the generals, catered for the expanding domestic traffic.

The driver, Rashidi, took Mensah to the five-star Hotel Proteus on Victoria Island. It was dusk. Other than at a pop concert, Mensah had never seen so many smiling faces and teeth. *I thought they were suffering*, he said to himself. But then he recalled that Fela Kuti song, 'Shuffering and Shmiling', about how Lagos people tolerated the most appalling public services, whilst their religious and political leaders hogged the best facilities. *Perhaps there is no ADHD here*, he thought, *because if what we are told is true there would be riots*. Rashidi pointed out the landmarks: the multi-billion naira developments on man-made islands to rival any in the world; and these not far away from the shacks of mobile shanty towns, erected every midnight after the guards had gone home to bed. Children hawking candles and groceries pressed against the locked car doors in the traffic. Mensah was going to buy some sweets as an act of charity, but Rashidi shouted: '*Oga*, stop, please, shopping malls, shopping centre – dey for buy something. No kill me oh. If anything happen he go be for my head.'

174

Mensah sank back into his seat, wondering how the little girl's family could make a living. The driver, as if reading his mind, said, 'God will provide, some done build house sef, you think say them no get money, some get pass you, no worry, ask *oga* when you see am.'

Mensah could just about make out what the driver meant. On the other side of the dual carriageway, drivers jostled nose to tail for the void created in the wake of a wailing ambulance slaloming through the snarled traffic.

At the hotel, Mensah had a shower and drank a bottle of water from the room bar. His skin reinforced with insect repellent, and his mind blank, he was prepared for nothing, but open to everything. Humidity engulfed him like palm oil. Perhaps he should have made notes from others' experiences, but what good would that have done? He would just play it by ear. *No tears*, he said to himself. *No matter what*. Twenty minutes later, they stopped outside the large steel gates of an estate. A porter saluted as they drove past. Mensah knew he should have tipped him but did not know how much to give. The driver called his boss on the phone for instructions. Then they came to a large pink house with a drive-through under which were parked three saloon cars and two Range Rovers; at least they looked like Range Rovers. Still petrol driven. Oil prices had plummeted with the move away from fossil-fuel-burning engines in the West, just when Nigeria had finally managed to commission enough oil refineries. The local barons who created and maintained the fuel production bottlenecks had moved on to other rent-earning activities. Providing potable water was lucrative. Water was the new oil, and even the Arabs were looking for ways in which they could convert their vast reserves of useless or surplus oil to water in summer. They used their empty oil wells as large rubbish dumps, pumping in waste from around the world.

Mensah got out of the car. He tried to plan how he should react. For Nancy it was a hug. For Marty a half hug and shake. So Mensah decided on a Marty greet. Bode was dressed in a *buba* and *sokoto* and a pair of slippers. He had just had a shower: minute sweat beads gleamed over his smooth, freshly shaven face. Mensah was struck by their similarity in build and how his father held his hands, left wrist slightly flexed and behind him as he leant forward to greet him, just like *he* did. There the similarity ended. The tips of their fingers collided in an awkward hand-shake. Then they hugged. Paternal ether transmuted Mensah's confusion into, if not love, something he had not felt before, which he had not expected and for which he was not prepared. Mensah fought his tears, successfully this time.

'My son, this big grown-up? I must be getting old,' said Bode, and laughed out loud. 'But Lagos life keeps me young, oh.' Bode swept Mensah into a large hall, decorated with a large mirror above which was an old photograph of a middle-aged woman in full traditional dress. 'My great-grandmother,' he said. Mensah nodded. 'You must be hungry, aeroplane food, particularly BA food, is not the most filling I hear. In my days, at least the stew-ardesses were pretty. But now they use robots, nobody buys food or duty free. Did you? Sorry, I didn't mean to be rude, I mean, you see, if they were human you might have been tempted.' Bode stood back, his outstretched arms on Mensah's shoulders. 'It's nice to meet you. I thought, what do you say? You are a blessing. How do you find Lagos? Different from Newcastle, I bet; how many there? Million, tops; we have twenty-five million, unbe-lievable – it just keeps going, like London did before the spoil-sports got their way. We'll not make your mistakes: if we need an airport we will get one; of course, we will have to break a few legs to make the omelette. Not legs, eggs, it's a local joke.'

Mensah smiled. 'I'm happy to be here, I can only stay for a week. I'd like to see the sights, if I may, when you go to work. Would I be able to borrow your driver? He seems quite nice.'

'Ha, what sort of question is that? You can commandeer the vehicle, the driver, every goddamn thing you want, are you not my first son? Look, my man, my work is not like yours: office or like that,' said Bode. 'I'm an entrepreneur, I'm always working.

I've passed the office-worker stage. They're going to make me a chief, oh. Why? Because I am a good engineer, maybe. Because I'm an excellent host, maybe, or socialite, or landowner, who knows? But I'll find a title that befits someone of my status in the community. I've been married twice since I came here. My family think I should always renew. I'm happy to see you, very happy. I think it's a miracle. Look at your ears and mine. You are my son all right. Let's eat. It will be half term in two weeks, then the children and their mum come down from the Ikeja area, near the good schools, to stay with me. When they are not here they can stay with my in-laws. When they finish the schooling who knows what will happen? This life is good, it suits me, no one in my head or ear all the time. Do you want to stay here for the night? There's plenty of room.'

'I'll come back tomorrow,' said Mensah, 'there are a few people I have to see to do with work; then I'll stay tomorrow, that is, if you don't mind.'

'Of course, ah, ah, what sort of question do you ask? This is Nigeria, not England. You don't ask your father whether he minds, I don't think Nigerians ask anyone whether they mind. *Do I mind?* Listen to this, my *oyinbo* son, man, incredible!' said Bode, laughing.

After a meal of rice and fried plantains with fried fish and beer, Bode asked, 'How's Hartley? He did a remarkable thing, a remarkable thing trying to save you. You know, he offered to look after you when things didn't work out between your mother and me. I left the area but always wanted to come back and then realised that we had done the best. Under the circumstances we did our best, oh. Those people wanted to finish us all, ah, ah. I'll talk to you tomorrow, it's getting late and I don't want that driver using my car as a taxi. At this time of the night I can time him there and back. Good-night, son.'

'Good night, Dad,' said Mensah. 'Dad' just popped out.

The next day, Mensah lounged around the hotel. He called Vince to tell him his news. 'What's he like?' asked Vince.

'What's *your* dad like?' said Mensah.

'I don't know, difficult to say,' said Vince.

'Exactly, I've only known him for a few hours, but he's nothing like me,' said Mensah.

Mensah spent the next day with Bode and his driver being driven around the old and newer parts of Lagos. Bode showed Mensah the Isale-Eko part of Lagos, where the indigenous people had lived for centuries. You could still see Brazilian influence on the architecture of the houses that had not been decorated for decades. Plans to turn the area into a mix of Jorvik Centre and the Beijing Hutong had been frustrated by the high level of street crime. Bode took Mensah to the Iga Idungaran – the palace of the Oba of Lagos, still a powerful influence on the local people. They lunched at the newly commissioned six-star Na Africa We Dey international hotel in Lekki and rode on the underground rail system between Yaba and Victoria Island. Bode introduced Mensah to several of his cousins. Most were property speculators. At the end of each day, Mensah crashed out on his bed into dreamless sleep.

The next evening, Mensah gave the driver a large tip, twenty thousand naira, just for fun, to see his reaction. The driver prayed for Mensah all through the journey to Bode's. After the evening meal, they tried a version of pounded yam with vegetable side-dish and snails. Mensah passed on the snails. Too risky if not cleaned properly. But he did not mind the beer. Bode had probably had a few before Mensah arrived. 'Do you want another drink? We have the strongest lager in the world. I thought I could drink, until I came to Lagos. Now I'm a wimp, oh,' said Bode.

Mensah sat on his father's balcony, the early evening anopheles mosquitoes circling over his head. In the background, a sudden eruption of cheers from a football crowd. In the distance, the blaring of horns – buses and minivans; the loud, feigned aggression and empty threats or '*shakara*' of the motor touts; the police vans and ambulance sirens wailing, ostensibly to reach a crime scene or a patient, but really switched on to get home early enough to watch the match or soap opera. All far removed from Gosforth, Newcastle life and the odd tinkle of the postman's bicycle bell. The sun set over telegraph and electricity pylons and the smoke from open-cooking deforestation fires. It was hard to believe that this was the same evening sun they shared with England.

'Hey, Mensah,' Bode called out from the living-room, glass eyed from downing another beer. He wiped his mouth with the back of his right hand and belched. 'You'll not read this in your newspapers and little was even written in this country. Yet large numbers of expatriate Nigerians were forced to leave Britain in a hurry. The government here failed to hold the British to account for its abuse of human rights. Our calamity, it was a tragedy, a disaster, a real palaver. Gradually, gradually, the climate changed, the political climate that is.' He paused, wiped his forehead with the back of his hand. 'The press caused it, but the economy was the foundation for our woes. They used to call it anaemic – we called it bloodless, as in bloodless coup, ha. As the economy went down, the trouble started. It was not the people's fault – they believed what they were told or read. These innocents were simply following the money. Millions had done so before them. Look at New Zealand, the United States, Australia. Were they not built on immigration and the decimation of the natives, the modern equivalent of those Amalekites, Jebusites in the Bible?

'I used to wonder what those Amalekites had done wrong, but that's another story. I digress. They call me king of digression. Speaking of which I need my vitamin supplements. Bode unwrapped a bag and took out four bottles of tablets and capsules. Mensah could make out that one of these was for arthritis, the others were multivitamins. Bode poured half a dozen down his throat, followed by a long draught of water. 'Ah, fortified,' he said, wiping his lips with the back of his hand. 'Where was I?'

'You were digressing about the Amalekites,' said Mensah.

'Oh, not that, I was making a point, ah, the government; traditionally a repository of the votes of immigrants, it cynically exploited this group, played them off against the indigenous working class; I prefer to call them the third class. It encouraged East European immigration, knowing that this would keep down wages. The third class non-EU immigrants were caught between the indigenes and the EU newcomers. Their own government invites in competition for their jobs and stands back as they suffer the backlash from the indigenes. They suffer for a policy that was not their design. But the government, like all governments, would not tell the truth. It wanted it both ways. To stay in power it would pretend that it was on the side of the workers; whilst undermining them. When the workers twigged, government blamed the foreigners. British jobs for British people or something like that. The one occasion when they nearly held their nerve was during the general election in 2010 when a lady asked the Prime Minister about 'all those East Europeans' and he quite correctly told her that there were British people abroad also. Then he had to go and spoil it by calling her a bigot while his microphone was still switched on.'

Bode interrupted his own story to ask Mensah, 'Are you all right – do you want anything – a beer or something? Let's go inside, too many mosquitoes here; are you taking your prevention tablets?'

Bode sent for some fried fish to go with his beer. Mensah tried some himself and asked, 'How did the people who left England cope?'

'Expulsion was the best thing that could have happened to some of the African diaspora,' Bode said. 'Expulsion forced them to confront their lives abroad. Many were second-class citizens and no better off abroad than they would have been at home. "Limbo" – bend over backwards citizens – we used to call ourselves.' Bode shifted in his seat, to get more comfortable. He wagged his finger in the air. 'Why are our people picked out for punishment wherever they are: East, West, communist, capitalist countries? Why do we, the poorest, pay extra wherever we go? For centuries our most valuable export has been people – dragged, pushed or driven out; treated like commodities. You know Goldman Sachs. Sacks full of money and influence. What do we have? Sacks of other people's rubbish and effluent. Eating shit, at home or abroad. Did you know slave owners forced people to eat shit in Haiti?'

Bode looked over his shoulder at a small bookcase containing half a dozen or so books. 'It's not there,' he said. He turned to Mensah. 'I wanted to show you a book by C.L.R. James. You know why we're treated like this? We black people don't have a state we can be proud of. It should be Nigeria. America serves its purpose still for white people; even the French will cherish American success. Can you see Americans siding with Algeria against France, with Iran against Israel? You are English, can you be Prime Minister? What is the test of whether you are a true citizen? When you have a Prime Minister of non-EU descent? As historic as Obama's election was, I will surrender all my worldly possessions when they elect a black George Bush. That's a test of successful integration. But our leaders have sold us into slavery again, sold our birthright, raw materials, oil, gold, uranium, then fought over the proceeds. What do we do? We turn all four cheeks – face and buttocks – to be slapped and defiled. After, we will hold some *yeye* commission and demand an apology. That will really stop them next time. Fuckers.'

'What's the solution? Revolution?' asked Mensah.

'No, first people need to be conscious, educated, they're blind. They don't know anything. In Britain you can afford to say, I don't like politics. Here, in a country like this – underdeveloped, developing, less developed – whatever they call us now, anywhere in which you are a visible minority, even a majority, ignorance can cost you your life. You must know what's going on around you.'

Mensah nodded in agreement. He could now see how political events had influenced even his relatively sheltered life. Mensah's interest encouraged Bode. Preening with the pride of a teacher whose student had finally caught on, his eyes glistened with passion and alcohol. He leaned back to down the last few millilitres of beer, pulled his large pantaloons down a couple of centimetres for comfort, and sat down again. 'Joseph, Joseph, bring me beer.' Bode scowled at the house boy. One beer bottle toppled over on the tray as the poor man hurried in, and he over-shot Bode's glass with the precious beverage, prompting another withering, disdainful glare.

'Sorry, sir, I'm not well . . . fever, sir.' Bode ignored Joseph and turned to his guest.

'Thieves and crypto-socialists held us back. I'm not just talking about Nigeria. Imagine a football team as socialist: everyone would have to have the same number of touches on the ball, no divi-sion of labour, no differential rates. How would that team compete, unless you broke the opposition striker's legs? Look, look around you: teeming, suffering masses, no electricity, no potable water, high infant mortality and maternal-mortality rates. Imagine, these are all black, eh! Then imagine that the small minority elite, who sign the inflated contracts, cart dollars and yuan around in suit-cases, own properties in Knightsbridge and Shanghai, but have no obvious legitimate source of income, were white, would Nigeria not be banned from all international bodies for racial discrimi-nation? Some people believe it is their birthright to rule and loot the country. Apartheid. We are the only country in the world, excepting perhaps North Korea, in which the President . . .'

'Excuse me, sir, said Joseph.

'What do you want?' said Bode.

'Excuse me, sir, Mr Buraimoh is here, wants you, sir,' he said.

'What did I tell you, what did I tell you? This stupid man, I told you I didn't want to see anybody; can't you see I have busi-ness?'

'Sorry, sir, I was confused as I see he be your friend, sir.'

'What did you tell him?'

'I didn't say anything, sir.'

Bode looked himself over and straightened his cap. 'Tell him to come in,' said Bode. Joseph tiptoed out of sight. 'Buraimoh was in England with me. He was an illegal, he got deported. No qualifications. Just comes to gossip, he's a councillor, next day political agent or importer,' he said.

'Bros Bode,' sang Buraimoh, bowing slightly, hurrying towards Bode, arms outstretched.

'How you dey?' said Bode. 'This is Mensah, visiting from England.'

'You're welcome,' said Buraimoh.

'Thanks,' said Mensah.

'We are discussing business; do you have any pressing matters?' said Bode.

'No, I just came to see how you were doing, the other matter, is delicate,' he said, glancing at Mensah. 'We can discuss next week.'

'Good,' said Bode. After a few seconds he said, 'Which matter?'

'My containers at wharf, cash flow is bad,' said Buraimoh.

'Call me on Monday, I'll see what I can do.' Bode stood up to shake Buraimoh's hand and ushered him towards the main door. Mensah got up, and at the door, Buraimoh turned, doffed his cap to the two men and disappeared into the night.

'Joseph, come and shut this door,' said Bode, and he smiled at Mensah. 'If you live here, you have to know how to deal with our people. They'll kill you with stories, there's no social security, so they have to survive. Buraimoh has no container, he thinks I'm stupid. I've checked.' Bode took a sip of his beer, made a face. Another servant cleared his tray; he pointed to the glass and the beer with his index finger and lifted two to the young man, who understood this as a request for two more bottles. Solomon bowed and returned with his order. Bode took a quick sip of beer, grunted and nodded his approval and waved Solomon away.

'If I ask Buraimoh to stay he will be here all night. He is good for parties, but not for business. It's not his fault, he has no real trade or profession; he got attracted to the wrong sort in England. He paid the fees to the correspondence college; the money disappeared. I tell you, the government knew about these bogus colleges but did nothing: they were a source of foreign exchange. When trouble started they claimed ignorance. Really? They didn't know what everybody else knew?'

Bode got up to go to the toilet. Mensah looked around the room, lit with two large, naked table lamps casting a penumbra over their chairs. He was beginning to feel tipsy and his vision was getting blurred, but he thought it might be considered rude to switch on the main lights. Mensah now understood one of his grandfather's diary entries.

By all means pray, pray for salvation, for wealth and happiness, but whilst you wait for God, ask your compatriots why they cheat you thus. Do not be distracted. When they ruined the economy in the 1980s they blamed foreigners and asked the Ghanaians to leave. A distraction, but many of you cheered. Do not let them get away with such a ruse again.'

He was referring to Nigeria.

Bode swayed back in. 'Ah, my child, where were we?' he said.

'On to the power supply,' said Mensah.

'Oh, yes, power, or light as we call it here. How did we get to talking about that? I was trying to tell you why we are victimised, let's park that.' Bode tried to sound casual.

'My mum, what happened to my mum?' said Mensah. Bode fell silent. He looked up at the ceiling.

'You are right, it is an important issue. I was going to come to it. Did you know?' Bode paused and looked at Mensah to see that he had his attention. 'Did you know? I was one of a set of twins; one in a million, one black, one white. My father was confused and bitter, although deep down he knew my mother was blameless. I know because I asked. I think he wanted out: of the marriage and the country. I can understand his frame of mind. Rachel, my sister, and I never got on. At school, when we were in the same class, we used to put our hands up to answer all the questions. Then one morning there's this teacher, Mrs Tipman. Anyway, I put my hand up as usual, so did Rachel and

184

one or two others. The teacher gave me this withering look; I was chilled to the bone. She just said, "We know you know – know-all – give the others a chance." Then she turned to Rachel to answer the question. I can remember what it was about: easy sum like two multiplied by three by three. Maybe a man would have done it differently, I don't know, but it was the way she said it, it cut to the bone. I never put my hand up in class again and I didn't tell Mum either. Rachel didn't understand, maybe just thought she'd won that day and I would have done the same. Fucking hell, man, we were seven years old. Even Mum, my own goddamn mum, expected more of Rachel than she did of me. You just know. Now it seems trivial, but I was so down, so to get my own back on the school, teacher and Mum, I stopped working. How silly it sounds now. I never really pushed myself hard after that, afraid of rejection perhaps, or just me, who knows? Funny how things affect a child, what do you think?'

Mensah felt a tinge of sympathy: nothing was straightforward. 'I agree with you, Dad, the teacher had a bad day, but you had more than a bad year.'

'It was more than a year, but when I saw that life would be impossible if Rachel got ahead and I became the bummer, I picked up, started working, not that I got any credit from anybody. Without my dad around, sibling rivalry savaged, then salvaged me.' With a careworn, distant gaze of sorrow, or reflection, and pursed round lips, he shook his head half a dozen times and, for a moment, was lost in his thoughts. When he looked up he said, 'Never mind, it's in the past.'

'Give me a second, will you, Mensah, I need to remind those boys what to buy from the market tomorrow. I nearly forgot, have to do everything. Bode called out for Joseph, but no one came. Mensah got up to find him, but Bode waved him down. 'I'll deal with them later, they're useless wasters, if there's such a thing. That Mrs Tipman, I wonder what she's doing now, MBE perhaps for services to the community? That's how it goes. My sister though, Rachel – sharp as a tack, so sharp she could cut herself, and she knew it – always had to be right. She'd look things up in encyclopaedias, dictionaries for weeks, over a point of fact. I called her the dog and bone girl. She applied to uni as Coulter, our mother's maiden name. We'd got over the serious sibling palaver, and we were happy for her. When she came up on holidays we kept out of the way. Somehow we just knew that's what she wanted. If she didn't, she would have said. Wouldn't you? You'd say, "Why do you go out when my friends are coming?" or "I would like you to meet so and so." I don't know what she told her friends, she didn't have many; we didn't care. She was still my sister, Mum's only daughter. She met John, I didn't meet him myself but Mum liked him. They had a son. I studied petroleum engineering and management and after my studies I worked for a few years. I met your mother at university. This boy, I forget his name, was hanging around her, but I won.' Bode was drenched in sweat. He wiped his face with his sleeve and finally took off his cap.

'I didn't know I had an aunt,' said Mensah. 'Marty and Nancy didn't say, I've had no idea, but Mum, what happened?'

'Ah, your mum, your mum,' he said. Mensah knew Bode was going to scratch his forehead. Then he braced his bent head against his left hand. 'Coming to your mum, your mum, Ruth, was named after one of your grandfather's favourite characters, Ruth in the Bible. A real daddy's girl: Daddy said this, Daddy said that; "go and marry your daddy," I said one day. I was fed up, frustrated. He's my dad, she said, as if I didn't know. I admit now, looking back, I couldn't handle it when your mother was ill – I was not a drinker; nothing like that, oh. The Hartleys tried to help. I told a close friend part of my story – you don't tell people secrets; he said even he, a quiet man, would have been jealous of the Hartleys if they offered help when he couldn't. I didn't say anything that day, but when I got home I knew he was right: deep down I was glad she turned them down. In the end they failed, but they tried, oh. Then I could see the same thing happening to you that happened to me. For me, no father; in

your case, no mother. But I didn't know what else to do. Rachel
didn't give me any slack. She kept blaming me, every time, the
same hassle – I should do something, be more responsible. What
could I do, oh? I still had to work, keep myself together. Did
anyone know what I was going through? One Friday evening, I
was visiting Mum with you and Ruth. Rachel came for the weekend
or something, or I thought just to have another pop. As she let
us in she gave me this look. I nearly flipped, but controlled myself.
Then, later on after tea, some girl on TV was crying because her
bloke had left her; I must have cracked a joke – plenty of fish in
the sea, something like that – just to loosen up, that's my way.
Rachel let rip, said I was just like Father, I was going to abandon
my family just like him. She called me a parasite and a coward
who could not face up to his responsibility, that I was a typical
Afro-Caribbean man who left his family whilst he enjoyed a selfish,
irresponsible life. I was sick, sick to my back teeth of her pious
preaching. I snapped. I told her she was a fake person. She did
not know or want to know what she was. I told her I was not
like her, hiding behind fair skin and a false name. We were in
Mum's living-room. There was no violence. I never hit anyone
in my life. I expected Ruth to support me. I don't know why.
Rachel was furious, Ruth was crying, you were asleep in a cot
somewhere. I remember thinking, who was looking after you?
Was Rachel so hard on me, to cut me off, to make her life neater?
I don't know; when you think so much you come up with many
crazy ideas.'

Bode stopped to get up and wipe his face. He tried to trap
some mosquitoes or nuptial termites in his clapped hands. He
grimaced, flicked his meagre catch on to the floor and sat down.

'I'm your father, you need to know this, I need you to know,
that's my duty. We lost you to the busybodies in the council. Oh,
for what it's worth, you need to find your mother. They closed
her hospital – to build apartments. There'll be records, I'll see if
I can help. I don't know where she is, but I'm sure if you found
me you can find her. Bad memories, bad, bad memories it brings

to me. When those days grip me, I can't sleep. I have my life. You have yours. Our youth has been messed up, we've missed out, but it was not my fault.' Bode slumped back in his settee, plumped up a cushion and placed it behind his neck. He stretched out, flexed his back and took off his sandals. 'You need moisturiser,' he said, looking at Mensah's bare, dry feet. 'Is the room too dry?'

'No, it's fine.'

'Do you want more fish?'

'No, I've had enough to eat. How did you get on when you came back here?' said Mensah.

'I came here to run my father's property business. I'm not starving. We pay very little tax, although we pay it in so many different ways – lack of infrastructure, graft, and so on, but I'm free here. No mask to put on in the morning. Some of our people there in England don't even take it off when they get home. What sort of life is that? Now I'm as happy as can be. I've met you, my son. I hear you're going to be a consultant. Well done. I know it's not easy. You look surprised. Your friend Vince told me. Are you getting married? Sorry to ask. In my family, we don't marry anyone unless she's pregnant. You should take that as a lesson, advice from the mother country. Our way saves a lot of *wahala*.

'I'm Nigerian by ancestry but British by birth, a BoND – British of Nigerian descent. I'm Bond, Bode Bond.' He laughed. 'Sorry, I just made that up. I'm digressing again. A Nigerian director is remaking some of the old Bond movies in Nigeria, with Nigerian actors. You could have all sorts of definitions: British of White Skin – BOWS, BOBS, BOYS – but it would be futile. Can you categorise like that? Yes and no. Each has religion, education, experience, life chances, luck, biology, temperament. I've been there. So will your children. We have a saying: Watch out for those who spread hatred under the cover of democratic freedom. Oppose them, by force, force of reason. You must find your own definition and identity. If one identity fails you have another, but for me it was draining. I think the same thing happens to minorities here but we are not that sophisticated. That is one thing learned from living abroad. I've done better than most, all considered – the coalition, your mother, all the rest. It was just as bad here under army rule when I got here – some of us thought we had fled from a spitting frying pan to the cauldron, but we survived singed, burnt, shrivelled, some diminished, others toughened and enhanced. First survive, then proceed, it could be a motto.'

Mensah stood up to stretch his legs, disturbing the moths swarming around his head. He clapped his hands in the local fashion to swat the insects, but missed, causing only a harmless vortex. 'Can I use the bathroom?' he asked, for a break. In the toilet, Mensah stared into the mirror and noticed a new weal on the side of his face from an insect bite. He flushed the toilet, washed and wiped his hands and returned to the balcony. The lights were on. Bode was wearing a clean, dry, beige, light cotton *buba*. He looked spent but relaxed, like a gold medallist after a gruelling marathon.

Mensah was drained. His father would not admit his feckless-ness, and Mensah had probably had too much to drink to artic-ulate what he wanted to say. He had a new father abroad in a foreign land, with half brothers and sisters that he was not yet ready to meet. They were his father's responsibility, not his. His father says she fell ill, it was not his fault, it was the government's fault, religion, vaccination. Maybe Mensah wanted to hear more detail, what happened first, then next, a story, not analysis, but now all he felt was anticlimax and embarrassment, as in the wake of meeting a hero. He missed Marty and Nancy. His allegiance was to them. Not to this father, Bode, who appeared to like the idea of having a son, but did not need Mensah except as a fulcrum for self-justification.

Mensah looked across the room at his father. 'I'm grateful you agreed to meet me. You know better than I do that many would not. There are many in the south-east of England, in particular, abandoned by Nigerian parents. But I've been through a lot myself. I was left to chance. That was not my fault. Odds were against me. Did no one think of that? What was to happen to this small boy whose mother was ill? How have I managed to get this far? Do you know how many children in care get even a minor qualification? How many leave scathed and traumatised? I suppose it would have been more convenient if I'd died. Am I worth, do I deserve, an apology? Yes, you called me a blessing, but I'm also a reproach. I've come all this way. You are right. You understand this need we all have to belong, to understand. Now I think I do. Everything I've heard has been from your point of view. What Rachel did, how you felt, what my mum did or didn't do. Whatever happened, there was a little boy in the middle of this mess. You didn't even have to have a child. And when things went wrong you knew my mum was ill but you still fled to your daddy. A grown man you were, you still needed your dad. Did you not think a little boy would need his daddy too? I could have fallen into the hands of a paedophile ring or those mercenary foster families and ended up as a statistic. Believe me, we read and hear about them. Disasters, then enquiries; each time we have one I think, *that could have been me*. Nancy and Marty made me the son you are proud of today. Yet you did not ask after them. They are my real parents.' Mensah's voice quivered.

Bode sat forward, swivelling towards Mensah. His hand shook when he raised his glass to his lips. 'It was not like that,' said Bode. You've misunderstood me, got it all wrong. I did my best. I loved your mother but I didn't understand what was going on. I never wanted to leave you, at all, at all. The council said they'd look after you. I hoped the council would do better than I could. I wouldn't have left if I was not sure. I didn't know life would be as hard as you said. I hope you understand. I'm sorry. But I've also been thinking. Would you be the same man if we'd brought you up in that country at that time? Would you have won prizes with your real parents? Think about it; we may have done you a favour. All the doors open to you now you may never have known existed. I hoped you would understand after you heard what I had to tell you. Believe me, from a father to son, it was not easy for any of us. We all took risks,' said Bode.

'I'm glad we've met, I've said my piece, it's been good,' said Mensah. 'Will the driver be able to take me back to my hotel? I have to prepare for some meetings with university staff tomorrow and will be flying out in two days.' Mensah had four days left but did not think he could take another night.

Back at the hotel, Mensah reviewed the evening's events. He asked himself whether this proclivity of his father and grandfather to abandon offspring was genetic or acquired. Some of the cousins he'd met were already grandparents in their early forties and on to their second or third families. Would he do the same? Would it not be safer if he did not have a family? For different reasons, neither of his parents were ideal role models. His mother was a patient: his patient. He could not hold her responsible for his fate. His father was too selfish. He had heard his father's version; from whom would his mother's story emerge? His aunt? Then Mensah remembered he did not know this Aunt Rachel's married name.

The next day he called Bode. 'Thanks, Dad, I didn't mean to be harsh on you, I was tired. Let's move forward. I'll come back after I've sorted myself out. I've got job interviews in the autumn. Give my regards to the family.'

'Good, son, safe journey, everything will work out, I hope you have better luck than us,' said Bode.

'What is my Aunt Rachel's surname?' asked Mensah.

'Timms,' Bode replied. 'She married one Dr John Timms. On the quiet. Mum went, I didn't.'

'Did you say Timms, Dad? Can you spell it?'

Bode spelled the name. 'Do you know them?' he said.

'I might know her son, we work together.'

'If he is, he's your cousin. Ha, ha, Allah works in mysterious ways, that's why family should meet; if he was a girl you could marry her by mistake,' said Bode.

191

'No way would I have anything to do with a girl like David,' said Mensah.

Mensah was relaxing by the hotel swimming pool when Vince called. 'Where've you been?' asked Vince.

'You know where I am, in Nigeria, maybe the reception was poor. What's happened?' said Mensah.

'Your mother's fine, she threatened to take her discharge when you did not turn up, but she's fine again. I went to the hospital yesterday. You need to come to see her as soon as you arrive. She's on the mend. The nurses sorted her out by telling her you were working, you hadn't gone away. But get your ass over here as soon as you can,' said Vince. 'I think the job's been advertised, I checked, it's in jargon, but I think it's the job you wanted. Let's go, there's also some ruckus about the contamination gene scandal.'

23

Rachel's Disclosure

Nearly ten years after the dyskeratotic gene scandal came to light, the government, with public support, continued to deny requests from academia and victims' groups for an inquiry. When the scandal broke, the Old Conservatives, embarrassed by their collaboration with the Nationalists, kept mute. Meanwhile, Labour's silence was for fear of alienating the working class. The labile and promiscuous Liberals waited for the wind to blow them. The experts had been wrong in predicting large numbers of deaths from the gene contamination and to the public an inquiry was going to be another expensive, useless, self-indulgent exercise. Letters to the editors made the same point. Measures had to be taken to get the country back on its feet. Everyone, not only the non-EUs, had made sacrifices, and those who did not like the policy had been free to leave.

Mr Jermaine Richards, a thirty-two-year-old prison officer with many features of the dyskeratotic syndrome, died after a chest infection. No one could agree whether this was the result of the contamination, a sporadic case or an unrelated condition. More captivating to the general public was a daily bulletin run for a month on the plight of a unique group of polar bears which, having shown signs of adapting to a small rise in global temperature, were threatened by a freak winter.

193

Rachel Timms was in her study preparing for the next day's meeting of the committee set up by the government to decide on compensation for the dyskeratotic gene scandal. John came in with a phone. 'It's David.'

'Hi, David, how's Jonathan?' said Rachel.

'He's great, just great, Mum. Mum?'

'Yes,' said Rachel.

'I want to apologise for the other day,' he said.

'Don't worry about it, it's nothing, you have your own life. You and Amanda have my, our, support, whatever you decide. It's the committee, it's sensitised me to genetic manipulation, like reports on food shortages or drought make you more careful about wasting food. I shouldn't have reacted,' she said. 'Tell Amanda really I don't mind, I'm over it, I'm sorry. I'll come to see you again as soon as I can, with your dad next time.'

'All right, Mum, look forward to seeing you.'

Rachel handed the phone to John and went back to work. John, relieved the tiff was over, asked David to bring Jonathan to the phone so he could wish him good-night.

'What are you still doing? It's not the committee again?' said John. He'd got bored with his book on golfing technique and wandered in to see whether Ruth would like to watch a play or sit with him.

'John, look, this contamination may not be an accident,' she said.

'What makes you think that?' he asked.

'Well, all the evidence points to some sort of deliberate contamination. We need to find out. Could be a crank working alone, but the science is too big for one person. It sounds like a long shot but hear me out.'

John sat down. 'I'm all ears,' he said.

'When I was a researcher there were rumours that Philip White had crazy ideas. Expelling social class five from the country, giving the *hoi polloi* a lie detector drug, forced sterilisation for benefit scroungers, imprisonment until the end of the recession or until there was a job for you – all White's ideas. Even Sugarcane laughed him out of court, but Sugarcane is wily; he could have been feigning. I worked with these people, some of them. They're vile, objectionable. But supposing some of these guys meant business, serious business? Whoever planned the contamination must have had access to the ADHD vaccines. If I'm right, some mad scientists have taken matters into their own sick hands.'

As she spoke she clenched her right fist. 'We need a judicial inquiry, but no one's biting. The committee work will drag on, the public, ambivalent at best, will become hostile. They've got better things to do than listen to some inarticulate victims whingeing and banging on about something that happened years ago. Remember Diego Garcia? Several of the guys involved with ADHD are still around, still top dogs . . . they . . .'

'What does the chairman think?' asked John. He put his open book face down.

'Don't make me laugh, our chairman, Sir Cedric Peasbody, is going to kick it all in to the proverbial long grass. Says we shouldn't rush to speculative conclusions. Wants us to adjourn and reconvene next year when we have more data from the Home Office. Burns-Savage. He resigned; had enough. I could also go quietly, or use the media to try to engineer a public inquiry, write a minority report . . .'

'Serve your tenure, and get out, keep your mouth shut, your head down, you're getting ahead of yourself. If Sir Cedric wants to bury it, let him, it's not your headache, we've got enough on our plate, I'm going to bed. Are you coming, sweetie?' He stood up, winked and looked down her cleavage, winked again, but she gave his hand a tepid squeeze and turned away.

'I've got to write this article tonight, no time,' she said.

'Good-night.' John tucked his book under his arm and carried some empty cups back to the kitchen. Then he sauntered off to bed like a chastened three-year-old. Committee work 1: John 0, again.

195

Rachel put the draft away and went to bed. John was already asleep. *Lucky man*, she thought. She got in to bed and was soon asleep.

The next morning she sent the draft off to *The Times*.

Justice for the Dyskeratotic Victims

An advanced economy should be large, wide, but funnel-shaped to direct contributions from the productive majority through a spigot to the truly needy few. Three decades ago, that model was turned on its head. In an unspoken, unwritten pact, the State used taxes from the lucrative, opaque, high-rolling, light-touch regulated financial sectors to service a burgeoning new set of entitlements and a broad-based dependent class created, or encouraged, by government. And at the bottom, immigrant labour filled the gaps. To support or subsidise constituents unlikely, unable or unwilling to make a contribution themselves, our leaders were content, even relaxed about importing from poor countries, those strong, young, clever, dynamic, rich, educated or able enough to add to our nation's coffers. As an insatiable government expanded, it needed higher taxes; and the private sector, more and more cheap labour. So the government turned a blind eye to financial sector excesses and to illegal immigration. When the credit crunch gate-crashed the party, the same politicians, like naughty teenagers, cast around for scapegoats and blamed the bankers who, hedged by huge bonuses against inflation, devaluation and quantitative easing, could look after themselves. And they blamed the immigrants who could not. To compound their dishonesty they conflated legal immigration, from the EU, which they had signed for and encouraged with European enlargement – which they still supported – with illegal immigration, which they had done little to control. With elections imminent, votes and seats at stake, out came sermons on race – printed by the press and spread by the Church and MPs – exculpating 'understandable' backlashes, preaching Christianity, cohesion, community and family.

The coalition underestimated the structural deficit and overestimated or misrepresented the savings to be gained by expelling the non-EU

196

immigrants. I remember the immense pressure on the government from international creditors to reduce the unfunded element of the deficit, particularly public sector pensions. But the coalition ignored our advice and the advice of independent experts not to carry out the manifesto promises they made in the first few months of that parliament.

The most productive of the immigrant community fled, commercial and residential property prices in the larger cities collapsed in their wake from the sudden glut in inventory. Services declined, particularly in retail and banking. Many new immigrants from the EU had less in common with the natives than the discarded non-EUs, except skin hue. Tightening of credit by financiers in revenge for windfall taxes, a vociferously critical press, dependent on the largesse of a handful of plutocrats, forced successive governments to sacrifice assets in appeasement. State provision of hospital care collapsed as companies, run, owned or advised by former Cabinet ministers, civil servants and general practitioners, cherry picked the most profitable institutions, leaving the rest to rationalise and amalgamate, and when these measures failed, to close. The numbers in the underclass, direct descendants of those left behind by the so-called economic revolution of the 1980s, plus teenage pregnancy rates and violent crime, continued to rise.

To buy time, distract the public, wrong foot opponents or placate pressure groups we were encouraged to 'think the unthinkable'. Most of these bastard products of the miscegenation of adviser and idea are aborted or strangled at birth. I know, I was there. I was a junior researcher with the Economic Forum and the monetary policy committee during the Nationalists' coalition when the ADHD vaccine programme started. But what if someone had followed on from thinking, to doing, the unthinkable? Surely, this could not happen here? But we know that far worse happened in the land of Beethoven, Goethe and Kant. A sprinkling of Nietzsche over a diet of nationalist and religious fervour, and off they went.

We set no limits on who can leave these shores for a better life. So when we say immigrants, by which we mean economic migrants, we are complicit. We say they are grasping, well so are we; threaten innocent lives, then so do we; bomb people – us too. Break the law,

so do we. Wife-beaters – so are we. They do not respect our reli-
gion, OK, but ask, tell me why they should. For many, of whatever
hue, it is a matter of good fortune to be born here, now. Should we
not be grateful for our blessings? If this should prove to be the end
of this epoch – with its national and racial privileges – and if some
find or consider themselves to be at disadvantage, should the new
arrivals fall, convicted and sentenced at the roadside court of native
frustration and entitlement? Let us reflect that income taxes fall dispro-
portionately on these first generation subjects. Many will not work
long enough cleaning our public toilets, hospitals and offices for the
pension for which they have now been asked to work longer to qualify.
Yet, how many of these people were high enough in government, in
the civil service or the law to influence, formulate or implement the
policies, the consequences of which they bear the greatest brunt?
How many?

Let us not repeat the mistakes of the haemophilia-HIV contami-
nation disaster or the injustice done to many Equitable Life policy-
holders or the victims of the wind farm catastrophe. Accidents, these
were. Should we not find out whether the dyskeratotic gene disease was
deliberately inflicted on our fellow citizens, by a rogue or by a cabal?
We need the answer to this question in the interest of justice for the
victims, to strengthen our democracy and the bonds between the citi-
zens of these isles, to live up to our ideals, to set an example to other
nations, to get to the truth, and because we know it is right.

When John came back from work she showed him the article.
'Where's the draft? You can't send this, they'll murder you.

'I've sent it,' she said.

'Oh, Rachel,' he said. He clenched his fist and brought it down
on the table; the loud crash of crockery startled Rachel into drop-
ping her pen. 'You've gone too far, too far. Bang, bang, bang
always, can't you go easy? Bang goes our way of life, all our
plans,' he said.

'You won't, don't, get it, ostrich man, these liberties you treasure
so much have to be defended, that's why I didn't show you the

article, I knew what you'd say, I was right, I won't give up until I've done what I can. The victims deserve my support.'

'At what price?' he said.

'We can afford it,' said Rachel, hands and lips trembling. She picked up the pen to write a note to remind her to call Oxford. 'Supper's nearly ready, go and get changed. You'll come round to my way of thinking in the end.' John grimaced and shook his head. 'Don't pull that awful face on me,' she said.

Rachel's article was published that Saturday. In the same edition was a rebuttal from the Home Secretary claiming that Rachel was arrogant to pre-empt the results of the committee.

24

Reaction to Rachel's Article

The next Tuesday morning, Rachel appeared on the eight o'clock slot of the *Arise* programme on BBC Radio. She explained her actions as calmly as she could in the face of hostile questioning from Ms Robish. 'Why are you so bothered about a condition that has so far claimed no lives? The country is recovering from a deep downturn, maybe not as severe as those you have witnessed in the past and for which as a former government adviser you share responsibility. We have four million unemployed. It's hardly the time to raise the plight of a few thousand with an obscure, artificial disease. What makes you think you are right when your chairman and several other members of the committee have come to differing conclusions? Could it not all arise from an over-active imagination or a personal vendetta against the chairman of your committee? Have you been not been passed over for a prominent position on the economic task force? Is this not arrogant of you?'

Rachel quoted the research from Professor Burns-Savage's team, claiming that contamination was either deliberate or the result of a very unusual accident.

'Unusual, but not impossible, as you know from personal experience,' said Ms Robish, closing the interview. The reference to personal experience could be an innocent coincidence, but Rachel thought she saw a smirk on Ms Robish's face.

To gather her thoughts, Rachel drove the long way home, past Gutcha, a waste disposal system invented in Britain, based on the human gut, which converted household waste into manure. She got home, perturbed, but relieved that she had made her case.

Rachel's unusual intervention, by one of its own advisers, forced the government, embarrassed by the coverage abroad, and pressure from Brazil, which had a new, large, prosperous middle class of African descent and with which it was to sign a lucrative bilateral trade agreement, into a partial U-turn. Through a written reply to a parliamentary question two weeks after her interview, it announced that it would consider a judicial inquiry into the scandal. Sections of the press were furious. Ignoring the scientific evidence, which was all in the public domain, they went on the attack. Rachel was a nutcase. One called her a terrorist. 'Rachel Timms' action is evidence that our enemies come not just from the disaffected or economically deprived youth, but from amongst the privileged in leafy suburbs.' Another paper claimed a scoop, accusing Rachel and her family of living a lie, foreigners biting the hand that fed them. According to the piece, Rachel and David hoodwinked the British people by hiding their origins. The authors found a former classmate of Rachel's, Mrs Penny Lover, who claimed that Rachel took her place at university. How they knew they did not say. An accompanying editorial mined the seam:

We support true, honest assimilation. In an open society we condone neither the wearing of veils, nor the assumption of false identities; the former to conceal and the latter to deceive. We condemn both practices.

'Thankfully, their deception did not succeed,' the editorial concluded. News must somehow have got out that Amanda and David wanted Jonathan to have blue eyes.

David was at work on the Wednesday, a week after Rachel's radio interview, when he came across the newspaper photograph of

Jonathan and Amanda, subtitled 'the hypocrite's grandchild'. He called Amanda. 'What on earth's this about?' he asked. 'What have your parents done, or was it just your mum?'

'No, don't start on me, it's your mum, she's stirred everything up, first with that article and then that interview she gave last week. She's campaigning for the gene-scandal victims. Not everyone agrees with her, as you can see. And they've come after us as well.'

'Are you sure?' said David.

'Of course I am, ask her yourself. Mum's here, she knows nothing of this, this mess. Will they follow us around now, will we be trapped? There's no one outside, thank heavens,' she said, lifting the blinds. 'But if this goes on . . .'

'I'll get home as soon as I can,' said David. He could not get through to his parents. Perhaps they were lying low as well. He needed some answers. Why hadn't they told him about the newspaper article? Perhaps they hadn't expected such a backlash. A hypocrite was the last thing Rachel was over this scandal. He granted them his mother was stubborn, but she was standing up against those who would bury the truth. David returned to work.

When David got home that evening, Amanda's mother, Mary Lockley, a former mathematics teacher who ran her husband's engineering firm, was sitting in the living-room, rocking Jonathan to sleep. Amanda had been crying. Mary's face was set in sympathetic anger.

'Hello,' he said to no one in particular. Amanda gave Jonathan's bottle to his grandmother and got up. Jonathan cried, so she sat down again. David went over to his computer to review his mother's interview. 'But what's hypocritical about defending the underdog?' he said. 'They're saying I deceived them. Rubbish. I've worked hard for everything I've got, on merit, not deceit, not on favours. Nothing they write will change that. What do my mother's views have to do with my competence as a cardiologist? As for this Bongo-Bongo land angle, it's ridiculous – a crude, imbecilic slander, and I have a mind to sue them. I just don't have the time for all this, I've got too much to do. I'll speak to Mum and Dad. We'll sort this out. It'll blow over.' He put his arm around Amanda. Amanda burst into tears again. 'Perhaps you should go to your mum's for a few days,' he said.

'I will,' she said.

Early the next day, David spoke to John, his father. 'I'm sorry Jonathan was dragged in like that,' said John.

'Is Mum there?' said David.

'Hello, David, I can't explain over the phone, you won't understand it like that. I need to see you.'

'That's odd, what's come over you, Mum, what's there to discuss that we can't talk about now?' he said.

'Look, we'll be up soon, in a few days, I promise, this weekend. Will Amanda be there as well?'

'Yes, she'll be back from her mum's.' Rachel was to find that weekend even harder than the radio interview.

Amanda gave David a special big hug before he went to work the next day. 'You're still the man I love and married, still the excellent, talented cardiologist. Nothing's changed. Your mum was doing what she thought was best, fighting for innocent victims. It couldn't have been easy. Don't blame her, blame the press. She couldn't have known this would happen. Call her and give your support,' said Amanda.

'We'll see her soon,' said David.

At work that week David was beginning to wonder whether his mother's views would affect his chances of getting the consultant post after all. So he called Professor Maginot. 'If it's any help,' said Maginot, I can tell you that for all the support the others can muster, they might as well not bother. I can't say more than that.'

25

Mensah back in Newcastle

Mensah got back to a typical windy, rainy Newcastle Monday morning. That evening he met Vince at a local pub, to take in the buzz: the low-pitched hum of static electricity from the old loudspeakers, eavesdropped snippets, the thud and clink of true and errant darts, the aroma of lager and cocky, pale, pregnant Geordie men in their short-sleeved white shirts propping up the bar. Mensah munched his genetically modified, sodium-free crisps; he frowned when the grating No. 2 song by The Leaves came on for the umpteenth time.

'You're shafted, unless we find a way out of this, some bargaining chip, weakness in their case, drag one of their chosen ones in, support from a boss, anything; you're shafted, fate has jumped out of the crowd to rugby tackle you on the home straight,' said Vince.

'Do you think I don't know that! How do I loosen its grip, get up and fight to the line?' said Mensah.

'Then think of something, God knows you've had time,' said Vince. 'I know it's serious, more serious than anything else I've faced; I don't like to use the word unfair, but this is *unfair*; it's unlucky, bleeding awful, a nightmare. First I'm told to give up on my career, then Mrs Patrick dies, then I'm a shoplifter in breach of hospital policy – you couldn't dream it. Pleading's not

on, probably futile and definitely demeaning – it's also undigni-
fied. My bosses won't support me, they cover their own back-
sides, leave juniors to stew. I've worked for some – Roger and
Douglas – they went the extra mile to look out for their juniors;
took responsibility for mistakes even when they could have ducked
out. I wouldn't count on Marsh; he's said to be angling to be
chief executive. His secretary goes out with a guy we know: she
says Marsh loves dishing dirt about his colleagues to the board
chairman, Li Tang. I can't see the hospital calling the dogs off;
impossible, never happened before. I pray that they'll lose the
files, but that's the stuff of wishful, outlandish Mensah dreams.
Waive the charges – even more fanciful. I don't understand why
they're accusing me of betraying patient confidentiality because
I never, ever take case notes off the premises. I know how seriously the hospital tracks these notes on their electronic system.'
He stopped to see whether Vince was following his argument.
'Vince, what do you think? If I can produce bank statements to
show I'd paid for the stuff, the detective may change his mind;
and withdraw the charges.'

'But they'll tell you that you were perverting the course of
justice, Mensah,' said Vince.

They waited at the bar for their next round. 'I've thought
of begging: pay-cut, extra shifts. But they'll take that as admission of guilt. Whatever way I pull at this web of allegations,
it threatens to choke me. I feel as if I'm in a noose. I'm really
angry, I haven't done anything wrong. Yet here I am plea-
bargaining; even if I accept that I breached confidentiality in
the hope that they'd drop the other charges I would have to
give up much more – the restorative-cardiology job – and when
it all dies down I might nab a degenerative-cardiology post. It
makes my head spin. Like a lost bird, a bird trapped in a conservatory. I feel as if, as I thrash about for a way free, I could
knock myself out. But I agree: if I do nothing I lose anyway.
Life's a bugger!'

'So you don't want another drink then?' said Vince.

'No thanks, I've changed my mind, Bacchus must wait. I've got other things on my mind – need to clear, not add to my mess.'

Each time Mensah examined the recording he thought he looked more and more uncomfortable. He knew why. That day, the only toilet on the floor was broken and, rather than keep the team waiting, he had carried straight on to Mrs Patrick's valve recon-struction. Mensah knew why he was edgy, he'd needed the toilet, but the hospital's forensic examiner could attribute his unease to the edginess of incompetence. After a morning jog, Mensah set off to see Mr Hudspith, the bank manager.

'What can I do for you, doctor?' he said, showing Mensah into his large upholstered office. 'You look as if your sector's doing well, what is the word – recapitalised?

'I'm decapitated if you don't help me,' said Mensah. 'There has been some mix up at a supermarket. I need dated and timed statements of all my transactions this year,' he said. Mr Hudspith looked at his reflection in the mirror behind Mensah.

'Are you sure we can't do any more for you, we've got some excellent new products, if you can spare a minute,' he said.

'Another time. Can you help me?' said Mensah.

'Of course, I'll get my staff to get it to you before the end of the week. 'We can send it in a coded format to a specific named officer at the shop; that should do. Let me know if you need copies, it shouldn't be difficult. I'll get the relevant release and authorisation forms.'

'Thanks, I'll see you soon,' said Mensah, making his way into the tranquil, post-rush hour Jesmond morning.

By the end of the day, Mensah was feeling much better for his minor achievements. Thinking his luck had changed, he called Ms Sherry who confirmed that the job had been advertised but reminded Mensah that he was not eligible to apply because he was still suspended from duty.

* * *

First thing the next morning, Mensah logged on remotely to his terminal to again look through Mrs Patrick's procedure. Trampling over and ignoring Mrs Patrick's autonomy was a more difficult charge to address. He hoped that the tapes would show that he was trying to do the best for the patient, but this was subject to interpretation. He had nothing left to do but to keep hoping and looking for a way out. The Defence Union was taking its time and, because Mensah did not think Vince would know what to look for, there was no one else he could trust or ask. He would have to rely on himself. Mensah saw that to an observer it looked as if he had barged David out of the way. Mensah hoped that anyone could see that it was not relevant to the charges against him. But, for the first time, he saw how nervous David looked as well and he had given up his place as first operator too easily. Then the recording moved on to Mrs Patrick's collapse and convulsions. How could anyone blame them for trying to resuscitate her when she had not expressed a wish not to be resuscitated?

Mensah turned to the scanned case notes. Hospital policy stated that every patient must give explicit written, signed consent to any intervention, no matter how minor. On one side of the consent form was Dr Marsh's name and a brief explanation of the procedure to be carried out; and on the reverse was a blank space where Mrs Patrick should have signed her consent. Marsh must have been distracted by Professor Radic. Mrs Patrick had not signed the consent form. The check-list showed ticks against all the pre-operative checks, including the signature, so the nurse must also have made a mistake or, less likely, tried to cover up. From what Mensah could remember of the hospital policy it did not seem to matter that Mrs Patrick had given implicit consent to the procedure by agreeing to come to the theatre. The hospital had broken its own rules. He printed the forms and called to tell Vince what he had found.

'If, through this technicality, I can extricate myself from the allegations about Mrs Patrick's care, I can make a reasonable fist of defending myself against the other complaints,' said Mensah.

'I think you may have something there, let me know if you

need any help. You know, general help, I don't understand the jargon, the technical stuff,' said Vince.

Mensah was waiting for Ms Sherry when she arrived at work the next morning. 'You shouldn't be here, Dr Snell. Applications will not close for another three weeks or so,' she said.

'It's not about that,' he said. 'I think I may have saved the hospital, everyone, a lot of bother.'

Ms Sherry beckoned him in to her file-laden office. Two large embedded monitors, labelled Scylla and Charybdis, dominated her desk. Everyone knew that she kept doctors' assessments and appraisal records on Scylla, but no one knew what she kept on the other – maybe it was just for effect. Ms Sherry was a large lady, a real woman, as she would be described in some parts of the world, and her chair wheezed when she dropped into it. 'Doctor, tell me again, what can I do to help?' She logged on to Scylla and watched the monitor for a few seconds to make sure she had typed in the correct password.

'I'm trying to respond to this complaint about a recent death in theatre,' said Mensah. 'I need to check my records against yours because I've got some queries to answer. As you can imagine, I've been under a lot of stress lately and my connection to the terminal here is not working properly. I need the data to reply to the allegations, to defend myself. My Defence Union also needs some information from the case records. I didn't want to use a colleague's workstation. It's confidential and I thought you'd be able to help.'

'What is it you want help with?' asked Ms Sherry.

'I just want to know if all the relevant forms had been signed – disclaimer forms, consent forms, blood tests and the WHO check-list.'

'I'll look on my system and let you know if there's anything amiss. It shouldn't be difficult. It'll take some time to get all the information and I have to be careful not to breach other clinicians' confidentiality,' she said.

'Thanks,' said Mensah, 'I'm extremely grateful, and if I'm right it will save you a lot of time and me all the hassle of a disciplinary hearing, but as you'll understand, my need is greater than yours. I appreciate your help, thanks again.' And he went to see his dentist.

Another week passed, and with about a fortnight to the close of applications and no news from Ms Sherry, Mensah was getting worried. He called Ms Sherry.

'Sorry, Dr Snell, I thought I'd told you. Don't you read your e-mails?' she said. 'I checked the process and forms, everything was up to date and signed, all in order: signatures, forms, everything. Sorry, I hope this addresses your question. Do you have any other concerns?'

'No, ma'am,' said Mensah.

'Then I wish you all the best,' said Ms Sherry. 'Thanks,' said Mensah.

'You're very welcome,' said Ms Sherry.

Mensah put the phone down and logged on again to the procedure page and documents. Ms Sherry was right, all the forms were signed and dated correctly, his tiny, flickering ember of hope extinguished. Yet Mensah was sure Mrs Patrick had not signed the form.

'I think when it comes to chicanery, your lot are just as bad as the press, the finance guys and the sex-traffickers,' said Vince. 'Why all this zigzagging for a bloody consultant job? Sorry, I know how much it means to you, I really do, but it's fishy, messy and all for what? It's out of proportion. From what I gather you've done nothing wrong, why are they putting you through all this?'

'I don't know, they seem to be going out of their way to get me. Maginot, you could say, was happenstance. Now this. Is it a coincidence, conspiracy? Or am I paranoid? They have me over a barrel,' said Mensah. 'I'll have a glass of sparkling water please,' he said to the waiter and nibbled at his bread roll. Vince wiped his hands and crunched into his apple. Suddenly Vince thumped the table, spilling his drink.

'I think I can see what they've done,' he said, splattering Mensah with apple. 'It's difficult to prove. It's illegal. But I swear they must have used Blue Peter software.'

'What's Blue Peter software?' said Mensah.

'Oh, there used to be a catchphrase in a children's programme a long time ago, "Here's one we made earlier", just to save time during the live show. When hospitals became big money-makers many surreptitiously kept all sorts of forms ready for inspections, regulatory and legal purposes. A duplicate of every paper transaction was kept on the system for three years. You couldn't alter clinical results; that would involve too many departments, and staff, but consent forms and such could be, what they called, "updated". A few years ago a hospital applying for a loan from the City was exposed by a whistle-blower. Big brouhaha, resignations, the lot, even one attempted suicide.'

'How do you know that's what happened?' said Mensah.

'I don't. Difficult, almost impossible, to be sure. The software's so good, even experienced experts may not spot spliced data or forms. The hospital would have had serious IT support to set it up and they almost certainly don't run the programme from the premises. Only a few members of staff in your administrative department will know what's happening, even your Ms Sherry may be in the dark about this. Although I doubt it.'

'How does all this help me?' said Mensah.

'I don't know yet,' said Vince.

26

Vince Goes Home

'I'm on my way, Mum, just leaving,' said Vince to his mother.

'I'm looking forward to seeing you, so is your dad, he hasn't seen you for nearly three months. I know you've been busy but you must both make an effort, we'll talk about it,' she said.

'That's the draw, isn't it, Mum, talk! You're not going to nag me about settling down and joining Dad's company again?'

'No, promise, but we care about you, that's why, you don't want Dad's work to go to strangers, do you?'

'No, but let's not argue about it, I'll be there within the hour. What turning is it again?'

'It's the first turning after the large silver birch after the post-box. You can't miss it.'

'I can, and I shall,' he said. 'See you, Mum.' He had to go that weekend. His mum had been nagging him for weeks. Vince did not like the narrow Northumberland country roads because he could not overtake the slow tractors and caravans.

He missed the turning and had to make a U-turn in the drive of a detached Tudor house, his red Jag convertible spinning on the gravel. The front gates to his parents' mansion stood at the end of a hundred-metre stretch of un-tarmacked road. A rabbit and a grey squirrel darted out of his way into the undergrowth, and his near front wheel lurched into a puddle, forcing him to slow to a crawl. A fine drizzle settled on his windscreen and he put the roof up, but not before bird's mess landed on his passenger seat. He cursed again.

Harry Mann added a holiday-inspired architectural feature to his mansion every year. This year's was an Italianate orangery. Rain meant they would all have to eat indoors, but it would give Vince an excuse to use the new Olympic-sized indoor swimming pool.

'It's the invincible Vince,' cried Jeremy as Vince walked in and took off his wet driving gloves.

'How are you, Jeremy, where's Dad?'

'He's around somewhere, he went for a walk, may have to send a helicopter out after him.

'He'll be back for lunch, always is,' said Vanessa.

'T'is Mum,' said Vince.

'Hello, my darling, you've lost weight,' said Vanessa. They hugged, patting each other's backs.

'It's deliberate, Mum, to help me find a wife,' he said.

'Stop it, I know you're teasing, wait to see what I've got you for lunch,' she said.

'Don't tell me: scrambled egg and toast,' he said.

'Oh, I'm hurt, that was ages ago, you won't let me live it down; no, some sea bass and a special Croatian sauce and, of course, apple crumble, to fatten you up: stodge, as you say,' she said.

'Mum, you're the best. Can I have a dip?'

'Of course you can, you'll find some swimwear in the changing room. Read the instructions though, you don't want to scald yourself,' she said.

After his swim it was time for lunch. Harry had come back from his walk. Vince thought his father had lost about a stone and was greyer, but it was his dad all right, dressed in a kimono. 'Hey, Home Office boy, what have you done this month? Caught any thieves, scroungers, terrorists, or are you not allowed to tell us?'

'Dad, nice to see you, no I don't catch them myself. I'm enjoying it, it's worth it: making the country safe so that you can make money to pay for us to make the country safe so that . . .'

'He's only teasing you, Vince,' said Vanessa.

'I'm only teasing Dad back,' said Vince.

'Let's have lunch,' said Harry.

'I second that,' said Jeremy.

After lunch, conversation again turned to Vince's future. 'The offer's open, Vince. Jeremy here is doing well,' said Harry. Jeremy blushed.

'Think about it,' said Vanessa. 'You're so good with people, you'd be a great asset to your dad. We're not getting any younger,' she said, glancing at Harry. He glared back. 'Dad's had a small scare,' she said.

'Oh, nothing much,' said Harry.

'What was it, Dad?' said Vince. 'Why didn't you tell me, Jeremy?'

'I didn't know,' said Jeremy.

'What are you doing in the company if you can't tell when Dad's ill?' said Vince.

'That's not fair,' said Vanessa.

'Sorry,' said Vince. 'What was wrong?'

'Well, if I can be allowed to speak for myself, my blood pressure was a bit high. I had to see that Marsh fellow at the Freeman.'

'You mean Dr Marsh? He's Mensah's boss.'

'Yes, your friend's boss, he does have more than one role in life, apart from being your friend's boss, you know; he treated me, he's your dad's doctor,' said Harry. 'Anyway, he was brilliant, explained everything ever so well, even I could understand, you know how thick I am. So I've got to lose weight, cut down on salt, but he's left me with Dr Crowther; I don't need to see Marsh, you see it's not that serious. I send him my best bottle of champagne and what do they tell me? Only that he doesn't drink. What does he do apart from work? What a waste of my best. Talking of Mensah, how is he?'

'He's fine in himself, Dad, having some professional issues, jobs . . .'

'Tell him to come and work for me, we could do with a medic,' said Harry.

'Harry, not everybody wants to be in business,' said Vanessa.

'Can't see why not,' he said. 'Spongers.'

'Vince, you're quiet, don't worry about your dad, he'll be fine,' said Vanessa.

'Just tired, late nights looking for this wife, Mum, not much luck, I'm afraid, and don't ask me to go back to Jeffer's manor for dinner because Rhianna, his daughter, is not my type.'

'I agree with you, son, no hips,' said Harry. 'What do you think, Jeremy?'

'Rhianna is a very nice girl, but I see why you are both right,' he said.

Later, after the meal, Vince explained that he had to cut his visit short. 'Dad, I've got to get back, we have a charity rugby match tonight,' he said. 'Mum, it's been lovely, Jeremy, say hello to Thomas and Cheryl for me, when they come back. Sorry I can't stay.'

'What's the match in aid of, how much will you raise? Stay and I'll pay it,' said Harry.

'You're very generous, I'll play anyway and you can send a cheque. It's for Save the Children and another charity, supports mental health in children,' said Vince.

'Kids, mental problems?' said Harry.

'Yes, Dad,' said Vince.

'You're a philistine, Harry,' said Vanessa. 'Pre-Neanderthal.'

'I'd use the term advisedly, don't want to insult the Neanderthals!' said Vince. 'I'm off.' And he set off down the front stairs to his parked car. Autumn had not yet displaced late summer; it would still be light when he got home. He did not have a rugby match. Marsh, his dad's cardiologist! That was a shock. He needed time to think. Marsh or Mensah. Marsh or Mensah – no contest! But Marsh and Dad versus Mensah was a tough equation. He had till Monday to make up his mind what to do if he was to help Mensah. Dad may not think much of the Home Office, but it gave him a way to tip the scales in Mensah's favour. If Mensah wished. Vince roared down the drive to the dirt path, waving to the receding forms of his parents and brother.

27

Marsh Out

Lunchtime, Monday, Mensah received a message from Vince to call him urgently. 'Are you all right?' said Mensah. 'What's the problem?'

'Listen,' said Vince, 'do you have a camera?'

'Of course I have a camera, you've seen it,' said Mensah.

'No, a proper video camera, not the toy ones,' said Vince. 'I'll lend you one if you want.'

'No that's fine, I've got it covered.'

'Have you got your consultant rota?'

'Yes.'

'Send it to me, now. You can manage that?'

'Of course I can, what's this about?'

'I'll tell you when we meet, tonight. I'll meet you at ten at the Third Green pub,' said Vince. 'Wrap up and wait for a man called Brown,' said Vince.

To keep fresh and alert for the evening's task, Mensah showered, shaved and had a light supper of chicken and a cup of coffee. Driving down the Great North Road he wondered what he was letting himself in for: a prank, or one of the impromptu parties Vince so enjoyed? Or a favour? But he trusted Vince.

At twenty-four past ten Mensah had been waiting in the car park bordering the football field just off Elswick Road for five minutes. He could hear late cheery birdsong over the yelping of a pair of dogs chasing after a posse of cyclists in luminous vests in the distance. The wind made it feel colder, but not cold enough for a jacket. Mensah was not cold, but nervous. He was going to drive round the block again, to kill time, but changed his mind when he thought someone might take his slot. He checked his camera again, cleaned the lens of condensation, replaced the cap and waited. Hunched forward, squinting through the windscreen, he was ready. With a click and a thud a man suddenly appeared in the passenger seat. Mensah nearly fainted. 'I'm Brown,' said Vince smiling.

'Oh shit, Vince, I nearly died. You're crazy. This is crazy, what's with dragging me here at this time of the day?' Vince smiled in the dark. 'It's not funny. I could do without this. I'm stressed enough as it is,' said Mensah.

'Hang on, hang on,' said Vince, 'I had to see whether you would go through with it. I wanted you to see for yourself. Wait and then you can have a go at me. Trust me.'

Ten minutes later a long-wheel-based Ford Britannia Estate cruised across the car park and came to a halt on the verge between the pitch and a path that ran along its side. 'Get ready,' said Vince.

'For what?' said Mensah.

'For what you are about to receive, sorry, see,' said Vince. 'Where's the camera?'

'It's on the most powerful zoom night-viewing programme, as you requested,' said Mensah.

'Good,' said Vince. You see the corner flag furthest from us, focus on that and I'll tell you what to do.'

Through his lens Mensah could just make out what looked like a man, his trousers just below his waist, pumping a spread-eagled man or woman – it was impossible to say. 'What do you see?' said Vince.

'I'm not sure why you ask, you know they're fucking. Do you come here often? I'm not into this sort of thing, Vince.'

'Hang on,' said Vince. 'Now, you see that estate, over there,

217

not that one, that one there, which came across us a few minutes ago. You probably didn't see it, the light one, focus on that,' said Vince. Mensah did what he was told. And gasped.

Dr Marsh was in the back of the estate. Next to him was a dog, which he stroked while looking through a pair of binoculars at the action in the car park about seventy-five metres away. He stroked the dog faster and faster and his pale bald patch flashed alternately oval and circle until, after a few minutes, it stopped. His orgiastic fit over. Marsh appeared to pull his trousers up. Then he clambered into the front of the car and drove away past the two men.

Mensah's mouth was as wide open as that of a hippo on the end of a reptilian blow job. 'Why would he do this in his own car, his own car, is he mad? He could be done,' is all Mensah could say.

'Look, drive home and I'll come after you, I won't be long. I know it's well past your bed time,' said Vince.

Back in Mensah's living-room, Mensah and Vince reviewed the footage, which was not as clear as the real-time images but showed Marsh's car and the coupling couple well enough. 'I didn't mean to alarm you,' said Vince. Every little handle we have on this may help; don't feel guilty. They say you should imagine your interviewers in their underpants; this will spare you the trouble.'

'But, Vince, shouldn't ask, but how do you get this sort of info?'

'How long have we known each other?'

'Nearly thirty years,' said Mensah.

'Well, let's just say I work in a vetting unit. We vet, usually important people, professionals like Marsh, celebrities, anyone who gives an important interview on the radio, anyone proposed for high office or for honours, for example, or troublemakers – extremists, those with entries in *Who's Who* and so on. I imagine the unit was set up to prevent establishment embarrassment. You don't want to knight someone to find that he is an Al-Qaeda operative, do you? It could be used in other ways, but that's not my business. There are several levels of clearance. Fortunately, mine extends to cover Marsh; there was some talk of him becoming chief executive or a big cheese at the British Cardiovascular Society. But you know if anyone finds out what I've done, if you tell a soul, I'll be toast. I'll keep the stuff and if you need it just ask. But never, ever tell anyone where you got it,' said Vince.

'You know I won't,' said Mensah.

Shrinking violets wither and die. Mensah knew he was caught in an unequal contest against powerful hospital machinery. Mensah thought what Marsh did in his own time was no one's business; but his own career was at stake. Invasive thrush thrives. Trembling, he logged on to the web page of a bespoke encrypted website designer, hoping his five hundred and fifty-six pounds would be well spent.

A few days later, Dr Marsh received a message by e-mail from the website of a Mr Gerry Lauder, of the *Hospital Medicine Watch* magazine, telling him that they were conducting a discreet investigation into the case of a vulnerable innocent junior doctor who the hospital was prosecuting for a breach of its policy. Mr Lauder went on to say that it was his understanding that the hospital had broken the law by using Blue Peter technology to conceal its breach of its own policy, whilst hypocritically pursuing the hapless doctor. In the interest of justice, if the hospital did not withdraw the case against the doctor within a week, the Trust's deceit and certain nocturnal activities by senior members of staff would be exposed to the full glare of public scrutiny. Footage of such would also be sent to colleagues, hospital shareholders and family.

'Why are you laughing? It was not easy for me,' said Mensah.

'I laugh because of the incongruity of it all: you, the photographer, the pornographer, sending dodgy e-mails, the whole shebang; and because you're learning. Thought, hoped you'd come round. Boot on your neck, you're stuck, man, you can't play by Corinthian rules. You roll and get into the trenches.' He turned serious. 'Wait and see, see what they say, they must react, do something, if they don't, escalate,' said Vince.

The next day, Mensah rang Vince again. 'No news, I might have to escalate if I don't hear soon.'

'Wait, a few more days,' said Vince.

'Tension's getting too much for me, I don't want to destroy Marsh's career, but if Ms Sherry doesn't deliver I'll go further, I'm in it now, feet first, and I mean it,' said Mensah.

'Wait two more days,' said Vince.

Two days later, Ms Sherry called Mensah. 'Do you mind coming to see me, doctor? I'll give you my personal number so you can call me if something crops up, but I'll look forward to seeing you at lunchtime; in my office.'

Ms Sherry was waiting when Mensah arrived. The receptionist had gone to lunch. Ms Sherry ushered Mensah into her office. 'You were right all along, I'm sorry,' she said. She opened the relevant files and showed Mensah the all too familiar paperwork again. 'I looked through the date sequences again on the master database and the integrated care pathway system. I must have made a mistake about the consent form, I should have gone through the sequence myself but my graduate trainee did some of it. Here, the signature's missing.'

'What does this mean, what happens next?' said Mensah.

'I'll argue that in the interest of justice and for procedural reasons it would be inappropriate for the hospital to pursue the investigations arising from Mrs Patrick's death and its aftermath,' said Ms Sherry. 'I'll prepare the documents and pass them on to the chairman of the clinical effectiveness committee, Dr Marsh, who will, in all likelihood, endorse my conclusions. You'll receive an apology. Good luck with your application.'

'Thanks,' said Mensah.

Ms Sherry went off to lunch. Mensah skipped back to his bike and pedalled home, wondering how it was that hospitals could make signatures appear and disappear.

28

John and Rachel at David and Amanda's

John and Rachel travelled up by train to Newcastle the weekend after her radio interview. After dinner Amanda went upstairs to check on Jonathan. David, John and Rachel were left in the dining-room. David was getting tired. He had been in to work that morning to check on Mr Reddick, a research subject who had been re-admitted with chest pain. Rachel cleared her throat, put down her glass of wine and looked at David. 'In life,' she said, 'there are many ups and downs, hills and valleys, trials and tribulations.' David looked up from his cup of coffee. What was his mother going on about now? Her advice and lessons about life tended to the elliptical. He hoped Amanda would stay upstairs. 'We've disagreed,' said Rachel. 'The seeds of some disagreements could be recently sown, but most serious disagreements have their genesis in the distant past, sometimes years, and between peoples, across centuries. Or let us call it "misalignment of opinion": results from events that took place before you were born. In life you have to make choices. For money, love, power, friendship, family. Some choices are deeply personal, rooted in high principle, religious faith, altruism, or in political ideology. Other decisions are grubby and shameful. If you are lucky you will not have to make the diffi-cult choices that may change the lives of the ones close to you. I'll explain.' John shuffled in his chair and leant forward. 'I'm sorry I threw a tantrum.'

'My actions years ago,' Rachel went on, 'were born out of love for you both. To protect you, and us. In the process other people may have suffered. I realised that later. If I am to be honest, I was also motivated by career. But I lacked the conviction or courage to do what was right.'

John started to say something. 'Wait, let me finish. I need to finish, then you can tell me where I went wrong. I have not been preoccupied by how I could atone for my errors, but I saw a chance to make amends. Public service, laudable, but not enough. So when I was appointed to the committee examining the implications of the dyskeratotic gene scandal I thought this was my chance to atone.'

John poured himself another cup of coffee. It was his turn to look round for Amanda. 'I'll come to the point,' said Rachel. She looked at David. 'When you chose the colour of Jonathan's eyes, it reminded me how this mess started. Physical traits motivated the Nationalists, broke up my family and led to my selfish cowardice. I was born a pair of twins. We were dizygotic twins. A rare set. Black swans. One in a million, they called us at the time. My brother was called Bode, dark as an average African–American politician like Banu Ceantemper II, say. As you can see I am completely the opposite. I seemed to take after my mum. Our father, Ibrahim Dacosta, half Nigerian of Brazilian extraction. Mum said with the passing months I got lighter and blonder and Bode got darker. I think it came as a shock to Dad – you know what some men say: "Mummy's babies, Daddy's little maybes" – something to do with his not understanding how we could both be his and yet so different. He had read about superfecundation and would not believe Mum and the doctors. Yet he refused to take a genetic test. Maybe there were already tensions. Anyway, they split up. My father left. Mother reverted to her maiden name, Coulter. Bode insisted on keeping the Dacosta name. Maybe to assert his identity. Or something like that. Mum said she understood. I kept mother's name. That's how we grew up with different names.'

Amanda walked in, sensed the tension, left to rummage in the

222

kitchen, muttered something about Jonathan and went back upstairs. Rachel paused for a sip of water and until she was sure Amanda was out of earshot.

'Bode and I never really got on. I didn't even invite him to my wedding. Anyway, he sort of didn't exist, did he? I knew Ruth quite well. She is, was, a gentle, sensitive and very religious woman. Devastated, crushed, she was. It was obvious to everyone, except Bode, that Ruth was having a breakdown. I didn't think he was doing enough to help her and I told him. So we fell out and lost contact. If I'd stayed in touch I might have been able to help, but I was angry with Bode and he was probably angry with me. I could have helped after the coalition dissolved and the ADHD laws were repealed, but Mum told me it was too late. Bode's son, Mensah, was in care. Occasionally, news came over the grapevine about Bode, that he'd gone to Nigeria and may have remarried. Looking back now, I can see how vulnerable they must have been. They were young, they had little support. That's another story. So I kept quiet, to protect you. I don't know where the boy ended up. That boy's fate is a direct result of the ADHD policy. I didn't save him then, but I couldn't let myself make the same mistake again. There's less at stake for us now than there was then. You're a grown man – with a family. You should understand. I couldn't wait. The chairman was about to bury the whole episode again, for another generation, perhaps forever. I couldn't let the government get away with another injustice. I wanted to wait until after your job interview before I told you; but the pressure on the committee to produce a report soon was too great. If I didn't act, the victims would have no voice, no establishment voice.'

David got up to lean on the dresser. 'David, were you listening? Why are you looking at me like that, David?

'Did you say Mensah?' said David.

'Yes, David, why do you ask?' said Rachel.

'It's nothing,' he said.

'I can see you're upset. Sit down. I'm sorry the media has been so cruel to you and Amanda and Jonathan. I didn't think they would go that far. That will blow away. You'll still have a successful life, better than many.'

Amanda had come back downstairs. She sat down next to David, glared at Rachel over the rim of her glass as she took a sip of water. It soon became apparent that she had heard everything. She cleared her throat.

'Excuse me, I didn't mean to intrude on this cosy party. Rachel, think how strongly you wanted to protect your family, your David, try to remember. Then can you imagine what I think of someone who puts her own guilt before my own son's happiness? I'm afraid I don't see it your way at all. I can't, and I shan't see how you can justify exposing us to this . . . this abuse, this calumny. You are an experienced woman, an economist. You claim to study and understand human behaviour. You know how government works, how the press works, you've dealt with them all your life, yet you were so naive to think your family would be spared; after your outburst. That you had a background that could be exploited and you did not tell David before you launched your crusade. John may not even have known what you meant to achieve by this, this "unburdening". Hello, didn't you know that you now had a grandson, that you just couldn't do what you wanted any more? Mum. She's suffered as well. Her friends mock her that her daughter married into a family of fraudsters. I don't mind, but you can see what this means for her and to her circle. If you're trying for expiation you've failed. I'm terribly disappointed. I'll never trust you with my Jonathan, ever again. Never. What you did then may have been selfish, but perhaps understandable. I can't judge you for what happened then, but I can for what you've done to my family now. And if this was your attitude then, maybe you do have course for remorse.'

David came over to pat his wife on the shoulder as if to calm her down and stop the torrent. She gave him back his hand.

'What you've done now may be all of a piece,' said Amanda. 'You didn't do too badly out of your initial betrayals: a husband, a career and family. How do we know you have not got some committee lined up now, that it is not all as selfless as you make out? Perhaps you've never done anything without an eye to your own advantage in your life. You haven't learned.' She swivelled round to look up at David. 'I'm sorry, David. I had to say it. These last few days have been hell, for me, my mum, even Jonathan. I'm going to bed, good-night.'

'Amanda, come back,' said David and John together.

'No, I'll see you later, sorry, David, good-night, John,' said Amanda.

David got up to follow his wife, a door slammed and Jonathan started to cry. A crestfallen David came downstairs a few minutes later. John and Rachel were in the kitchen clearing up. 'David, your wife hasn't heard the whole story. She's jumped to conclusions. I'm sure she'll understand,' said Rachel.

'I don't think so,' said John.

'Let me get this off my chest. You can crucify me later,' said Rachel. 'I started work as a researcher in the Economic Forum and have held several jobs in the Treasury in policy-making roles.'

'We know all that,' said David.

'When the Nationalists formed their coalition with the Old Conservatives I was afraid that I would be outed, I would lose my job and that you could be in danger. I was privy to some of their discussions. I knew how their minds worked. I sat through hours of meetings listening to their vile language and pretended to work, write, think, research, anything not to draw attention to myself. I told John something like the ADHD vaccine was on the cards.' John nodded. 'We couldn't be sure that we would be exempt. The ADHD programme started about eighteen months before you were born, David. If someone exposed me you would be vaccinated as well, at least that's what I thought. I was determined that nothing was to jeopardise your start. It worked. We escaped. Nothing was going to risk that. John, you knew all this, but you didn't know why I was so adamant that I didn't want to have any more children. I kept all this secret from you, I'm sorry.

225

You would have pressurised me to look for my nephew, and to me that would or could have been suicide. Remember, I knew how the coalition worked. I had to take the risk, I'm sorry. Really sorry, I've said enough, I'm hoping you'll both understand.' She drained the dregs from her wine glass, looking around for more.

'Mum,' said David. 'What are you saying, what am I hearing? You might as well say Dad's not my dad. Do you know, I don't know what to say! Disappointed, let down, disgusted, I've never let *you* down. And, Dad, you've let *me* down.'

John started to say something, but David shouted him down. 'I'm gutted, gutted, that you didn't trust me until your crisis. From where I'm standing, this looks like a self-indulgent, self-flagellating guilt trip, a free lunch for you. You owe them nothing. Between Jonathan and a group of strangers there should be no contest, except to this special forces saintly grandmother. I can see how your committee works and my remarks may have upset you. Couldn't you tell the difference between government policy and a parent's wish to give their child the best start? You did once.' He raised his voice and turned towards the hallway. 'As Amanda said, we are now in the same position you were in: a young family, a young son who also wants, needs, the best start in life. Why should that be risked? Why have you risked it? Amanda and I weren't to know. About your past, this heavy stuff between you and a twin brother. How were we to know? Sorry. We're sorry, but we were just doing what we thought was best; just like you were. When he grows up, Jonathan will probably condemn us for choosing the wrong attributes. That's a parent's fate. I understand that. I'll not sacrifice my son's prospects or my career to your cause. I've never failed at anything in my life, but I will if this gets out. Couldn't you wait until after the interviews? You knew the reaction, but you had to sacrifice my career, not yours, to this, this crusade. A few more weeks wouldn't have made much difference.'

Rachel listened, forehead in hands. David pulled his chair back to sit in it sideways. 'Did you want to punish me?' he said. 'You think I'm privileged and should put up with, welcome, this set-back because it's nothing like your new flock have had to endure. You're taking your guilt and anger for what happened to all those people out on me. Now do you feel better, do you?' said David, leaning over his mother.

Rachel looked straight into David's eyes. 'I'm not punishing you for anything. When you were a baby I used you as an excuse for my silence. Now that you're old enough, I don't have that alibi. This flock, as you call them, had no control over what was done to them. How would I face myself if I again failed to speak up? I would deserve worse condemnation if I'd lost my nerve again, and, more importantly, I would condemn myself again.'

David got up. 'Do you know how this has affected Amanda? They took photographs of her with Jonathan to print in the papers and called him the hypocrite's grandson,' he said.

'I'm sorry about that,' said Rachel. 'The media will be censured for its behaviour. I'm really sorry; for everything.'

'How could you leave Dad out? When would you have told us? When Jonathan went to school, or at his wedding? I'm going to bed, to get my head round uncles, nephews, a cousin in care, silent victims – can all this be my fault?' asked David. He tiptoed halfway up the stairs, turned round, and came back downstairs.

He stood in the dining-room doorway, arms on hips.

'Something's been bugging me. We have a Mensah at work, doesn't sound as if he was in care, but he's the right age and was brought up here. Jesus, Mensah could be my cousin. It just gets better Mum, just what I need, a fucking long-lost cousin in the same hospital department, going for the same bloody job.'

'David, calm down,' said Rachel.

But David had stormed back upstairs, ignoring Amanda who was in Jonathan's room trying to get him to sleep.

After a quiet breakfast the next morning, John and Rachel left for the airport by taxi.

29

John's Response

The older a secret, the greater its explosive impact. John unloaded the luggage in silence when they got home. He abjured confrontation. Rachel was Rachel, he would never win. 'You're quiet,' said Rachel.

'I've nothing to say,' said John.

'Come on, John, spit it out, don't you make life difficult for me as well. What are you thinking?' said Rachel.

'No cause is bigger than my, our, son's welfare,' he said. 'All these years, you kept secrets away in your head. How many years have we been together? I'm shocked, dead, numbed. David made his case. You did too. You know I'm not good with words. You know. I resisted a row at David's. It wouldn't do for us to argue there, would it? I don't think much of your crusade either. You kept this to yourself for nearly four decades. I didn't know you as well as I thought I did then; how do you think I feel? I was shocked and humiliated last night. Twin brother, father in Nigeria, David has an uncle, a cousin. You wouldn't have told us if the media had not forced you to, would you? You could have told me before we went up to see David, certainly before your newspaper article. You've taken me for granted. Where is this nephew? We may be able to make amends. Only posterity would judge whether you were right not to look after your nephew. I'm open and broad-minded enough to understand why some so strongly oppose *in vitro* fertilization in those capable of conceiving naturally. I understand why you don't like the selection of presumed advantageous traits, as you say "like choosing sweets in a supermarket". Your exposure to the Nationalists sensitised you to Aryanism, I understand all that completely. But you are being oversensitive and unfair.'

'Why do you say that?' said Rachel.

'Because David insists that their choice of blue eyes was an innocent afterthought. It was not social or aesthetic. Knowing him, knowing Amanda, I have my doubts, but that's not the issue, it doesn't matter. None of us is perfect. I wish you would understand that. I'm trying to understand why you hid your family from view, all this time. Yes, I can see why in the early days after the coalition, but for decades?'

John stormed out. He closed the door, but it bounced back open off a doorstop. He walked up to the top of the road and for twenty minutes sat on an empty grit dispenser. He did not want to go to the pub, he did not want to talk to anyone while he was feeling this way. So he went for a run around the block, a familiar route. When he got home, an hour and a half later, he could see that Rachel was preparing their traditional peace offering: dumplings. He could also smell baking. Anger, in spite of itself, was smitten by associative gastronomy. He gave Rachel a hug – more a grasp – and went up for a shower.

Later, during supper, he asked, 'You've told me everything?'

'Yes,' said Rachel.

'Why didn't you tell me?' asked John.

'I didn't think you needed to know, I wanted to protect you from yourself. You would have tried to help and made it worse. That's what I thought. Did I do the right thing? No, now I know I was wrong. I've let you and David down. David will not be the same. We will not be the same to him.'

'We can help David if we pull together,' said John. 'I'm sure we can, but you'll have to give up this dyskeratotic protest. Finish

229

what you've started, then stop. No more interviews or articles. I'm sure the patients' group will understand if you want to spend more time with your family; after the sacrifices you've made. I love you, for who you are, I don't really care about anything else. If you want, we can scale down our work, downsize, maybe look for your nephew. Find out whether your Mensah is the same Mensah David was talking about. And if he isn't we can keep looking, but that's if you want to. If he's fine, it may reassure you, give you closure, and if he's not we can help. But let's not rush, and for heaven's sake don't go barging in to David's hospital. For all we know, even if this Mensah is your nephew, he's built his own life and may be just as shocked as we were. I'll cancel my lecture engagements so we can plan this together.'

Rachel squeezed John's hand, and went to the oven to check on the date and walnut cake. 'I've seen her a few times,' she said.

'Who?' said John.

'Ruth,' said Rachel.

'Where?'

'At the hospital: when I go fell-walking up there I see her at the hospital. It occurred to me once while I was up there that I could help, at least visit. I didn't tell anyone who I was, I just attached myself to the volunteers, Friends of the Hospital,' said Rachel. 'I explained to the sister in confidence because I didn't want to deceive them, and they let me come as long as I was not exploiting Ruth or being nosy. I wore a wig, blonde curls.'

'Rachel, I don't know what to say. You said you'd told me everything, now this.'

'It wasn't important, and I only saw her once or twice a year when she was in hospital, I don't think Ruth recognised me, I didn't visit her at home,' said Rachel.

30

Mensah Returns to Work

With ten days to the close of applications, Ms Sherry confirmed that Mensah could return to work. When Mensah reported to the intervention suite for duty, Mrs Viv Knight, the secretary, handed him his security badges and the week's rota. Mensah scanned it quickly. 'Hey, it's all drug study work, I have only one instead of three restorative interventional sessions this week. Where's all the valve work I used to do? That can't have all gone in a few weeks?'

'It's not for me to say, Mensah. Dr Timms draws up the rota now, have a word with him.'

'I will,' said Mensah.

Quizzical looks greeted Mensah as he scrubbed up to help the professorial team with a drug trial comparing the effect of a new anti-ischemic agent on cardiac arteriolar and venous circulation. 'Nice to have you back,' said sister.

'Thanks, not sure about all this drug work, I'm being done up,' said Mensah. He threaded the third guide wire round a corkscrew in the millimetre-diameter distal branch of Mr Albright's cardiac vein as Dr Paul Board, the specialist registrar, watched. A smaller, more distal vein would give more accurate results, but Mensah felt rusty and did not want to push his luck; a perforation could cause severe bleeding or damage to the underlying muscle. 'I'm chickening out here, we'll get some good data from

this vein, if they don't like it they can come and do it themselves.'
He was not going to give anyone another excuse to suspend him.

Mensah's PDA went off. 'Please come to the physiology department. Mrs Luger has fallen off the treadmill and landed on Trace. You know Trace: she's twelve weeks pregnant. She's so tiny; I think she's cracked a rib or two.'

'Why doesn't the trial coordinator sort it out?' said Mensah. But Trace could be hurt; he could deal with the berk who had arranged such a mismatch later. Mrs Luger, a rather large woman, was still breathless when he arrived.

'Sorry, Mrs Luger, the treadmill was too strong for you, thank you for taking part. Are you all right?'

'I'm fine, I hope your colleague is all right. I warned them I was never good at sports; my legs are too short. I've never walked that fast in my life.'

Mensah was about to tell Mrs Luger that she was on the easiest stage of the protocol, but thought better of it. 'I'm glad you're all right, we'll get some scans done to make sure you haven't broken anything. Jerry, can you take Trace and Mrs Luger in your buggy please?' The two women sat in the buggy side by side and Jerry drove them to their tests. 'Don't forget to go to the occupational health department,' he shouted after Trace. Trace nodded, one hand on chest, the other on her pregnant abdomen. 'Are you going to fill in an incident form, whose trial is this?' asked Mensah.

'It's one of David's,' said Patrick, the trial coordinator.

'I think you should,' said Mensah. He would too. Amanda, one of the other coordinators, probably wouldn't; she liked David, so he would have to rely on Patrick, perhaps even Trace and Mrs Luger, to report the incident to trigger a formal complaint against David. 'I'm off now, back to theatre, glad everybody's cured.'

At lunch, Mensah sought David out in his new office on the consultants' floor. 'Do you like my new office?' David asked.

'The rota's lopsided. You've fixed it, haven't you?' said Mensah.

'I've done no such thing, just doing what I'm told. Adam

Maginot and David Marsh asked me to; they said it would be more efficient; didn't want you rushing back into RC until you were back into the swing.'

'And when did they expect me to get back into this swing?'

'Don't know. I guess that's for you to say or decide. I don't suppose . . .'

'Well, tell them I'm ready.'

'Tell them yourself,' said David.

'I will,' said Mensah, and he walked up the stairs to the professor's office. The professor was not in, and by the time he got there Mensah had thought better of confronting the two senior consultants.

Later, Mensah was sitting at his workstation wolfing down an illicit sandwich when he was surprised by a tap on his shoulder from Nurse Daviniesta. 'Hello,' he said, attempting to cover his guilt, and embarrassment, by making a clenched fist across his face. 'I know you are on the infection-control team, I was just going back to . . .'

'Never mind.' She smiled, moving a little closer than was needed, and with a slight brush against Mensah, she sat down on an office chair. She swivelled towards him, legs together in elegant repose. 'Sorry to intrude, I'm working on an audit of perioperative infections. Every four months, as you may know, I take samples from all the operators to check for bugs – MRSA and so on – to reduce hospital-care-associated infections. I also help in theatre. Could you spare me a few minutes to help with my data collection for the next audit meeting? As you work with all the consultants who use the theatre, it would help my presentation – make it more personal, more authentic and interesting if I knew the preferences, you know, whether the consultants prefer particular manufacturers of theatre equipment. We will be going to tender soon and we want to make sure you all get what you want wherever possible,' said Daviniesta.

'Can't you extract the data from the database?' he said.

'I looked, what I need's not on the database,' she replied.

Mensah was not sure whether he wanted to help anyone with anything. He would end up doing all the work for nothing, save for the odd nodded acknowledgement. *They flew up the greasy pole while he propped it up*, he'd read somewhere of duped juniors. This was the second time Daviniesta had asked him for help with a project. 'I have a lot on my plate at the moment, I'm sorry, I don't think I can help you, ask one of the others, or I can ask one of the registrars for you,' said Mensah.

'It won't take long – I just need your help to make sure I've got the right information and that I understand the material. It should be a doddle for you,' said Daviniesta.

'I'm sorry,' said Mensah.

Daviniesta got up and turned away, hurt more than she cared to admit. She had got him wrong. Daviniesta was cross with herself because she felt humiliated; Mensah, because he had lost his composure. His grandpa's advice rang in his ears: 'Never let anyone see how upset you are, ever.' He remembered reading this in the old man's diary: 'You have not been born in a phase of human history in which you will succeed in life by losing your temper.' Mensah could not explain why he had been so dismissive of Daviniesta's project. Perhaps because she had not asked how he felt after his return to work, perhaps because he felt he was being used: she was trying to use her wiles to get him to do what she wanted; or because he cared for her more than he wanted to admit but was frustrated that he had not taken the initiative, and if he worked on a formal project with her, he risked his longings collapsing into the boring platonic. Daviniesta, on her part, had Mensah down as cheerful and open but now thought he was an obnoxious, selfish, chippy Geordie.

To assuage his guilt for his rudeness, Mensah took lunch at the same station whenever he could, hoping that Daviniesta would ask him again. When she did not come he sought her on the nurse's floor. 'Daviniesta is on holiday,' said Mrs Monmy, the tutor.

'Would you be so kind as to let me know when she might be back, because we should be working on an audit presentation.'

'She told me about that . . . she has gone off the idea and was thinking of asking one of the trainees to take it over. She'll be back next week,' said Mrs Monmy.

Drat, boobed again, thought Mensah.

Mensah had been quiet until his coy request. 'Vince, promise you won't laugh,' said Mensah. They were on the quayside nursing canned drinks and looking over the Tyne at the gleaming Baltic Centre. Mensah did not feel like going out, but Vince had convinced him to come out to enjoy the autumnal lights.

'I won't laugh, but I can't promise, what have you done now?' said Vince.

Mensah told Vince about Daviniesta. 'I find myself thinking about her, all the time,' Mensah said. 'You know I was speaking to the ward sister at my mother's hospital the other day and I imagined I was speaking to Daviniesta. I forgot to ask when my mother would be discharged. It's the same at work: at the mortality and morbidity meeting I did not take in a single detail, not a jot, luckily I did not have to present. It is as if nothing else matters. I'm afraid that in this mood I'll make a balls up of an angiogram or reconstruction. That's frightening, I can hardly stop work. I'm all right on the surface but all over the place underneath, simply not right. I don't even feel like clubbing. All my hormones are normal; I've checked the receptors as well: they're all good so it's not that. I'm not ill, but I feel off centre, off beam, I'm teetering, but without stabilisers. I thought I saw her on the street the other day, but it wasn't her. I'm edgy, jumpy. I should be preparing for this interview but I can't seem to concentrate, it's as if I'm coming down with something all the time, but I'm not sick. Yet I can't go back to being normal. Where is she? I don't know where she is. Logic says she is on holiday and will come back, but fear tells me different and fear is winning.'

Vince stood up to go. 'Sit down, you're not going, I've not finished yet,' said Mensah.

'Don't worry, I wasn't going anywhere, just teasing,' said Vince.

'She smiled at me, once, but I can't wait for her to do it again. I want it to happen again; the way her eyes light up – I want to see that it was not a dream. I hope she's not angry with me out of contempt, but in exasperation. Then I may have a chance of getting back into her good books.'

'Her pants,' said Vince.

'No, well yes, and that too, but not like that. It's not just lust, I might be getting a Madonna complex, that's what's so frightening. What if she doesn't like me? She might be on holiday with her boyfriend or lover. She's probably having a whale of a time on a yacht on some sun-kissed island while I stew here,' said Mensah. 'I imagine her with him, whoever he is, and want to puke.'

'It could be a she,' said Vince.

'You're not helping,' said Mensah.

'What's wrong with me? In Nigeria they'd call this magic, someone taking hold and control of your mind.'

'You asked me not to laugh,' said Vince. 'But you are funny. You need to find her, and don't mess about. As for a boyfriend, don't let that bother you, almost everyone is in some phase of an attachment, a relationship of sorts. You can't wait for an absolutely free agent to come along, if such exists. Even free agents are in what I call virtual relationships; there's someone, near or far, dead even, they still feel for. But if she's married, that's another question, move on. Promise me, though, that you will not fail to try. I'm curious. It's called growing up, my son.'

'You're patronising me,' said Mensah.

'See if you still believe that in a few weeks,' said Vince. 'Remember the Sierra twins you pined for as a boy? Well, this is the grown-up version.'

'What do you know about it?' said Mensah. 'Enough, more than you do,' said Vince.

* * *

Mensah could not see what was happening to him. The rationalist unravelling, his cerebral cortex rearranged by remote control. He could not explain it, but he had lost the curiosity to look up his symptoms, and even if he had the inclination, he would not know where to look. These chemical reactions, pheromones, bio-magnetic signals, physiological or psychological, whatever they were, they drew him to Daviniesta, inexorably, as wasps are drawn to light, and Christmas embraces turkeys.

31

David's Turmoil

David did not remember how he used to poke fun at minorities. He did not ask himself whether he would have called the Ghanaian locum anaesthetist a smoked Irishman or asked Mensah to get his togs if he had known what he knew now. He did not ask whether he had taken for granted his expectations of himself and others of him. He had never doubted that these were his birthright or questioned whether his achievements were influenced by his mother's decision. But others now seemed to, or so he thought. He had recurring nightmares. In one, he was a bird about to fly the nest. In the split second before he leapt off, he looked round to his parents for reassurance, but found they had turned into serpents. A voice told him that he had no choice but to flap hard and fly, flap hard or die, flap hard or die. In another dream, millions of blue-eyed babies flew towards him as he hurtled round a wind tunnel in a prototype sports car until he was brought to a shuddering halt by the impact on the windscreen of a brown-eyed baby, its arms encircling tentacles. David woke up once with a start at five o'clock for fourteen terrifying minutes, his heart beating wildly and rapidly in atrial fibrillation. No one else at work could remember any of their nightmares. 'Count yourself lucky that you get any sleep. Good lord, you even remember your dreams!' said Dr Kitner, a pathologist, himself a new father.

To Amanda's dismay, where he used to roar in like a lion and, after victory, emerge like a mouse, David's carnal attempts simulated the flaccid futility of trying to poke the soft end of plastic treasury tags through a bulk of misaligned punch holes. So he avoided humiliation by pretending to work on his letters or read a book, and he developed a sudden interest in the *Book at Bedtime* slot on the radio. He had a surreptitious slug of whisky before he got into bed, and drowned the aroma in toothpaste and aftershave. In desperation, he scoured the delicatessen's shelves for supplements but was too embarrassed to ask for advice or write himself a prescription.

One evening, David came out of the bathroom to get into bed to find that his radio was disconnected, his book hidden away and Amanda sitting up with arms folded. 'I've had enough of this,' she said. 'And don't tell me you are tired or busy because you're not. Have you got someone else? If you have, tell me,' she said. 'None of this is my fault. You may or may not get the job, but that's not my fault. You said yourself that your mother's views and what she said do not change you as a person or as a cardiologist. I've supported you; all the way. I was there with you. Now I'm at the end, the absolute end of my tether. You don't enjoy my food; even Jonathan, our son, you seem to tire of after a few minutes – no more bathtime play, nothing. Haven't you noticed he has stopped crawling to you? Don't do this. We can be happy, job or no job. Seek help. I will. Let me help.' She leant towards him for a kiss, but he turned away.

'How do you know I'm not tired? Can't you see how much I've got on my plate? I've got to overturn disciplinary points I got the other day for swearing when I learned that the supplier of our surgical gloves was to be changed. I'm not sure I like these new clothes you bought after you had Jonathan. They make you look frumpy. The other day I saw a speck of blood in the toilet basin again. You know how it puts me off. We agreed, no blood, you're not a teenager,' said David. 'I asked you to suspend your cycles until we are ready again for another child, but you refused.'

Wounding retaliatory retorts considered and discarded, Amanda bit her tongue. 'Sort yourself out,' she said, turned her back and pretended to go to sleep. But when after an hour she could not, she went to lie on the spare bed in Jonathan's room.

David wondered whether Amanda still wanted him. After all, if the tables were turned he would not accept a pig in the poke. She had taken him as a package. But was he still what she wanted? Had he detected a new contempt in her voice last night or was she just angry or sad? They had chosen the right traits for Jonathan but could not hide or erase his racial heritage. They hoped it did not matter. At least, that is what the mainstream politicians said. But could Jonathan be turfed out with the turn of the economic tide one day?

32

The Selection Process

Professor Adam Maginot, head of cardiology, chaired the monthly meeting of the senior cardiac consultants in the magnificent new boardroom lined with photographs and paintings of eminent consultants who had worked at Freeman Hospital. A few, like Mr Lindsay, still visited the hospital to gossip and pass the time. This meeting was to choose a preferred candidate for the consultant in restorative cardiology to be appointed that autumn. Their choice was not binding on the selection committee, but in a sense it was because most of the appointments foisted on the consultants failed. But the consultants had made a few ricks themselves. Mr Edison, in respiratory medicine, was nicknamed 'Elbonics' for the ruthless way in which he got rid of three of the consultants who appointed him.

'This is an international hospital earning us millions of pounds, an asset to the country, to the area and to us. We are custodians. Look around you,' he said, pointing at the portraits of former consultants. 'These are the giants on whose shoulders we stand, and some of us rest, the founding fathers of our hospital. Think of our reputation. Whatever we think of the world outside, think of what they think of us. We have an international clientele, an important constituency in the Middle and Far East in particular. They have an image of this country. You've met some of these clients yourselves. You've heard me talk about this before. I agree, we are no longer a country of bowler hats and warm beer, but if that is what the customer wants, and thinks, in this competitive world it has never been more important to meet their expectations. Health tourism demands a unique experience, unique to the host country. It is in that sense that I appeal to you to consider carefully the merits of the candidates for the post in restorative cardiology,' said Professor Maginot.

Dr Marsh squirmed in his seat. Professor Simon Rodell spoke softly: 'Adam, I see and understand your point of view, but we are a teaching hospital, not a museum. As for this tourism business, they can go visit the Tower of London and Hadrian's Wall after we have fixed their dodgy valves, not before. First, let us base our choice on the agreed criteria for assessing trainees, let's use these and not be unduly influenced by wishy-washy custom and tradition. Are they now going to pick our staff for us? We have three excellent internal candidates: Mensah, David and Lisa. No doubt we will attract a few more when the advert formally goes out. Broadly, there are two approaches to this sort of appointment – we define the job and choose someone to do it, or we choose the person and make the job fit them. I favour the former. It seems to me to be more objective. Let us not rush and decide anything today as we all agree that there will be little to choose between the . . .'

'Simon, character, essence, chemistry – these are all important too,' said Dr James Devilish. 'I agree with Adam. Choosing a colleague involves several subjective factors, these are the intangibles. Remember, this is a relationship that can be closer and certainly longer than most marriages. It's probably as costly if you get it wrong.' Dr Guardian, head of imaging, flinched inwardly. He was on to his third family, but he was heir to some earldom and could afford it. Devilish went on: 'Even in this technological age, post-modern some call it, we do not choose our partners by the book. I don't expect to fall in love with my colleague, but I'd like to be able to get on with them. Science combined with intuition, intuitive science,' he said, looking pleased.

'Then why do we bother filling in all those assessment forms?' asked Dr Cracknell.

'To see who has the basic qualities to be appointed; after that it depends on indefinable criteria,' said Professor Maginot.

'Adam, we'll fall into the old trap again, we lost our freedom to appoint because we did not move with the times. This all sounds like the old system by the back door – the talk, walk, look, think like me policy,' muttered Professor Rodell.

'Why don't we wait a bit longer, before we make a recommendation?' said Dr John Dickens, cardiac pathologist.

'Because, unlike you, we are not used to thinking in geological time,' said Dr Bell, cardiac-care-unit supremo, 'we need to make up our minds, so that we can place the unsuccessful candidates as soon as possible. It will be unhelpful both to the candidates and to our reputation if we cannot resolve this matter quickly. We could end up with an unhappy ship. Everyone's here, so can we have a show of hands?'

By the end of the protracted meeting, four new candidates were added to the shortlist for the consultant job. An extra post had been added based on the European mainland for a year before returning to the main hospital base in Newcastle – the consolation prize. Piotr Polanski from Poland had somehow managed to get himself into several photographs with Professor Maginot at the European Society of Cardiology meeting in Krakow that autumn and was on the shortlist, as was a Dr John O'Donotstent. Mensah and David were also shortlisted. Lisa did not apply. Perhaps she had had the same talk from Professor Maginot. No one seemed to know much about Hong and Saluter, the other two candidates.

In the week before the interview, Mensah received a good luck card from Mrs Baker, a patient he had treated for a serious post-operative infection. There was also one from Mrs Wallace, the patient who had known him as a boy.

243

33

Interview Day

Mensah got up at two o'clock in the morning on Thursday, interview day. He went to the wardrobe to make sure that his blue suit and white shirt and the tie Nancy had bought him for Christmas were still where he had left them three hours earlier. The shirt's collar was made of special absorbent and biological haem enzyme that dissolved blood specks and stains from shaving nicks. Its designer, Harry Leviathan, was the unofficial patron saint of interviewees during the recession. The shirt fell off its hanger. Mensah grabbed it, but not before the left cuff swept the floor. 'Oh, boring,' he said. He switched the main lights on to inspect the shirt, but he could not find the clothes brush. Shirt in his left hand, he walked sideways through the doors to the bathroom to wash his right hand, dried it on a towel, inspected it to make sure it was dry, could not be sure, sat on the bed with the shirt held as high above his head as he could manage and blew his hand dry. Satisfied, he brushed the specks of dust off the shirt sleeve, but he could still see a faint residual imprint. He looked for a replacement, and when he could not find one gave the sleeve another wipe. A tube of correction fluid left by the previous owner on the top wardrobe shelf caught his eye. But it was solid. Then he wondered why he had not put the shirt back in the wardrobe while he washed his hands. 'What's wrong with me?' he said.

He put his tie up against the shirt and, standing in front of the mirror, put the tie on. He did not like the length and it took him four attempts to get it right. He loosened the tie with the bow intact, and hung it over his shirt hanger. He put a pen in his outside suit pocket, then inside, then out again, sought another pen to put inside and secured the pair of trousers on to the hanger with a peg. It was three o'clock. Mensah turned his attention to the threadbare vest he wore for all his interviews. With the radio tuned to Radio 3 on low volume it took him two movements of a sonata by Bach to decide that he would not wear his lucky charm singlet, but he would keep it close, in the back of his car. He shrugged his shoulders; he was not going to get this job anyway, but he shuddered to dispel the thought, recognising in it his dad's influence. He listened to another half an hour of Radio 3, went back to bed, got up at four, shaved, nicked himself and sat with his chin in a towel for fifteen minutes.

At six he had breakfast. Then he drove up to the hospital, slowly. He did not want a collision to upset his plans. He paid for his ticket and sat in the car for an hour waiting. The library did not open until eight thirty. He gathered his papers, checked the interview times again and looked in the vanity mirror once more. Daviniesta. Flicking the vanity mirror back to, he turned round and could not have sprung out of the car any faster if it was on fire.

'Daviniesta, Daviniesta,' he shouted, running after her. She slowed down, cocking her ears to the left. She turned, saw him and stopped.

'Hello,' she said. Mensah wanted to crawl back to the safety of his car, but he could not give up now.

'I, I saw you,' he said.

'Yes, I can see you too, you look smart,' she said.

'I'm attending the consultant interview this afternoon,' said Mensah. On a fresh autumnal morning after a nice shower and a cool shave he felt as hot and sticky as a freshly minted bottle-fed baby's turd. 'Did you have a good break?' he said. He did

245

not want to evoke sunny warm lands and passionate lovemaking by saying holiday.

'Yes, I did, very, thank you for asking, are you going in to the hospital?' she said.

'Yes, I am,' said Mensah, and walked beside her to the main hospital entrance. Just as he was going to ask her out, he remembered that he had left all his papers in the briefcase in his unlocked car. 'Oh, no,' he said.

'What's wrong?' she asked.

'I'm sorry, I've got to go, you smell nice, I've left my briefcase in the car, please can I see you about the project audit, and a drink one of these days – you were away – if you want to, that is; if not, just put it down to interview nerves, I'll call you.' He hurried off before Daviniesta could reply.

David kissed Amanda and Jonathan. 'You look the part. I like your new suit, when did you get these shoes?' she said.

'I feel the part, the suit's Italian,' he said. 'If they're right, Maginot and co, if they're right there's nothing to fear. It's an open one, no quota, no burka, no affirmative action or diversity issues, just a straightforward contest. Shouldn't have a problem. One more kiss?' he said, pointing at his lips. Amanda kissed him. David hopped into his car and arrived at the hospital in fifteen minutes.

'Hello, sister, I've come to see Mrs Hay,' he said.

'We weren't expecting you, Dr Timms, we thought you were at the interviews. It's going to be a walk-over,' said Sister Wright.

'I just came to say hello to her; hello, Mrs Hay, I won't see you properly today, I'll see you tomorrow, sister will explain.'

'My word, doctor, if only I were a few years younger . . .' she giggled.

'Steady on, ma'am,' said sister.

'Right, I'm off now, see you tomorrow. And who knows? In another guise!' said David.

'Good luck, but you don't need it,' said the sister.

In the interview waiting-room David recognised Hong from his drubbing at the World Congress, and O'Donotstent he had seen around. Piotr Polanski from Poland was either late or had dropped out.

Mensah was already there and conversing with the other applicants. 'Hi, we met at Harrogate, at the Bio-magnetics in Coronary Intervention study day,' said Mensah.

'That's right, I hear you're one of the internal candidates,' replied O'Donotstent.

'Yeah, but not always a good thing, more pressure,' said Mensah.

'Anyway, good luck, I've never been to Newcastle, looks a nice city.'

'Great city, I was born here, if you get the job, I'll show you around; if you don't, it will be even more of a pleasure,' said Mensah.

'You're on.'

'Mind if I look at your newspaper?' said Mensah.

'Go on, don't read them, rely on radio, but the headline grabbed me.'

'You mean the law to get people back to work at seventy-five if they've been retired for more than ten years? Or if they won't their relatives will have to pay more tax. It'll never happen.' Mensah took the newspaper to the window, and scanned it quickly. O'Donotstent was right: it was full of rubbish. Through the heavily glazed windows Mensah could see, but not hear, the school run traffic. Daviniesta intruded. Mensah extruded her from his mind. But she kept returning like a software pop-up ad. Mrs Farr, an assistant in the human resources department, came in.

'Good afternoon, doctors.'

'Good afternoon,' they murmured.

'You'll be called in alphabetical order. Sir Li Tang, chairman of the board, will chair the panel. There are eight other panellists. You know Ms Sherry.'

Ms Sherry bowed. 'I'll be in the room to help the interview run smoothly. The chairman's there to ensure fair play. You will

247

be notified by PD the next day and a formal offer of contract will be sent through the post. Any questions?'

'When will the successful candidate be expected to start?' asked David.

'Three months after the formal offer of appointment,' said Ms Sherry.

O'Donotstent emerged from his interview with a rueful smile. 'They're bastards, especially Maginot,' he said. 'You'd think I'd never met him, beastly man.' Mensah knew that old trick, designed to put off the remaining candidates. He ignored the Irishman.

Years later, when asked by friends, David could still recall many of the questions, and his answers. Maginot started:

'Where do you see yourself in five years?'

David said, 'I see myself building on your foundations; leading a scientifically, clinically and commercially successful and expanding multidisciplinary team, taking medical care from the test tube and the laboratory to the bedside; and from the bedside to the laboratory, using every clinical encounter as an opportunity for service, teaching and research.'

('I really also wanted to say I would get rid of that obnoxious toad Mrs Winalotte. That I would sack Westerman – he doesn't know a test tube from a tube test; just regurgitates what others tell him at conferences. I wanted to say to the hairy one sitting in the corner, half asleep, his name escapes me – Jacobi, something like that – I wanted to say, "What are you doing here! All you do is edit children's science books and obstruct progress." But I didn't, daren't.')

Rodell asked: 'Why are you the best person for this job?'

'My record speaks for itself.'

'And what is this record, if I may crave the chairman's indulgence?' said Rodell.

'I've always been top of my class, one of the youngest, won many prizes, and have excelled at each point of my training. I don't make excuses, but I don't see why I should understate my achievements; by any measure I am the best for this job.'

Rodell, arms folded, rolled his eyes and sighed. Marsh smiled. The others were busy scribbling.

('I felt it was in the bag, we were acting out a charade,' David later confessed.)

Bell asked: 'Should doctors receive bonus payments?' David had wanted to say: 'Eggheads like you will make up the rules, do little work, divide the spoils and leave those at the coalface worse off.' Instead, he said, 'I support a system that rewards hard work as long as it does not detract from the wider and primary responsibility to patient care and the organisational ethos and it does not undermine teamwork. Criteria for bonuses should be pre-specified and changed every few years to reduce gaming.'

At one point in the interview, David caught Maginot's eye, but the professor looked away. 'Adam Maginot was an excellent actor, no one could have known what we had discussed or what he was thinking, he put up a convincing charade, talk of inscrutable,' said David, later. 'He even asked me what I would do if I was not appointed. I was going to say he was joking, but I said I would continue to improve my qualifications and experience and had discussed the possibility with my referees and hoped not to have to take their excellent advice.'

Mensah noticed that some of the boardroom's artefacts, paintings and vases were Chinese and Japanese. Maybe, if he was successful, he would have his portrait up there one day.

Marsh asked Mensah how he would deal with a difficult colleague. Mensah wanted to say: 'I'm not sure why you ask this question. Have you been out with the dogs again? How did you get the hospital to change its position on my disciplinary points?' He said instead: 'First, patient care is paramount. If patient care is not jeopardised, a difficult clinician is defined by the viewer's vantage point. If I am correct in assuming that the colleague in question is difficult all the time then the normal rules of everyday social intercourse should suffice – subtle pressure from those who understand the person to improve the working environment.' He wanted to add: 'The head of nursing governance and performance drives me mad with all that jargon manager speak – "piece of work", "unpick the data", "blue sky thinking"; all that cheek-splitting, undoing the Gordian knot gobbledegook.'

Next question: 'How do you justify your expensive speciality when many in the world barely have enough to eat?'

Mensah hated that sort of 'why do we have the Albert Hall and the Royal Opera House when we can build schools and hospitals?' type question. Normally, in a pub, he would refuse to join in the argument, or, at home, he would shout at the radio, but he was neither in a pub nor at home and Lady Ballarum was not the radio. 'I can only do what is best for each of my patients and hope that philosophers and politicians can answer your question, ma'am. As I understand it, other measures – continuous revolution, oppression and violence, to ensure equality and equality of access in society – have been tried and failed.'

Lady Ballarum looked puzzled. Mensah thought he sounded pompous, but he did not care; it was what he thought. The chairman coughed, raised his brows at Dr Bell, who nodded. He had no supplementary questions.

To Professor Maginot's predictable question about where Mensah saw himself in five years, he gave his rehearsed answer. Of course, he really wanted to say: 'I'm not sure whether I'll still be around – I applied for this job because it was the next step in my career. What would you have me do, apply to be a security guard? You know where I should be or where you want me in five years, in the gutter somewhere, or doing some lackey's dead-end job. If I do fall ill I'll retire; the day I retire I'll do a hand-brake turn in a Bugatti Veyron in the consultant car park over and over again until the tyres go bald. I'll take my last official ward round, then return wearing full African regalia – wig on head, *agbada*, a cap, chains, the works – jiving to a heavy beat on my MP player, wearing large earrings, with a South London walk, pretend hip-hop limp on the left leg, a large, artificial, pendulous bosom that smothers the patients when I bend over to examine them so they can neither see nor hear me. And after that, on my last day, I'll register my cardiology escort service, providing support for patients with heart disease on their holidays, and when we get to the first port I'll check them into the nearest hospital while I complete the cruise and collect them on my way back. If I'm not married I'll apply to be chief experimenter for new street drugs; if I am I'll write smutty books for the suburbs.'

Professor Maginot thanked the candidates on behalf of the committee, and the official members of the panel and the board chairman, Sir Li Tang (in the United Kingdom for the autumn and whose absence had delayed the process), retired to vote. Representatives from the medical colleges did not have a vote and were free to leave.

The vote was split, with Mensah and David tied in first place. Marsh had been surprised to see that Maginot had voted for Hong. *What was he playing at?* he thought to himself. After a complicated process of recasting votes, in which the result still remained tied, Sir Li Tang was left to cast his deciding ballot. It all hinged on this.

Sir Li Tang spoke in a clear voice; he did not need a microphone. 'I thank you all for taking the time to attend and make up this appointments committee. I know how busy you are,' he said. 'I see how difficult it is for us to choose between such talented candidates. It's not the first time we have seen this problem. There's indeed nothing to choose between them. In this situation it is customary for the chairman to go for, to plump for one or the other candidate.' He stopped and took a sip of water and waited a few seconds to make sure he did not cough. 'As a major, *the* major shareholder, our approach has been to do things differently – a new beginning, every day,' he said, quoting the company motto. Marsh thought he saw the chairman smile again. He was usually very serious in public. 'I see that these candidates are excellent and have your strong support. Choosing one over the other could, or would be divisive. Perhaps Mensah displays a greater capacity for empathy, and a collegiate approach but may be too good to be true. David exudes an old-fashioned dash of brilliant self-confidence. Their achievements are humbling. Undoubtedly they have the ability to succeed in any field. But no candidate has been able to land a knockout blow, and we have to think of the long-term interest of the department, the hospital. What do we do? Divide the hospital, the department, down the middle, or do we look for another solution? I always look to tradition in this situation; your western tradition, our eastern ways, at face value they are far apart, but we have a lot in common, including a sense of compromise, and it is in this spirit that I am going to make a suggestion. Some of us will be disappointed whatever I decide, but let's think of Freeman and our patients. May I suggest Dr Hong. He's also excellent, but underestimated because he's, as you say, self-deprecating. His body language is submissive, almost apologetic, but he is learning how to carry himself here. I believe, know even, that his appointment will be exciting and, as you say, he ticks many boxes. Shareholders, especially in the Middle and Far East, will be thrilled that we have drawn from a wide pool of talent. Many more from afar will come to these shores for treatment knowing that our outlook has changed. I can almost guarantee that you will be more likely to get the investment we need to improve the already excellent cardiac facilities, particularly the genetic transfer modular theatre.'

Rodell tapped his fingers; he had not seen that coming. Marsh stared at Maginot. Jacobi could not hide his glee. A coup, it was not such a boring stitch-up committee this time.

Li Tang continued: 'Therefore, I strongly advise you to appoint Hong. Even if we had not arrived at this stalemate I would have made the same call. In my opinion, he answered the questions at least as well, if not better than the other candidates. He also has an unblemished disciplinary record and is unlikely to be embarrassed by political association.'

Marsh raised a finger. He was going to say something to support David, then changed his mind and put it down again. It might have come out wrong and it would be politic not to oppose the chairman. His heart sank. If the main shareholders could hijack a clinical appointment then there was little chance of his being appointed chief executive. For all he knew his web stalkers could start again, but he had not heard from them since the consent form affair. He wondered whether the chairman knew about his night-time escapades. Now he understood why Li Tang had been so cross when he'd learned that the charges against Mensah had been dropped. But Marsh did not think he had a choice. Li Tang must have always wanted to get his own man in on the quiet but had been forced to break cover by the stalemate. Or maybe he had engineered the deadlock with Maginot. Whatever happened, there was nothing they could do but to obey the chairman. He held the purse strings. To obstruct him would be self-immolation.

'Should we vote?' said the chairman. On the third vote, Hong was unanimously appointed to the post of consultant in restorative cardiology at Freeman and honorary associate professor to the University of Shanghai at Durham. The consolation-prize post was left open.

Professor Maginot gathered his papers. He went up to the chairman. 'Congratulations, sir, excellent summary and biblical conclusion, if you don't mind my simile.'

Sir Li Tang bowed. 'Difficult decision but correct, I leave it to you to placate your colleagues, but it was in everyone's interest that we got this right. We'll have to work harder on future appointments; this was a bit too close for comfort,' said the chairman.

'Ha, I agree with your thinking, sir, but with your support for the post we discussed, I can protect your investment in our hospital; I'm done with pure basic research,' said Maginot.

'Take care of Marsh, he looked very unhappy in there,' said the chairman. 'He hasn't been himself lately.'

'Don't worry,' said Maginot. 'I'll talk to David, he'll understand. Are we still meeting at the Park later? Golf this weekend?'

253

'I'm sure we can fit in a round,' said the chairman.

'Adam, can I speak to you for a minute,' said David Marsh.

'Oh, hi, it's you, what a turn-up in there,' said Maginot.

'Never mind, you stitched it up with the chairman, didn't you! How can you live with yourself?'

'I don't know what you mean, we all supported whom we thought best; I can't see what you're making a fuss about,' said Maginot.

'You're a two-faced, scheming . . . Scarpia, you knew how we were likely to vote. You voted for Hong to curry favour with the chairman. Why? To be chief executive? Or are you so insecure that you did not want David to get it? I've never trusted you, or your ilk, always on the make; we used to cherish talent, from what I have seen it's now all down to native cunning. I hope you're very proud of yourself; if you are, accept my congratulations,' said Marsh.

'Call me what you like, you're not going to be chief executive of this hospital, I am; welcome to real life!'

34

Post-Interview

David Timms was on his way home in his car when he got the message that the job had gone to Dr Hong. *At least Mensah didn't get it either*, he thought. He could not face Amanda yet; he had failed. What would she think of him? David got out of his car and sat on a park bench, watching the school children stream out through the school gates. He noted that the school had a high homogeneity index, one of the new indices used to calculate government grants. He would now have to face all those staff tomorrow who had thought the job was his. Some had already started to address him like a consultant. The incompetent ones – the pygmies – would be really pleased. They could gloat, but he had no time for them. What did they know?

'Where've you been?' asked Amanda when David got home.

'Nowhere in particular,' said David. 'I didn't get it. Some Chinese man got it: Hong,' he said.

'Hong? How?' she said.

'I'll have to wait for the debriefing to find out why. I can't believe what's happened. Skulduggery, I'm sure; you hear these things but you never think it'll happen to you. Well it shouldn't, what do they want? Hong, who had been torn apart at the World Congress, who can barely speak intelligible English, he's landed a plum job whilst I have nothing. I dare say even O'Donotstent and Mensah were stronger candidates,' he said.

'What will you do?' asked Amanda.

'What will I do, what will I do?' He scratched his head. 'I don't know, if they're right about another recession, new appointments at the Freeman are unlikely for some time, could be a year; I'll have to find a job somewhere else. They said my mum's profile wouldn't have made a difference, but I don't believe them. How could Adam Maginot let me down? He promised me everything would be fine; not once, several times!'

'Well, take your time, don't rush or do anything silly,' said Amanda.

'I'm hardly in a strong position to do anything,' he said. 'I've been shafted, what will people think? They've made me look really silly. I could have applied for that job in London Dizzy John got last week. I could apply to the "supermarket and super-hospital integrated partnership" created by Tesco in the Far East. But I was promised this job. All my hard work, dashed hopes, useless, what do they want me to do? Just because I don't take nonsense. I have high standards, and now I've got to work with these same people after what they've done. I'll never trust that toad Maginot ever again, ever.'

Amanda picked Jonathan out of his cot and hugged David to her while David leaned against the wall in the hall, seething.

'I'm sorry you didn't get the job, but you don't know why yet,' said Rachel, and she handed the phone over to John.

'Better luck next time, son, that's life, we've all been through it; shame it should happen this way. You'll get a better job, you'll see,' said John. John did not like the sound of his son's disappointment.

After they'd put the phone down John took Rachel to task. 'Rachel, everything pointed to a successful interview; that hassle over your article didn't help, it put David off. At least accept that much,' he said.

'What practical difference does my guilt make?' said Rachel. John grabbed his sweater off the armchair and went for a walk.

David spent the next two weeks trying to avoid his erstwhile mentors: Maginot, Marsh and the others. They avoided him as well. Clinical meetings were dry affairs. Camaraderie with a soon to be member of the elite was replaced by embarrassed formality and correctness. Only a few consultants wished him better luck. David wrote a letter of resignation, kept it for a day, thought better of it and threw it away.

Two weeks after the interviews, the maximum period allowed by hospital policy, David went to see Maginot for debriefing.

'It's got nothing to do with you, or what you said, David, old chap. Your answers were excellent, but it was how it came across, body language. You must have read the *Handbook of International Interview Technique* by Han and Jost? No? For example, you should have bowed your head ever so slightly when you addressed the chairman the first time and not stared at him so aggressively when he addressed you. In a multicultural setting, world, the correct eye contact is important. At times your voice was too loud and your hand gestures palpably confrontational. But it was still very close. I'm sorry it did not go your way; I tried but – I shouldn't be telling you this – but some of the others were not as supportive as they might have been.'

'You more or less guaranteed me the job, perhaps it affected my performance. You're sure it had nothing to do with recent publicity about my mother?' said David.

'Absolutely not,' said Maginot. 'Don't even think that, it was just bad luck on the day and you know how we feel; I'll have to prepare the ground better when another job comes along. I'll let you know what's happening here; you may have to wait, but you'll get another shot, I'm sure,' said Maginot.

'Maginot's never mentioned this Chinese etiquette or interview book before,' David said to his dad next time they spoke.

'Never heard of it,' said John.

'Have you heard of this book, Rachel?' he shouted.

'No,' she said. David could hear her in the background.

'Keep your head down until something comes along. We'll be ready, book or no book, next time,' said John.

'Perhaps there's something to be said for that old Burka system,' said David.

At home, Amanda was as solicitous as ever and Jonathan was a cuddly consolation. Bedroom stirrings remained unmet aspirations.

Mensah was not surprised when he received news of his rejection, but it still hurt. He stopped at a fast-food outlet, SirKi, bought a half-sized cup of their latest cold tea and reviewed his day. He wanted to call Daviniesta but thought he might whine and put her off. He would call her when he felt better. His phone rang. Before he could answer it he felt a sting on his right cheek. He put his hand to his cheek, saw that the culprit was not an insect but a piece of paper cup flicked across his table by a pair of smirking spotty teenagers. Mensah lost it. Seeing the change in his demeanour, the set of his jaw and the frown on his face, the miscreants legged it through the side entrance. Mensah gave chase, not knowing what he would do if he caught them. On reflection he was thankful they escaped, for he was so angry he could have killed or been killed. These kids carried knives. Trembling, he returned to his seat, relieved that his bag and jacket were still there. The phone call was from Daviniesta. 'Shit,' he said.

'None of the standard questions were particularly challenging, Nancy,' Mensah said that night.

'Bad vibes, too much on your plate,' she said.

'We don't know what the others have to deal with, do we? It just didn't go very well, I was not nervous enough, no edge, just flat . . .' he said. 'At one point there was this smirk on Maginot's face, made him think he was toying with me. I gave an example about evolution, you could see him thinking, "You're no Darwin."'

'You weren't as keen as you were, were you?' said Nancy.

'I was, desperate, wanted to sort this out, then get my mum out of hospital; I had it all planned,' he said. 'They weren't going to have me, whatever; I should've known.'

'But from what you say, it was a turn up for the book, wasn't it?' said Nancy.

'Sure was, couldn't have predicted that, David will be gutted. My heart bleeds. Hats off to the chairman, Sir Li Tang, for wangling his man Hong the post, if that's what's happened. Doubt whether a westernised Nigerian would have had the nerve. He would have wanted his man to be twice as good as the others; anyway, that's what my dad says would have happened.

'If that's what the chairman's done what's the point of the debriefing, Nancy? It'll be a waste of time. Absolute waste of time. I'll tell Ms Sherry I'll take the two disciplinary points and when another position comes up we'll try again. I'm not counting any chickens, but I'd rather not leave Newcastle now I've got my mum to think about. Why should I move? Even the sage of Gosforth, Maginot, went to school in Newcastle, then Durham and back to Newcastle, and he was already hosed and dried and appointed senior lecturer by the time he went off to spend a sabbatical year in New England. But things were more predictable in those days; look how they shafted David, he must have thought he was one of the boys,' said Mensah.

'Are you sure you're all right?' said Nancy.

'I'm fine, really, Nancy, I've learned a lot these last few weeks. What I can take, how much I can take.'

'I know, Marty said that too, that you've come through; he's not worried about you, in a funny sort of way. He says he's now confident you can cope. He's really proud of you, he doesn't say it, but he is,' she said.

'Thanks, you've made me feel much better. I was dreading tomorrow, going back and seeing everyone, now I can go back to work, just carry on as if nothing's happened,' he said.

The next morning, a few of the consultants commiserated with Mensah, assuring him that he would soon get a consultant job. Mensah responded by saying the best man won and thanked them for their support and kind words. That evening Mensah went to see Ruth. She was ready to be discharged.

'Are you happy? You're not looking your real self,' she said. Mensah smiled, but Ruth could see that it was false. 'Don't worry about me,' she said. 'The nurses have done a great job, I've got you back. I don't know what they've done, but a lot makes sense now to me, thanks to Jesus.' Mensah groaned. 'I'm going home in a few days, will you come to visit me?' asked Ruth.

'Of course I will, and I'll bring Nancy and Marty as well. You'll love them, and Vince, my friend. He helped me find you,' said Mensah. He thanked the nurses, left a large box of chocolates for the other patients. Minutes later, Vince called to ask whether Mensah would like to meet his new girlfriend, Patricia.

35

Daviniesta and Mensah

Friday night, a week after the interviews, Mensah and Daviniesta were going out to dinner with Vince and Patricia. As both pairings were new, neither woman could claim precedence. Patricia was a designer and lecturer at Northumbria University. After dinner, Vince dropped Mensah off and Daviniesta got out too. Mensah waved his friends goodbye, front door keys in one hand and Daviniesta's hand in the other. She gripped his hand with just the right amount of pressure and smiled. As he brushed past her in the hall, her moist lips, half open mouth, the bright tip of her tongue and shiny, wide, defiant, but soft, inviting eyes, his penetrating gaze, the scaffold in his trunks, strong broad shoulders, film of perspiration and aftershave ignited coeval passion into flames. She grabbed him round the neck and he carried her up the stairs.

Postprandial, coital and alcohol, Mensah dozed and dreamed of a debate in the House of Commons on cuts proposed by government to improve male sexual efficiency. Daviniesta smiled and watched Mensah sleep. When he woke up she was still watching him. 'Phew,' he said, relieved. 'Hi there, must have dozed off,' he said. Daviniesta smiled, brushed a hair from her mouth. He kissed her on the forehead and slapped his slimy cock on her inner thighs like a paint brush. Still some hyperaesthesia, but a faint tingling told him he would soon be ready. 'He'll be back, he says,' Mensah said to Daviniesta, looking down at his half tumescence. 'His boss will be back, too, on my back, knees, begging,' Mensah said, kicking Daviniesta's shoes on to the floor.

'You know, we were meant to be together,' she said. 'I was gutted when . . .'

'Shush . . .' said Mensah. 'I'm sorry, it was my fault, I was preoccupied by I can't imagine what. Am I forgiven? I'll do any project you want, but not now. Look what you've done, my prick's gone all soft again. Resolution number one, there should be no work talk in the bedroom, swear?'

'Swear,' she said and kissed him on his tip. Prick pricked up. She took aforesaid boner and buried it again.

36

Committee Revelations

'Phew, at last I can get some rest, I hope I've sent everything they'll need,' she said to John before she crashed into bed. Rachel had just e-mailed the last of her submissions to Mrs Elizabeth Desborough, secretary to the Simmonds Inquiry. 'I didn't know I had so much stuff,' she said.

'Don't forget it goes back so many years, from when you were a baby economist,' said John. 'When do you give evidence?'

'They'll tell us soon, Mrs Desborough will e-mail us with the order of play in a few days,' she said. 'Exciting, isn't it?' she added.

'Only exciting?' said John, switching the lights off.

In the first few days of the inquiry, only about a dozen protesters, half of them committed, the rest incidental, accidental or curious, stood outside the Courts of Justice. But their targets were hustled into court by a secret entrance, and by the end of the first week, with no one to boo or heckle, the agitators melted away.

Inside, in the half-empty courtroom, the gallery could have done a lot better watching snow thaw. After a day and a half of arcane procedural wrangling, they finally got some action when Sir Timothy Moloney, a Home Office permanent secretary, was asked a few questions about procedure, who attended which sorts of meetings and how policy was formulated and passed down. Following this, a junior civil servant explained the background to the vaccine programme.

On the second day, Philip White ('Philip the philosopher'), the brains behind the coalition's economic and social policies, was called to give evidence. Now, the public thought, they would start to get some answers, and if no answers, at least some fireworks. Mr Fright Hunter Q.C., counsel to the inquiry, asked White to explain his links to Bootsaleiger, the company that supplied the ADHD vaccine. White said, 'I did nothing wrong, these were legitimate business transactions entered into between His Majesty's government and a private company. I had nothing to do with the procurement or the execution of these contracts. By the law of this land, this still pleasant land worth fighting and dying for, I will be vindicated. I am an ordinary patriotic Englishman whose crime is to challenge an establishment that is leading us into the abyss. All I have done is try to improve the lot of my countrymen and look after my young wife and family . . .'

'Thank you, Mr White, I will have to stop you there; are you saying that you have no knowledge of payments made to this company?'

'I have no knowledge of any invoices, sir,' he said.

'How well do you know Sir Stuart Farrington?'

'He is a researcher. He worked at Bootsaleiger,' he said.

'Is that all?'

'Yes, I have just told you, I thought I made myself clear.'

'Is it not the case that whilst you were an adviser to the Home Office you produced several ideas for consideration by the Nationalist Party including the sterilisation of unfit mothers and immigrants?'

'I did no such thing,' said White.

'Was it not your idea to vaccinate young men of Afro-Caribbean descent with the ADHD vaccine?'

'It was a collective decision,' he said.

'But it was your idea?'

'It was a collective decision.'

'Can you explain how the ADHD vaccine came to be contaminated with the dyskeratotic gene?'

'We do not know that this was a contamination.'

'Well, can you explain why every patient who had the ADHD vaccine also had the dyskeratotic gene?'

'Maybe those people were born with the gene.'

After twenty minutes of unproductive probing, Mr Fright Hunter called his next witness: Sir Stuart Farrington.

Sir Stuart, wearing a dark green shirt, loud pink tie and a light grey suit, had to be escorted to the stand by an orderly. He took off his glasses to polish, but dropped them. When he resurfaced, flushed and panting, peering through the largest intact pieces of lens, he was ready. Sir Stuart described his research into the ageing process, how he had simulated premature ageing in the laboratory.

'How well did you know Mr White?' asked Mr Fright Hunter.

'I know Mr White, he helped me when my company was in trouble.'

'Did your research involve this dyskeratotic gene, about which we have heard so much?'

'Yes,' he said.

'Did Mr White enlist your help in producing a model of this gene that could be used in humans?' Sir Stuart looked up, was going to answer, but rubbed his left wrist. 'Could you explain . . .' he said. He stopped and just said 'No.'

'Did you ask Mr White why he was interested in your research?'

'No.'

'Research of such potential commercial and scientific importance and you want us to believe that you were not curious?'

'I was curious, but I didn't ask,' he said. Sir Stuart dropped his hands and stood up straighter.

'In hindsight, do you not think you should have?'

'In hindsight, yes.'

'What did you think when you heard that vaccinated patients had been contaminated by the dyskeratotic gene?'

'I thought it must have been some sort of accident.'

'It did not cross your mind that the large quantities of this gene or material that you had helped to produce may have been, let us say, misappropriated?'

Sir Stuart rubbed his wrist again, looked straight ahead into the distance. Just when he was going to be prompted, he said, 'I, I, was, I thought, a lot of things: that it had been stolen, it was an accident, a mutation, a reaction between the ADHD vaccine and the patients in some way.'

'But you did not think that Mr White had anything to do with these events?'

'No, sir,' he said.

'And we should believe you?' said the Q.C. with an arched brow.

Sir Anthony Budd Q.C. took the part of the hyena to Hunter's lion, to take the flesh off Sir Stuart's testimony. 'Did Mr White ever use your company to make payments to other parties?'

'I don't know, sir.'

'Do you know of any payments made by Mr White's organisations to other parties in connection with the ADHD vaccine?'

Sir Stuart looked uncertain. 'No, sir, I do not know of any payments, I was not concerned with finance,' he said.

'For the record, can you speak up please, Sir Stuart.'

'I'm sorry, I've had a sore throat, I meant to say I can't remember,' he said. He looked down at his hands. Played with his fingers.

'Do you want a drink?'

'No, thank you,' said Sir Stuart.

Sir Budd established that Sir Stuart had thought he was working on a secret official project, perhaps a war project, he was not sure, but he did not think it was official government policy.

'These letters and e-mails show that some Ministers of State were aware of the project, the same ministers involved in the ADHD project.'

Sir Stuart looked shocked. 'This is the first I am hearing of ministerial involvement, honestly, I was just doing my work, I am not political. Can I sit down, please, please?' He pulled on his shirt, black with perspiration, crumpling his tie. 'I'm not feeling at all well, water please, can I have a glass of water?' If he'd had a mother, she would have dragged him off there and then in her arms. As it was, an usher had to do. The proceedings were adjourned.

John Timms was attending a multidisciplinary meeting at the Priory when Rachel called him. 'What's wrong?' he asked, mouthing a silent 'Rachel' to his colleagues as he left the room. They nodded out of sympathy, or understanding. 'You don't normally ring me at work,' he said.

'Don't fret, it's just I had to tell someone,' said Rachel. 'It's Stuart, he's not turned up.'

'Turned up where?'

'At the Simmonds Inquiry, that's where, I was going to follow him some time this morning or afternoon. He was looking peaky yesterday, he's done a runner, done something silly, been run over, I hope he's just ill with flu or a heavy cold, it's odd, doesn't make sense; I saw him yesterday,' she said. 'Everybody's here the day before they cr . . .'

'Hold on,' he said, as a porter walked past. 'Okay, carry on, what's happening now?'

'Someone's just said the police have circled his block of flats. He has a pad in London, near Kensington. I'll wait for news from Mrs Desborough, but I don't think we'll be doing any business today,' she said. 'I'll let you know what happens.'

'Be careful,' he said. For her sake he hoped Sir Stuart had not been murdered.

Rachel was watching the hourly bulletins when John got home. 'The BBC says when the police broke into Stuart's flat he was already dead, they won't give any more details.'

'There's not much you can do then, what's for dinner?' said John.

'Is that all you can think about?' she said.

267

'No, but it is all I can think about at the moment,' he said.

'You'll just have to think a bit longer, I'm not ready yet,' she said.

'I've had just as bad a day as you have, if you don't mind let's order a Tesco,' said John.

'I hoped you would say that,' she said, passing him the take-away menu. 'I'll have the usual,' she said.

'The usual it is then,' he said.

Lord Simmonds suspended the inquiry, but Sir Stuart's death roused the hitherto indifferent public. *The Workers* paper ran an editorial: 'Fear, guilt or cowardice?'

On the *Weekly Scrutiny* a member of the audience asked the panel whether Sir Stuart was murdered, either by his former accomplices to shut him up or by opponents of the ADHD programme. There was applause and murmured assent from the audience, but to hoots of derision the police commissioner said, 'I am not at liberty to discuss the case, the post-mortem has not been completed and we await the final report. When the facts become available you, the Great British public, will be the first to know . . .' Then, 'maybe second,' he added.

Mr Peter Fenton, a left-leaning journalist, said he thought 'Sir Stuart may have been compelled to take his own life, through pressure exerted by his accomplices or unknown others, it depends on what you look for; yes, he may have died by his own hand, so for neatness you say he was not murdered, but suicide can be murder by proxy. I am no expert, but it strikes me that there are far too many of our scientists, and God knows we need them, scientists with links to government projects, who take their own lives. Why?' Applause.

'There you go. You people are never tired of peddling conspiracy theories, with nothing better to do, you beaver away at your screens looking for people to smear,' said Lady Fraser-Pounds. 'When all's said and done you'll find that this poor man took his life because the strain he felt was intolerable; none of us can imagine what could have made him take his life, which is what it looks like; anyone seeing his performance at the inquiry could tell he was in distress. Remember this: he has a family.' She turned her head up to the camera. 'To Sir Stuart's family, we are grateful for the service he provided to our country, our thoughts are with you at this difficult time.'

Except for a few murmurs of approval, the audience was silent. David Bell, Q.C. said a statement from the police was crucial: 'This wild speculation will continue; it helps nobody – the public, the families, the vaccination victims – for people to come on air,' he turned to Fenton, 'to spout the sort of nonsense we heard from our journalist friend here. We still have a judicial system, unlike the sort of system that he and his ilk would impose on us. The police commissioner will release his findings and you will all have the opportunity, I hope, to make up your own minds when Lord Simmonds completes his inquiry.' A titter and hissing and weak applause followed.

A week after *Weekly Scrutiny*, and with increasing clamour to hold a public inquiry into Sir Stuart's death, the metropolitan commissioner, Sir Rupert Peter DePallister, announced on television that Sir Stuart had been found dead, slumped in an armchair, both his television and his radio still switched on. 'What killed Sir Stuart? Television-repeats revolver,' went the joke. The commissioner went on: 'The post-mortem examination showed that he died from ingesting a concentrated form of a cell-denaturing anti-telo kinase, which is said to hasten body-cell death. A number of documents which may be of potentially great assistance in helping us with our enquiries – criminal and civil – have been found. I cannot divulge their contents. I shall pass these on to relevant parties including Justice Louis Simmonds.' To questions about whether Sir Stuart's death was connected with the ADHD or dyskeratotic gene contamination he replied, 'No comment.'

Lord Simmonds reconvened his inquiry three months after Sir Stuart's death. White's second appearance closed the Strand. Rival

269

protesters, the police, the curious and the unconcerned competed for ascendancy on the streets in the early July sunshine. The more polite posters read 'Justice for the victims of eugenics', 'Coward White face us', 'Murderers, Holocaust deniers'. In support of White and his colleagues, an equally motivated and determined group turned out dressed as Knights Templar.

'White is our man, he's a patriot, a hero of the working man; never mind what they say he's done, he has more guts than all those poxy lawyers in there. Three lions' hearts he has; he is the man to save England; he's the only one speaking for us, defending this country from Islam, communism,' said a White supporter to a television reporter outside the court.

In the tussles between protesters and the scramble for the few public gallery seats, one man was knocked unconscious by a flying object. Probably a bottle thrown by a rival group, claimed the police; by a police baton, claimed the protesters. Television replay footage was inconclusive. The man survived.

'Good luck, Rachel,' said John. 'You're sure you don't want me to come with you?'

'You'll make me nervous, more nervous,' she said. 'I've been well briefed by the lawyers. I'm relieved in a way, I'll say my piece and the rest is left to the tribunal; and public opinion,' she added. 'I've got my papers, I know where to meet the escort, she's Special Branch. She takes me round the back, to avoid the crush and the tomato throwers. I've got a tomato-proof jacket, but it's better to avoid them.'

'I'll be thinking of you,' said John. He kissed her on the head and went upstairs.

'I'll be gone by the time you get dressed, bye,' she said.

'Bye,' he said.

Rachel lingered a bit longer, savouring her cup of tea before she went to catch her train.

Sir Geoffrey Knowles Q.C. led the questioning. 'I'm sorry for what your family had to go through for your public spiritedness,' he said.

'Thank you, Sir Geoffrey, it's very kind of you, it's all behind us now, we hope,' she said.

'Well, it was very brave of you, can you talk us through your career and what sparked your interest in the ADHD vaccination programme?'

Rachel told him about her jobs at the Treasury and Home Office during the Nationalist coalition.

'We hear a lot of ministers and advisers being advised to think the unthinkable: can you recall some of these ideas?' he said.

'Yes,' said Rachel.

'Do you mind giving us some examples?'

Rachel took a sip of water and looked straight at the Q.C. 'I was responsible for collating and summarising some of these ideas for my superiors, and ultimately I believe these were passed on to the relevant minister or ministers. Just as Sir Timothy described. In the first two years of the coalition, Mr White's think-tank was the most prolific source of ideas.'

'How do you know that these were Mr White's ideas?'

'He signed many of the documents himself. Perhaps he wanted the credit for his iconoclastic ideas.'

'Bitch,' said a woman in the gallery. She was removed. Rachel waited.

'Go on,' said Sir Geoffrey.

'One of White's unthinkable ideas was to reduce the size of the underclass by sterilisation and deportation. He argued that just as students were asked to withdraw from courses from which they would not benefit, people, regardless of ethnicity, should be paid to leave or be removed from Britain. If, after four unbroken generations of association in a rich country with all the opportunities for self-advancement it provided, they were still dependent on the State, they should leave or agree to be sterilised. The minister rejected this proposal out of hand as unworkable and politically unacceptable; he scribbled those words over the paper.

271

I remember quite vividly because it was the first time I'd seen a minister's handwriting.' Mirthful murmuring wafted down from the gallery.

'Thank you, Mrs Timms, may I ask you to give us some more examples of the ambience at the time, the sort of policies put forward?'

'One idea, which I believe followed on from discussions about banning the burka, was to introduce the new drug Verifide into the water supply. The drug is supposed to make it very difficult to hide your true feelings. The proposal was leaked,' she paused, and Sir Geoffrey smiled, ever so briefly. 'Water company executives saw the proposals; the more liberal wing of the government argued that those who could afford it would avoid the public water supply, so only the poor would be compelled to tell the truth. So the policy was rejected.'

'Which of White's ideas was accepted then?'

Rachel took a deep breath. Behind her an asthmatic wheezed. Rachel took in another breath, reassured it was not her wheezing. 'White came up with his rebalancing strategy. The country needed socio-demographic as well as economic rebalancing. This was his big idea, the initiative he was most proud of; the least politically fraught and the most economically attractive of all his ideas. He planned to use the ADHD vaccination as a vector for "rebalancing" the country's ethnic composition. Discouraged by the vaccine, birth rates amongst the immigrants would fall, many would emigrate, and the population would return to some ideal homogenous norm.'

'Could you elaborate, what did you understand him to mean by this policy?'

'As I understood it, the political objective was to reverse what they called Labour's deliberate policy of using massive immigration to create a clientele state. His economic rationale was that the dyskeratotic gene allowed you to live long enough to contribute to society but you die before pensionable age, leaving the State with a windfall. This windfall would be used to raise the tax threshold and salve the consciences of the beneficiaries. In the end, basic infrastructure, law and order and security would remain State funded, but there would be no need for a public-sector-funded social security system or a National Health Service. The executive would be kept at arm's length: to allow them deniability.'

A man clapped, another turned round and slapped him, and the police expelled them both. Rachel looked up, waited until the commotion died down, and avoided the hostile gaze of a severe woman sitting in the aisle.

'And if they were caught, or exposed?' asked Sir Geoffrey.

'I admit to speculation, but I am told that the inquiry has access to the minutes of these meetings. They hoped that a two-parliament coalition government would give them enough time to implement the policy. After that, they could argue that it was all a mistake, a cock-up, some contamination in the ADHD vaccine, an ill-conceived scientific experiment. Even if they were exposed, five years of their policies would have such profound and long lasting socio-cultural and economic consequences that it would be worth the risk. Public relations firms, one based here and one in America, would be lined up to defend them. I believe that friendly newspaper editors were to be invited to dinner to be briefed or sounded out, but I don't know whether these ever took place. An appendix to their proposal went something like this: "Set against the ranting of the poor, angry, inarticulate victims, there would be no competition; the Gaza strip, Burma, Nepal demonstrate what you can get away with."' She went on. 'I left the Treasury to return to academic life; dissenting voices must have been defeated. I realised what might have happened when the ADHD scandal broke.' She took another sip of water, holding the glass in both hands to still them while Sir Geoffrey exchanged files with Mr Fright Hunter.

'Are you ready to continue?' he asked.

'Yes,' said Rachel. 'Why did you think the dyskeratotic gene contamination was not an accident?'

'While researching my book I came across the results of a study by Professor Burns-Savage showing that nearly all recipients of the ADHD vaccine had telomere shortening. Oxford- and London-based researchers published similar results. Yet the literature was clear that except by using particularly virulent nanovectors, extreme radiation or exposure to some novel kinases, it was difficult to produce such a high penetration in the laboratory. I thought that these findings could only be due to a deliberate, or an extremely unlikely and unusual, contamination. Professional caution dictated that the scientists wait for the results of their own ten-year study and more government data. The Home Office, citing national security, is yet to release these figures.'

'Is this the same Professor Burns-Savage who served on the committee and will be giving evidence at this inquiry?'

'Yes,' said Rachel.

'Do you have any other reasons to doubt the official explanation for these events?' Rachel shifted her weight from foot to foot in her fashionable, but uncomfortable shoes.

'I was granted access to Treasury and Home Office files to carry out research on my book on social policy and pensions. During the course of my research I found that the department of health appeared to have paid over the odds for the ADHD vaccine. I thought this was because this was a new vaccine and the government was in a hurry, and I did not give it much thought until the scandal broke. When I heard about the contamination I went back over my figures with a firm of accountants, Colls and Stone. From their calculations they suspected some skulduggery, corruption, misappropriation, perhaps. Putting the science and the accounts together, so to speak, I thought the contamination and the irregular payments could be connected.' Rachel folded her hands in front of her, smiled, bowed and went back to sit with the other witnesses.

When Philip White was recalled to give evidence, Mr Fright Hunter went straight on the attack. 'Good morning, Mr White. Sir Stuart

was a far better scientist than he was a businessman, was he not?'
he said.

'Good morning, Mr Hunter, nice to see you again, but I don't
know what you mean about Sir Stuart,' said White.

'We have his bank statements and correspondence around about
the time you bought his company, Mr White.'

'I know that,' said White.

'Did you not pay close to three million pounds to clear Sir
Stuart's debts when the banks refused him credit and his company
ran into trouble?'

'Yes, I did, as a humanitarian gesture,' White said, lifting his
head. Mr Hunter harrumphed, pushed on his glasses.

'Shortly afterwards, a subsidiary of yours bought Sir Stuart's
company for less than half its market value. Is this correct?'

'Strictly, no, the purchase price was the market price. It is what
he would have got for it; he perhaps got more,' White said.

'Did you not then sign an agreement for Sir Stuart to lease
back his company and his main residence in return for his collaboration with you on projects to exploit the findings from his
research?'

'Yes, I did, to impose commercial discipline on a very brilliant
scientist,' said White.

'Did Sir Stuart not stand to lose his house and status – everything he had worked for – if you disagreed? In other words, he
had more to lose than you did if you disagreed?'

'No, he was better off than when we first met,' said White.

'So you would not conclude from the evidence that Sir Stuart
was so desperate to keep up appearances he agreed to all your
proposals?'

'No,' said White.

'Was Sir Stuart represented by independent advisers?'

'I believe he took independent advice before he approached
me,' said White.

'Did you meet any of these advisers?'

'No.'

'Did you use your influence with Sir Stuart to get him to produce the dyskeratotic gene for your own clients?'

'No.'

'How do you explain these documents, the inflated invoices submitted by Bootsaleiger – through subsidiaries, including Sir Stuart's shell company – to the department of health to supply the ADHD vaccine?'

'They must have been planted by my opponents to smear and ensnare me when they murdered Sir Stuart,' he said.

'We know Sir Stuart was not murdered,' said Mr Hunter Q.C.

'We don't know for certain,' said White.

'The sums, less those you paid to the intermediaries, have been traced to offshore accounts in your name, sir,' said Hunter.

'Sirs, my learned friend, this is a witch-hunt. Argh . . .' White gripped his neck and collapsed to the floor.

A woman screamed, 'He's dying, they've killed him.' Mrs White, watching from the gallery, fainted. Paramedics got to White in seconds and carried out a quick check of vital signs, oxygen saturation and an ECG.

'Okay, clear the way, we're off, let's assume heart attack, Tommy's,' said Mike, the senior paramedic, as they strapped White to the couch and wheeled him on to the ambulance. Siren blaring, the crew headed for St Thomas's Hospital at breakneck speed through the London traffic.

Rachel could not believe her eyes. She felt for White, but with one witness dead and another ill, she wondered what she had let herself in for. After the chamber cleared, she made her way to Charing Cross station via the secret side entrance.

For four days, St Thomas's medical director attended the daily press conferences with nothing new to say other than that White was in a stable condition. After a week, Dr Ian Anscombe, chief medical officer and Czar for Public Understanding of Medical Science, announced that White was suffering from a form of dyskaryosis. He based this on a consultation with the government's chief general practitioner, Dr Ash Roberts, who had 'seen more of these cases in the community than any number of consultants', and without talking to the cardiologists and neurologists directly responsible for White's care, who had found nothing wrong with him.

'As you know, this is a condition with an uncertain outcome and prognosis. I would counsel caution in discussing this so as not to cause hurt to the many thousands of His Majesty's subjects also afflicted by this disease,' said Anscombe.

'Is his caused by the same gene that triggered the ADHD contamination?' he was asked.

'Not that we can say for certain: this is a syndrome, many conditions look the same but are caused by the different agents,' he said.

'Then why do you refer to the other thousands of victims?'

'I merely wanted to suggest that we avoid causing offence,' he said.

'Any further questions?' said the chief executive.

'When do you think Mr White will be able to return to the Simmonds Inquiry?'

'Too early to say, we'll have to see. Lord Simmonds may have enough to complete his report,' he said. 'I'm afraid that will have to do,' Anscombe concluded, retreating into the hospital foyer, escorted by the chief executive and the hospital medical director. The sidelined specialists did not care; it did not matter what the minister said as long as he did not throw grit into their caviar.

With White's departure, and with Lord Cazenove dead, and Colville – a hunched, shuffling, mumbling witness who, as one paper put it, 'did not even know how to lie' – repeatedly contradicting himself, the inquiry lost momentum.

Four months after the inquiry closed, Rachel was heading home in the rain, after a trip to the new enterprise and business centre in Stratford. Just as she was going to board the train her phone rang. 'Could I speak to Rachel Timms, please?'

'Speaking.'

'Oh, hello, sorry to trouble you, it's Brian Slattery from the *Financial Times*. I'd like your reaction to the report, Lord Simmonds' report.'

'Sorry, I can't talk at the moment,' she said, hanging up. Rachel grabbed the evening paper from a news-stand, left the change and dashed on to the train. 'No conspiracy' read the subsidiary headline over a six-inch, half-column article describing Lord Simmonds' conclusions that the contamination was the result of an unusual and unexplained train of events, and there was no evidence of a conspiracy involving Mr White or anyone else. 'What caused it then?' she muttered to herself, casting the paper aside. The gentleman sitting opposite gestured at the newspaper and Rachel pushed it towards him.

The news was no different when she got home: the commentators were in no doubt there would be no indictments, no prosecutions, because it was all an accident. She called David. 'David, have you heard?'

'Yes, no wrongdoing,' he said. After a moment's silence he said, 'Happy now, mother? Can we now get on with our lives?'

'We've been through that . . . can I see you?' she said.

'I'll call you,' said David.

She heard John come through the front door and got up to meet him. He kissed her. 'Sorry, Rachel, we had a late admission, staff, couldn't help it; I heard about the whitewash. Do you ever see this sort of thing go against the government?' he said, taking off his jacket. 'We should've known: they decide if, they decide when, who chairs, who serves, terms of reference, the lot. Come on, Rachel, could you lose an inquiry if you were in charge? Even I couldn't.' He winced as he sat down to take off his shoes.

'John, don't be so cynical, this review cost the taxpayer ten million pounds, its final report runs to two thousand pages. But, of what? It's full of balderdash. Can't believe it, they put us all through this to come up with such hogwash. He says mistakes were made, but no evidence for wrongdoing. He found Stuart's suggestions plausible: that it could have been a mass reaction, some sort of virus! Over all the other evidence I supplied. He seems to agree that there was some sort of agenda for the ADHD, but he says that their "willing an event does not prove they caused it". I'm gutted, I thought there was a strong enough case to indict Philip White.'

John shrugged. 'Don't know, they keep telling us it was an inquiry, not a trial; they'll come up with some deal, I guess,' he said.

Rachel sat on the second stair, head in hands, knees up to keep her warm. She flicked a hand out between the banisters at a spider's web, banged her knuckle, hissed, and blew on it. She got up to go to the kitchen. 'Well, not much we can do about it tonight, I'll rustle up something for us to eat.'

'Good idea,' said John. 'I have an idea, a website. Whenever there's a government inquiry, invite the public to write the final report in advance, lock up each entry, and the entry closest to the official report is the winner. Only anoraks would enter, but the results would be interesting.'

Rachel waved a spoon at John. 'Your game isn't going to help the victims, or my nephew,' she said.

'I'll be back down soon, my back's hurting. I'm trying out this new man corset,' he said, halfway up the stairs.

'Your life's so simple,' she said.

'So was yours,' he replied.

Rachel was watching the latest news bulletin when John came down in his baggy trousers and a jumper. 'You'll make yourself ill, going over this farce, just forget it, have a glass of wine. Let's try the good stuff Mr C bought us,' he said. John poured them each a glass of the red wine.

'I won't give up, they need to fight for adequate compensation; at least the government hasn't set its face against that,' she said.

'Do you want anything else with your meal?' he said. 'Rachel, what are you having?'

'Sorry, what did you say?'

'I asked you whether you wanted anything else with your meal: water, cream?'

'Whatever you're having,' she said.

'I'll get some sparkling water for you. Seeing you're not having any wine, I'll have yours,' he said.

After supper, John loaded the dishwasher and went to the television room to select a film. 'Should we watch this one? Just got it; I typed "boring psychiatrist and his glum wife who happens to be an economist" on their website and they sent me this. *Assizes Matters*, it's called; don't know what it's about – porno and law combined it seems.' He set it up, but when he came to fetch Rachel, she had gone to her study. 'I'll watch it on my own then,' he said.

The Times did its usual stuff when it came to its conclusions on the inquiry:

Another Fine Mess

We have come to the end of yet another expensive public inquiry into the abstruse, this time an alleged conspiracy to cause a rare, but life-threatening disease that in thirty years has not claimed a single victim. Yet, one witness, a senior scientist, is dead and another, a talented and enthusiastic public-spirited entrepreneur, is gravely ill. We wish him a speedy recovery.

Lord Simmonds, in his wide-ranging but circumspect report, has not allowed himself to be distracted by those who see a conspiracy in every Whitehall inglenook or civil servants as mendacious racists. His conclusions, that first, there was no conspiracy to contaminate or poison or do any harm, and second, that we do not have the tools to explain the scientists' findings, are balanced, well considered and just. We welcome the chief medical officer's speedy announcement of an increase in the grant to the Medical Research Council for research into gene therapy.

At the heart of the research, the production and commercial exploita-
tion of gene therapy for age-related conditions, was a man, Sir Stuart,
whose performance at the inquiry raises serious questions about his
ability to work under pressure. Had he lived, we may have learned
more of his role in the accident. That the cack-handed scribbles of a
callow young man struggling to make a name give rise to shock today
is testimony to the progress made by our democracy in the last thirty
years, but he was only doing his job. No matter how unpleasant to
some, debate is the lifeblood and bedrock of our democracy. It must not
be stifled.

Sir Cedric Peasbody, who counselled caution, but was overruled by
hysteria and humbug, has been vindicated. In a mature democracy like
ours the ad hoc, arbitrary and political basis for these inquiries is unac-
ceptable and unsustainable; the system must be overhauled. Detached
forensic examination of matters of such national importance should
never again be subjugated to expedience, whim or arrogant self-right-
eousness.

In response to the report, the president of the Association of British Insurers, Mrs Deidre Steed, asked what happened to the government's promise to underwrite the insurance policies of the victims of the contamination. The minister replied, 'Decisions made before the Simmonds Inquiry will have to be reviewed. Compensation will be considered for those in genuine need, but we will supplement monies raised by the victims' families.' He was referring to an anonymous donation of over two hundred thousand pounds to fund the routine annual check-ups recommended by the experts.

After a few weeks of deliberation the government announced that payments in compensation would be capped at twenty-five thousand pounds per victim. 'A fair outcome for the victims and the taxpayer,' said the Prime Minister.

Also, in the wake of the report, Mr William Conserverie, the thirty-five-year-old MP for Reigate and Banstead, tabled a motion supporting an extension of the delay of the release of secret papers from twenty to fifty years. *Clever*, thought Mensah. Under the existing provisions of the twenty-year rule, whole paragraphs and pages were expunged from the record at the discretion of nameless, faceless officials. At school he remembered Stephen Gould, a sixth former. Stephen, now a political researcher, had won the English oratory prize for his attack on the system. To Stephen – and Mensah agreed – the whole system was part of a sanctimonious propaganda machine. Even when papers were released, the culpable – for cock-ups, for conspiracies, or for both – would be dead, well into their dotage, or could or would not recall the events: likewise, the victims. But with rising life expectancy, the victims and protagonists, or perpetrators, could still be alive and professionally active thirty, even forty years after the relevant events and could be brought to book. So extending the limit to fifty years would buy more time.

Dan Grounds and Norman Hastings, two of White's accomplices who had fled and been granted political asylum in Russia to spite Britain, with which it was having one of its public, but ultimately unproductive spats, quietly returned. One underling hung himself. His leader, White, was discharged from St Thomas's to convalesce in a 'sympathiser's' Devon cottage. Shortly after, a civil suit for crimes against humanity, brought by families of the victims, collapsed. White was said to be too ill to testify. 'My client wishes those who are suing him well; he knows how they feel as he suffers from the same condition, and I might add that Mr White's illness, as he did not receive the ADHD vaccine, is indirect evidence that there was no conspiracy,' said his lawyer, Mr Ronald Haylor.

37

David and Mensah at Loose Ends

'Tell David I'm in the library if he wants me,' said Mensah after his case.

'Why don't you wait, it'll go much better if you scrub up together,' said the sister.

'Can't be that sure, he has his own way of doing things, he'll call me if he needs me, just as I would.'

'When's the last time that happened?'

'Never, I'm off,' he said. David had been watching Mensah's progress on a monitor and did not want to go in to the suite until his cousin had finished and left. If only his mother had kept her mouth shut. Everyone knew that they were avoiding each other, but did not know why.

'Oh, hi,' said David to Mensah when they bumped into each other at the lifts. 'Are you good?'

'I'm good,' said Mensah, 'see you.'

About four months after the interviews, Maginot asked David and Mensah to decide how to implement a new working time directive for the junior teams. Neither was looking forward to the meeting. David thought the initiative would lie with earlier arrival and was as relieved to see that Mensah was not in the library annexe as Mensah was to find David there when he arrived. 'Hello,' they said together.

'Another directive,' said Mensah.

'Yes, another new government plan,' said David. 'Do you think we should sell it, or put it, to them?'

'I'm not that fussed, they can do what they like with their rotas,' said Mensah.

'Why have they asked us to do it, when it's really Hong's call?' said David.

'I think it's Maginot's idea. A joke, he wants to put us together to see what happens, you know, with all the recent kerfuffle,' said Mensah.

'Yes, it's been interesting in a crazy sort of way. I'm sorry about the dyskeratotic contamination; my mum was sure it was deliberate. Don't know what to say; I hope they find a solution to it,' said David. 'How are you?'

'I'm fine, thank you,' said Mensah, touched but wary.

'The press had no business dragging your son into it,' said Mensah. 'I'm fine and getting sorted out, we'll see what the government does in the end. Give your mother my regards. Before I forget, how did Hong wangle the job? I was rowing against the tide anyway, so I'm not surprised that I didn't get it . . .'

David bristled. 'Between you and me, I don't think I can stand it here any more. I'm thinking of leaving. Everyone's whispering behind my back, about my family, the job, and I've had a few run-ins with Hong over the allocation of work and the on-call rota. He's head, is he not? He spends more time showing delegations around than doing any work. Marsh and the others appear to be happy to carry him, but it's we who have to do the donkey work.'

Mensah bent to pick up a piece of paper, reading its contents before he tore it up. He looked at David. 'Just destroying incriminating evidence. I'm not sure what to do either, but we'd better get back to this rota thing before the boys and girls arrive,' said Mensah.

'Right, nice to have a chat, I'll tell mother,' said David. He switched the projector on, and Mensah logged in.

After the presentation, they cleared up in silence. 'See you,' said David.

'OK,' said Mensah.

A favourable exchange rate, clever marketing and the rising cost of healthcare elsewhere attracted thousands of overseas patients to the United Kingdom, making health services one of the most profitable economic sectors. Medical schools charged higher and higher 'economic' fees until only the children of the truly wealthy could study medicine. Inflated fees, fuelled by mergers and acquisitions, earned chief executives six-figure bonuses, evidence, said the commentators, that Britain now had one of the most vibrant and exciting health sectors in the world.

Professor Adam Maginot was to be the new chief executive of Freeman Hospital. Dr David Marsh would retire before the end of the year. Mensah rang Vince to tell him the news.

'Just what I thought, but you won't understand,' said Vince.

'Try me,' said Mensah.

'Well,' said Vince, 'there's more to these appointments than you would imagine. Maginot is as crafty and patient as a heron eyeing a fish pond, and as greedy. Someone, perhaps backed by majority shareholders, has played this trick before. They gain access to human resources' computer systems, manipulate candidates' eligibility through disciplinary points, or dig dirt up on the candidates, or God knows what. Do a Blue Peter in reverse, for example: make signatures disappear. I found out by accident, some guy, you may have heard of him, Zac Blitz – establishment guy, right tie, etcetera; anyway, he's bang on for this top job at the New Harley Street Chambers. Unopposed, no internal candidate and the rest of the country didn't think it worth even applying. What happens? They parachute this girl in from God knows where. He runs home to Lord Blitz, his dad, crying foul. The group says globalisation. Dad's not having it, starts proceedings, tries to keep it quiet, but someone leaks it that he was suing for racial discrimination. But the top geezers, Sir Richard Morton and the others, had covered their backs. Anyway, it all blew over; interesting, though. Hold on, my other phone is ringing. I'll call you back.'

After waiting an hour, Mensah called Vince and they arranged to meet at the Foxy Lady pub. 'I didn't want to talk over the phone. Your paranoia's catching,' said Vince. 'I think the shareholders wanted Hong all along. They kept dirt on local candidates on either Scylla or Charybdis, to use; the same M.O. they used at the New Harley Street Chambers. Ms Sherry, Maginot, Marsh – one or all of them – were in with the shareholders, perhaps Sir Li Tang himself, to get the strong candidates to withdraw or knobble them in some other way. So, your goose was cooked when Maginot failed to convince you not to apply. David's mum's crusade was probably enough to doom him, but they would have found something else to use. Maginot did the rest. Only heaven knows how he shafted Marsh to get the top job.' Vince winked at the young woman who had been staring at him. She looked away coyly and blushed. Her friend nudged her playfully.

'When's this food going to arrive?' said Mensah, peering through the service hatch. To his relief, a waiter soon headed their way with their order. 'Go on, how did he, Maginot, wangle all this?' said Mensah.

Vince's face flushed with excitement. 'My contacts say Li Tang used them both, but Marsh came off worse. He didn't like Marsh's vibes; personal chemistry and all that. Thought he was shifty. I don't think he knows about Marsh's extracurricular activities. Maginot may just have been hungrier and craftier.'

Mensah rolled his eyes in disbelief. 'These people, these people, they're incredible. Where do I go from here? If I move I could end up in exactly the same position, grass for foraging elephants to trample,' he said.

'You may not always come up against the anointed, you've got to take your chance, it'll all work out,' said Vince.

'Ah, sugar level up, I'm feeling better,' said Mensah, dabbing his lips before another morsel of dumpling.

'Remember how you used to fret?' said Vince. 'Things are working out with . . .'

'. . . Ini,' said Mensah.

'Yes, her, Ini, as you call her; who's laughing now? Apart from this job business, you're sorted,' said Vince.

'I can't believe it, I can't,' Mensah said. 'Ini, she's perfect. Her real name's Davina, but her dad said he had to add the Iniesta after the brilliant Spanish midfielder who scored the winning goal in the 2010 World Cup final. I don't have to pretend. She laughed herself silly when I explained why I got a birthday card on the twenty-second of the month when my real birthday is June the fifteenth. She knows what I want. I think I know what she wants. Pretence, mimicking, second guessing, not for me any more; if I want to buy flowers, I do, and if I don't, I don't. No hassle – sing, dance, work or play, she enjoys it all. You haven't seen her smile. Grandpa says a smile is better than a hundred face-lifts. Try it at work, on anyone: no matter how careworn or old a face, a smile lights it up. Ini has the best. I die, I cry inside when I think of her as my widow, that is if she'll commit, but she knows. I've told her about my mother, my dad, I wasn't even afraid, I'm not afraid to grow old now. I knew. I knew she would understand. I met her parents. They live near the coast, near Bamburgh Castle, lucky people. I told them everything – ADHD, dyskeratosis, everything. They were worried. Which parent wouldn't be, but they didn't flap. Why did their daughter want to marry someone with a death sentence, but I told them how I had come to terms with it. But Ini is a brick. Just right. All those girls, you just knew, inside, it would not work. Others say what they think, but I knew how I felt, how I really felt. All that time I was just not ready. Still can't stop thinking though: does this mean the ADHD vaccine has worn off, or does it not affect love, or was it all a mirage? Maybe it didn't do anything in the first place? Will it come back to ambush me? I'm immune, I can take anything life throws at me. Sorry I'm banging on, but you started me off.'

Vince held his friend's hand. 'Come on, eat up, I've nearly finished while you've been babbling on; I'm happy for you, for both of you. I told you you'd be fine. Listen, I've come to a decision. I'm chucking my job, I'm going to work for my dad. And, I'm getting married.'

'You bastard,' said Mensah. 'When?'

'When you're ready, too,' said Vince. 'Let's have a double wedding!'

Mensah looked into his friend's moist eyes. 'Yes, yes, I'm sure Ini would love that,' he said, pretending to inspect his fork's harvest.

38

Ruth Comes Home

Apart from a few kamikaze riders, the roads were deserted early on the Saturday morning when Mensah set off to pick up Ruth. Snow was banked up six feet high high on each side of the road, higher where the snow ploughs had cleared the road. Mensah drove slowly down the middle of the road looking for grip in the fresh snow, praying to the laws of physics to protect him. A madman on a motorbike charged past and nearly crashed into an abandoned car. Only one mile further and he would be there. He had chosen the wrong day to pick up Ruth from the hospital, but he could not let her down. Even if he had to sleep there he was not going to leave the hospital without her. He chugged on, careening from precarious tyre-hold foot by foot, block by block, through the natural and plough-made valleys of snow.

He turned into the hospital road. Not gritted either – the council could not afford it – but the locals had a sign up, saying they would dig you out for a tenner. He did not have a tenner, only twenties. He would pay if he had to, but he made it, sliding to a halt past and oblique to his target. Relieved, he crept round to the boot, changed into a pair of boots, crunched, crawled and slid his way to the ward like a toddler on skates.

'Is it cold enough for you?' said Staff Nurse Henman.

'Sure is,' said Mensah. 'Here, this is for the ward, thanks a million, all of you. Where's Ginny?' Mensah handed over a large box of chocolates and a voucher for a new television for the ward.

'Thanks very much, I'll pass this on to sister. Ginny's off duty today,' she said. 'Your mum's in her room, she's just had her breakfast; I think she's been up all night, excited. Silly thing to say really, to you, but I hope you take it in the right way: she's a lovely lady.'

'Thanks, I hope to get to know her,' said Mensah. 'What happens next?'

'Well, we need to check that her blood levels are right, that the follow-up appointments with Dr Lamb are made, and that she has all her belongings with her. Won't be long. Wait here please.' She hurried off down the corridor, arms folded across chest in reflex protection against the cold, but the wards were boiling. He looked down the corridor so that he could see his mother emerge. When their eyes met, she smiled, a broad, eye-lid lifting, heart-warming, heart-stopping smile. They hugged.

Nurse Henman carried a bag past them to the nurses' station. A few of the other nurses came out to wave goodbye. Mensah held his mother at the arm to support her back to the car. Then they set off for home. The snow had frozen over again, but somehow, after two and a half hours of steering-wheel-gripping anxiety and slithering progress, they made it to Ruth's.

Mrs Dexter was waiting. Ruth and Mrs Dexter hugged; for a minute they just rocked in each other's arms. 'You look good,' said Mrs Dexter.

'Pat, this is my son, Mensah.'

Mrs Dexter started to cry. 'Don't know what to say, look after your mother, she's had a rough time.'

'Don't be silly, it's all going to be fine, we're here to look after each other. Is my room warm?'

'Yes, of course, I know how you hate the cold,' said Pat.

'Just like me,' said Mensah, 'can't bear it. Rather smell than die, I say, when I wrap up; I've got five layers on, you know.' He followed a few paces behind his mother.

'Don't be shy, come in,' she said. She chucked her bag on to the single bed. The faded green curtains were drawn. Mensah saw that the skirting was cracking and peeling and a book was wedged under one of the bed's legs. In the corner was a dining chair with a faded dark orange cushion cover and a Bible on it. He took the Bible off and laid it on the bed. Ruth watched. 'Sit down here,' she said, patting the bed beside her. 'Now, do you want a cup of tea? Pat's got a lot in I'm sure, she's always ready. She knows what the occupational therapists want: she's there on the ball. I've known her for a long, long time.'

They went through to the neat, but tiny kitchen. Ruth flicked on the kettle, watched it for a few seconds. 'It's the same kettle all right, a bit slow, but we can't bring ourselves to buy another one; we've wasted more in electricity than it would cost to get a new one,' she said.

'It doesn't matter,' said Mensah.

'No, it doesn't,' she said. 'Where's Pat, she's not gone out in this weather? Pat, Pat,' she called. Pat had gone out. So they drank their tea on one of the worn two-seater settees in the living-room.

'Do you want me to get anything else for you?' said Mensah.

'No, I'll be fine, I can look after myself you know; you mustn't fret, really I'm fine. What's happened, it can happen to anyone; it's luck, bad luck; we just have to cope; we'll see, but I'm not a baby. I won't burden . . .'

'Stop, Mum, just let me help, if I can; if I can't, I can't. I don't want you going out and falling in this weather, that's all. I'm not a baby either; I've been . . .' His voice nearly broke. Ruth waited until Mensah had composed himself.

'Mensah, there's a lot you don't know about me. We don't know each other. I may be here in this place, but I'm not stupid, I understand what this means; I may not know the details of your life, but I have seen life, I know its outline, broadly. Don't forget I used to work with children, those in care in particular; you are a credit to have got where you are. I'm proud of you, and I hope you will not be ashamed of . . . me.'

'Never,' said Mensah. He took the cups to the kitchen to wash in the icy cold water. When he came back, blowing on his hands, Ruth had got out a photo album.

'I lost some of yours, but here we are with Grandpa and Grandma and Bode.'

'I saw him,' said Mensah. He waited for her reaction.

'It's OK, he's your dad, where did you see him?'

'In Nigeria,' he said, and he told her about his trip. Ruth stopped him to ask about the odd cousin or acquaintance.

When he finished she said, 'You know more about him than you know about me; you even know about Rachel. In such a small country like ours it's a wonder that so few knew about her; is it good, or bad, that we each mind our own business? Where's Pat? We usually decide what to watch at this time of the evening in winter; history, crime, comedy, we draw lots. Summer's different: we go out to the coast, National Trust. Maybe she thinks you're going to spoil our routine. Oh, guess which one's me.'

Mensah scoured the photograph of teenage girls; he did not want to get it wrong. Then he saw her: the nose, the eyes, the high forehead. 'That's you, Mum.'

She grinned. 'I was seventeen, just before A levels. There's Matilda, she did Law. I always wanted to be a doctor. Dad was a doctor, he had a tough time but he made it, told me stories in an oblique way, didn't want to frighten me or discourage me; he always said always have something to look forward to – a target, an experience. If you don't want problems, don't want progress, he used to say.

'I saw him too,' said Mensah.

'You saw Dad?' said Ruth.

'I did,' he said.

She was silent for a minute. She looked up as if in recall. 'Mum died, I wasn't there. Just shrugged, I think they said I just shrugged when I was told; never really mourned her properly with Dad.' She paused again. 'We must go and see him.'

292

'We will, I promise, just let the weather improve. I'll call him, but driving there now in winter would be murder.' His phone rang. It was Ini.

'Who's that?' said Ruth.

'My girlfriend,' said Mensah.

'I see you've been busy,' she said.

'So will you be, when you settle down again,' said Mensah. 'Will you be all right? You've got my number, I'll stay in tomorrow, and the next week is our week on call, but I'll be in touch.'

He hugged her and made his way down the wet staircase to his car. Another hour in the car and he was home. He jumped on to his bed, buried his head in the pillow and sobbed.

Mensah's working week passed without incident, though there was a near miss when the cocky trainee took on more than she could swallow and Mensah just happened to be around to bail her out. Not a word of thanks from the dangerous ingrate, but he was getting used to that. On Saturday afternoon, after a trip into town, he set off for Ruth's against the tide of black-and-white shirted football fans heading for their weekly homage at St James's Park.

Ruth made him a snack of fish and a few chips and a cup of tea, and a glass of water 'to clean your teeth,' she said. Then they sat down on the two-seater settee. Ruth spoke slowly, watching Mensah's reaction. At first, Mensah could not help listening for signs of illness or side-effects in Ruth's speech, but he was enchanted by his mother's face, her lips, the creases in her cheeks, by every inflection, pause, hesitation, turn of phrase; by how, when searching for the right word, she cocked her head to the left. Within an hour, he was on the floor, legs outstretched, slapping her knee, clapping and rubbing his hands in glee as she changed from patient to mother.

'You're not going to get fat like your dad, are you? Because if you do, you'll have that pot belly thing some Nigerian, I would say all, men have. It won't look good on you at all. When I was young I liked the tall athletic boys, can't understand how Bode and I got together. Dad was fierce: no boys; Mum was more reserved. It's hypocrisy really: how did they meet if the girls were not allowed to see boys? They say it's different for girls, but I don't agree; girls have brains, they should use them. Dad and Mum met at work. Typical in those days, to meet at work, you know, doctor and nurse. In their case it was over a bedpan; really, how romantic! Mum was so naive, or so she said, timid even, and I believe her. Dad helped her put a urinary catheter into a woman. Men were allowed in those days as long as a chaperone was present. My mouth's dry, can you get me some water, dear?'

Mensah loved it when she called him dear. He hurried back with the glass and, as there was no stool near, in his eagerness he nearly spilt the water by offering the glass to her unprepared hand. She smiled. 'Mum didn't mind boys coming to the house, because I didn't go out much. Most of the boys at our school – Harry Mann, Tony Bosworth, Jim Hagler – they were boys who came for help with their assignments. They were always behind. I think they had a rota of girls to visit, because we were more diligent, still are, I hear.'

Mensah nodded. 'I'm afraid so,' he said.

'Dad didn't like Harry. Flash Harry he called him, which wasn't fair. I knew he liked me because he used to come on his own. Mum didn't mind, but dad was, well, he did what you would expect a dad to do; if he didn't like someone, he'd hang around, ask about their work, their parents, prospects, anything to put him . . .'

'Harry Mann, that's Vince's dad, I'm sure; dark features, funny hump on his back from playing in the front row, yes, I'm sure. I'll ask Vince. That's really funny,' said Mensah.

'So off to medical school I went; one or two clinical prizes, commendations in clinical years. Hated the basic stuff; medical school humbles most of us, so many outstanding people. I thought I was good until I went to Newcastle University. Anyway, I loved paediatrics and I became clever again. It's what you enjoy that brings out the best in you; I'm practical: you don't do paediatrics for the money. What's yours?'

'Cardiology.'

'Maginot did cardiology,' she said.

Mensah gasped. 'Maginot, you said, he's one of my professors.'

His mother nodded. 'Adam, a professor, crafty bugger! Adam should have become a diplomat, a spy, not a doctor. Did his work in the middle of the night; hid specimens away in his locker to dissect on his own; jumbled up books in the library so no one else could find them. Within a week he knew all the lecturers' first names.'

'I've had a bit of a run-in with him,' said Mensah.

'Be careful,' she said. 'Speaking of which, Bode; can't remember how we met – it was a slow burner. Ah. Yes, it was one of those BoND events Dad had been keen on for years. He'd attended a BoND to BoND – you know, British of Nigerian Descent or what- ever – wedding in Durham. He was really taken in by the colour; took loads of photographs: Yoruba traditional dress in Durham, relatives from all over the world, food, even "spraying" money as they do in Lagos. Anyway, Dad took me to this mixed wedding – BoND girl and local lad; you could see that Dad was not that keen, but it was his friend's daughter, and he had to go for moral support. He took me to show off and to introduce me to a BoND. I knew what he was doing.' She paused for a drink.

'Ah, that was just right, you're sure you don't want another cup of something, darling?' Mensah shook his head. 'I went out with Bode out of politeness, to please Dad; show him I'd made an effort.' She smiled. 'You know the rest: from out-of-sight love bites.'

'I don't know the rest, Dad didn't say that much really, what happened?' said Mensah.

'Everything happened, but it shouldn't have been like that for us. Recession, depression, credit crunch, coalition, political change; just part of life, society. We would have weathered it like anyone else, better than most, we would have been fine on one salary if we'd had to manage. But the coalition blew our plans out of the water.'

Mensah waited for more, but Ruth looked as if that was all she had to say. 'My dad, what was he like?' he said.

Ruth's eyes narrowed and she turned towards her son again. 'You'll have to make up your own mind; can't take what I say as gospel. Don't look or think of him through me, he's your father, can't change that.' She looked down at a spot on the carpet. 'I've been no better or worse a mother than he's been a father,' she said.

'Mum, don't say that, you were ill.'

'I know, but facts are facts, whatever their cause. Whether mental cluster bombs grew inside me or were lobbed at me from outside, same difference: I disintegrated.' She paused again, looked at her distorted reflection in the blank television screen, then up at a cornice. 'Spiders, hate them,' she said.

Mensah took her hand. 'Mum, tell me, when I was little, did you come to see me?'

She sighed, brushed some fluff off a cushion, plumped it and put it on her lap. 'I did, I think twice; but the authorities said it was on condition that I went back to live with Grandpa and Grandma; they said I couldn't see you if I didn't. And if I did go while I was under their programme, I would lose my accommodation and they'd move you away, far away. So I had to stop coming. On your birthdays I . . .' Suddenly, her voice sounded crackly and as flat and distant as one of those digitally remastered, old 1920s classical recordings. 'Don't know how that's supposed to make you get better.'

'Is that why you were crying? That's all I remember,' said Mensah.

'I don't know why I was crying, darling, I'm sure I wouldn't want to upset you.'

'Did I get my hands dirty a lot, did you wash them for me?' said Mensah.

Ruth waited. She looked into his eyes for clues into what he wanted to hear. She knew the truth, but she sensed that the truth was not the right answer. 'No, I can't remember, but your memory is better than mine, I'm sure you're right,' she said.

Mensah squeezed his mother's hand. 'Thanks, Mum, I remember it very well, it means a lot to me.'

'You mean the world to me,' said Ruth.

Mensah got off the floor, brushed his trousers and returned the crockery to the kitchen. 'I need to speak to Grandpa soon, I promised,' he said. 'I'd like to take you to see him, you'd like that wouldn't you, Mum?'

'Very much,' she said.

Mensah clapped his face in the manner of a boxer readying himself for the ring. 'Then let's do it. I'm here.'

'Yes, let's do it, I'm here too, for you,' she said.

39

To Grandpa's

'Vince, what do you think? I'm going to take my mum to meet Grandpa,' said Mensah in the shower after tennis.

'Hand me that towel, will you,' said Vince. 'It's a great idea, the sooner you take her the better, or you'll start to get cold feet,' he said. 'Mensah, what about this job at the RVI?'

'It's hotting up: rumours are that a foundation's been set up like the Bobby Robson one, this time for restorative cardiology, by some grateful patient, industrialist. He wants something less commercial, something that the local people can afford, but they're not sure what they want. I'm throwing my hat into the ring, no question. I don't think they'll appoint before the end of summer. What's the weather going to be like this weekend?' said Mensah.

'Same: no snow, same north-easterly winds; it's going to be cold. I just look up the States and assume that'll be us in two weeks. Let me know how it goes,' said Vince.

Mensah had just turned off the highway when his mother said, 'You're quiet.'

'Oh, I'm trying not to get us lost, I've only been here a few times, the roadworks throw me,' he said.

'Oh, look, the purple crocuses and snowdrops are out, aren't they pretty? Delicate, fragile, yet survivors; year after year, no matter what, they poke their little heads through the snow, proud in their little clusters. Aren't they resilient? It's a miracle: one minute all this slush, the next minute, precious beauty,' said Ruth.

They turned into the 'Departure Lounge' at exactly three o'clock. Mensah switched on his radio to find out which match would be featured on the live commentary. Leeds, Bolton: two kick-and-rush teams; he would not be missing anything. He locked the car, overtook Ruth before she got to reception.

'How are you, Dr Snell?'

'Snell, of course, Snell,' said Ruth, 'I'm so used to Mensah; you must take me to see Marty and Nancy soon.'

'Straight up; the doctor will see you now,' she said in a mock doctor's receptionist's voice.

Mensah was not sure whether it would be better to catch his grandfather unawares, just appear to him, tap him on the shoulder to break the ice, forestall awkwardness. They were just going to knock on the door when from behind them Grandpa said, 'Looking for me? I had to go to the top of the hall, my tap's come loose and I didn't want to risk leaving it running.'

'I can fix it for you, Grandpa.'

But the old man had been smothered by Ruth. In the hall, Mensah's stooped grandpa and a swaying Ruth were locked in an uneven embrace, tears on the diagonal down each other's backs, silently ululating sniffles, convulsions, a few seconds' break for air, then re-engagement, each clinch stronger than the last, until Mensah said, 'Let's go in now. Where's that broken tap of yours, Grandpa?'

'It's fine,' said Mensah after his inspection.

'They must have fixed it,' said his grandpa. The old man had seen them arrive. He had not wanted to wait for an awkward reunion either so he had walked halfway up the hall to lie in ambush, so that he could come up on them instead. Ruth and her father sat on the bed holding hands. He wiped her tears; his tears dried on his face. All they felt, needed or wanted to say passed through hands and their carbon-copy eyes. For him, these were memories of happier days, as a young man hand-in-hand with his Ruth at Eldon Square shops, at Paddy Freeman's Park feeding the ducks, waiting up for her when she was late; and of the dark days of filial loss and ADHD from which she had seemingly been retrieved. Her jumbled memories were of her dad, carrying her piggyback at the Hoppings; dressed as Santa, handing her presents; with her mum and dad at prize-giving day; he, Dad, kissing her head better when it ached, licking her salty cheeks when she cried; and more, all good, the bad memories banished, beyond recall or crowded out by the good.

'Found you, Mensah found you, he found you,' said her dad.

'Sorry, Dad,' she said.

'For what? It was we who failed; we fought hard, very, very hard, though we lost.' His face creased into tears.

'Dad, it wasn't your fault. Thank Marty and Nancy. What could have happened if Mensah hadn't been with them, if they hadn't found him?' The old man sighed and looked away. 'Is something wrong?' she said.

'No, he's got a lot on his plate, has Mensah: his job, he may even be getting married; we don't want anything to happen to him.'

'I know that, I don't want him harmed either, I am his mother.'

'I've not got long left,' he said. 'I don't have much left and whatever's left over after I've gone the government will take; new rules they say. Just wish I'd bought that Ferrari when I could.'

'One day Mensah will buy one and you can go for a spin. Oh, poor Mensah, he's outside, it's snowing, blizzarding down. I hadn't noticed, he must be freezing. I know where you are now, I'll come; if Mensah can't, I'll come by myself.' She squeezed his hand.

'That'll be good. If you could, can you ring the bell, please, Ruth? For my tea and tablets.'

When the tea arrived Ruth signalled for the girl to leave and she laid out her father's tea. She kissed him and tiptoed back out of the room, keeping him in view for as long as she could.

'Ready?'

'Are you all right?' said Mensah. Ruth nodded, suppressing a sob. He switched off the radio. Rubbish match, as expected. They drove in the dark, accompanied only by the car's drone and the crunch and squelch of layers of snow under wheel.

'Don't bother to get out,' she said when they got home. 'I've got a bit of a headache, I'll have an early night. Thank you for taking me to Dad, he looked quite well, everything considered.' She knew she was going to cry. 'I love you.' She kissed him on the forehead.

'Love you, Mum, I understand, wrap up, love to Pat,' and he skidded off back home.

40

Revelation

After the previous day's visit to his grandfather, Mensah thought
he needed a lazy day in, to take stock. Dr Lamb was sure Ruth
could handle meeting her father again, but if Mensah was worried
he should let them know. They could then tighten up on monitoring her blood levels and motor activity. So far, there had been
no problems. Mensah rang the ward nonetheless, to leave a message
for the duty doctor to pass on to Dr Lamb. Fortified with a hot
cup of tea and a bacon and egg sandwich, he trudged stiff-legged
in his boots through the fresh snow, but after ten minutes of
snowy monotony he turned round for home, wondering what to
do next. His phone rang. Ruth. 'How are you, Mum? Are you
just getting up? I'll call you back, I've been for a walk, for the
fresh air, to clear my head. I'll be home soon, it's freezing.'

When he got home, he called Ruth. 'It's me, did you sleep
well, Mum?'

'I did, I was so exhausted, everything, seeing Dad, the trip,
anticipation. I crashed out, but I woke up early, couldn't get to
sleep after.'

'It's probably because you went to bed too early,' he said.

'Yes, probably,' she said. 'Things pop in to your head at that
time of the day, when you can't sleep.'

Mensah felt his heart palpitate. 'What popped in, Mum?' he
said.

'Well, Grandpa, he seemed worried, about you. It may be nothing; you know, you feel things, even unsaid. Anyway, this morning I remembered a game we used to play, Dad and me; we called it "cousin". If we saw someone on TV, in a book or anywhere, and you thought they looked like somebody you knew you shouted, "Ah, that's so and so's cousin", and you got a point if the other person agreed immediately. You didn't get the marks if you had to think about it or argue. A bit of fun; argy-bargy. Anyway, I was shopping in Elba's, the department store, recently, and this TV picture caught my eye. There was this woman on telly, a brief news item, or documentary, something like that, giving testimony to a tribunal or inquiry. But for her dark hair, she looked the double of the woman from the League of Friends who used to visit me in hospital. Didn't come often, but she was vaguely familiar, this woman on TV. Maybe it's the way she blinked, even with different hair; lineament so similar they could be sisters. In the game, I'd have pressed Dad for more than a point for her. This morning, it came back to me: not the woman, but the moving subtitles; that's what must have caught my eye first – some inquiry about the ADHD vaccine.'

Mensah's knees wobbled. He sat down, free hand trembling.

'What's it about? Mensah, are you there?'

'I am, Mum; everything's happening so quickly, didn't want to bring that all back again. It's behind us, have a good day, I'm going to have a nap, read a book . . .'

'No, Mensah, I'm your mum, I want to know. What's this inquiry about, what's new, what's going on? Grandpa said you have a lot on your plate. Is this part of it, what he meant?' She whooped. 'Annabel, Annabel, that's the name of the woman who used to visit me. Can you find out for me, Mensah? Anyway, I'd like to meet her again, tell her my good news, could you do that? To thank Marty and Nancy as well, of course, but Annabel also; I'll ask at the hospital next time I see the girls. I hope she's all right because I haven't seen much of her lately. You'd have met her.'

Mensah thought for a moment. He wanted to tell Ruth everything. If he did not and she found out about the dyskeratotic gene scandal, he would lose her, and her trust, so early in their reconciliation, and if he did tell her, would he lose her anyway if she relapsed? No Vince, no Marty, no Nancy, no Lamb to advise him. He had to decide. 'Mum?'

'Yes, son.'

'Mum, that woman, the woman on telly, she's Rachel Timms, my dad's sister, used to be a member of the government's economic task force. She's got something to do with the inquiry, she's fighting for compensation for us,' said Mensah.

'Why?' she asked.

'I don't know,' said Mensah. 'I haven't been following it.'

Ruth was silent. 'Can I come over?' he said.

'Well, yes, the place is a tip, but yes, why not? I'll tidy up. When are you coming?'

'I'm on my way, it depends on this wretched snow,' he said. On his way, Mensah wondered how and what to tell Ruth. A loud beep from behind him urged him to move on at the traffic-lights. 'What's the hurry?' he said. As he got closer to Ruth's he became more resigned to his plan. She was going to find out anyway; it might as well be from him.

When he got out of the car, he put on his bravest face and a clinician's smile ready for when Ruth opened the door. Ruth just about heard the door bell above the whine of the vacuum cleaner. She switched it off to make sure she'd heard right and let Mensah in. 'You made it,' she said. They hugged. 'What's this about the inquiry?' she said when Mensah sat down. 'It's bugging me, I can handle it you know, I've had lots of counselling about ADHD; it won't do any harm to know what they're thinking. If it's compensation then you've earned it, I've earned it, they should pay,' she said.

'I don't think it's that, Mum,' said Mensah. 'Mum, I just remembered, can you write your name on this piece of card? Thanks, I'll keep it by my bed.' Mensah took a quick glance at Ruth's handwriting. He thought it looked fine. He felt mean playing a trick on her to see whether he could detect any signs that she was not well or incapacitated. 'Mum, you are getting ahead of yourself.'

'How?'

'Well, let's think this through. We have three issues: ADHD, and two women; one is a woman you've seen at the hospital and the other, this woman on TV, yes?'

'Yes,' she said.

'The TV woman is my aunt, my dad's sister.'

'Are you sure?'

'Of course I am, she's fighting for compensation for the ADHD patients. It's got nothing to do with the other woman.'

'Gosh, Bode's sister, I didn't recognise her,' she said. 'Wow, can't believe she was on TV, I don't suppose she would want to hear from us now. But what's the compensation for? It looked like quite an inquiry from the bit I saw, it . . .'

'It's bits and pieces, just going over old ground; I don't think it's good for you to go there again.'

'It's funny you should say that, Mensah, that is about the only part of this that I can revisit. I had so many counselling sessions about the vaccine that I can face anything about it they put before me about it. So, what are they saying? Forget the woman for the moment; I can ask the girls about her.'

'They made some mistakes,' he said.

'What sort of mistakes?'

'They don't know the long-term effects, doses, etcetera. They're looking into whether mistakes were made, just logistics, you know: if we had an epidemic, whether they could do things better.'

'So what's Rachel got to do with it? She's not a scientist.'

'That, I'm not sure. I didn't follow it. I have issues as well, don't like to think about it, Mum.'

'Sorry, son, it was silly of me to go on, we'll put it behind us. Is that why you came?' He nodded, rubbing his hands against the cold, but it made him look sorry. He was sorry. 'You see why

I didn't want to talk about it over the phone; let's not talk about it again.'

'I promise,' she said.

'You're sure you're all right, Mum? I can stay if you want.'

'Oh, you go, you need some time to yourself.'

He sat, quiet, taking his time to put his driving gloves back on. 'Okay. I'm ready now. Bye, Mum.'

Mensah called round at Marty and Nancy's on Tuesday evening to ask their advice. It was snowing again. 'If you were ill and you didn't tell us, I would be gutted if I found out elsewhere,' said Nancy.

'If it would make you ill would you still want to know?' said Mensah.

'Yes, I would, without doubt, I would take the risk; it might not make me ill, it might give me focus, make me better. I could get worse if I found out by accident. Have you asked the doctors?' she said.

'They weren't sure, they left it to me,' he said. 'What does Marty think?'

'Marty's not sure, he's afraid, but I think he agrees with me. If she finds out from somebody else, and with all the publicity that's on the cards, you'll be in real trouble; that's what could cause a relapse.'

'I'll think about it,' he said, but he had made up his mind.

After work on Wednesday, he called his mum. 'Mum, about the other day, can I come around on the way from work? We could buy a take-away; if Pat's around we'll buy her one as well.'

'Okay, Mensah, I'll be expecting you. How was your day? I thought it was your on-call day today.'

'Yes, but it's not resident on call, this one, you can float; the present crop of juniors seem to know what they're doing. I'll be there soon.'

He knocked on the door, Ruth ushered him in. Pat was out, but would be back soon. 'Mum, I'm sorry, I didn't tell you the whole truth about the ADHD vaccine.' No reaction, just a quizzical and almost imperceptible raise of the head.

'What's the truth?'

'They think it was contaminated, by some rubbish, no, a gene; it's supposed to make you age faster. No one's ill yet, but many of us go to dentists and orthopaedic and eye doctors for check-ups; I've been fine.'

'What do you mean contaminated? My son, my Mensah, what have they done now? Wicked, wicked people they are; they take my son and poison him, the . . .'

'Mum, I'm fine, they're not even sure whether anything will come of this thing; we're all fine, but there's this talk of compensation: some people are looking to the judicial inquiry to give them closure, find out who did it, cock-up or conspiracy, that sort of thing,' he said.

Ruth buried her face in her hands. 'But, you could be ill. I was supposed to be looking after you. You've not even started to live; when did you find out?' she said at last.

'When I was a house officer.'

'All that time, all that time you've been alone, what are we looking for? Oh, here's Pat.' The door opened and Pat came in carrying a shopping bag.

'Pat, how are you?' said Mensah.

'Oh, look, Ruth, what's happened?'

'Nothing,' said Ruth.

'It's not nothing, out with it,' said Pat. 'Come here.' She gave Ruth a hug. 'What's wrong? Should I call the hospital?'

'No,' said Ruth. 'I'm allowed to be sad, just like anybody else, they'll inject me with their stuff if they think I'm ill, I'm not, I'm angry. My son's a target and I couldn't do anything to stop them. If only, if only, who's responsible? I'll kill them, I'll . . . I won't have it, I'll sue . . .'

'What's wrong?' Pat asked Mensah.

'Sort of bad news, but it's old news, it's just that Mum's just heard,' he said. 'I don't expect you to know about it.'

'What is it?' said Pat.

'Some vaccine mistake they made when I was small; Mum's just found out, it's nothing,' said Mensah.

'Good,' said Pat.

Ruth blew her nose and sat up straighter. 'I'm fine now,' she said. 'Honestly. We'll pull through, I'm not going to crack again. They won't win. Good luck to the inquiry . . . Your phone, Mensah; you go to work, don't worry, Pat's here.'

Mensah answered his call and headed for the hospital. A confused patient had somehow managed to dig out the pacemaker inserted earlier that day. When Mensah arrived, the woman had the pacemaker generator in her hand, wires still connected, oblivious to all the fuss. Her next of kin had gone on holiday; she screamed every time Mensah got close. Theatre was busy. In desperation, Mensah shot her with a tranquillizing needle, gave a shot of antibiotic, retrieved the box, soaked it in disinfectant for five minutes, re-implanted it on the ward and put her arms in a sling. He went home.

First thing the next morning he called Ruth again. 'I knew you'd call, what time is it? Aren't you supposed to be at work? I've done some reading. I wish you'd told me. Does Grandpa know?' Mensah did not reply. 'You told Dad, you didn't tell me, look at it this way . . .'

'Grandpa found out, I had to tell him,' he said.

'If it was your child, would you not want to know?'

'Sorry, Mum, it won't happen again, it's not on my radar as much as it used to be; it's because I've accepted it. I don't think about it so much except when it's in the news. You can come to the clinic with me. I'll tell Ini you know, it'll take the pressure off if they know you know.'

'I know you're trying to help, to protect me, but don't. Have a good day. It's Ini, isn't it? Love to Ini as well, then. Where's her name from?'

'From football,' he said.

For three weeks, Mensah called his mother every morning

before he went to work and last thing at night. 'Am I one of your patients?' she asked. 'You keep checking on me, it should be the other way round.'

Her holiday to France with Pat and her daughter broke the habit. Satisfactory reports from her clinic appointments and from Dr Lamb's blood tests meant that Mensah could relax. Relax until she turned the tables on him by asking whether he was going to marry Ini. 'Be fair to her, make up your mind, are you going to allow this dyskeratotic gene to hang over you forever or get on with your life?'

41

Mensah at Home

'If I had this dyskeratotic gene thing the dentist would not have spent the best part of an hour trying to get this tooth out,' said Mensah one weekend. 'Mum was getting worried because it was taking so long. She said she was tempted to knock on the door to find out what was going on.'

'Don't get carried away now, Mensah,' said Daviniesta.

'You should have been there. You know how small the dentist is, well, she started off gently, a smidgen of local anaesthetic, small forceps, then she produced larger and larger ones. I was smothered by perfume and her boobs, maybe a new form of anaesthetic. At one point she was pulling so hard she literally had her knee on my chest until it slipped on to my crotch – friction burns on chest and squashed balls. I winced, but didn't want to let it show. She got it out in the end. My jaw was hurting and boggy. She said it will soon go down but I won't be able to chew properly for a day or two. And the lesson in all this? I've got nothing to worry about. Checks were good, I feel good, let's start a family, you know that song.'

'There's no such song, you made it up; even if there was it's hardly the basis for having a baby.'

'Oh, Ini, what's stopping us? I'm ready. I'm ready, I'm ready, you know I'm ready.' He danced a little jig to his silly song, but his sore jaw or head made him unsteady.

'It's a big step to decide on the back of one dentist's appointment. Calm down, let's be serious,' said Daviniesta. 'We've got a lot to think about. Pre-implantation genetic diagnosis: have you thought about that?' she said.

'Of course I have, what do you think? What with what's happened to me and my mum. What sort of question is that? Have I thought about it? I've thought of little else. What a question, Ini, maybe you don't see how much this means to me, more than it means to you, obviously.'

Ini came round to hug him. She put her hands round his neck to knead his chest. 'That's why I want us to think about it properly. We need to think this through: all the genetics, you, how it fits in with what the doctors say about your condition, everything. We need advice. If we go genetics and all that, what should we try to eliminate? Big diseases? What if we leave something out and the baby gets it? Lots to think about. Or do we just take pot luck like our parents did?'

Mensah nodded. 'I sound like a hypocrite, but I want my baby to have the best start. If it means manipulation, so be it; if we do nothing, he or she will ask why she was the only one in her generation with cystic fibrosis or some other serious monogenic condition.'

'I agree,' said Ini, 'but where will we draw the line? If we chose all the traits we could, just because we can, like some oil baron in Harrods, would the result be a child or our own little experiment?' she said.

'You're right, but I'm going to have a baby,' he said.

42

Rachel Calls Mensah

'Amanda will still not have me at theirs, you know, even now they've moved down south,' said Rachel. 'I was planning to go while you were away at that conference,' she said.

John frowned. 'I thought we sorted that out. I spoke to her and to David only the other day,' he said.

'She was just being polite to you. Jonathan's walking, he's got four teeth and can shout a bit, but she won't let me see him,' said Rachel.

'Should I call her?' said John.

'Last time I called her on a Saturday she gave the impression that I was spoiling her weekend; she said something like Jonathan was all wrapped up to go out but she would have to unwrap him to speak to me, I should call back in five minutes. I did,' said Rachel. 'I don't know, I'm beginning to wonder myself: was it worth it? But it's easy to say now; what was the choice, not to do anything again?'

John patted her on the shoulder. 'You've sacrificed a lot: your government work, your nephew, dad, now son, grandson, or more,' he said.

'I know that,' she said. 'But I've still got civil liberty work and the tie-in with the Chinese. They like my independence. And the Africans have woken up at last, formed a joint raw material nego- tiating body to get a better deal, and have asked me to help. The

Nigerians called me Dacosta when I met them at the High Commission. It tickled them. Dacosta. There was a Vera Cruz on their delegation.' She gazed through the conservatory at the grey squirrels hopping out of the way of an unsettlingly healthy and frisky fox.

'I've not heard from Bode,' she said. 'You'd think with all that's happened . . .'

'He's not heard from you either, has he?' said John.

'No,' she said. Were time, distance and culture too high a barrier between the twins to climb for kinship?

John slung his jacket over his left arm. 'Do I cut the grass or go for the papers? If I go for the papers, I'll have a lazy day. No, I'll cut the grass, and then go for the papers; half price they should be by then. Might pick up some discarded sections of the *Financial Times* or *Telegraph;* I could pay someone for the business and arts section, and save money,' he said.

'Your life: so complicated,' she said.

'I agree, maybe the job made me this way, make mountains out of molehills . . .'

'Radio's far better than the press,' she said. Radio in one hand, she went to deadhead the flowers.

When John returned with the newspapers, Rachel was well into her gardening, with her apron on and her long-sleeved pruning gloves. She looked heavy-eyed. 'You haven't been at the anti-histamines again, have you?' he said.

'Just a little to be safe, you know what happens when I get stung.'

On Rachel's radio, John caught the snippets of a trailer for a charity-work programme. 'I've been thinking,' she said.

'Not another impulse, you're not going on *Weekly Scrutiny?*' he said, looking at the radio.

'No, nothing like that, but I've pushed this as far as I can; I need to mend. I've decided to contact everyone: David, Mensah; they can turn me down, call me names if they want, I'll do it,' she said.

John put his papers down on the garden bench. It was wet. 'Oh, I've ruined . . . Oh, it's all right, only the money section, I haven't any money,' he said. 'Let's think this through: will this new initiative be on your terms or theirs? You're calling them; maybe it won't make them any better. They've got their own lives. We know Mensah's fine; he's probably better off than our David with the stuff he's had to deal with lately. All I ask is think about it, send him a Christmas card or something, wait, take it easy. Don't go diving in feet first again.'

Rachel pointed her secateurs at John. 'I'll . . . I don't like this attitude you have that everything I do now is wrong,' she said.

'I'm not saying that, I'm saying these are real lives, real minds, not theoretical goods and services, not economics,' he said.

'I know that, why do you think it's so hard to know what to do?' she said.

'Then why don't you ask before you do it? Then even if we don't agree, we've had time to warn everyone, prepare. You charge in and we clear the mess or live with the mess.'

'That's not fair,' she said, and as she turned round she caught her shirt on a thorn. 'Drat.'

A few weeks later, Rachel and John were lying on loungers enjoying a quiet Saturday evening. John had just finished the crossword puzzle and gone in to pour them another drink when: 'John . . . John, come here please,' said Rachel.

'What's wrong?'

'Nothing, I'm going to call Mensah, David's got the number for me.'

'Are you sure?'

'That's what I said I would do; clear up all the loose ends I can. Here we go.' Rachel put her book down and dialled the number.

'Dr Snell here,' said Mensah.

'It's Rachel, Rachel Timms, David's mum,' she said.

'Oh, hello, is everything all right?'

'Yes, thanks, you're Mensah, aren't you? You used to work with David, my son? Do you know who I am?'

'Yes, I did, I do, it's very good of you to call. Are you still in Surrey? I guess you won't have much need to come up North now David's down there,' he said. 'Amanda's still here, I hear,' he said.

'She'll be joining him as soon as he's settled in at St Thomas's,' said Rachel.

'Thanks for calling, ma'am, it's very nice to hear from you at last. I'll tell Mum; Dad's in Nigeria.'

'I know, all the best,' she said.

'To you too,' said Mensah. He waited for Rachel to hang up. 'That was Rachel,' he said.

'Who's Rachel?' said Daviniesta.

'My aunt.'

'Didn't know you had an aunt,' she said.

'I didn't either, until recently,' he said.

'When did she know she had a nephew?' she said.

'It's a long story,' said Mensah.

43

Philip White

'Good evening, my friends. Patriots. As you know, I've been ill, gravely ill, but thanks to your support, the support of my family and hundreds of years of breeding I can stand here in your presence once again.' He paused. A stifled cough from the top table rang round the dark room. In the dimmed spotlight, White stood in his open-collared white shirt; his stubbled scalp gave the impression of rejuvenation, rebirth after calamity, the conference theme of the Albionic Society. 'I am feeling better, but is our country? We have no spare country, we have no roots elsewhere. These are grave times for Battleship Britannia. She's heading for the rocks with incompetents at the helm. Blinkered leaders, blinking leaders.' He paused for effect. A few titters from the dark seats at the back. 'Leaders oblivious to, or unable to confront the rising threat of robbers, pirates, stowaways and vermin assailing Britannia, to ravage her stores, and, when these stores are spent, gnaw at her proud timbers, her structure, supports, traditions and customs. Why should we hang on hoping for the best? Why should we trust the fate of your children and grandchildren to this rudderless class?

'We led the world in language, philosophy and science. I, for one, will not stand idly by and watch us sink or throw our people on the scrap heap to make way for those who share not our history. Why should I? They did not live through or fight our wars, they cannot, don't, share our ways, our freedoms, they cannot.' He sipped some water. The compère wiped a tear from his eye. The chairman, Mr Ed Mandrake, winked his approval at Mrs Julie Bansard, the publicity secretary. Gordon Ferry, he of the True Brit radio phone-in, was in tears.

'Set our easy self-deprecation against the militant rant of the Islamists, compare Songs of Praise with the guttural, hacking loudhailer; our understated Christian against their gaudy festivals. Our county cricket, banter and debate and their tribal, sectarian honour killings and foaming, wild-eyed hate. Our love of animals against their ritual slaughter, the spinsters on bicycles riding home from evensong against the burka-clad slaves. Think of warm beer and cricket on the village green, the premature daffodils in winter, the cock robin in spring, the long days in summer and the autumn when we draw in. We, a nation of Supermen, can and will bear the burden of the less fortunate, ordinary men, ordinary nations. We can and will bear our burden, bravely, but we must be free to choose. To choose, as free peoples, before we capsize, how much of this cargo we can safely carry. Until we do, let the burden stay abroad; and not, like weeds on our lawns, oil spilt on our shores, flood waters on our moors, engulf, overwhelm, swamp or suffocate this land, our fair Albion.'

To wild cheers and a standing ovation, led by Dr David Timms, White raised his head to the lights and a white-gloved fist to the aisles. Ten minutes later he was led down the aisle through the cheering audience into the back of a hired limousine by the compère, Mr Tobias Willoughby.

Vince switched off the footage and went to bed. Not one for Mensah.

44

House Party

Six months after his appointment as head of the new department of restorative cardiology, established at the RVI by the Pattinson Cardiac Trust, Mensah received a call from Professor Maginot. 'Mensah, how are you, how's it going?'

'Fine, and how are you too, professor?' said Mensah.

'Well, very well, I'll get to the point,' he said. 'This city's too small for two RC departments. We should cooperate, combine forces, share facilities, you know, that sort of thing. We've got the facilities already, shame to duplicate them,' he said.

'Professor, most of your clients come from overseas, there's little for the local people. This department is an opportunity to provide services for local people with serious cardiac disease. The nearest similar facility is in York. The locals can't afford the Freeman; if we amalgamate, we'll be swallowed and they'll be back to square one. Anyway, it's not in my gift, I'll talk to the executives and trustees,' said Mensah.

'Please do, you're welcome back here any time. We'll create a chair for you; just say, and we'll accommodate you. No need to compete, doctors shouldn't, that's for retailers and shoe-shine boys.'

Mensah wanted to say his father was a shoe-shine boy, just to embarrass the professor. 'I'll think about your offer, professor, it's nice to speak to you,' he said.

'I think you should, we could make life very difficult for you,

you know. You haven't got staff yet; how will you attract them? We could offer them much more money. Can you afford a bidding war? It'll be quite a struggle against an established outfit like ours.'

'Really?' said Mensah. 'Professor, I've overcome worse odds than that.' He put the phone down.

'Is everything all right, Dr Snell? Should I make you a cup of coffee?' said Flora when she walked in a few minutes later.

'I'm fine. Just don't like people throwing wood chippings into my cereal.'

Flora smiled. 'Could do with some chippings . . . can I go now?' she said.

Mensah nodded. 'Have a really good weekend. I know I will,' he said, clearing his desk.

Saturday morning. Contrails, towed as if by airborne ships, pierced wispy clouds in the pale-blue spring sky. A man cursed at his hibernating lawnmower, his mood not helped by the sound of his next door neighbour's starting first time, and a bare-midriffed teenager, trying her first few spliffs beside a skip full of discarded flotsam, sneered at Rose, the squash champion going on a run. Ruth and Ini had just returned from shopping for more baby clothes at 'Bairnies' on Gosforth High Street.

'Hello, we're back, is anybody in?'

'Shush, now look what you've done, he's up again, the little pest, you runty you; your mum's back with Grandma,' said Mensah. 'What should I do, do you want to feed him or should I try?'

'You bicker, I'll feed him,' said Ruth. 'Okay, Mum, don't give him back until he's asleep.'

'It's a deal,' she said, taking little Marty off his daddy.

Mensah waltzed back from the kitchen with a bib. 'There, that will keep you both dry,' he said. 'What are you making for later?'

'Don't you worry. There'll be enough for everyone, including you. Grandpa doesn't eat much, it's Vince and you we have to fear. Anyway, you can fill up the cracks with lager,' said Ini.

319

'I'm a responsible Dad now, can't just drink myself sober any more,' he said.

'Try for one night,' she said.

At six, Vince arrived, with Grandpa Omughana.

'Dad, Dad, come in, Dad, we've been waiting for you; we made you your special rhubarb crumble, but you must eat your greens first. Where's Patricia, or should I say Mrs Mann?'

Vince blushed. 'Morning sickness, terrible, she's in a foul mood,' said Vince.

Mensah's grandpa took his scarf off and slipped out of his enormous jacket. 'Hello, girls, I'll eat anything but greens at my time of life, I've earned it, I'd like all the unhealthy butter and cream or I'm going back home.' He chuckled and shadow-boxed unsteadily in the hall mirror. 'If I was brave enough I'd try a spliff or two, but no, I'm high enough as it is, seeing you all here. I'm so high on adrenaline I'm exhausted.'

'Do you want to have a kip next door? It's quiet, we'll take your case, there's plenty of room here, we've got two spare rooms,' said Ini. 'We'll wake you up when we're ready to eat.'

'All right then, point me in the right direction. My old friend Dr Buckold will be coming later; he said he'd pop in, you don't mind?'

'What's his tipple?' said Ruth.

'If I told you, he'd kill me: battery electrolytes to vintage Dom Perignon – he'll drink anything,' said the old man. 'Where's Mensah?' he said.

'He's just gone upstairs with little Marty,' said Ini.

'There he is, daddy from hell, preening and prancing . . . like a Ferrari prancing horse,' said Grandpa Omughana.

'You're obsessed by Ferraris, Dad,' said Ruth.

'I can think of worse obsessions,' he said, laughing. 'I'm off, call me when you want,' he said, heading off next door to sit in an easy chair in the corner of the dining-room.

'My mum and dad are on their way, when are Marty and Nancy coming?' said Ini.

'Any time now,' said Ruth. 'Nancy called to ask me while we were out. Oh, is that them? Hi, we're here,' she said, waving.

After supper, Ini, her mum and dad – Paul and Susannah – Mensah, Marty, Nancy and Vince played the latest console-based game *Pandoramion*. Grandpa Omughana sat next door in the dining-room with his old hospital colleague, Dr Buckold, who had come back to live near his daughter just over the road. Ruth went upstairs for a nap. After all their guests had gone, her father went to bed and Ruth helped to wash up.

'Do you want me to bring you a nightcap?' Mensah asked Ini as she carried Marty upstairs.

'No, I've had too much to eat and drink as it is; bring your glass and I may have a sip before I clean my teeth,' she said. A tipsy Mensah followed her upstairs with his glass of wine. He watched her put Marty back into his cot. Then he dipped his finger in his glass of wine and touched it to his little Marty's philtrum. 'A toast: to a better start in life than mine, than ours,' he said. 'Hear, hear,' he said in a deep voice, responding to his own toast. He flicked his electric toothbrush on, started to clean his teeth, then flicked it off again. 'Marty's start may be better than mine, but I can't say much for his old age. With the state the economy's in, he'll have to work till he's a hundred. Ini, look what's happened.' Mensah put on a sad face, opened his mouth wide so Ini could see the gap where his incisors should be. She gasped. Premature tooth loss: one of the early signs of dyskeratosis. Ini's lips trembled and her eyes filled up. He sat beside her for a minute, then saw that he had gone too far.

'Look,' he said, and showed her how he did the trick. 'The dentist taught me,' he said. Ini hit him hard twice on the chest with her fist.

'Never, never do that again, that was cruel.'

'I'm sorry, I wasn't thinking, I guess I was relieved that I had an excellent check-up last week,' said Mensah. He kissed Ini. 'I love you, thanks, I had a wonderful day,' he said.

'Do you love me more than the rainbow, more than the sea, more than the itsy-bitsy in with me?' she sang.

'Yes, more than the rainbow . . .' he replied.

'Is everything all right?' said Ruth from across the hall.

'Yes, Mum,' he said, giggling.